A SHIMMER OF HUMMINGBIRDS

W9-COX-580

The Birder Murder Mystery series

A Siege of Bitterns
A Pitying of Doves
A Cast of Falcons

STAY CONNECTED

#BirderMurder

abirdermurder.com

@birddetective

A BIRDER MURDER MYSTERY

A SHIMMER OF HUMMINGBIRDS

STEVE BURROWS

DUNDURN
TORONTO

Copyright © Steve Burrows, 2017

All rights reserved. No part of this publication may be reproduced, stored in a retrieval system, or transmitted in any form or by any means, electronic, mechanical, photocopying, recording, or otherwise (except for brief passages for purposes of review) without the prior permission of Dundurn Press. Permission to photocopy should be requested from Access Copyright.

All characters in this work are fictitious. Any resemblance to real persons, living or dead, is purely coincidental.

Printer: Webcom

Library and Archives Canada Cataloguing in Publication

Burrows, Steve, author
    A shimmer of hummingbirds / Steve Burrows.

(A birder murder mystery)
Issued in print and electronic formats.
ISBN 978-1-4597-3530-9 (paperback).--ISBN 978-1-4597-3531-6 (pdf).
--ISBN 978-1-4597-3532-3 (epub)

    I. Title.

PS8603.U74745S5 2017   C813'6   C2016-904867-5
                                              C2016-904868-3

2   3   4   5   22   21   20   19

Conseil des Arts   Canada Council
du Canada   for the Arts

Canada

ONTARIO ARTS COUNCIL
CONSEIL DES ARTS DE L'ONTARIO
an Ontario government agency
un organisme du gouvernement de l'Ontario

We acknowledge the support of the **Canada Council for the Arts** and the **Ontario Arts Council** for our publishing program. We also acknowledge the financial support of the **Government of Ontario**, through the **Ontario Book Publishing Tax Credit** and the **Ontario Media Development Corporation**, and the **Government of Canada**.

Care has been taken to trace the ownership of copyright material used in this book. The author and the publisher welcome any information enabling them to rectify any references or credits in subsequent editions.

— J. Kirk Howard, President

The publisher is not responsible for websites or their content unless they are owned by the publisher.

Printed and bound in Canada.

VISIT US AT

dundurn.com | @dundurnpress | dundurnpress | dundurnpress

Dundurn
3 Church Street, Suite 500
Toronto, Ontario, Canada
M5E 1M2

For Flora and Gene,
from whose story came my greatest gift

ACKNOWLEDGEMENTS

I am grateful, as ever, to my editor, Allison Hirst, my publicist, Michelle Melski, and to Kirk Howard and the rest of the great team at Dundurn. Jenny Parrott, Margot Weale, and the staff of Oneworld Publications in the U.K. have worked tirelessly to introduce the Birder Murders to new audiences, and I thank them for all their efforts. Michael Levine, Meg Wheeler, and Bruce Westwood at WCA offered much valuable advice and insight. Mike Burrows cast a careful eye over the text, David Arango did likewise with the Spanish phrases, and Graeme McLeod, as usual, was my consultant on all things vehicular. My thanks and gratitude to each of them.

I was fortunate to join members of Toronto Ornithological Club and North Durham Nature on a birding tour of Colombia, organized by Geoff Carpentier. In Colombia, the staff and facilities of EcoTurs and ProAves provided us with great opportunities to experience the country's bird life. Particular thanks are due to Andres Trujillo. Over late-night beers in birding lodges, Andres's thoughtful comments and suggestions helped me to resolve many plotting challenges. By day, his expert guiding skills helped our group to find over five hundred bird species, including fifty species of hummingbird. Both the guide and the tour company in this story are the product of the author's imagination, and bear no resemblance to any characters or institutions I encountered in Colombia.

Finally, my love and thanks go to my wife, Resa, for her unfailing enthusiasm and support. I now consider her uncannily accurate predictions for each book almost a ritual; one might even say, Resa's rite.

1

The cold lay across the land like a punishment. Along the lane, the grassy verges bowed with their burdens of frost, and lacy collars of ice fringed the edges of the puddles. On the far side of the lane, beyond the hedgerow, the skeleton shapes of bare trees lined the boundaries of the fields. Stands of pale grass moved uneasily beneath metallic skies. Winter was stretching its fingers over the landscape, and if it had not yet drawn them in, to clasp the land fully in its grip, the time was surely near.

The street lamps along the lane were already on, shining through the grey light of the fading afternoon like tiny suns. Suspended in their light, ice crystals spiralled like shards of shattered glass. From the window of a small cottage, a man watched a girl's progress along the lane. The lace curtain hung from his fingertip like a veil. "Prospect, Erin," he said without turning. The man's shoulders were hunched slightly, as if he might be expecting a strike from the tension that seemed to hang in the room like a presence. "This could be the one."

From the armchair behind the man, Erin offered no opinion. A kitten mewled around the legs of the chair, looking for an affectionate pat that wasn't forthcoming. At the window, the man's eyes tracked the girl's approach carefully. She was perhaps eighteen, a youngish eighteen, though, slightly-built, with hardly an ounce of adult bulk on her delicate frame. He wondered if she was a runner. But there was no sign of well-developed muscle tone, no athletic spring in her step. Besides, it hardly mattered. Those boots she was wearing, all pointy toes and high heels, would not be much good for running over the uneven cobblestone surface of this laneway. Not that he intended to give her the chance.

"Yes," said the man, nodding softly to himself, his eyes flickering slightly as he watched her. He could feel the pressure building in his chest. The hair at his collar was damp with sweat and the dryness in his mouth made it hard to swallow. Stage fright. He closed his eyes for a moment and took a deep breath. He was surprised to find it affecting him like this. He had been over the scenario many times in his head. He should be calmer than this. But the heart holds surprises for even the most disciplined minds, and now the moment of truth was drawing close, the doubts were starting to flood in.

The girl was closer now, and he could see the wispy trail of her breath as she chatted on her phone. *Distracted*. Not ideal. He wanted her to know what was happening, to take it all in, to be aware of everything. His eyes moved to the greying sky beyond her, and then switched anxiously back and forth along the lane. *No one*. He turned his attention back to the girl, perhaps twenty metres away now, no more. If it was going to be this one, he had only a few seconds. Cap, jacket, open the door and run. Her head would spin around at the sound of his approach, just in time to see him bearing down on her. A momentary look of confusion on her face? Panic? Terror? And then. Over. It would be done. He could feel the pulse throbbing in his temples. *This has to be done.* His heart was racing. *You have to do it.* He clenched his fingers into his palm, feeling its wetness. But still he hesitated.

"I don't know, Erin. This one? Or not?"

Not.

He let out a pent up breath and withdrew his finger, letting the curtains fall back into place with a delicate shimmer. From behind his lace screen, he watched the girl pass beneath the street lamp outside, still chatting on her phone. Her breath spiralled up in the cold air, seeming to him like whispered prayers, drifting up to heaven. She would never know how close she had come.

It was the light. It was important, perhaps the most important thing of all. It needed to be right, and it wasn't. Not yet. The man saw the mug on the window ledge in front of him and a bolt of alarm speared his chest. What if he had left it here, in his rush to get outside? He picked up the mug and carried it wordlessly into the kitchen. As he walked past the armchair, the kitten let out a small bleat. It looked for a moment as if it might follow the man into the kitchen, but in the end it jumped up onto Erin's lap and curled itself inside its tiny tail to go to sleep.

In the kitchen, the man set the empty, unwashed cup carefully in the sink. He peered out the kitchen window, checking the narrow garden as it ran down to the boat dock. He could feel the cold winter air coming in through the neat hole in the glass panel of the door. On the far bank of the river that ran behind the cottages, a pair of Mallards was hunkered down, blending in to the pale, brittle reed stems. Nothing else moved.

The man sat for a long time at the kitchen table, watching as the day retreated into the half-light of dusk. There was a large part of him that didn't want to do this. But something else had taken over. His actions were no longer his to control. His breathing had begun to quicken again. He steadied it. He felt tiny droplets of moisture running down his temples. Sweat. DNA. Bad thing.

He stood up quickly and walked back into the tiny, neat living room, now sheltering pockets of darkness in its corners. "We'll leave the lights off for now, Erin," he announced. He approached the bay window and peered through the curtains again. All the other cottages had lights on now. From outside, this one would look like a missing stone in the necklace of lighted windows that ran along the lane.

The man checked his reflection in the window glass; the brown leather jacket with its soft corduroy collar; the cap, tilted far enough forward to hide the plastic lining. And the greying goatee, with the little horns on the moustache. He gave the beard a downward stroke with his thumb and forefinger, as if to ensure it was in place. From the corner of his eye, he caught a flicker of movement, and he turned quickly to see a woman walking slowly down the lane, carefully picking her way between the puddles. Not up from the village as he had always envisioned it, but coming from the other direction. Panic started to rise within him. This was wrong. Why hadn't he ever considered this? *Pull yourself together*. What did it matter? She was taller than the other one and slightly older; a year or two. More woman than girl, this one. His mouth felt dry, and he dragged the back of his wrist across his lips. His breathing was shallow and rapid. A whisper of doubt flickered across his mind. Would she put up a fight? Try to grab him? No, he thought, the twilight, the shock; they would do their work. It would all happen the way he had planned it.

The woman was getting closer. Another fifty metres and she would be directly beneath the street lamp outside. Darkness all around and just that tiny pool of yellow light spilling onto the cobblestone lane like a spotlight on a stage. He watched her approaching. She had picked up her pace slightly and was hunched against the evening, as if something in her subconscious might be whispering about the dangers a quiet lane like this could hold. He wondered where she was going. Home after a hard day's work? To the pub to meet her friends? Or her boyfriend? It didn't matter.

He sat at the window, his right knee bobbing up and down like a piston, resisting all his efforts to control it. His heart felt like it might explode from his chest. He was finding it hard to breathe. The mantra built in his mind, like the roar of an oncoming train. *This has to be done. You have to do it.*

"Here's where I have to leave you, Erin," said the man over his shoulder, not taking his eyes off the woman outside. His mouth was dry again and he licked his lips to moisten them. As the woman approached the pool of light beneath the street lamp, the man stood up. He ran to the front door and snatched it open. The door banged back against the wall of the cottage, but the woman was already looking in his direction — that primeval mechanism, perhaps, alerting her to danger? It was already too late. The man sprinted toward her. She stared, frozen in terror, as he closed the gap. Less than five metres now, with no signs of slowing. The woman raised her hands defensively, bracing for the impact. The man exploded into her, lowering his head and smashing his cap into her face. The impact lifted the woman off her feet and sent her flailing back against the street lamp, snapping her head back hard against the post. Lying on the cold ground, stunned, she heard rapid footfalls; the sound of running. She raised her head and managed to focus in time to see the man sprinting away down the centre of the narrow lane. His escape rang off the cobblestones until, like the assailant himself, the sound finally disappeared into the night.

From behind the screen of the net curtains, the sightlines from Erin's armchair to the street lamp were unobstructed. The woman was still on the ground, sobbing softly now, reeling from her injuries. She was beginning to shiver, too, as shock began to seep into the places where her fear had been. But Erin didn't go to her, or call out to check if she needed help. Nor did she reach for a telephone to call for an ambulance, or a police officer. Erin Dawes did not respond at all. The dead never do.

2

The heat was waiting for Chief Inspector Domenic Jejeune, enveloping him in its sultry embrace as he emerged through the glass doors of the international terminal. He stood for a moment on the sidewalk, adjusting to the mirror-like glare of the sunshine, as he searched for a driver to guide him through the casual, yellow-taxi chaos of Bogota's El Dorado International Airport.

Despite the heat, Jejeune felt a lightness that he had not known for days. The shadowy world of hedging and half-truths was behind him now, sloughed off like dead skin. He was here, in Colombia. Whatever was going to happen, whatever was waiting for him, it could all begin now.

A taxi driver approached, an older man with a lined face and a crooked, world-weary smile. Before he could reach Jejeune, two other drivers swooped in, vying for the fare. They were younger, hungrier, and Jejeune watched as the three men held a spirited negotiation for the right to claim the prize as their own. His thoughts turned to three other people who had wrangled over his fate recently; one he should not have deceived, one he could not, and one he would not.

"Black Inca, Chiribiquete Emerald, Green-Bearded Helmetcrest," recited Lindy Hey, absently bunching the ends of her long blond hair with a fist as she read the list once again. "My God, Dom, this isn't a birding tour you're going on, it's a trip through the enchanted forest. These names alone make these birds worth travelling all the way to Colombia to see. Well, almost." She offered him a wan smile. They were standing by the bed, side by side, methodically packing his travel kit. His departure was still a couple of days away, but Lindy was not a person to leave things till the last minute.

She waved the paper at him. "Will you see these when you're over there, do you think?"

"The ones on that list? Most of them. Probably." He hesitated. "Perhaps."

Lindy gave him a look. Another time it might have made it all the way to exasperation, but Dom was leaving soon, and she had already determined to make things as comfortable between them as possible until then. Besides, she already knew the reason for his uncertainty. "It depends on how much of your trip is actually going to be about birding, you mean? Have you decided yet what you're going to tell DCS Shepherd when she asks why you've chosen to go to Colombia at this particular time?"

"It's the dry season." Jejeune waited for Detective Chief Superintendent Colleen Shepherd to look up from her paper hunt. "It makes access to remote areas easier."

Perhaps even those that exist inside us. But even though the thought went unsaid, it was clear from Shepherd's expression that she suspected there was more behind Jejeune's impulsive decision than he was telling her.

The DCS let herself stay occupied with hunting through the various papers on her desk. The task seemed to be a constant feature of his visits to her office these days, as if all the shuffling might give her eyes something else to do, rather than looking at him. Both would tacitly acknowledge they were not enjoying the most cordial of relationships at the moment, even if neither was willing to broach the subject openly. As a result, most of their conversations now teetered on this tightrope of strained politesse, where eye contact was avoided as much as possible and conversation carried the clipped terseness of those who would sooner move on.

"Nothing else going on?" Shepherd straightened finally from her task and looked squarely at him. "On the domestic front, I mean. Everything's okay, I trust ... between you and Lindy."

Jejeune managed to hide his startled look from his DCS, but not without some effort. "Fine." Even to him, the answer seemed to lack the conviction he would have liked.

"It just seems a bit sudden, that's all. I can't imagine what that girl of yours makes of this zipping off to foreign climes to watch birds with Christmas just around the corner. Still, I suppose she has more than enough events of her own to attend. She seems to be very much in demand these days, I must say. Every time I open a newspaper, I see something about her."

"Exactly. I doubt she'll even notice I've gone." Jejeune offered a smile, grateful that Shepherd's scrutiny of his motives seemed to be behind them.

The DCS seemed to consider his comment. "As a visiting police officer, I assume you'll be informing the Colombian authorities of your trip. Just as a courtesy, I mean. How long you plan on being in their country, where you'll be going, that sort of thing." She paused for a long moment. "And, of course, the reason for your visit."

"Birdwatching."

Deputy Consul Carmela Rojas made her pronouncement in a way that suggested she might have been expecting a different answer from Jejeune. Behind her, Sloane Square was enjoying a crisp, bright winter day. Sunlight danced off the woman's dazzling white blouse as it slanted in through her office window.

The Deputy Consul for Legal Affairs looked up from the form she was consulting, her dark eyes searching Jejeune's face. She was about his height, though the way her straight black hair hung down her back made her seem taller. It wasn't a hairstyle Jejeune would have necessarily associated with the prosaic business of diplomatic liaison, but then he doubted Carmela Rojas would have any difficulty being taken seriously by her male colleagues.

She set the form delicately on her desk, face down. It was a signal that she wouldn't need to refer to it again. Jejeune suspected she had committed the details to memory long before he received his invitation to enter her office. Rojas walked around the desk to take a seat behind it. She gestured for Jejeune to sit and he settled opposite her, the liquid shine of the rosewood surface glistening like a pool between them.

"This birdwatching tour, it is with Mas Aves."

It wasn't a question. Jejeune said nothing.

"May I ask why you chose to inform the Colombian authorities of this visit? You are aware that, under normal circumstances, a British subject, or even a Canadian one," she flashed a smile at him, "does not need any special permission to visit Colombia?"

"I didn't want there to be any misunderstanding … about my reasons for taking the trip." Jejeune's expression seemed to suggest they both knew choosing to visit a country where his brother was under an international extradition warrant made these anything but normal circumstances.

Rojas nodded slowly. "This is perhaps wise. Although a visitor's visa is issued on arrival as a matter of course, it is done, as you may know, at the discretion of the immigration officer. The decision would be easier for such an officer if he could be reassured that you have listed all of the areas you plan to visit, for example." She paused for a moment. "But we will come to this in a moment. I see you will be travelling alone? Your partner has no wish to accompany you to Colombia?"

"You know I would, if I could." Lindy paused in the act of rolling up a lightweight shirt. "I will, if you want me to. There's still time. I could see if I could get a last-minute deal."

Jejeune offered her a smile and shook his head. He took the shirt from her and tucked it into his pack.

"If only it didn't have to be now," she said. "It's just so busy for me."

"I know."

"But it does have to be now, doesn't it? Because if you miss this Mas Aves tour, it means another six months with no …." *Closure?* It wasn't a word Lindy used. But it was what she meant. She held on to a bottle of insect repellant as she handed it to him, so he would have to look at her. "I get it, Dom, really I do. You need to see it all for yourself, the locations, the birds. You need to try to understand how Damian managed to get himself into this awful situation." Lindy gave him her special look, the one designed to show empathy and support, but that could never really suppress a little shadow of doubt behind all the reassurance. "You know things will be all right? Between us, I mean. Nothing is going to change that," she said gently. "Not what Damian did, nor the circumstances, nor anything. Whatever you find out, or don't find out, we'll still be okay."

But it was a question, and Jejeune had heard it as such. "Okay," he repeated unconsciously.

"Are you sure you can't discuss any of this with Shepherd before you go? It might be better. In case anything happens out there."

"Not now," said Jejeune. "Not yet. Maybe …" he tailed off, unsure what he meant to say next.

Lindy paused and looked at him. "She'll get it. You know that. Colleen Shepherd is a very bright person. She's going to make the connection whether you spell it out for her or not."

"Colombia," said Shepherd, leaving room after the word with a long pause. "And it's really that good for birds, is it?"

"Over nineteen hundred species. More than any other country in the world," said Jejeune over-brightly. "There's an incredible range of habitats, you see. Plenty of room for speciation." If he could keep the conversation out here, among the technical details, it might prevent her from venturing elsewhere with her inquiries. Jejeune felt uneasy about his manipulative methods, but deceit by evasion seemed preferable to outright lies — to the deceiver, at least.

"Birds." Shepherd's tone suggested she now lumped all avian life in with the hardened criminals it was her job to deal with on a daily basis. "You know Eric's off on some birding jaunt with Quentin Senior again? I swear, the man sees more of him these days than I do."

Eric. So that was it. Shepherd's partner was pursuing birding with all the zeal of a new convert, and she was still adjusting to his frequent absences. Not many things could have made Jejeune's request for leave to go on this trip any more difficult, but Eric's newfound love of birding was probably one.

Shepherd seemed to realize she had veered into personal territory and swung the conversation back abruptly to the matter at hand. "Well, if you must go, I suppose we can manage without you for a while. You are due some leave, after all. I'll put the paperwork through this afternoon. Just make sure Sergeant Maik is up-to-date on everything before you get on that plane."

She looked down at her desk, and for a moment it seemed as if she was prepared to let the conversation end this way. But as Jejeune made his way to the door, Shepherd called out. "Domenic."

She rounded the desk and came toward him. The two of them stood awkwardly, hovering between a hug and a handshake. *There should be a word for this moment*, thought Jejeune. In the end, the DCS settled for a hesitant stroke of his arm, a gesture that added an unwelcome frisson of intimacy from which they both recoiled slightly.

Retreating to a more formal tone, she said, "Do be careful. Try not to leave any little pieces of yourself in Colombia. I want you whole and intact on your return. Just as you were."

Were, he noted. Like when she first brought him onboard, the high-flying Golden Boy, with his celebrated successes newly tucked under his belt and the carillons of national press acclaim still ringing in the air. But not as you are *now*, perhaps; distracted, uncommitted, weighed down by the burden of past secrets.

"You make no mention of Chiribiquete National Park on your travel itinerary," said Carmela Rojas, still seated behind her exquisitely figured desk. "You are aware you would need a permit to travel to this area." Her steady gaze held him for a moment. "Under the circumstances, I do not think the park authorities would be prepared to issue this to you."

"I have no plans to visit Chiribiquete," Jejeune told her.

Rojas's expensively manicured eyebrows rose slightly. "And yet, it is not simply for birding that you wish to visit Colombia. On this I think we may agree."

"I would like a better picture of what happened," conceded Jejeune. "I'm hoping someone at Mas Aves can provide some insight."

Rojas inclined her head. "Perhaps. But you will not find anything in these insights to help your brother. I am aware that you have an excellent reputation for uncovering evidence that others have missed. This will not happen in this case. A full and impartial investigation has already been conducted. You must accept the facts in this case, Inspector Jejeune. Your brother committed a serious crime in our country, and his actions were responsible for the deaths of four people. Of this there can be no doubt."

Despite her forthright manner, Rojas's expression showed compassion. The woman deserved the courtesy of as much honesty as Jejeune could give her. Of his thoughts, though, she was entitled to no part. "I am willing to accept the facts in this case," stated Jejeune. "But where there are gaps in the account, there are no facts to accept. Yet."

She waited, matching Jejeune's silence with her own. At first, it seemed she was prepared to turn it into a contest; a battle of wills. But finally, she placed her hands on the edge of her desk and pushed herself back slightly. "You are saddened by your brother's situation. This is understandable. I have a sister. We are very close. *Amigas del alma*, we say — soulmates. I would feel the same. But your brother is a fugitive from justice in our country. An international warrant has been issued for his arrest and extradition to Colombia. We cannot permit entry to anyone who might be in a position to give any assistance to this person."

Jejeune was silent. These were the terms of entry; reassurances, the same ones he would have sought if he had been in her place.

"I am not in contact with my brother," he said, "and I don't know where he is."

Carmela Rojas inclined her head slightly. It was a non-committal gesture, but to Jejeune it had the feel of one that had served her well in past negotiations. "Then I am sure an affidavit to that effect will ensure the Colombian immigration authorities grant you a visitor's visa upon your arrival. Enjoy your stay in our country, Inspector Jejeune."

Jejeune emerged from his reverie to find a taxi driver waiting patiently for him. It was the man who had first spotted him, the older one. His claim on the new arrival had apparently prevailed, and there was something about the thought that gave Jejeune some small sense of satisfaction, as if fairness stood a chance in this country, as if natural justice was recognized. He climbed into the little yellow vehicle and gave the driver the address of the hotel.

The busy streets of Bogota drifted by like a carnival procession; vibrant and dynamic, pulsing in the clear tropical light. *Colombia*. It was a long way to come for answers. Especially when Domenic Jejeune did not even know yet what his questions would be.

3

Outside the window of the cottage, the cold winter light hung with menace. But it was here, in the comfortable, well-ordered interior, that the dissonance of murder charged the air. Here, within these whitewashed walls and the low, dark-timbered ceilings, and this still, silent fireplace, the emptiness lurked in the room, as if something had been removed from the atmosphere itself now that victim's body had been taken away.

The world of Erin Dawes was still on view, in her possessions, and her photographs, and her furniture. But they had lost the axis on which to revolve. The objects in this room merely existed now, without context, without purpose. Though most of the decor and furnishings in the cottage were unremarkable, one item stood out. Beneath the single bay window sat the dark mass of a vintage 1950s Chubb safe.

Detective Constable Lauren Salter picked up a heavy metal figurine from an occasional table beside the armchair and studied it closely. It was a striking yellow bird with black wings. On the base on the ornament, a small plaque bore a simple inscription: *Norfolk Gold*. Salter wondered what it had been in its former life, when Erin Dawes was still alive to give its existence some meaning. A cherished gift? A souvenir of a happy time? Or just something Dawes had picked up for herself, on a whim as she passed by, perhaps, because the bright yellow colour caught her eye. Whatever it had once been, it was now merely more detritus of a life ended early.

"It breaks your heart a little bit at a time, doesn't it, this job?" said Salter sadly, looking down at the figurine.

"It can," said Sergeant Danny Maik quietly, "if you let it."

She looked at him now, at his broad back as he rested on his haunches examining the steel-grey safe, an imposing, impenetrable mass. Perhaps a shell was necessary in this job, but what if it trapped too much inside you? Once Salter had thought she might be able to overwhelm Danny Maik's protective layers, conquer them with words and kind gestures, with love. But only sadness made it beyond Maik's defences; sadness and his Motown songs. She was beginning to accept that he was always going to remain the same protected fortress, as impenetrable as the grey safe at the far end of the room. Perhaps it was time to move on. Life was too short to wait for miracles that were never going to happen. Another wave of melancholy swept over her as she considered the figure again.

"We don't have birds like this out here, do we, Sarge?"

"I've never seen one," said Maik over his shoulder. "But then, I'm hardly the one to ask, am I?"

Salter shook her head. "No. Plenty of odd-looking birds around here, but none like this, I'm sure of it. So what's this all about then, d'you think? *Norfolk Gold?* A bit of wishful thinking? Artistic licence?"

Or a clue? It looked like a high-quality work, collectible. Although it was weighty and solid, it would have fit into a pocket easily enough. The thing was likely worth a few quid at the local pawn shop, if not on eBay. So why hadn't the killer taken it? A clue, or not a clue? Salter wasn't even sure it mattered anymore. As she replaced the ornament, she tried to suppress a sigh, but part of it escaped anyway. If Danny Maik noticed, he gave no sign.

She turned her attention to the leather wallet poking out from a handbag beside the chair. SOCO had murmured about a lack of physical evidence left at this scene, but there was nothing but evidence, if only you had the wit to interpret it. A wallet tucked hastily into an open handbag. Tiny shards of paper peering from the edges of closed drawers in the oak sideboard. There had been no watch or ring on the body they had taken away, although a photograph on the occasional table showed Erin Dawes wearing both. A robbery then? A life taken for a few valuables and some small change? She looked down at Danny Maik as he remained hunched in front of the safe. *I might not be able to reach your heart, Danny, but I know that will.*

It was just the two of them in the cottage now. The uniformed constable who had first responded to the call had long since made excuses of being needed elsewhere and sidled away. The SOCO team, too, appeared to be in an uncharacteristic hurry to complete their task and escape this oppressive sadness. Even Danny had been unusually terse when they told him how long it would take to get someone to open the safe.

The lamps burning inside the room did little to dispel the gloom hanging low outside the window. Perhaps it was this that had winnowed its way into Maik's mood. But perhaps it was the journey they had just made together. Salter shied involuntarily from the memory. They had driven back in silence — no music, for once — from the small house, the shabby living room where they had stood shoulder to shoulder watching the silent pulse of disbelief, followed by the abject abandonment to sorrow, to feelings of pain and loss that would never leave the aged parents from this point on. Danny, as always, had managed to strike that balance of sympathy and strength that she knew she could never master if she delivered this news for the next one hundred years. And she knew, too, that you could only find that balance with practice, with having done it so many times before, standing there and letting bereaved ones drag you into their pain, even as they drew some small support from your own strength. Lauren Salter spent most of her days wishing she could either protect Danny from the world or wrap herself in the reassurance he brought. Though she was beginning to acknowledge that neither would ever come to pass, the feelings were never as strong as when she watched him amid the devastating sadness he had chosen as his role to deliver.

"Strange DCI Jejeune didn't mention we were getting a sub in," said Salter suddenly. "He said nothing before he left?" She didn't need the confirmation, merely somewhere else to direct her thoughts.

It would have been strange if he had been aware of it, thought Danny. But he was fairly sure, due to its absence from the myriad instructions Jejeune had tossed his way before leaving for the airport, that the DCI had no idea someone would be coming in as a temporary replacement. Colleen Shepherd had never been shy about lighting up the stars when she had a major announcement to make, and whatever you thought about her approach, at least you usually knew what was in the offing at Saltmarsh Constabulary. But the casual way she had come alongside Danny's desk that morning to announce the impending arrival of the new officer suggested this wasn't news she intended to broadcast to a larger audience. Not yet, at least. And you had to wonder, if you were a suspicious bugger like Danny Maik, whether there might just be a reason she hadn't made the DCI privy to her plans in advance.

In truth, he would have expected Shepherd to bring in a senior officer to stand in for Jejeune. That an extra body was going to be needed had been clear enough to all of them since DCS Colleen Shepherd had posted the new duty roster a couple of days before. With DCI Jejeune on his holiday, there was a large detective-inspector-shaped gap at the head of the

Saltmarsh Serious Crimes investigation team. With this murder to investigate now, it could not go unfilled.

"No reflection on anybody here, Sergeant," Shepherd had told Danny. "I hope you know that." Shepherd leaned over Maik's desk earnestly, treating him to the soft scent of her perfume. "It's just that the DCI's absence leaves us a little bit light to do a *full and proper* on this cottage murder, especially with Detective Constable Holland out on compassionate leave."

Maik understood. Until recently, the words *compassionate* and *Holland* were not candidates to appear in the same sentence. Although a girl he cared for had died, Tony Holland had been back on the job a couple of days after, a little scarred, a little damaged, but determined to show the world he wouldn't be bowed by it. But Maik knew these cases, the water-off-a-duck's-back brigade. These were the ones you found one day with their heads down on their desks, faces bathed in sweat, shaking uncontrollably. It was Maik who had advised Holland to take some time off, and he was pleased the constable had, for once, listened to him. Salter was right. This job could break your heart. The trick was, every now and then, to let it.

Danny heard the familiar chirrup of Salter's iPhone, and turned to find her looking down at the device. "Text from the DCS. She says the new bloke is on his way over. Should be here any minute. He wants to meet us and do a run-through here at the scene. At least I found out his name. It's Laraby."

"Laraby?"

Salter misinterpreted Maik's look of surprise. "I know. It might be a bit easier to take our temporary detective inspector seriously if he didn't sound quite so much like an Ikea cabinet."

"You could always call me Marvin," said a voice from the doorway. "It's what my friends would call me. If I had any, that is."

4

Laraby stood in the doorway, making no move to enter or introduce himself further. Salter took a second to assess the man temporarily drafted in to act as lead investigator in Jejeune's absence. He was perhaps a couple of decades older than the DCI, but still in good condition: trim and fit. There was an easy self-confidence about the way he held his frame; upright, shoulders slightly back, as if daring the world to bring on its little assaults so he could show he was ready to deal with them.

Behind him, the uniformed officer who had driven him, a lad who himself looked like he shouldn't have been driving unaccompanied, hovered uncertainly as he waited for further instructions. Laraby seemed not to notice, so Danny Maik dismissed the officer with a short nod of his head. The sergeant, it appeared, would be seeing to the new DI's transportation arrangements from now on.

"Sergeant Maik and Constable Salter? You two were first in after discovery, I understand?"

Their silence told Laraby he was correct.

"Initial impressions?" He softened his demand slightly with a trailing smile. "Best part, sometimes."

Perhaps Salter's embarrassment was heightened by Laraby's unwillingness to dwell on her faux pas; her neck and ears still held a noticeably rosy glow. Nevertheless, it was clear she would need to go first. Danny Maik was still looking as if somebody had told him the investigation was being taken over by Sherlock Holmes.

"It looks like a burglary gone ..." Salter hesitated. *Wrong* did not begin to cover the heartbreakingly sad scene they had encountered. "We think someone broke in through the back door expecting the place to be empty, but then found her here, possibly asleep in the armchair. Smothered her with a pillow and then had a riffle around. There's evidence that some personal effects have been taken; jewellery and such. And the drawers in that sideboard have been searched."

"TV and electronics?"

Salter shook her head. "It looks like whoever it was might have been disturbed before they had a chance to get them away."

Laraby looked around the room. "Murder in a pretty little village like this," he said, shaking his head. "Doesn't seem right, somehow. How did we catch it, anyway?"

"A call from a neighbour three doors down. Out for a late-night stroll. She saw the door wide open and called the station."

Laraby glanced across to Maik, as if checking whether he might have anything to add. He didn't, but he was looking at the new DI as if he might have more than a few questions of his own.

"This stroll…?" Laraby asked him.

"A well-established routine." Maik seemed to be paying out the details reluctantly, as if suspicious of exactly what Laraby might do with the information once he had it. But his tone suggested he was comfortable enough with his earlier verification that Laraby could be, too.

Laraby came around behind the armchair and hunched slightly, following the line of sight. The dark mass of the safe beneath the window was in direct view. "Killed here?"

There was a beat of silence between the men which Salter felt compelled to fill. "It looks like the location of the suffocation, forensic confirmation pending. We found a pillow on the floor by the chair. No signs of a struggle. Mind you, a high chair back like that, an approach from behind. If the killer got a good hold, it would be difficult to put up much of a fight."

The DI nodded without speaking. "So, what do we know about our victim?"

Still Maik seemed reluctant to answer any inquires not specifically directed his way. Again, Salter stepped in. "Erin Dawes, thirty-eight, owner and sole occupant of the property. She's lived in this village all her life. Went off to university, bought this place when she came back, and she's been here ever since. Never married. No kids."

Laraby picked up a photo from the table. "This her?" He considered the photo for a long time, and was still looking down at it when he spoke. "Good looking woman, but never married. Anything in that, I wonder?"

"Other than she had some common sense?"

Divorcee, Laraby's smile seemed to say. But there was more irony than bitterness in the constable's response now. If she wasn't completely over the break-up, she was well on her way.

"Not much of a social life at all, that we can see," continued Salter. "About the only thing we could find was an investment group called the IV League."

"Ivy league like those American colleges?"

"In a way. The same derivation of the name, IV, *four* in Roman numerals. This lot actually spelled it *I, V,* though. But there's no meetings in her diary for the past couple of months, so either she left, or they've disbanded."

"Let's find out which, shall we?" Laraby nodded and moved to set the photograph down on a small side table draped in a floor-length floral cloth. The sound seemed so perfectly co-ordinated to the inspector's actions that at first they all assumed it was the squeak of a loose table leg. But a faint movement of the cloth caused Laraby to bend down. He fished beneath the hem for a few moments and emerged with a tiny kitten in his hand.

He held it up to eye level, the squirming form dwarfed by his hand. Laraby didn't look happy, but to his credit, he didn't take it out on the animal. "Looks like it's starving," he said. "See if there's any milk in the fridge, will you, Constable?"

"Milk's no good," Salter told him with authority. "It'll want water."

He handed the kitten off to Salter and watched her disappear into the kitchen with it before turning on Maik.

"I thought SOCO had done a sweep of this place." The tenor of the statement was unmistakable.

"There's a cat door in the kitchen," said Maik evenly. "I imagine the kitten was outside when they were here and came back in after they left. They wouldn't have missed it. The SOCO crew are a bright bunch. They know what they're doing."

Laraby nodded to himself slightly. The legendary loyalty of Danny Maik — unwilling to let anybody take any liberties with the SOCO team's reputation, even in their absence. Laraby considered the hulking form, now turned slightly away from him in examination of something else in the room. *I'll bet I could enjoy working with you, Sergeant Maik*, he thought.

Laraby pointed to the figurine of the bird on the small table beside the chair. "This lot has all been dusted by those Mensa members from SOCO, I take it?" He hefted the figurine and distractedly tapped it against the cupped palm of his other hand as he gazed around the room. Maik's eyes followed the metronomic rise and fall of the yellow and black bird.

Laraby looked at the safe. "That's a formidable piece of hardware for any domestic dwelling. Any reason this woman would need a six-hundred-pound safe in a quaint country cottage like this?"

Salter answered from the kitchen doorway. "She was an accountant ... sir." She added the title as an afterthought, but Laraby either didn't notice, or didn't mind. "She did a couple of on-site jobs at local companies, a half-day here and there, but mostly she worked from home."

"Took it seriously, by the look of things." He pointed to the kitchen. "Point of entry?" he asked. Maik nodded and followed the DI into the other room. For a moment, the two men stood shoulder to shoulder, peering intently at the hole in the glass panel in the kitchen door.

"What do you reckon on that kitten, Constable?" asked Laraby finally, without turning round. "Can we find it a good home?"

"I can try."

He nodded absently. "There was a mug, I understand, in that sink over there. You said there was no sign of a struggle. Any evidence of a sedative?"

Maik was still staring at the weed-lined path beyond the back door. "No, but there was recoverable DNA on the mug." He turned so his look found Laraby. "The SOCO team has already sent it for analysis," he said. "Results should be back within a couple of days."

Laraby raised his eyebrows in what might have been admiration. He gave another short smile and returned to the living room. Maik and Salter trailed after him, leaving the kitten in the kitchen to lap at the saucer of water she had set down. "DCS Shepherd tells me the ME's already finished his preliminary examination of the body. Any signs of recent injuries? Cuts or bruises? Burns? Broken bones?"

"Nothing at all. She seemed to be in very good health. A couple of tattoos — not gang, not military. We checked, just in case, but they weren't in our database."

Laraby pulled a face. "Be easier these days to have a database of people who don't have a tattoo." He stroked his chin with his fingers "So the safe is in plain sight; the intruder must know any valuables are going to be in there, yet there's nothing on the body to suggest any attempts at coercion or torture. Why kill the woman without at least even trying to get the combination from her? I can well imagine they're not the most sophisticated bunch of villains you'll ever find, out here in a picturesque little spot like this, but still...."

Salter flashed a look at Maik. What the hell was Laraby on about? Killers made illogical choices all the time. Panic, fear, a loud noise outside; there were any number of reasons why he might have killed her if he didn't have the luxury of time. He was just a bit too full of himself, this bloke, with his *picturesque* this and his *quaint* that and his *pretty* the other. How many ways was he going to find to tell them he thought they were just bumbling village coppers whiling away their time in some picture postcard irrelevance out on the edge of nowhere? She searched out Danny Maik's eyes for some sort of agreement. But Laraby hadn't finished speaking yet.

"That bolt is up high on the kitchen door, very odd place for it. I don't remember seeing one in that position before. And yet there was just the single hole cut in the glass, right next to it." He shook his head. "I despair sometimes, the luck these villains have? Why can't nice coppers like us get breaks like that?" Laraby thought for a moment and turned to Maik. "It's a problem, isn't it, Sergeant? Do you want to tell the good constable here what it means, or am I still being put through my paces?"

Maik looked at Salter. "Whoever cut the hole knew where to find the bolt. It suggests they'd been here before."

Laraby nodded. "But expecting there to be valuables hanging about when there's a perfectly good safe in here? Now that suggests otherwise." Laraby leaned back slightly and slid his hands into his trouser pockets. He looked at Salter. "You see my point."

She did now. Deliberately or not, somebody was sending mixed signals. And that meant investigating the murder of Erin Dawes was not going to be anywhere near as straightforward as it had once seemed.

5

Jejeune stood on the sidewalk outside his hotel and watched his taxi disappear into the miasma of traffic. The heat was building, and there was a steady bustle of activity on the streets as people hurried to get their tasks completed before the warmest part of the day arrived. Soon, things would slow to walking pace as Bogota drifted toward its afternoon somnolence. The city would wait for the heat to lift once again from the mountain-rimmed plain with the advent of evening.

After checking in, Jejeune hefted his pack with one hand and ducked into the darkened, air-conditioned bar off the hotel lobby. He ordered a coffee and settled on a stool in the far corner, a place to observe unobserved. On the other side of the room, a man was leaning forward in a low-slung wicker chair, forearms resting on his knees. His dark hair was slicked back, framing a lean face with strong, defined features. The seats facing him were all occupied by people leaning in to listen. The man was addressing the group casually, making sure he engaged each of them in turn; a man giving instructions he expected to be followed. He was about Jejeune's age and build, but he had the raw muscularity and weathered features of a man who spent his days outdoors. The tanned arms showing beneath his short-sleeved khaki shirt hinted at special toning; martial arts training, perhaps.

The man had registered Jejeune's entrance, and he turned to look at him now. There was no hostility in his gaze, only a deep, intense interest. He was not wondering why Jejeune had come to Colombia, or why he had chosen this tour company. He thought he knew. But did he? Even Jejeune wasn't entirely sure himself. There was more to it than just the need to be here, as Lindy said, to see it all for himself, so he could understand, somehow, the heartbreaking truth of his brother's predicament. *Whatever you find. Or don't.* This country had been on his radar since his earliest days of birding. Part of him wanted to believe that he might be able to immerse himself in this birding tour, to experience the joy of it as the other participants undoubtedly would. But perhaps that, too, was just the shadowy wish of a mind awash with whispered questions and travel fatigue.

Jejeune raised his coffee cup in a small gesture of acknowledgement, but neither man made any effort to close the gap between them. The detective regretted slightly that he'd lost the opportunity to study Armando Perea unobserved, to note his *tells*, the little giveaways in his gestures and habits. For reasons he couldn't have explained, Jejeune had a sense that any advantage he could gain over the man who was going to be his guide for the next few days was going to be important. With a final nod in Perea's direction, Jejeune drained his coffee, picked up his pack, and headed up to his room.

Emptying out his pockets, he took out a crumpled sheet of paper and stared at it: the bird list, in Lindy's handwriting. A few scribbled words that had made this trip possible, because of the assurance it had allowed him to give Deputy Consul Rojas: *I am not in contact with my brother. I don't know where he is.*

His mind drifted to the clifftop path beside their cottage; a safe, quiet place to let his swirling thoughts return to normal. It was the only written communication he could ever remember that had left him literally speechless. He had looked at the sheet of paper for a long time out there, with the winds buffeting him, threatening to tear the precious note from his grasp and send it floating out over the sea. It wouldn't have mattered. Because by then, he knew the contents by heart: *Black Inca, Chiribiquete Emerald, Green-Bearded Helmetcrest*, and two other names. Hummingbirds, he knew now, endemic to Colombia, found nowhere else in the world. At the time, their significance was not clear to him. But as a message, even then, the words had meant everything. They were a response to a statement, blurted out in frustration a few days before. "If I even knew Damian's list of target species on the trip, that might tell me something."

It did. The list told him that Lindy had found a way to ask his brother, that she knew, somehow, how to reach him. Even now, he marvelled at Lindy's guile in revealing it to him. Because inevitably, as soon as you received a list like this, your mind was going to be flooded with questions about how and when and where. But if Lindy had thrust the list into your hand just as she was leaving — *Popping out to the shops for a bit* — and had also, for the first time in living memory, left her phone behind, well, then, you might find yourself with time to reconsider exactly what you wanted to ask. Because you might realize, as you peered out over the sea, and the keening wind made your eyes water, that not knowing would allow you to keep a gossamer thin veil of deniability, so you could look into the eyes of your DCS, if she asked, or those of a deputy consul like Carmela Rojas, and be able to tell them honestly that you didn't know where your brother was, that you were not in contact with him.

So when Lindy returned, wearing that faint pirate smile that told him she was prepared to keep any secrets he allowed her to, all he could do was cup her face in his hands with a tenderness even he was surprised he possessed, and draw her in for a long, silent hug that could have gone on forever.

Jejeune checked his watch, then took out his phone. The familiar voice answered on the second ring. "You got there okay then?" said Lindy, in that jaunty tone she seemed to reserve exclusively for him. "So, what's Bogota like?"

"Thriving. There's new building going on everywhere — roads, services, office blocks." Domenic strode to the window as they chatted and looked down onto the street below. Crowds of people gathered amongst the bodegas and the traffic, conversing, trading, negotiating; the beating heart of human interactions. "There's a great enthusiasm about it all, too, like the country is heading in a new direction and everybody's buying in."

"Sounds terrific. How was your flight?"

The conversation moved on to this and then the weather, Jejeune countering Lindy's description of the cold and dreary north Norfolk winter with an account of the bright, sunny cityscape he now found himself looking out over. It was communication, nothing more; holding hands across the vast expanses of the globe that separated them.

"Met anyone interesting?" asked Lindy.

Jejeune could hear the uneven breathing patterns as she moved around the house, sorting through mail, folding clothes, putting away dishes, all with her phone resting on her shoulder, clamped into place by her cricked neck.

"I saw the tour leader, but we haven't spoken yet. How about you? Any new men in your life?"

"Tons." Lindy told him. "In fact, even today there was some geezer with a shaved head and an interesting line in neck art hanging around outside the office. If he's there again tomorrow, I'm going to ask Eric if he wants me to interview him for a feature on prison tats."

"I meant at your events. Old flames."

The Circuit, they were calling it, the steady round of appearances that had come her way since winning a prestigious national journalism award. In the beginning, Domenic had accompanied her, but he had cut an increasingly isolated figure on the periphery of her circle, as she reconnected with colleagues from earlier in her journalism career. Though she denied it vehemently, they both knew she would enjoy her time much more without the distraction of having to flash solicitous glances his way every five minutes, so he had started finding himself unavailable when her appearances came up, until he had finally stopped attending them altogether.

"I really do wish I could have been there with you," said Lindy. "There's just something so enchanting about that part of the world. No wonder all the great magic realist writers come from Latin America. Marquez, Allende, Uslar Pietri. You'd better be careful, Inspector Jejeune. Strange and wonderful things can happen in the world of magic realism."

"Like you becoming a birder, you mean?"

"You're confusing magic realism with fantasy, darling, and that's one fantasy of yours that just ain't a-happenin.'" Lindy's frivolity seemed to give way suddenly, and there was a beat of uneasy silence. "Danny Maik dropped by," she said finally. "He said he just wanted to check I was okay, see whether I needed anything."

"That was nice."

"Not to mention unexpected." She may as well say it. She knew Domenic would be thinking it anyway. And he would be waiting for an explanation. "It took a whole side of a *Motown Chartbusters* album before Danny got around to telling me the reason for his visit. An entire side!" she repeated for emphasis. "Broken hearts, betrayals, unrequited love. Those poor Motown singers didn't have much luck in the old romance department, did they?"

Jejeune waited.

"This case," said Lindy carefully, "the lady who was found murdered in one of those cottages that back onto the river. Colleen Shepherd has brought somebody in to handle it."

Jejeune still said nothing.

"It's Marvin Laraby."

In the street below, the stream of life continued to flow. People wandered back and forth, interacting, touching other people's lives, perhaps once, perhaps as a daily ritual. But Domenic Jejeune's mind was not on them. It was moving back into the past; ahead, to what this news might mean for the future. His future.

Lindy's voice jolted him back to the present. "Are you still there? I don't think you can read anything into this, Dom. As Danny understands it, Laraby just happened to be available. As soon as you get back, he'll be given the old heave ho and everything will be *as you were*. I just thought you should know, that's all."

Lindy hadn't said she thought he would *like* to know. A good journalist chose her words carefully.

"It's okay," said Jejeune easily. "Like you said, by the time I get back, Laraby will probably have the case wrapped up and be on his way. Whatever else he might be, Marvin Laraby is a very good detective."

There was another beat of silence as Lindy digested this. Or perhaps listened for something else.

"Listen," said Jejeune finally. "If it's okay, I'm going to get going. I want to have a shower and get some food. I've got some studying to do. The birds of Colombia await, and I want to be primed and ready to seek them out."

Lindy let the phone rest in her hand a long time after Jejeune ended the call. He was good at a lot of things, Domenic, but false levity wasn't one of them. The birds of Colombia might be awaiting him, but she knew he was likely to be considerably less primed and ready to seek them out now he knew Marvin Laraby had just re-entered his life.

6

Marvin Laraby stood at the front of the incident room in Saltmarsh Police Station, tall and straight-backed. He had his hands in the pockets of his suit trousers, flaring his jacket back behind him like a small cape. He held his head back slightly as he stared out over the assembled officers. A man who enjoyed looking life in the eye, the posture said. It added to an overall attitude that told you he had probably already faced most of the things you were likely to encounter in the course of your career, and you could trust him to steer you right when you needed him to.

"Now, I can appreciate you're all used to working under the watchful eyes of the media, whenever there's a high profile case in this part of the world." He paused a moment. "There's a lot to be said for that. Every time the DCS is required to brief the Directorate of Public Affairs for a press release, that's another opportunity to shine a spotlight on a case, another chance that a member of the public will come forward with useful information. But I might as well tell you right off, I don't seem to attract that kind of media attention myself." There was a faint glimmer of something in his deep-set eyes, though he didn't allow it to reach his face. "So what I do instead is make sure the little bits get done properly — checking alibis, verifying details, interviewing witnesses. Bit of a nuisance, I know, all that note-taking, and not very flash, but the thing is, in most of the cases I've worked, and in all of the big ones, getting a result has depended on it. No magic, no clairvoyance, no intellectual gymnastics, just people doing their jobs properly. So while it'll be a bit of a change of pace for the next little while, if you're as good as the DCS tells me you are, I'm sure none of you will have much trouble adjusting."

Laraby paused and looked around the room, waiting for someone to contradict him. No one did. From the open doorway, DCS Shepherd nodded appreciatively. There were a lot of ways to get the opening gambit of a temporary assignment wrong. Striking a tone that found the sweet spot between authority and approachability was a rare skill. The way he seemed to have instantly struck a rapport with the troops went some way toward helping Shepherd understand why DI Marvin Laraby was in the running for promotion to DCI the next time an opening came up.

The sound of Laraby clapping his hands together echoed round the room. "Right, let's get to it, then. So how do you want to go about this? I tell you what I think, you tell me where I'm wrong, and we take it from there?"

"Sergeant Maik usually leads us through the briefing," Salter said, looking around the room as if for confirmation. Maik had readied himself to stand when he caught sight of Laraby's upraised palm.

"Why don't you do it, Constable? You were at the scene both times. You've done the backgrounds. I'm sure the sergeant wouldn't mind you taking centre stage for once. Besides, female victim, a female officer's perspective on this can't hurt." He flashed a flat grin that came to rest in an empty space somewhere between himself and Danny.

Salter flickered an uncertain glance at Maik, and then at Shepherd. Maik was impassive, but the DCS eased herself up off the door jamb. "Why not, Constable? After all, for once we seem to have a viable line of inquiry."

Laraby nodded. "On the face of it."

Shepherd's expression suggested she might have preferred something a bit more unequivocal from Laraby. But given the normal lack of any sort of input from Domenic Jejeune at these briefings, she undoubtedly looked upon Laraby's contribution as something of a bonus anyway.

Salter ran over the findings as she had related them to Laraby in the cottage the day before. She ended on a hesitant note that had both Laraby and Shepherd looking at her.

"There was a figurine in the room, a yellow bird with black wings. It looks expensive but the killer didn't bother with it." She paused and looked around a little. "The thing is, the plaque said the bird was from Norfolk but I'm pretty sure it isn't." She shrugged. "It's probably nothing, but …" But they'd been taught to look at *probably nothings* before, especially ones concerning birds.

"I can't see that it's worth a formal line of inquiry." Shepherd surveyed the room briefly to see if anyone had a different opinion. "But if you wanted to have a look at it, I'm sure nobody would object." She turned to Laraby. "Anything come of that lead you called me about on your way to the site? Something about cat hairs on the victim's clothing?"

Laraby shook his head and cast a significant glance at Maik. "That's gone down the crapper, I'm afraid." A slight pulse of unease passed through the room and Laraby inclined his head slightly. "Apologies, ladies and gentlemen. It'll take me a bit of time to get used to the genteel ways of the countryside."

But it was not the vernacular that had them off-kilter. The SOCO team hadn't given him the information about the cat hairs, so if he knew about them on his way out to the site, that left Mansfield Jonus. But the Saltmarsh forensic medical examiner was notoriously cagy about releasing information until he had concluded his findings. Whether Laraby had obtained these early details through intimidation or persuasion, it was an impressive feat for someone who had only just got his highly polished brogues under Jejeune's desk.

"Okay, let's look at our victim, Ms. Dawes. That armchair she was found in. It was all set up to watch the goings on of the world outside. Any chance she nosed in on something that might have gotten her in trouble? I've heard about these seaside villages. All sorts of naughtiness going on behind the curtains. Anything to suggest she made a habit of knowing what her neighbours were up to? Any disputes on file?"

Salter shook her head. "Nothing at all. Erin Dawes seems to have been a polite neighbour who mostly kept to herself. Quiet, unassuming."

"Good job she didn't live in her parent's basement, or I might have been looking at her as a serial killer, with a profile like that," said Laraby. "How about her work? She was an accountant. Could she have uncovered some dodgy financials belonging to one of her clients?"

Once again, there was an uneasy shifting in the room. Shepherd watched with interest as the swell of discomfort drifted in Salter's direction. The constable was the one who seemed to have all the rapport with the new DI. It was going to be up to her to voice their misgivings. "So you don't think the motive was burglary, sir?"

Laraby's expression suggested it might be a bit early in the proceedings to be telling them what he thought.

"This investment group she was a part of, what do we know about them?" Maik asked.

Salter looked uncomfortable at this reversal of roles, this running the show while Danny Maik stayed on the sidelines and asked questions. She consulted her notes, though nobody really believed she needed to. "It appears the IV League was formed to purchase shares in a tech sector company called the Picaflor Project. It's a fairly new enterprise but it seems to be doing very well. Three of the IV League members contributed fifty thousand pounds each, and the fourth contributed land of equivalent value."

"Land? What for?" Both Shepherd and Maik looked like they were ready to pounce, but Laraby was first in with the question.

"No idea, but the payments were used to buy options on two hundred thousand pounds worth of shares in Picaflor, at very preferential rates."

"We should have a word with other investors in this IV League," said Laraby decisively. "Do we know who else was in the group?"

"Gerald Moncrieff, Amelia Welbourne, and Robin Oakes. All three are … local."

Danny Maik had a formidable stare when he chose to use it. This new man's was something different, softer, and yet at the same time equally compelling. It held enough inquiry to have Salter faltering slightly.

"It seems like a bit of an odd mix, that's all. They're all members of what you might call the local landed gentry. Well-to-do, a bit upper class, if I'm being honest. Sergeant Maik thought …"

"… it might be something worth looking at," completed Maik. "It's heady company for an accountant from a modest background."

Laraby nodded thoughtfully. "I assume Dawes is the one who contributed the land in lieu of the funds."

"No, sir," said Salter. "It was Robin Oakes. Erin Dawes appears to have paid in the fifty thousand along with Welbourne and Moncrieff."

Laraby's expression showed interest as well as surprise. "Okay, the sergeant and I will go to see what this Robin Oakes's land contribution is all about. In the meantime, let's get full backgrounds on all the principals. And listen, one more thing. Any result we get on this is going to belong to each and every one of us in this room, no matter where the final breaks come from, so let's work together, yeah? Make sure you share everything, make sure everybody is in the know with what you're doing, what you're thinking, where you're taking your investigations."

Shepherd watched Laraby from the doorway as he gathered up his notes and walked over to consult with Maik prior to them heading out. Leading from the rear, they called it, showing them he didn't mind being in the shadows as long as they got the result they were looking for. Even in the short time he had been there, it was clear to the others that Laraby was one of them. It was no wonder so many top brass still considered working one's way up through the ranks to be the preferred method of reaching the senior levels. Unless, of course, you had the helpful hand of the Home Secretary to guide your progress. She smiled to herself. She was being a bit unfair to Jejeune. He certainly had his own talents, and if she suspected that, even at this early stage, Laraby might win the People's Choice award, Domenic possessed detective abilities that were, as far as she was aware, unmatched anywhere in the police service. And since policing was not now, and never had been, a popularity contest, she knew where her own preferences lay. But it had been an impressive debut, nevertheless, and if Marvin Laraby's results matched his performance today, he would certainly be one to watch.

7

The sweep of the encircling mountains was barely visible through the early morning haze, a signal that, if the temperature was pleasant enough now, another warm day awaited the residents of Bogota. Domenic Jejeune sat on the rooftop terrace of his hotel, looking out over the haphazard tapestry of tiles and corrugated sheets that made up the roofscape of the city. Here and there, the canopy of a green tree pushed up through the mass like a weed through a patch of concrete. Below him, the city was slowly awakening, but the noise levels were still muted, and from somewhere an unfamiliar bird call drifted up to him. *Unfamiliar.* These birds, this place. Unfamiliar, too, was this feeling of impulsiveness, of acting without really understanding his motives. He wondered where it might lead.

Jejeune took a slow sip of his coffee and watched the Eared Doves effortlessly riding the updrafts. All around the perimeter of the terrace, plants Lindy struggled to nurture in tiny pots at home spilled from terracotta planters in luxurious abundance. At a table on the far side, the other six birders Jejeune had seen in the bar the previous evening were enjoying an animated discussion. They were from Barcelona, and although they had made friendly gestures to him as they passed, the gravitational pull of their mother tongue drew them inevitably toward each other's company.

Armando was at the head of the table, his back to Jejeune. From here, the detective could see the colourful web of tattoos that spiralled up the guide's arms. Jejeune thought about Lindy and her tattooed man. He remembered the moment of her return to the cottage, how delicate and fragile her body felt, like a bird's egg, as he enfolded her in his embrace. He was a long way away, and the world was filled with such dangerous and unpredictable things. Lindy was bright and resourceful, but she was also effortlessly beautiful and appealing. It wasn't difficult to imagine her attracting the wrong kind of attention. He felt the urge to protect her well up in him. But protect her from what?

A hand on his shoulder startled him from his thoughts, and he heard a low voice behind him, close to his ear. "Hey meester, you wan' buy some Colombian product. Bery good, bery stron'."

The pathetic predictability of the approach caused a wave of despair to rise in Jejeune. He was disappointed, too. Colombians were fully aware of their country's reputation, and everything he had read suggested the citizens were diligent and alert for behaviour that reinforced such negative stereotypes. He turned to decline with a suitably regretful smile, but his expression morphed into one of shock as he looked at the speaker. "I knew you'd find suitable employment one day," he said with a delighted smile.

"That'd be a 'no', then?" asked Juan "Traz" Perez, setting his coffee cup on the table and settling into the chair across from Domenic's.

"What are you doing here?" asked Jejeune warily as he sat. As delighted as he was to see his old college friend, he had already rejected the idea that this was a chance meeting. *Met anyone interesting?* "Lindy," he said.

Traz looked sheepish. "She told me you were coming here and I thought it was about time I did some birding in Colombia myself. Lots of endemics down here. Besides, I've heard your attempts at Spanish before. How far you gonna get around here telling the waiters they've got a *grassy arse* every time they bring you a beer?"

"Lindy asked you to look after me?"

Traz nodded solemnly. "She's paying me two hundred dollars a day, plus expenses. I got the rate from *The Rockford Files*," he said, conjuring memories of the detective series whose reruns, along with pizza and beer, had been a staple of Friday nights in the two men's college dorm.

In lieu of a response, Jejeune tipped his ear toward the same unfamiliar call as before.

"Great Thrush," said Traz, sipping his coffee. "Better learn that one in a hurry. You'll be hearing a lot of it." He nodded at the *Field Guide to the Birds of Colombia* on the table in front of Jejeune. "You're going to need something better than that first edition, too. Luckily, I'm the kind of friend who thinks about such things. I picked you up a brand new copy of the second ed." He paused and looked at Jejeune significantly. "Of course, all this presupposes that you are actually down here for the birding."

Jejeune looked at his good friend across the top of his coffee cup. Domenic Jejeune was not inclined to deceive Traz, but it would have been a waste of time in this case anyway. The man across from him could read him as well as anyone he had ever known, Lindy included.

"Your name, this country, this tour company. You don't need to be Jim Rockford to work this one out, JJ. Nobody is going to think this is a coincidence." Traz reverted easily to Jejeune's college nickname, as if the years had simply fallen away. "I don't know what you're hoping to find, but everybody will know this trip is not just about the birds."

"It is for now," said Jejeune simply. "What else did Lindy tell you?"

"She said if you wear black socks with shorts and sandals, I have her permission to shoot you." Traz looked directly at his friend, his dark eyes unblinking. He let his gaze rest on him.

There are places neither of us want this conversation to go, it seemed to say. *But I'll tell you if you ask.*

Domenic returned Traz's stare. He knew once he had crossed the threshold of knowledge, he could never go back. He chose to stay in his illusory state of denial, for the moment at least. He let his eyes drop, and then raised them again quickly at the sound of a scraping chair.

"May we join you?"

The man was older than Jejeune by a generation. His grey hair was swept back neatly from his forehead and almond eyes sparkled from behind large steel-rimmed glasses that seemed to suit his slightly fleshy features perfectly. "I'm Carl Walden." The hand he extended was soft and perfectly manicured.

Traz stirred to rise, and Jejeune was surprised at the excessive courtesy until he caught sight of the woman standing behind Walden. "This is Dorothea," said Walden, looking at the woman as if for permission to introduce her, "my daughter."

"I've been Thea to everyone but my father since I was about fifteen," she said pleasantly, shaking hands. She looked to be in her late twenties. Her pale khaki outfit was simple and unflattering, but Thea Walden carried her lithe body with confidence. Her face was framed with long black hair that hung straight to her shoulders. She had higher cheekbones than her father, and more attractive, angular features, but she had inherited the older man's eyes, deep-set and almond-shaped.

Traz smiled gallantly as he wheeled a chair around for her to sit in, and Thea responded with a warm, open smile of the kind which Colombians seemed to have a never-ending supply. She wore no jewellery or makeup, but she seemed to be having no trouble holding Traz's attention anyway.

"I'm guessing you must be Inspector Jejeune, the police detective I was told would be joining us?" Walden offered a pleasant smile along with the inquiry.

"Domenic," said Jejeune easily.

"And I'm Juan Perez. Better known as Traz." He didn't seem to particularly care whether Walden caught this information. It wasn't offered in his direction. Traz passed a hand lightly over his hair, but he needn't have bothered. From his neatly arranged hairstyle to the out-of-the-box freshness of his tan shirt, Jejeune's notoriously tidy friend had lost none of his panache, despite the building Colombian heat.

"Your name is Spanish, but you are not?"

"I live in St. Lucia now, but I grew up in Canada."

"You two are friends, then?" Thea looked between the two foreigners.

"We just met," said Jejeune quickly. If Traz was right in suggesting that the tour company might suspect his motives for being here, it seemed important that they knew he had come here alone. If he had not come to cause trouble, he would have no need to bring reinforcements.

"It must be nice to have a daughter who shares your interest in birding." This time, Traz had directed the comment to Walden, but it was Thea who responded.

"We went out quite often when I was young, but we haven't been birding together for a long time."

"My daughter is recovering from a bad experience," said Walden gravely. "I am hoping this will be a time of healing for her."

Thea gave a light laugh and rolled her eyes theatrically. "He makes it sound like a traffic accident. It was a break-up. A long-term relationship." She dismissed the subject with a wave of her hand. "I believe he just wanted an excuse to bring me on this trip."

"The truth is, we don't get to spend as much time together these days as I would like," said Walden. "Dorothea and her mother live here year round, but I have to split my time between Bogota and my practice in Tucson, Arizona. But we both have good memories of the birding trips we used to take, so I thought we should use this time for a little bonding." Thea cast her eyes demurely toward her lap, and Walden seemed to pick up on her discomfort. "Anyway," he said, "enough about us. This is your first time in Colombia, I'm guessing. How come you chose Mas Aves for your tour? I didn't think the company was that well known in the U.K."

"I heard about it from someone," said Jejeune simply. There was silence as he stared at Walden, trying to turn his look into one of nonchalance and not quite succeeding. Traz picked up on his friend's unease and stepped in.

"For me, it was the website. It's very well done. Everything laid out nice and clear. Comprehensive reports on all the reserves."

"It's a pity you don't read Spanish," said Walden. "Some of the trip descriptions on there are wonderful. Almost like poetry. I told them they should put English translations on there. It might attract more foreign birders."

Thea had turned her attention to Jejeune. She seemed to be regarding him with a particular interest, playing her eyes over his features almost as if she was looking for something. Traz was fairly sure his friend wouldn't be interested, but he was taking no chances. "The inspector here was just telling me about his girlfriend. She's a journalist. What was her name, Lois something?" asked Traz, wide-eyed. "Lane was it?"

"Her name's Lindy," said Jejeune, avoiding eye contact with Traz. "She would have liked to see Colombia, but she's very busy at the moment. She won an award and she's very much in demand these days."

"It's interesting you should both choose careers that are concerned with revealing the truth," said Walden, fixing Jejeune with another of his inquiring looks. "I imagine it makes for some interesting discussions at the dinner table. Which techniques work, which don't."

There was something about the direct nature of the question that troubled Jejeune, but he was spared the need to respond by the trilling of Walden's phone. The older man pulled a face as he looked at the screen. "If you'll excuse me, I have to take this." He stood up and walked away to lean on the wall of the terrace, gazing out over the city as he conducted his call.

"Work," said Thea, watching him leave. "Always work."

A good-natured uproar swelled at the far table. Armando was holding court and the Spanish contingent was in his thrall. Thea flashed the group a look. "Much of this tour will be conducted in Spanish, I imagine. But you two don't have to worry. Armando's English is excellent. And I'll be happy to fill in anything he misses out."

"That would be terrific," said Traz. "I'll make sure I stay close by, just in case I need to ask you something." It was the second time in as many minutes he had allowed Thea's misunderstanding to pass uncorrected. Jejeune didn't know why his friend was choosing to remain silent about his ability to speak Spanish, but he was certain it was a conscious decision.

Walden returned to the table, but he did not sit. "My apologies. Thea and I have to leave, but tomorrow is a free day for us. If you have no other plans, perhaps you will allow us to take you to a place called Casa de Colibries. I think you might enjoy it."

Jejeune's input was apparently not required. Traz accepted enthusiastically on their behalf, and sealed the deal with a formal handshake to both. Jejeune followed suit, but he was silent as he watched the couple walk across the terracotta tiles toward the elevator. He leaned on the low wall of the terrace for a moment and looked down. On the streets below, Colombians were negotiating their way through another roiling, chaotic colourfest of a day. They were so comfortable with the intimacy of reduced personal space, with the physical contact of hands on shoulders, on forearms. But they guarded their inner lives carefully. Perhaps it was this dissonance between the cultures, the contrast between this Latin reserve and Carl Walden's American openness. All Domenic knew for sure was that he spent his career looking for human behaviour that didn't quite fit. And the encounter he had just had with Carl Walden had set those tripwires trembling.

8

A wispy trail of white steam drifted up from the front of Maik's Mini as it idled in the forecourt of the bed and breakfast. Maik had smiled slightly when he had been given the address: *The Birder's Roost*. He rolled down the window, allowing the crisp coldness of the morning air to swirl in. The soft harmonies of The Four Tops drifted up to him from the speakers. Laraby came down the steps at exactly eight o'clock. The old soldier in Danny appreciated the other man's punctuality and the sharp neatness of his appearance.

"It's like a house of horrors in there," said the DI as he squeezed himself into the Mini. "Stuffed birds under glass domes, pictures of them all over the walls. Even the rooms are named after birds. I'm in the *Dotterel Suite*. What the bloody hell's a Dotterel, anyway?"

"It's a shorebird. A fairly uncommon one for these parts."

There was a glimmer of amusement in Laraby's expression as he turned to look at Maik. "Got you caught up with his birding nonsense, has he?"

"Not exactly," said Maik shortly as he eased the Mini away. But if Laraby was anticipating more details about Maik's half-hour wait on a blustery clifftop while Jejeune tracked the small group of birds back and forth along the shoreline, he was in for disappointment.

"So what can you tell me about this Robin Oakes?" asked Laraby, leaning forward to turn down the music slightly and earning a sidelong glance from Maik for his efforts.

Maik shrugged easily. "The family has been a part of the north Norfolk landscape for centuries, but the last couple of generations have lived overseas. America. They have some strong ties over there, apparently. Over the years they've sold off most of the estate, so there's not much left now; a few hundred acres at most. The old manor house and outbuildings were all destroyed by a fire in the sixties and never rebuilt. When Oakes inherited the property a few years back, he decided to return to the U.K. He moved into the gatehouse — the only building still standing — and he's lived there ever since. It matches the persona he seems to have chosen for himself: flamboyant, non-conformist, slightly off the grid."

"A fifty-year-old playboy," said Laraby sourly. "I'm starting to love this bloke already. Does he have an actual job?"

"He's highly rated as a photographer. Exhibition quality, showings, galleries, that sort of thing. Leads the lifestyle to go with it. A string of celebrity relationships, seen in all the right restaurants …"

"Nothing to concern us, though, in this hedonistic lifestyle of his? No drug convictions, no punch-ups in public places?"

Maik shook his head. "He seems to take his photography fairly seriously, by all accounts. He's got a name for himself with the local environmentalists in particular, documenting the local wildlife and scenery. They're among his biggest supporters." Maik tilted his head toward the car window and nodded toward the high stone wall beside them. "This is Oakes's property we're driving alongside now; Oakham, the ancestral family seat. The gatehouse is about a quarter of a mile further on down this road."

Laraby looked out the window of the Mini at the wall blurring past. "Down to a few hundred acres, you say? At most?" He shook his head in mock sadness. "Heartbreaking.

Makes you wonder how some people can find the will to get up in the morning, doesn't it?"

Maik wheeled the Mini into a drive that passed beneath an imposing stone archway. The ivy-clad gatehouse was showing the wear and tear of having protected the Oakes estate over the centuries, but it was still an impressive structure. Built from the same stone as the wall, it seemed to grow out of it organically, rising three storeys above the archway under which Maik now parked. A studded oak door was set into the inside wall of the arch; the ground floor entrance to the gatehouse. There was no answer when Maik knocked, so the two men continued through the opening on foot. They emerged into the estate grounds. Ahead of them a long, straight driveway led their eyes to the ruins of a once-magnificent building. From somewhere in the woods to the right, the sound of rapid-fire clacking tore through the still morning air. The two men went in to investigate. As they arrived, a pale shape ghosted away between the dark tree trunks. In seconds, the ethereal being was swallowed by the low light in the interior of the forest.

Oakes heard the men's approach and turned to greet them, a large-lensed camera cradled across his body. "Barn Owl. Roosts down amongst the Manor House ruins most of the time. I rarely get to see him in the deep woods like this." He tapped the barrel of his lens. "Doubt I got anything useable, though. Light's not co-operating today, I'm afraid." He approached the men and extended his hand. "Oakes, by the way. This is my land you're on, actually." He was a tall man with the kind of square-set jaw and high forehead that would ensure his good looks lasted as he aged. He had a robust handshake and a winning smile he used to good effect when he looked you in the eye. His neatly trimmed goatee lent a touch of raffishness to his appearance, but it was easy to imagine Robin Oakes inhabiting the social world he did. He had a charisma that would make others want to be in his presence.

Maik handled the introductions. It wasn't necessary to explain the reason for their visit. Violent death was enough of a stranger to most people's lives that when it darkened anyone's horizon, a visit from the police was to be expected. Still, Oakes seemed particularly unnerved about the appearance of the two officers.

"Isn't Inspector Jejeune the chief investigating officer around here?" he asked. "I would have thought a case like this would have merited his involvement."

He had directed the question to Maik, but Laraby fielded it. "Detective Chief Inspector Jejeune is off on his holidays at the moment," he said brightly. "So it'll be me asking the questions on this one. Live alone here, do you, sir? Just you and this great big estate?"

"Just me, Inspector," said Oakes amiably. He cast a glance around the woods. "No wife, no little 'uns. From either side of the blanket." He gave Laraby a wink and made a show of looking around the forest again. "Seems to have gone a bit quiet in here. Shall we walk over to the gatehouse?"

He dismantled his camera equipment and packed it away, meticulously setting each component in its own segment of a long padded bag before zipping it up and shouldering it. As he led the way, picking a path over the leaf litter, Maik regarded him carefully. If he was going to come up with a stereotypical uniform of the landowner class in these parts, the flat cap, cowboy boots, and corduroy-collared leather jacket would hardly have been it. Better suited for swanning around the nightclubs of London, Danny would have thought. Barely serviceable for a day duffing about in the woods taking photographs.

As they emerged onto the driveway, Oakes stopped. To their right, the ruins of the old manor house took on a stark desolation under the flat morning light. A maze-like warren of stone walls spread out low across the area, their tops crumbled away into ragged fringes. Large blocks of masonry lay strewn around the site like bomb damage, bleached and weathered by decades of exposure to the ferocious elements along the north Norfolk coast.

"What can you tell us about your involvement with Erin Dawes?" asked Laraby without preamble.

"I didn't know Erin that well, you understand. Only through our mutual investment in Picaflor. We didn't socialize, obviously."

"Obviously," repeated Laraby, with more emphasis than Maik would have thought absolutely necessary.

But if Oakes thought so, too, he chose not to let it show. He set the shoulder bag on the ground with exaggerated care and let his gaze rest on the policeman for a long moment. "Look, it's bound to come out, so I may as well be perfectly up front with you. Erin Dawes and I didn't always see eye to eye. There were aspects of her character that I found, shall we say, unattractive. She was fractious, confrontational. Not traits I find particularly appealing in anyone." He looked at Maik, as if perhaps he might find more understanding for his position with the sergeant.

"Confrontational about what?"

"Most things. To tell you the truth, I always got the impression that her background was a bigger issue for her than it was for any of the rest of us. Her social standing never came into it, as far as we were concerned. I mean, she brought us the deal in the first place. We were happy enough to have her be a part of it. But that didn't seem to be enough for her, somehow."

"This deal with Picaflor," said Maik, "can you tell us what it involves?"

"Drone technology, Sergeant. Cutting-edge."

Laraby snorted derisively. "Blimey, they told me down The Smoke that I should set my watch back twenty years when I got to Norfolk. Sorry to be the one to break it to you, but drones are already up and running. Even police departments are using them these days, which must tell you how far past the cutting edge they are."

Instead of responding to Laraby's sarcasm, Oakes merely nodded indulgently. "The company we have invested in is looking at new applications for the technology. Specifically, how drones might be used in large-scale reforesting projects." His smile was still in place, but it seemed to have an edge to it now.

"These confrontations with Erin Dawes, they weren't anything to do with her having to come up with fifty thousand pounds in cash as her part of the investment, while all you had to do was contribute a bit of land?"

"Not my decision, old fruit," said Oakes brightly. He seemed to have tired of Laraby's antagonism and was prepared to respond with some calculated provocation of his own. "I was prepared to fork out the cash, just like the others. But Picaflor asked for the land in lieu. Offered me fifty thousand quid's worth of options against it." He nodded toward the hillside beyond the ruined manor house. "Twenty-five-year exclusive lease. Ideal test site for the project, apparently." Again, he took his explanation to Maik. "The idea is to stitch together two tracts of ancient forest by reforesting my land, which lies between them. I can't pretend to understand all the science behind it. Your boss might, though, from what I've heard. When did you say DCI Jejeune is returning?"

A trail of thunderclouds crossed Laraby's features. "He didn't. Where were you on Saturday night, Mr. Oakes?"

It was a jarring change of direction, of the type DCI Jejeune might have appreciated. Perhaps he had even learned the technique from Laraby. From what Maik could tell so far, there was precious little else of similarity between the two men's interview methods.

Oakes drew himself up to his full height and faced Laraby squarely. There was genuine hostility in his eyes now; all pretense of politesse gone. "Exactly what are you implying?"

"I'm implying I don't know where you were on Saturday night," Laraby said evenly. "No need to get all defensive,

Mr. Oakes. It's a question I intend to ask every potential suspect in this case."

Maik watched closely, but if Laraby's words were meant to unnerve Oakes, they seemed to have failed. He drew a breath and looked at the detectives. "On Saturday night, the night Erin Dawes was killed, I was here at home, alone. I was going through the photographs I had taken that day," he said. But his eyes didn't. They flickered momentarily up and to the right until he was able to bring them under control and turn them on the two men again.

"So instead of questioning people who have no motive whatsoever for wanting Erin Dawes dead, can I suggest you apply your limited police resources to finding those who might have one."

"Thank you for that, sir," said Laraby. "I'm going to have my sergeant put that down in his notebook right away." He turned to Maik. "Remember, Sergeant — two *p*'s in *apply*. You have a nice day, Mr. Oakes. We'll speak again soon."

The two detectives strolled back to the car in silence, their footfalls deadened by the hard, cold earth of the driveway. "Not a very good liar, is he, our Mr. Oakes?" Laraby said without looking up. "You saw the eyes? So I suggest our next step would be to find out what he's lying about."

"Do you have any previous background with him, sir?" asked Maik.

"That bit of argy-bargy, you mean? Not exactly DCI Jejeune's soft shoe shuffle?" He stopped and looked at Maik. "I've dealt with this lot before, with their condescension and their distain and their smug superiority. You let them get away with thinking they've got the upper hand, and by the end of the interview they'll have you apologizing for disturbing them."

Maik had seen plenty of distain in his days in the army. And superiority. But he hadn't detected much of either in Oakes's demeanour, at least not until Laraby had provoked him. On the other hand, Oakes's mention of Domenic Jejeune hadn't gone down well at all. Given the history between the two detectives, that was understandable enough. Any suggestion that Laraby might somehow be a second choice to DCI Jejeune would certainly touch a nerve. Maik could see how that might be enough for the new man to start putting himself about a bit. He just hoped it wasn't going to be an ongoing feature of this investigation.

9

Jejeune was sitting on the patio of the hotel in the dappled morning sunlight, watching the Rufous-collared Sparrows pilfer crumbs from the breakfast buffet. He mentioned it to Lindy as he waited for the waiter to bring him his coffee.

"No birds in this restaurant, unless you count these ceramic ducks on the wall," she replied. "No idea what species, in case you were wondering. They don't look like Mallards, though."

"The ones in Malvern's? I think they're meant to be Teal. What are you doing down there, anyway? Gone to check if they've solved their punctuation issues?"

They had initially been drawn to the seafront café because of a couple of eccentric apostrophes on the chalkboard outside. Lindy had a pedant's eye for such things and drew a tiny glow of private amusement from them, so she had slipped her arm through Domenic's and steered him inside. The glorious view out over the glittering waters of Saltmarsh harbour had won them over immediately, and while Lindy couldn't wait to order anything that came with *bean's* or *mushrooms'*, the rest of the food proved enough of a draw to have them stopping in whenever they went for a walk along the waterfront. Still, it was a long way for her to have gone for lunch on her own, especially when the grey November skies would have been showing the harbour in its most unflattering light of the entire year.

"Just fancied having somebody else serve me a meal for a change," she said breezily, before changing direction abruptly. "Aidy's been given the elbow," she announced. She said it as if Domenic might know who Aidy was. Now was not the time to ask. "Thirty-one years with the same publication, and he goes in last Friday and gets the DCM."

"DCM?"

"Don't Come Monday."

Jejeune nodded his silent thanks as the waiter delivered his coffee. He sipped it cautiously before spooning in a generous amount of coarse raw sugar. He could imagine Lindy's sad expression as she delivered this news. For all her pragmatism about her profession and its ruthless ways, the cutthroat, bottom-line nature of life still seemed to catch her off guard at times. She suddenly seemed vulnerable, alone there on the far side of the globe, exposed to the world and all its injustices.

"Seen your tattooed man again?" he asked casually.

"Relax, Dom, he wasn't my type," she said, willfully misinter-preting his interest. "So, where are you off to on your *jour-ney*?"

Across the miles, Jejeune imagined Lindy's impish grin and smiled. The word had found its way onto her radar recently, having cropped up in conversations with her friends rather too often. Everything these days, it seemed, was becoming a journey, from night-school courses to hospital stays to job searches. Lindy had quickly tired of the affectation, and now rarely missed an opportunity to overuse the word, even using it to describe a trip to the shops. Her *grocery journey*, she called it.

"I'm off to a place called Casa de Colibries, and then tomor-row we set out for El Paujil. How about you?"

"Nowhere special. A couple of interviews, local media." She watched a young couple walking slowly along the edge of the harbour, arms linked, hunched against the biting winds. They were leaning into each other, as if their love alone could shelter them from the elements. "I miss you," she said suddenly. Outside, she saw a person approaching the café from a parked car. "As nice as all this long-distance love is, I want you home as soon as possible so we can go out on a proper date. You know, one where we sit across from each other in a fancy restaurant while we both text other people.... I'll call you later. Bye."

Perhaps on a different day, Domenic might have reflected on the abruptness of Lindy's dismissal. But sitting here, with exotic bird calls carrying to him on the warm air and the soft breeze riffling the vegetation, it wasn't long before the bleak, metallic greyness of Saltmarsh harbour faded from his thoughts and he was drawn once more into the gentle ambience of a sunny Bogota morning.

"Thanks for finding the time to do this," said Colleen Shepherd, taking a seat opposite Lindy. She pantomimed an order for tea to the young waiter behind the counter, letting her glance linger over the pastries in the glass display case before eventually deciding against one. Lindy waved a palm toward the waiter to indicate she wouldn't be tacking anything on to the order.

"I have to say, you do seem to be in demand," said Shepherd. "Every time I open a paper or turn on the radio these days, there seems to be something about you."

"Big story, small town," said Lindy easily. "Not that I'm complaining. I'm loving every minute of it, truth be told." She offered a smile that showed she was.

Shepherd looked around, taking in the wide vista through the window. The slight tint of the glass made the cloud-laden sky even more ominous. Beneath it, the waters of the harbour rose and fell like mercury. "I haven't been in here before," said the DCS. "I imagine it must be beautiful in the summer."

"Harder to get a table, though, especially with a view like this."

They leaned back slightly as the waiter set a tray on the table. Shepherd reached for the teapot and began to pour. Lindy watched her carefully. It seemed to her that Colleen Shepherd, in a phrase Lindy had recently added to her repertoire, had got her jazz back. The last few times Lindy had seen Shepherd, the DCS's disillusionment with Domenic had been palpable. There had been an air about her that suggested she felt she was owed something better, perhaps even that she had somehow been the author of her own misfortune by investing so much in her chief inspector. Now, despite having resolved precisely nothing with Dom as far as Lindy was aware, Shepherd seemed to have a new vitality about her. It was good to see, and Lindy wondered if it might augur well for better relations with Domenic when he returned.

"Have you heard from Domenic?" asked Shepherd, handing Lindy her cup. "I'm happy to report he's managed to avoid calling us every five minutes to check in. So many people seem to think their workplace will fall apart at the seams if they take a few days off. I'm sure they don't realize what an insult it is to the people who are still there at work." She offered Lindy a smile. "Which is not to say he isn't being missed, of course."

"I'm sure this new man you've brought in will be able to take up the slack until he gets back, though."

Shepherd took a sip of her tea and nodded. "Marvin Laraby. He seems to have settled in quite nicely. He worked with Domenic at the Met." She looked at Lindy over the rim of her teacup, eyes wide in query.

"Dom was at the very end of his time there when we got together," said Lindy, holding eye contact with Shepherd. "I may have heard of him, but I don't remember meeting any of the people Dom worked with."

Behind Shepherd, the couple had disappeared, gone to seek the warmth that even their love couldn't provide on a day like today.

"I'm sure you must be wondering why I asked to meet," said the DCS, drawing Lindy's attention back to the table. "What I actually wanted to talk about was Eric."

Lindy shifted slightly in her seat. On the long list of things Lindy would have wanted to avoid discussing with DCS Shepherd, the intimate details of her relationship with Lindy's boss came very near the top.

"I'm wondering what I can get him as a gift for Christmas. Something to do with birding, obviously, since that seems to be all he ever thinks about these days." She gazed into her teacup as she stirred it and spoke without looking up. "You know he's in the Scilly Isles with Quentin Senior at the moment? Some rarity or other dropped in. He did mention the name, but I'm afraid …"

Lindy smiled her understanding. Both women knew she would have been able to complete the thought. She had voiced it often enough herself. "Welcome to the widowhood," she said.

"I imagine you've become accustomed to Domenic jetting off to see some bird or other. Colombia, for example," said Shepherd, "it's an interesting choice."

"It's one of the top birding destinations at the moment." Even to Lindy, her answer had the ring of a prepared response.

"It seemed to come up so suddenly," said Shepherd. "I think that was what surprised us all most." She gave Lindy the same stare as before. Pleasant, benign. A conversation topic, it said, nothing more.

"I think he'd been considering it for a while, to be honest," said Lindy. Because being honest, or as close to it as you could manage, was always safer around a clever woman like Shepherd. "So … a gift for Eric? Wow, you don't ask me the easy ones, do you? Well, clothing is out, obviously, since, as far as I can tell, the goal for birders is to try and look as much like vegetation as possible. I can't say I'd want to be held responsible for the way Dom looks when he goes out. How about equipment? A spotting scope?"

Shepherd shook her head. "Eric seems to have pretty much all he needs in that department," she said. "I've been looking for ages, but I can't seem to find anything."

Lindy wondered how long "ages" was. She didn't have Shepherd down as a patient shopper, but then, everybody had layers. Lindy watched the dark, oily waters sluicing around in the harbour. In the flat, overcast light, the sea's movement seemed ponderous, deliberate. It occurred to her that, for a person with Shepherd's prodigious responsibilities, dedicating a large slice of your life to such a frivolous concern was odd, to say the least. To say nothing of going to all the trouble of phoning Lindy at work to schedule a meeting way out here. Either Eric's gift had taken on a significance that eluded her, or Shepherd had another reason for wanting to meet today. What that reason might be, Lindy wouldn't have liked to say, but a feeling of uneasiness was beginning to build within her.

"I really will have to bring Eric out here when the weather warms up." Shepherd, too was staring at the water, as if mesmerized by its motion. "Listen to us," she said suddenly. "Two bright, accomplished women, and all we can find to talk about is the men in our lives."

Unless that had been the purpose of the entire meeting after all, thought Lindy. But men? Or man? Because while Shepherd's dilemma about Eric had ostensibly been the reason for the meeting, it seemed to her that talk about Domenic could have remained completely outside their purview if Shepherd had wanted it to.

Lindy lifted her cup and drained it. "I should be going," she said, reaching for her bag. "Let me give it some thought, and I'll get back to you."

The bill had already been settled, but Shepherd, despite her pressing duties, seemed inclined to linger. When Lindy left, the DCS was deep in thought, staring out over the gunmetal waters of Saltmarsh harbour, as if the slow rolling swells might hold the answer to her dilemma. Perhaps they did.

10

Jejeune had not seen Traz at lunch in the rooftop restaurant, but his friend was already waiting in the ground-floor lobby when the detective emerged from the elevator.

The afternoon sunlight flooded the space, reaching even the far corner, where Traz had positioned himself for a perfect view of both the elevator and the lobby doors. He looked as effortlessly neat as ever, and if his freshly pressed turquoise shirt might have been out of place on the rainforest hikes that were to come, it certainly made a striking impression now as he lounged casually among the lobby's tropical decor.

Traz rose and walked toward Jejeune, but continued past him to greet Thea Walden as she came in through the lobby doors. Her father followed. Both were wearing motorcycle helmets and carrying a spare. Carl lifted his visor as he handed a helmet to Jejeune. "Bikes will be the best way to get through the Bogota traffic at this time of day," he said. "I hope that's not a problem for either of you."

They walked outside where twin Kawasaki KLRs sat beside the front doors of the hotel. "The rules of the road are a little different out here," said Carl to the two men, "so just hang on tight and leave the rest to us."

Having recently denied their years of friendship, Jejeune realized that it would be but a small matter for Traz to trample him into dust if he made any move for the pillion of Thea's bike. As he climbed aboard Carl Walden's, he wondered briefly if the breadth of Traz's grin might cause wind drag.

Progress through the sprawling arteries of Bogota consisted of sporadic acceleration and sudden braking for yellow cabs, delivery vans, and municipal trucks. But once they were clear of the central commercial district, Walden and his daughter opened up the machines, the 650cc engines roaring with the strain as they began a steady climb up the side of the caldera. They flashed past an unbroken frieze of low breeze-block structures, houses, and shopfronts, shuttered now against the midday heat. Washing lines hung like colourful bunting from the corners of awnings that teetered unsteadily on spindly legs. Yet even these modest properties protected their facades behind elaborate iron grilles. How closely we protect our possessions, thought Jejeune, no matter how little we have.

As they crested the rise, Carl Walden lifted a hand and pointed ahead. Jejeune patted his shoulder to let him know he could see the Cezanne-esque blocks of colour sprawling up the hillsides. La Calera — their destination.

Bright sunlight painted the wall of Casa de Colibries, shining on an elaborate latticework frame filled with flowering plants and bushes. One or two looked vaguely familiar to Jejeune, but none were in his limited plant vocabulary.

The four of them were sitting at a wrought iron table in a large courtyard, beneath the mottled shade of a cypress tree. If the building itself was a jarring mix of architectural styles and materials, there was a pleasing harmony about the courtyard. Low stone benches and adobe walls blended perfectly with the well-kept gravel paths and neat gardens of cacti and succulents.

"I can see why you like it here," said Traz.

Thea nodded. She was sitting with her feet on the edge of her chair, resting her arms on her tanned thighs. She cupped a glass of guava juice in her hands. "Much of this property was constructed with materials rescued from old, derelict buildings," she said. "I think it is so important to preserve your country's heritage. How else can you understand where you have come from?" Like the building itself, Thea's speech displayed influences from different sources. Her formal sentence structure clashed with her easy use of idioms; a person who had learned English from a native-speaker, but spent most of her time restructuring it for Colombian ears.

"So how's your coffee?" Traz asked Jejeune. His friend had forgotten to add the qualifier *Americano* when ordering, and Traz was enjoying Jejeune's struggles with a drink the colour and consistency of engine oil. He had already added half a jug of cream and now he reached for two packages of sugar. He took a sip and made a face. Traz saw the Waldens watching with amusement.

"You want me to ask if they've got any maple syrup?" he inquired unsympathetically.

Jejeune's response was interrupted by the appearance of a spectacular hummingbird at a flower just behind them. Its small green form trailed a long black tail at least the length of its body. Jejeune stared in wide-eyed amazement. It was hovering so close by, he could hear the faint buzz of its wings.

"Black-tailed Trainbearer," said Carl Walden casually. "One of the easier ones to identify here. There's a Green-tailed, too, though they're not as common."

Common. The word served to remind Jejeune once again that he was in a place where such astonishing sightings were the norm. He watched other hummingbirds zipping around the air space, streaks of jewelled lightning, darting in to feed at the flowers before spinning away to the safety of the surrounding trees.

Traz made a show of looking around, taking in the sun-dappled courtyard and the carefully landscaped garden, with its bank of flowering shrubs and its low walls. The shadows of the tall trees behind them created bands of shade that lay across the courtyard like dark streams. "This is some place," he said to Thea. "Do you spend a lot of time here?"

"Not now, so much. I used to come with my father ..." She faltered, as if she had intended to say more, but decided against it. Hesitation seemed to flit between the girl and her father like the brightly coloured birds carving the air around them.

"But sadly, my work doesn't allow me to get out these days as much as I'd like to," said Walden.

"A practice, you said. Law?" Jejeune's casual tone did nothing to disguise his interest.

"Clinical psychology, though much of my work is academic now. I'm on the faculty of the National University of Colombia in Bogota. My practice in Arizona is mainly long-term clients. I'd like to wind down, but the bond between a patient and a psychologist is not one that can be easily broken. It takes time, a gradual weaning process. For both parties, if I'm being honest." It was clear Walden felt he had said enough about the subject. "So tell me, Inspector, what do you make of this place, sitting here as these wonders of nature spin about our heads? It's a far cry from your black-and-white world of criminal investigations, I imagine?" Walden smiled, just in case anybody thought his question smacked a little too much of interrogation.

"It's incredible," said Jejeune sincerely.

"A shimmer, that's what they call a collection of hummingbirds, isn't it?" asked Thea. "Such a lovely English word."

"A shimmer of hummingbirds. It's perfect," said Traz. "Fleeting, here and then gone in an instant."

"Perhaps like the truth you seek in your work, Inspector.

Only a moment to grasp it before it disappears forever." She offered Jejeune a strange smile, playful but perhaps with hidden depths. He found it vaguely disquieting, and offered a trite comment to dispel the feeling.

"I never imagined I'd ever see so many hummingbirds up close like this."

Traz laughed. "*Casa de Colibries* means House of Hummingbirds, Inspector. It was a pretty safe bet there'd be some hummers here."

Thea turned her head in interest. "You know this word, *Colibries*?"

Traz shrugged uneasily. "I've picked up the odd one here and there."

"Still, this is not a Spanish word I would have expected you to have known." Thea's tone was pleasant, her inquiry suggested interest, nothing more. But behind his steel-rimmed spectacles, Carl Walden's eyes seemed to be watching Traz with an intensity that went some way beyond casual curiosity.

"What can I say?" Traz extended his hands to enhance his nonchalance. "Hey, that's a Woodstar, right? White-bellied? See it, Domenic?"

They spun their heads to follow the direction of Traz's finger. A tiny bird hovered at a fuchsia bloom, as if suspended from an invisible wire. They watched as it dipped its beak delicately into the flower and then reversed away.

"Flying backwards." said Traz with genuine admiration. "That's what fifty wingbeats a second will get you."

"My father will tell you they're wing rolls rather than beats. It's what gives hummingbirds their astonishing flying skills," said Thea, looking at Walden. She shrugged. "But I still prefer to see it as just another one of nature's miracles."

"Colombia's magical realism, alive and well in its hummers," said Traz. "Like the Sword-billed Hummingbird. I've never seen one, but they tell me it's incredible, the way it dances in the air with such a massively long bill."

The waitress came over to collect the empty cups and the group waited for her to complete her task before continuing their conversation. At a nearby bush, two birds jousted for a moment, the sound of their whirring wings filling the air around them. The waitress paused and watched them, smiling. "They move so fast. It's like they're so busy, they only have so much time to get their work done."

"Are those Sparkling Violetears?" Traz asked her.

The waitress shrugged. "Possibly. Or Green. Sometimes it is hard to tell." She turned to look at the Waldens. "Only Mariel could tell us for sure, no?"

The look between Thea and her father was brief, but Jejeune did not miss it.

"Who's Mariel?"

"Mariel Huaque, a former guide for Mas Aves." It was not clear whether Walden intended to offer any more information, but the waitress stepped in anyway.

"She can even identify individual hummingbirds of the same species."

"That would take some doing, surely," said Traz, careful to keep any note of disbelief from his voice.

Carl Walden's momentary intake of breath was followed by a soft smile. "It's true. Mariel was a patient of mine. She came to me after she fell and hit her head on a rock." He shook his head. "Something as simple as that; a twenty-eight-year-old woman falls and her life changes forever." He paused in thought for a moment and looked at his daughter. The meaning was not lost on the men. Thea would be about the same age as Mariel was when she had her accident.

"She was in a coma for two days, and when she woke up she found she could see the world differently. Things slowed down, she was able to take in details, no matter how fast something was moving. It's a condition known as acquired savant syndrome. Everything she saw left an impression in her mind, like a vapour trail of pixels. At least, that's how I understand it. She never was quite able to articulate her experience clearly. I used to bring her here to test her skills. I would videotape the birds, then later, back at the lab, she would tell me what she had seen and we would run back the films in super slow-mo to compare them. Her observational skills were near-perfect."

Walden seemed to recoil slightly from his memories and neither Traz nor Jejeune felt any desire to push him for further details. Thea, too, seemed uneasy at the mention of Mariel, though Jejeune could not have said quite why.

"It's getting late," she announced suddenly. "We should probably get going if we want to miss the worst of the traffic on the way back."

"You don't want to wait a while to see if a Sword-billed Hummingbird shows up?" Traz seemed reluctant to see the visit end so soon.

"I think it will not come today," said Thea. She picked up her bag and, with a thin smile at the men, began walking in the direction of the parked bikes.

As they negotiated the switchbacks along the edge of the caldera, descending into the fading twilight hanging over Bogota, Jejeune reflected on their day. Despite the glittering array of hummingbirds on show at Casa de Colibries, he had found their visit troubling. The conversations with the Waldens, and between father and daughter, had been full of false starts and half-formed ideas, as if there was always more lying beneath the surface. It left Jejeune with a sense of twirling in a breeze, moved by unseen forces, strange and unsettling.

Thea signalled to a parking area along the side of the road and Walden guided his bike to a stop beside hers. He went over to speak to his daughter, who had taken off her helmet and was sitting astride her bike, shaking her long hair free of tangles. Traz approached Jejeune and the two men stood before a low wall looking out over the city, nestled in the black bowl of the plain.

"Some view," said Traz.

"Any idea what today was all about?"

"Maybe not you, for once. Apparently, couples come up here to picnic in the evenings. It's considered something of a romantic hotspot." Traz pushed out his bottom lip. "I've had worse signals. But even if it was about getting to know more about you, a little curiosity is to be expected. I'm sure they recognize your surname. Damian's was a pretty well-known case here, JJ. Any Colombian of Thea's generation who is as interested in her country's recent past is going to know about indigenous rights issues. Damian Jejeune's name is going to be a part of those conversations."

Traz strolled off to join Thea, leaving Jejeune alone to gaze out over the vast, sprawling plain below. The lights of Bogota lay before him like a carpet of diamonds. He thought about the people who lived in the homes they had passed on the way out. People in love, caring for their children, living life. Daily human commerce, the universal language of existence on this planet. How would they feel about the deaths of indigenous Karijona people? Sad, their hearts broken a little at the thought of innocent lives lost. But would they condemn a man to ten years in prison for it? A decade in a hellhole like the notorious La Tramacúa?

There was a blast from a car horn. A man in a passing car shouted something at Thea and she shouted something back. Harassment? Possibly. But like so much else out here, the truth was a shadow, hiding in the grey margins of uncertainty, until Domenic Jejeune was unsure what was reality and what was merely the product of his own imagination. Walden called out to them and the two men walked back to the bikes. Tomorrow they would begin the tour. Perhaps clarity was waiting for Jejeune in the lowland rainforest of El Paujil. Or perhaps only more uncertainty.

11

Laraby rubbed his hands as he got into Maik's Mini, making a show of enjoying the warmth inside the car. Maik had turned down the music as Laraby climbed in, but it was still loud enough for the detective inspector to comment.

"So who's this, then? Barry Manilow?"

Maik pinched the bridge of his nose between his thumb and forefinger as he put the car in gear.

"It's Jimmy Ruffin, one of the early Motown artists."

"Motown, eh? My ex used to like that stuff. Thelma Houston, Lionel Ritchie."

"As I say," said Maik with the kind of restraint that could cause a person injury, "I tend to listen to the earlier artists."

"What was the name of that Motown group? Had one or two big hits?"

Like most people who discover an unexpected curiosity in their interests, Maik was keen to encourage it. He quick-fired a couple of suggestions. "The Temptations? Junior Walker and the All Stars?"

Laraby shook his head slowly. "It'll come to me," he said. He turned to take in the passing countryside. While he seemed content enough this time to at least let Jimmy Ruffin continue at his present volume, if the DI had any further concern for what became of the broken-hearted, he showed no sign.

They continued their journey along the country lanes in silence, the pale daylight flickering between the bare branches of the hedgerows like a black-and-white film reel. Neither man spoke again until Maik turned off the road and began bumping the Mini over the rutted surface of a long driveway.

"Blimey, what have we got here?" asked Laraby.

In the centre of the large field in front of them, an inflated dome sat on the brown, frost-hardened soil like a giant white eggshell. Beside it, dwarfed by the smooth white mass of the structure, was Lauren Salter's Toyota. Maik drew up alongside and the two men got out. Salter pointed to a large sign in block letters next to the door. DO NOT ENTER. RING BELL AND WAIT.

"I did," she said, "and I am."

The bone-chilling wind drove low across the treeless landscape, cutting into the officers as they huddled in the doorway. Trails of breath curled around their heads; smoke from the warm fires of human souls.

"Enough of this," said Maik, "we'll wait inside." He pushed open the door and stepped in, followed by the others. Even in the dim half-light of the interior, Maik could see that the dome was immense, bigger even than it had appeared from the outside. He found himself standing on what he took to be a running track that ran around the outer wall, although there were no lane markings. The track enclosed a space that Maik estimated was comfortably big enough to house at least eight football fields. But there was no turf, natural or otherwise. Instead, a latticework of grid wires divided patches of soil up into small squares.

Maik was still taking it all in when he heard the cries of alarm and from behind somebody struck him full force in the small of the back. He collapsed forward into one of the soil squares, feeling the weight of the other person land on him. A loud sound filled the air beside his head, and through a blur of confusion, he heard a voice over a loudspeaker. "Kill them. Kill them all. Now!"

Maik's instinct, hard-wired into him over years of training, was to roll toward cover; to move, to escape, to do anything but lie there and make it easy to be shot at. But whoever had attacked him had him pinned to the ground. He reached back with an elbow and slammed it into his assailant's face. There was a cry of pain, and the other person slumped off Maik's back and onto the ground beside him. Maik rolled away, to give himself more space for his next blow. But it never came.

The bright lights snapped on with a loud metallic click. "Stay exactly where you are," ordered the voice over the loudspeaker. "Don't move. I'm coming over."

Maik helped Salter to a sitting position and offered her his handkerchief. "I'm sorry, I didn't … I heard …"

Salter was bleeding heavily from her mouth and nose and she pressed the handkerchief to the area firmly. Maik hoped it was the blow that had caused the watering eyes, but he wasn't sure. On the ground a few metres away lay a metallic four-legged contraption about the size of a serving platter. All across the interior of the dome, other disks fluttered to the ground like falling leaves and settled onto the soft black earth. *Kill them all*, thought Maik. He heard the sound of running footsteps on the track and looked up to see a young man in jeans and a sweatshirt hovering over them.

"Exactly what part of DO NOT ENTER didn't you get?" demanded the young man angrily. "Do you realize you've just cost me an entire day's work? I'm going to have to recalibrate the whole damn fleet now, you morons."

His lack of concern for their condition, compounded by the indignity of sitting in the dirt, after Danny Maik had just smacked her one, was more than Salter was prepared to put up with. She snatched the handkerchief away from her face angrily and rounded on the man. "What the bloody hell do you think you're playing at?" she snarled fiercely. "You could have taken his head off with that damned thing."

Having satisfied himself that both of his officers were going to survive their ordeal, Laraby stepped forward and reached out a hand to help Salter up. He suspected Maik might want to take care of himself.

"Look, we've been through all this with you people before," continued the man, speaking as if to children. "We have secured all the necessary permits. They are registered and on file. So if there's nothing else, perhaps you can let us get on with our work. Goodbye."

He made an impatient ushering motion with his hands; the same one Salter had seen farmers use to get sheep off the local roads at times. But she was not going anywhere just yet. "What permits? Just what are you up to in here?"

"It has to do with controlled drone flights. Ring any bells?" said the young man in a tone that had Salter looking like she might want to start ringing a few bells of her own.

"I'd suggest you change your attitude," said Laraby darkly, "before you find yourself arrested for reckless endangerment."

"What, because some old fool chose to ignore a clearly posted DO NOT ENTER sign? What did he think it was, an eye chart?"

Maik had rolled to his feet and was eying the man-child stonily, as if he thought he might need to identify him again at some point. The young man retreated slightly under his stare.

Salter was still dabbing at her mouth, but it didn't seem to be staunching the flow of blood. "You all right, Constable?" asked Laraby. "Do you want to press charges?" He gave her a cheeky smile. "Against either of them?"

"Constable." A look of panic crossed the man's face. "You're the police?" He held up his hands defensively. "Hey, look, I'm sorry. Okay? I thought you were those bozos from the council again. They're up here all the time. I swear, it's as if they think we're conducting alien autopsies in here or something."

"I think we'd better start by having a word with the person in charge of this facility," said Laraby.

"You're having it."

"You're Dr. Amendal?" Laraby's surprise was obvious. In his defence, the person standing before him looked even younger than the fresh-faced constable who'd given him a ride to the cottage a couple of days before. The man's lank hair framed a thin face of uncertain complexion. His large black-rimmed glasses seemed almost a statement of defiance against the world's opinions — of him and everything else. Behind them, intelligent eyes flickered back and forth as he sought some sort of understanding as to how his well-ordered world could have gone so catastrophically off course in such a short space of time.

"Perhaps we could go into your office?" suggested Laraby.

Amendal gave a short laugh and fished a phone out of his pocket. "This is my office," he said. "I'm okay to chat here, if you are."

Laraby looked at Salter, who was still holding the handkerchief to her face. It was soaked with blood now. Laraby fished in his pocket and produced another one. "Well, perhaps you've got a toilet where the constable can get herself cleaned up, at least." He nodded at the man's phone. "I presume those aren't in there as well."

Amendal directed Salter to a small cubicle at the far end of the complex, and she left, brushing the dirt from her clothes with her free hand as she went.

Maik was doing the same thing as Laraby turned to him. "Want her to bring you a glass of prune juice back, Sergeant?" he asked with a smile.

Amendal held up his hands again. "Oh, hey, that 'old' comment. The light in here sometimes, it's …"

"Any chance we could get on with this while I've still got all my faculties?" said Maik gruffly.

"Sure. Of course. What is it you want to know?"

Laraby looked out over the gridded quadrants spread out across the interior of the dome. "Why don't we start with exactly what it is that the Picaflor project is doing?"

"We're going to use drones to undertake large-scale tree replanting programs," said Amendal. "Humans currently cut down about fifteen billion trees a year. With the best will in the world, no planting initiatives are going to come anywhere close to replacing that number, but with our technology, we can at least do a hell of a lot better than we are currently. We're going to be reforesting massive tracts of land, more than could possibly be covered by conventional methods. We're talking about thousands of hectares, many in remote, inaccessible areas. It's going to make a massive impact on the problem of carbon emissions."

"I'd heard it was old-growth forests that were important for carbon storage," said Maik. Laraby's look let him know he was in no doubt from whom Maik would have heard this, but Amendal seized on the chance to make amends with the sergeant.

"Right, absolutely. Yes, well done you, Sergeant," he said enthusiastically, earning perhaps not quite the look he'd hoped for from Maik. "Old-growth forests are vital for the carbon they're already storing," he continued in a slightly chastened manner. "Chop them down and you'd release all that carbon into the atmosphere. But with the right rainfall and soil fertility, new-growth forests can absorb more than ten times as much carbon from the atmosphere. It's because the trees use it as part of the photosynthesis process as they grow."

"And how do you propose to go about this mass planting?" asked Laraby.

"First we send out mapping drones to conduct aerial surveys and produce detailed 3-D images of the area. Then planting drones follow pre-set routes and sow the seeds. The drones can plant thousands of seeds per day at a fraction of the cost of traditional hand-sowing methods."

"And Picaflor has cornered the market on this technology?"

Amendal inclined his head. "There are other projects out there, but this one has the edge."

"Really. Why's that?"

"Well, mainly because it's got me." The statement was delivered with the flat detachment of a phrase from a textbook. Amendal seemed to take no ownership of it. He certainly seemed to have no intention of impressing anyone with the remark, least of all himself. "Of course," he continued, "there are people who know more about tropical species mix, soil fertility, and all that. But if you're looking for someone to program drones to fly specific patterns under pre-set conditions and payloads, I'm who you come to. I know more about this stuff than anybody else."

Maik had retrieved one of the dormant drones from the earth and was turning it over slowly in his hands. He didn't have much expertise with the things, but he had seen one or two. This one was of a design he had not seen before. It was painted in a matte black finish. The four wings were light and flexible, but the central hub, which housed the camera unit, was surprisingly heavy and unyielding. If it had caught him on the head on its fly-by, it could have caused him serious injury. He handed it to Amendal.

"You haven't asked why we're here today, Dr. Amendal," he said. "In case you were wondering, it's in connection with the death of one of your investors."

"No it isn't."

Laraby's face showed his surprise. "I beg your pardon?"

"I presume you're here to talk about the death of that woman at the cottage. She wasn't an investor."

Maik shared the DI's astonishment. "Her records suggest otherwise," he said. "She was part of a group called …"

"The IV League. Yes. They were going to invest. They were offered options on a block of shares worth two hundred thousand pounds. But they never took them up. We had the offering documents, filed the final prospectus, set up the fund transfer protocols, everything was set to go."

"So what happened?"

Amendal shrugged. "No money is what happened. We waited, but the option deadline came and went and no funds ever showed up."

Laraby pressed. "There's no mistake? You're sure about this?"

There was an eloquence about Amendal's look of contempt that almost made Maik smile, despite the seriousness of the situation.

"That's a considerable shortfall in funding," he said. "How did you make it up?"

"There's no shortage of people who see the potential in this project. The money was never going to be a problem. It was failing to secure the land that caused the setbacks." Amendal paused — *hesitated* might have been Maik's word. "But, we made some adjustments. We were back on track within a few weeks."

Maik and Laraby looked at each other. Amendal's response had caused the sort of small whisper in the ether that DCI Jejeune might have chosen to pursue. But Laraby had other ideas. "We heard it was Erin Dawes who took the options deal to the IV League. Were you dealing with her directly?"

Amendal shook his head. "No, I hired an investment broker, some clown named Connor James." He pulled a face. "Big mistake. That tract of land at Oakham would have been ideal for our purposes. We were counting on it heavily. James came in here all flash and fast talk, guaranteed me he could get the IV League investment. *Guaranteed it*," Amendal repeated for emphasis. "Needless to say, he's not my investment broker any longer."

Laraby saw Salter returning along the walkway. She was still dabbing at her mouth and her top lip looked puffy, but she seemed to have been able to stop the bleeding.

"Thank you for your help, Dr. Amendal," he said. "We'll let you get back to your research. I take it you're not still in contact with this Connor James, but would you happen to still have his details?"

"You might be able to find him at the Saltmarsh marina. He has a boat down there." Amendal took out his phone and scrolled through the contacts until he reached the right one. He handed his phone to Maik, who noted down the information.

Outside the dome, the three officers huddled in the doorway again, sheltered slightly from the raw winds that seared across the land, if not the cold temperatures they brought with them.

"Have a look into Picaflor's financials, will you, Constable, once you've got yourself sorted out? Just in case Mr. Amendal is mistaken, after all. The sergeant and I will see you back at the station."

Laraby turned to Maik. "But first, what do you say we put on some of that nice disco music of yours and have a tootle on down to the marina for a chat with Mr. James?"

12

The narrow coast road lined with stone cottages wound through a small village. Laraby watched as the homes flashed past, their curtained windows like eyes staring back at him.

Maik was quiet, his face set like stone.

"It was an understandable reaction, Sergeant," Laraby told him. "I'm sure Constable Salter will be none the worse for wear." He looked across at Maik. "Clocked her a good 'un, though. You clearly haven't lost your edge. Good thing, too. You never know when it might come in useful, a skill set like yours."

Maik remained silent. He preferred conversations where he knew either the purpose or the direction. So far, this one was short on both counts. "The marina's just down this lane," he said unnecessarily, turning up the music as insurance against any more idle chatter.

Beyond the car park, the light played off the water in quick-silver flashes. The detectives walked along the wooden dock to a well-appointed cruiser berthed at the far end. Laraby indicated the name on the stern: *The Big Deal*. On the deck, a tall, wiry man was wrangling a heavy piece of equipment into position. He looked up as the detectives approached. Despite the cool conditions, there were beads of sweat at his hairline.

"Connor James?"

"These days. And I'll bet you're the police, come to ask me about the accountant that died."

"Who was murdered." Laraby's gentle correction didn't seem to hold any admonishment. "Shouldn't this boat be in dry dock by now?"

James rolled his narrow shoulders easily. "Ah, you know how it is. The water won't freeze properly for a couple of weeks yet. I might get another couple of trips in." He looked up at the overcast sky, as if seeking a clue to its intentions, and reached for a butternut jacket in scaled leather. "You'd think crocodile skin would be all right in the wet, wouldn't you? But I don't want to take any chances if those clouds let loose. You'd better come on down."

The two men followed James into the hatch, ducking under the low bulwark. They emerged into a small, lavishly appointed cabin with a leather-upholstered bench seat running along one side and rich, dark wood panelling around the walls. It struck Maik that James hadn't allowed a single wall-hanging to spoil the effect.

"Walnut," announced James. "And that's genuine calfskin on those benches." He made an expansive gesture with his arms to embrace it all. "Not bad for a kid who left school at thirteen, is it? I never done no good there, but that's because I never found out what my talent was until I was out in the real world."

The two detectives waited patiently.

"I read people."

"The magazine?" Laraby's face was showing no expression when Maik's sidelong glance reached him.

"Mock all you like," said James indulgently. "I understand their needs, see. And then I bring them together. Mostly them that has money with them that wants it."

Laraby cast another glance around the sumptuous interior

of the boat. "With a bit left over for you at the end of it all?"

James shrugged. "My up-front fee is nothing to write home about. The real pay-off is in the back end. A tidy little percentage when their venture pays off."

"Risky, though, I would have thought," said Laraby. "Not only are a good number of those ventures going to fail, there's also the deals that never get made. The ones where you put in all that work and then the investors walk away at the last minute. That must be frustrating."

"You're talking about the Picaflor deal, the IV League investment group." James looked at the detectives frankly. "I'll admit it; I thought I had that one. For the life of me I can't see why they never followed through." He opened the small cocktail fridge and took out a soft drink. He waved it in the direction of the detectives, but both declined. He opened the can and took a long drink.

"Sugar water," he said, setting the can down on the counter. "I should know better, I suppose, a grown man like me. But I don't have a lot of other vices, so where's the harm, eh?" He took another swig and set the can down again.

"You never asked why they didn't make the investment?"

James pulled a face. "It happens. Small-timers trying to pretend they're the next Richard Branson, until it's time to come up with the cash." He shook his head. "I have to admit, though, this group didn't strike me that way. I'd have had a small flutter that the deal was going to go through." He smiled again. It appeared to be a default setting with James, though it seemed genuine enough. "As a broker, there's not much you can do when somebody decides they don't want to play anymore." He shrugged his shoulders. "It's frustrating, but there it is. Part of the game, innit?"

Maik made a point of looking at a large black-and-white photograph propped on the bar, beneath the spot on the wall where it had obviously been hanging until recently. It was a close-up of a Barn Owl staring directly into the camera lens.

"Is that one of Robin Oakes's?"

"Gave it to me as a gift. In happier times, when it looked like we'd all be doing a deal together. I'm just packing it up for a gallery in Norwich. I hate to seem ungrateful," he said, "but I can probably get half a grand for it."

"Five hundred for that?"

"Nobody buys photographs anymore, Sergeant. They buy photographers. Same with artists. And Mr. Oakes is flavour of the month these days, especially out here." James took another sip of his drink. "Listen, I like art as much as the next bloke, but if I can pay three figures for a painting and get four when I sell it, I couldn't care if it was done by Damien Hirst or some elephant with a paintbrush stuck in its trunk." He considered the photograph. "I suppose it's nice enough, but it's best not to get too attached to things, I find. Clouds your judgment."

"Does that go for your investors, too?"

James eyed Laraby carefully. "Now why would you ask a question like that, I wonder?"

"I'm a detective," said Laraby. "Asking questions was in the job description."

"The vast majority of my clients are widows looking to invest their husbands' life insurance payouts. Hazardous occupation, apparently, being a husband. Significantly reduces your life expectancy. The thing is, they're not all elderly, these widows. Some are still in their prime. I'm single, healthy, normal appetite." He shrugged. "It happens. I'm not going to give you a list of names, but if you ask specifically, I'll tell you yes or no."

"Erin Dawes."

"No." James inclined his head. "Good-looking woman, mind you. Nicely put together. But she wasn't interested in any of the fringe benefits." He smiled. "She never had her eyes on anything but the prize. She wanted those Picaflor options in the worst way, though. I can tell you that."

"How can you be so sure?" asked Laraby.

"It's my game, innit? She had that uncertainty at first. It's what I watch for. It's easy to get carried away when you talk about money. People's eyes light up like pinball machines and their common sense goes out the window. But the ones who have some reservations, they're the ones who are taking the idea seriously, considering it. If I can win them over, answer their questions, they'll be keepers."

"And you're usually right, are you?" asked Laraby in a tone that suggested he wasn't wholly convinced.

"Often enough." James gave them a cheeky smile. "I'll bet I could guess exactly who both of you are, investment-wise." He looked at Maik. "You like a safe bet, no surprises. You, on the other hand," he tilted his can in the direction of Laraby, "long odds wouldn't faze you, as long as the payoff was worth it at the end." He raised his eyebrows in question, but neither man seemed inclined to confirm his assessment. Neither one denied it, though, either.

Outside the window, patches of sunlight lay on the surface of the water, lifting with the gently moving swells. The large boat rode them easily, a gentle rocking motion the only hint that the men were on the water at all.

Laraby seemed to be considering the information he had heard so far, sifting James's salesman's bluster from details he could find a use for. "So there's no doubt in your mind," he asked finally, "Erin Dawes was convinced the Picaflor investment was sound?"

Laraby seemed to be asking all the questions Danny Maik wanted answers to — unlike Jejeune, whose thought processes were so obscure you weren't even sure half the time if you were investigating the same crime. It was a strange feeling for Danny to be on the same page with his lead investigator. It had usually been like that in the early days, when he was learning his craft, following the tried and true methods laid out before him by a string of distinguished, if unremarkable, detective inspectors. But it wasn't a feeling he'd enjoyed much since DCI Domenic Jejeune had come onto the scene in Saltmarsh.

James took another long drink. "To be honest, by the time we'd finished chatting about it, I had her down as leading the charge, doing my job for me when the IV League got together for a final decision." James shook his head. "Apparently she just wasn't able to get them to go along with her, though."

"Why do you think that was?"

"Who's to say? It's their money. They can do what they like with it. I have to say, I doubt they got a better offer. Options that looked set to yield twenty percent once they were exercised? Let's just say, if they found a better return than that, I've got a long list of clients who'd be interested."

"I'm having trouble understanding the structure of this land deal," said Maik. He didn't give a convincing impression of a man who had trouble understanding many things, but James let it go.

"New one on me, too," he admitted. "But the terms were straightforward enough. Picaflor was prepared to offer options on two hundred thousand pounds worth of shares, as long as they got that particular tract of land as part of the package. The other one hundred and fifty had to be in cash."

"And Picaflor intended to use it as their test site, replanting the area between remnants of forest on Gerald Moncrieff's property on one side and Amelia Welbourne's on the other? But Dawes was the one who put the IV League together," said Laraby, nodding to himself. "She chose the members. You met the group, I take it? How did they get along?"

"As you might expect; three rural aristos and her. No love lost between her and Oakes, in particular. Always at loggerheads, those two."

Laraby's eyebrows went up a notch. "Any idea why?"

James shook his head. "No. But money in a business relationship is like water on a boat. If there's the slightest crack, it'll find it." He made a production of sweeping the overlarge dial of his wristwatch into view. "Listen, I don't want to rush you off, but I need to get this package away to the gallery. Feel free to come back any time you like, though. If it's a nice enough day, we can even take the boat out for a spin."

He accompanied the men up onto the deck and they shook hands. As the detectives stepped from the boat ramp, James called out to them. "Oh, about that photograph. Probably better you didn't mention it to Mr. Oakes when you see him. It'd only hurt his feelings." He gave them a wink before disappearing below deck.

"I'd say Mr. Oakes will soon have a lot more to worry about than an unwanted photograph, wouldn't you, Sergeant?" asked Laraby as they walked toward the Mini.

Maik knew what he meant. When Oakes had talked about the land lease, he had used the present tense. Which meant that, as far as he was concerned, he was now holding fifty thousand pounds worth of extremely lucrative stock options. Maik had no doubt Laraby was relishing the prospect of informing him otherwise. But another thought struck him as they walked. And he had little doubt this one had already occurred to Laraby, too. If Robin Oakes still believed he held those options in Picaflor, it was likely both Amelia Welbourne and Gerald Moncrieff did, too. And unlike Oakes, their contributions to the IV League coffers had been in cash.

13

From the top of a tree on the edge of the clearing surrounding the lodge, a Crested Oropendola broke into its curious gulping call, pitching forward with its wings held out like a cloak. Jejeune stopped on his way to the breakfast area and stared up at the bird, enthralled. It took him a moment to come to terms with the fact that he was actually here, in the rainforest, witnessing such an exotic, eccentric display.

Bogota seemed a long way away now, but the trip to El Paujil had been an enlightening one. Signs of national pride were everywhere along their route; even in the smallest villages flags flew and walls and lampposts were painted in the tricolour yellow, red, and blue. But the chain of police and army checkpoints was a sobering reminder of the country's troubled past, and perhaps even offered an explanation of sorts for the new outpouring of patriotism.

Traz was stirring a coffee, deep in thought, when Jejeune approached the breakfast buffet. "The group at the next table," he said in a low voice, "they've been talking about that guide, Mariel. She was the tour leader when a couple of them came here before. They make her sound pretty good, JJ. Phenomenal, in fact."

Jejeune was quiet. They both knew birding, like every other pastime, acquired its share of giants, beings touched with greatness, who strode their world like princes. *World-class birders,* he had heard them called, as if it was some standard you could reach if only you worked long enough, diligently enough. Perhaps it was. Jejeune poured himself a coffee and cast an eye at the table, where Armando had joined the group and was now talking to them earnestly. "Is that what they're discussing now?"

Traz shook his head, but kept his voice low. "He's giving them his *I'm here for you* speech. You know: *you are my clients, my job is to make you happy. If you need anything, just ask and I will make it happen.* He pulled a face. "If he works as hard finding us birds as he does on getting his tip, we'll hit six hundred species on this trip."

The two men took a table on the far side of the patio. Traz nodded at Thea as he saw her approaching along the gravel pathway. "Straight for me." He shook his head in mock pity. "I almost feel sorry for her. Poor woman can't help herself, so strong is the attraction."

"Like a moth to a low-wattage bulb," said Jejeune, suddenly finding something in his arepa that was worthy of his attention. He doubted Traz could have given Thea a warmer welcoming smile if she was bringing him money.

"Your father not joining us?" Traz didn't sound overly distressed by the prospect.

"He has some calls to make." Her resigned expression suggested a well-established pattern. She made her way over to the buffet table and Traz watched her go.

"Oh, yeah," he said to Jejeune, like a man suddenly remembering something important, "I'm going to need that book back. I've promised it to her."

"The book you brought all the way to Colombia to give to me? As a gift?"

"Yeah, well let's just say it's been re-gifted. She was very grateful. She said she's been looking everywhere for one. Besides, you still have the first edition."

"You said it was useless."

"No. It'll be fine for someone of your level."

Traz rose to greet the returning Thea, but Armando intercepted her, reaching out to relieve her of her plate and following her to the table. He set the plate before her with a flourish and a winning smile as she took her seat. Jejeune noticed Traz's own smile had dimmed considerably.

"You enjoyed your visit to Casa de Colibries?" asked Armando pleasantly. "Though I'm told you missed the Sword-billed Hummingbird. This is very sad."

"We did okay," said Traz with a defensive petulance that made Jejeune smile. "We saw plenty."

Armando inclined his head slightly. "Still, it is a shame you could not see this bird. It would leave you," he turned to Thea and touched his bunched fingers to his lips, "*sin aliento.*"

"Breathless." Thea let the word roll sensuously around in her mouth. "Can something really be so beautiful that it takes away your breath, I wonder?"

Armando placed a flat palm against his heart. "Speaking for myself, I think I can say that it can."

"*Chulo,*" announced Traz. Jejeune was already familiar with the Colombian slang for the Black Vulture, but when he searched the skies, there was no bird to be seen. Besides, if Traz had seen one, he'd managed to do so without looking up. Armando seemed not to notice. He rose and treated them all to another of his lizard smiles. "Excuse me, I must get things ready for our hike. Departure in twenty minutes. Okay?"

Jejeune noticed he had not bothered with an English translation of his speech to the other group. Maybe he just thought the better tips would be coming from the Spanish birders.

The hike was well-chosen for so early on the tour; the modest grades and well-groomed trails provided a gentle introduction for a group still coming to terms with the rigours of rainforest birding. It meant that the more elusive birds of the deeper cover would almost certainly not be found today, but a continuing procession of flycatchers and seed-eaters carried the group along contentedly from one sighting to the next, and the occasional company of raucously screeching Blue-Headed Parrots overhead offered enough tropical flavour to keep everyone fully engaged.

Jejeune was at the back of the pack. He had been hiking alone for some time; pausing occasionally to peer into the deep tangles of leaves and vines that lined the edges of the trails, looking for telltale flickers of movement. Traz had moved ahead to chat to Thea, and grudgingly, her father, and had kept pace with the slow but steady progress of the rest of the group. They were still within sight, but the distance was widening.

The overloud crashing of a falling Cecropia leaf caused Jejeune to raise his binoculars and look up into the canopy. A passerine flittered through the branches briefly, but backlit and silent, it was impossible for him to identify the bird.

"White-bearded Manakin." Armando's voice startled Jejeune and he snapped his bins down swiftly. "A good bird," acknowledged the guide. "You did well to find it. This is not like birding in England, I think. It is challenging, no?"

"It is challenging, yes," said Jejeune with a smile.

"This is secondary growth, denser and darker than much of the primary forest cover. It seems impossible that we can find birds in this. But your eyes will soon become accustomed to it. The birds are here. You will see them." Armando paused, perhaps to listen to a faint bird call. If so, he failed to identify it to Jejeune. "But other things you are looking for," he shook his head, "these you will not find."

Jejeune straightened and looked at the guide. "And what might those be?"

The rest of the group had trudged on ahead and were about to disappear around a bend in the trail, but Armando showed no interest in them. His focus was fixed on Jejeune.

"Excuses to take away your brother's guilt."

The faintest of breezes stirred the vegetation. The group had disappeared from view. It was just the two of them, standing opposite each other on this exposed path, the morning sun warm on their shoulders. A call, possibly the one Armando had heard earlier, came to them now from somewhere in the forest. "White-tipped Quetzal," said Armando. "A beautiful bird, but very far off." He paused. "Your presence brings back bad memories for this company, Inspector. For the guides, too. If you had to come to Colombia at all, it would have been better if you had not chosen to tour with Mas Aves."

"The company could have refused to take my booking," Jejeune pointed out reasonably.

"They wish to show they have nothing to hide. But many people feel ashamed that they did not do more to stop your brother. Your presence raises again feelings of guilt in them." He shook his head, like a man trying to free himself of such thoughts. "The truth is there is only one person to blame for your brother's crime. He is the person who took the sick man to Chiribiquete, despite being denied a permit by the authorities for them to travel to the area."

"I am simply trying to understand the whole picture, what caused him to do what he did." Jejeune realized his own undeclared motives were unfurling before him as he spoke. He was beginning to understand, finally, his purpose in coming here.

"Your brother was being paid three hundred dollars a day. This is a great deal of money for any guide, even the very best. To take this man to Chiribiquete would have been a seven-day journey. That is a lot of money to lose." Armando looked at Jejeune. "The moment he took a sick man into the land of the Karijona, your brother became responsible for the deaths of those four indigenous people. This is your whole picture, Inspector Jejeune."

Armando spoke dispassionately, almost kindly, but he left his eyes on Jejeune for a long time after he finished speaking. Jejeune let his own gaze wander up the trail to where the others had so recently departed from view.

"You are right," said Armando. "I must catch up with the group. If you are here to find birds, Inspector Jejeune, I will do all I can to help you."

But if not? Armando did not need to finish the sentence. Jejeune would get no help in trying to find someone to lessen his brother's guilt. The detective understood. He had no reason to expect anyone else would want to see Damian escape justice. Perhaps not even his brother himself.

The sudden noise in the undergrowth had both men turning together to see a large iguana trundling clumsily through the leaf litter. In a world where so many creatures moved stealthily and silently, the animal's ungainly progress seemed recklessly out of place.

"Please do not fall too far behind the rest of the group, Inspector," said Armando as he turned to leave. "The rainforest can hold many dangers for the unwary."

Jejeune detected no hint of threat in the air on this warm tropical morning. But then again, Armando knew this rainforest far better than he did. Perhaps there were dangers the detective just couldn't see.

Armando didn't join the group for dinner, but his comments circled Jejeune's mind in an unending loop as he sat at the table with Traz. His silence didn't go unnoticed, and his friend understood its cause. Jejeune had confided in him the essence of his conversation with the guide as soon as he had returned to the lodge. Traz had known Damian for a long time. If anyone could judge Armando's views on Domenic's brother, it was him.

"It's just talk, JJ. I mean, okay, we both know about Damian and money. But there's no way he would have taken that man into Karijona territory if he had known he was sick, no matter how much money was on offer. You know that."

Did he? Jejeune looked beyond Traz into the velvety darkness that had descended around the lodge, listening to the trills and buzzing of a thousand different insects. The air retained the remnants of the day's warmth, but Jejeune could draw no comfort from the tropical evening. He left the remains of his beer and bade the group goodnight, leaving Traz to sidle toward Thea's table, brandishing the *Field Guide to the Birds of Colombia, Second Edition* like a trophy.

Traz wasn't long in following Jejeune to the room, but his friend was already in bed when he arrived.

"I think it's fair to say she was impressed," said Traz with a wide grin. "Just so you know, I'm going to suggest the two of us take a stroll on the north road tomorrow night, just to give the book a trial run." He gave his friend a look of exaggerated innocence.

"There are supposed to be Lyre-tailed Nightjars up on that road. Maybe I'll come along."

"No, you won't. And I wouldn't wait up either." Traz sat on the edge of his bed and lapsed into silence, as if he was considering telling Jejeune something important, but had not yet reconciled himself to it.

"What?" asked Jejeune.

"You know why Walden was so interested in how we came to choose this tour company?" asked Traz quietly. "Because he's a shareholder. I heard Thea mention it to him on the trek this afternoon."

Jejeune nodded slowly. Of course. How else would he be in a position to advise Mas Aves what to put on its website? And who could have told Armando they had missed the Sword-billed Hummingbird at Casa de Colibries? It explained, too, the strange atmosphere that had shrouded their day there, the feeling of being scrutinized by Walden. Jejeune wondered how long it would have taken him to put the pieces together if Traz hadn't uncovered this information. Important or not, he couldn't shake the feeling these were details he should have picked up on himself, much earlier.

Traz climbed into bed and switched off the light. "I wouldn't read too much into it, JJ," he said. "I imagine the company just wants to be sure if you have any questions, there is someone close at hand to answer them." He gave an elaborate yawn. "Anyway, we'd better get some sleep. I hear it's going to be a long day tomorrow."

Traz didn't offer any further details, and he was asleep almost as soon as his head hit the pillow. But Domenic Jejeune stayed awake for a long time, staring into the darkness above his bunk. Thinking.

14

It could have been a plinth, a grey slab of granite set on the cliff edge sometime in north Norfolk's wayfaring past. But it moved as the two officers approached, half-turned toward them, and Salter could make out the shape of a person in a long grey duffle coat. Having acknowledged their presence, the woman turned back to resume her study of the sea. Laraby and Salter continued over the hard, uneven ground toward her, heads bowed against the fierce winds coming in off the water. On either side of them, row upon row of low white stakes stretched out over the undulating land like half-finished crosses on some vast burial ground. Looking closer, Salter could see each stake had a small sapling tethered to it, though the trees were too short yet to be troubled by the winds. Their wrath was saved for taller targets. Like people.

"How's your mouth, everything all healed okay?" asked Laraby as they walked. "I get the impression Sergeant Maik was mortified about what happened."

Salter's top lip was still puffy and she touched it gingerly. "It's fine," she said. "Cheaper than collagen, anyway."

Laraby smiled. "Ever think of moving up the ladder to Sergeant yourself?" he asked casually. "There's nothing wrong with a bit of ambition."

The elements disguised any surprise Salter might have felt at Laraby's inquiry, but she still took a second to compose her response. "It's always been in the back of my mind, I suppose, but it's not what I'd call a priority at the moment, what with my son Max and all."

Laraby seemed to consider the constable's answer warily. "Well, if you ever do decide, here's a bit of advice; get yourself a specialty. The service loves a specialist these days. You could do worse than this drone business. Most officers treat any new technology like it's radioactive. You become a specialist in this stuff, and you'll find yourself in demand."

"Noted." Her tone suggested the topic was closed, and Laraby received the message.

As they approached the woman, Laraby called out her name and his own, but Amelia Welbourne didn't turn from the sea. Perhaps the DI's words had been snatched away by the wind. The two police officers joined her, standing shoulder to shoulder, watching the heaving mass of olive water twist into mounds, spewing out great spumes of white foam as they exploded back into nothingness.

"It was a storm like this that exposed the underwater forest," said the woman without turning from her vigil. Laraby's expression suggested he was searching for metaphors in her words, but Salter knew what she was referring to.

"An ancient forest, sir, about ten thousand years old, they think. Some divers discovered the remnants of it when a storm shifted the sand on the sea bed." She turned to Welbourne. "It's just off here somewhere, isn't it?"

Welbourne raised her arm and pointed to the southeast. "About two hundred metres offshore. It was called Doggerland, an immense oak forest that once stretched all the way to the continent." Welbourne's eyes continued to play over the rolling waters. She was tall but small-boned, and the combination gave her frame a particular kind of frailty. And while Salter suspected all three of them had high colour in their faces at the moment from the sharp bite of the wind, Welbourne's looked of a more permanent sort. There were traces of the same red blushing on her neck when the winds whipped her mousy hair away. Her overall appearance suggested a delicate constitution, of the sort that might be tested to the limits by the demands of managing a large property like Sylvan Ridge.

"Any particular reason you're out here on a day like this, Ms. Welbourne? Looking for something special out there?" Laraby had to raise his voice over the blustery wind, but he managed to keep the tone pleasant.

"I walk my property every day, Inspector," she called back, "in all seasons, rain or shine. This land has been in the Welbourne family for many generations. It is a part of us, and we, a part of it. I owe it a duty of care."

There was a resolve in her voice that made Salter rethink her earlier assessment. Determination went a long way toward the success of any enterprise, and the Welbournes must have had a fair supply of it to be able to hang on to a vast swath of north Norfolk like Sylvan Ridge for centuries. A sudden gust of wind took Salter off guard and rocked her sharply.

"We are investigating the murder of Erin Dawes," said Laraby. "We know you were part of an investment group with her, the IV League." Having declared exactly where he stood, the detective fell silent. He knew the information would influence whatever Amelia Welbourne chose to tell them now. And that suited him perfectly. Less messing about with irrelevances that way.

"Indeed, we were both part of the group," she conceded carefully, "but I had no dealings with Erin Dawes beyond that. Not personally, not professionally." Welbourne wore the expression of someone who believed an expensive education and well-established pedigree might inure one from this sort of prying. "That said, I shall be forever grateful to her for bringing us this wonderful opportunity."

"The Picaflor project, you mean?" Salter stole a glance at Laraby. "You were enthusiastic about it, then?"

Welbourne turned from the sea, a strand of her hair almost hitting the detective in the face as it whipped around in the wind, causing him to snap his head away sharply. "The chance to reforest areas on a large scale? The loss of our forests is one of the great catastrophes of our age. I have rarely been so proud to be involved in helping a new project get established."

Again, Salter flicked a glance at the DI, but there was more information to be gleaned while Welbourne was still in her state of ignorance. "Did all of the IV League members feel the same way?"

"The financial return was obviously Erin Dawes's major concern, but I believe she did also appreciate the inherent value of forests." Welbourne stooped to pick away a remnant of grass that had become entangled around one of the saplings. It seemed like a futile gesture in the face of these winds, but Salter understood it for what it was, the need to nurture something you cared for.

"What inherent value?"

"Ecosystem services, Inspector. Climate regulation, flood control. Not to mention the sheer sense of inspiration and fulfillment one feels when surrounded by a stand of mature trees. Surely, the spiritual nourishment one receives from a forest far exceeds any economic value."

"I'm sorry, you've lost me." Laraby's smile came just soon enough to reassure Welbourne that perhaps there was a soul in there somewhere after all. "And the others?"

"Robin seems as unconcerned about this as about most matters of consequence in his life, to be frank. Personally, I felt his contribution to be the most valuable of all. To give us the opportunity, through the use of his land, to re-establish an unbroken swath of forest, to link these two ancient remnants once again." Welbourne stared off into the distance at the thought. "Magnificent." She tossed her head slightly, sending her wispy hair swirling in the wind once again. "Gerald expressed the gravest reservations about the project, though, of course, he did eventually come round."

"What reservations might those have been, then?" asked Laraby, stirring with interest.

"Drones. He's vehemently opposed to them."

"But he agreed to invest in the project despite this?"

Welbourne gave the two detectives a narrow smile. "Gerald Moncrieff never met a pound he didn't like, Inspector. The projected returns on offer overwhelmed any philosophical objections he might have had. I won't stay invested, myself, you understand. I'm not a fan of the stock market. I believe there are times when you have to ask yourself just how much bother you are willing to go to in order to get extra money that you don't really need. But I am glad that I have been able to help such a worthy project in its early stages."

Laraby turned to stare at the sea, steadying himself against the blustery wind. He seemed mesmerized by the waves, racing toward their ceaseless suicide against the boulders at the base of the cliff. Salter knew he was preparing himself, not just to deliver the news, but to sense the first reaction, the unguarded response, before anything could sweep in to mask it. She prepared herself, too, watching Welbourne's thin face carefully.

Laraby turned to Welbourne. "Can you think of any reason Erin Dawes would not have gone through with the purchase of the options in the Picaflor project?"

"None at all." She drew her head back slightly. "What on earth do you mean?"

"Ms. Welbourne, the investment was never made."

Unless acting was high on the list of subjects they taught at Welbourne's finishing school, her surprise was genuine. And profound. She brought a slender hand up to her mouth. "This is dreadful news. Simply awful."

"As I'm sure the death of Erin Dawes was to you," said Salter, continuing to watch the woman's face carefully.

"What? Yes, of course." Her mind seemed to be reeling, unable to take in the news. "But to lose this opportunity…. So the reforestation project on Robin's land has been abandoned?" She looked distraught, even as she fought to retain her dignity, as her breeding seemed to demand.

"I believe Dr. Amendal was able to make other arrangements for test sites," said Laraby. "So you never asked to see the investment documents?"

She shook her head numbly. "It's not what one does, is it, check up on one's business partners? Erin Dawes assured me the investment would be made by the deadline, and I would hold the agreed share options in the project. I gave that side of things no more thought."

What sort of a world did these people live in, wondered Laraby, where a fifty-thousand-pound investment was on the side of things to which someone gave no more thought. "We were wondering whether Ms. Dawes's decision might have anything to do with her relationship with Robin Oakes."

Salter had never had the benefit of finishing school acting classes, so there was no question the surprise she showed was genuine. Nobody she knew at the station was wondering about this. She looked at Laraby, but he was focused on Welbourne.

At first, the woman said nothing. Laraby waited patiently, seemingly oblivious now to the raw winds that buffeted the air around their heads. Welbourne found something across the fields that captured her attention. On the horizon, a single tree stood like an ominous black scarecrow, silhouetted against the white sky. But other than that, there was nothing of interest that Salter could see.

"Were they involved in a sexual relationship, Ms. Welbourne?"

"I couldn't say."

"But it's possible?" pressed Laraby. "You couldn't rule it out?"

Salter felt vaguely uneasy. It was quite a distance from putting words in a person's mouth in an interview to doing it on a witness stand, but once you had started on that path, you had already taken the most important step.

Welbourne was silent, weighing the inspector's question. "Anything is possible, I suppose. Robin's casual relationships have been well-documented by the press." Welbourne softened her face into the kind of smile that did nothing at all for her own appearance. "But really, I have to say, Erin Dawes was hardly Robin's …"

"Class?"

"*Type*, Inspector. She and Robin did not have what I'd call compatible personalities. He has raised indolence to an art form. She was, shall we say, animated. They spent most of their time defending their approaches to life. If there was any physical attraction between them, they kept it very well hidden."

She seemed to consider her remarks and turned a little to allow her look to add weight to her comments. "I refuse to believe Robin can have been involved in Erin Dawes's death, Inspector. That is what you're implying, isn't it? It's unthinkable. You should know I trust Robin Oakes utterly. I have always found him to be an honourable person, of impeccable background."

"If he ever applies for a job with the police services, perhaps I'll come to you for a character reference," said Laraby testily.

"You don't understand, Inspector. Robin Oakes could never have committed a crime like this. He's simply not that …"

"Type?" offered Laraby. "Thank you, Ms. Welbourne, you've been most helpful." The inspector delivered the words with finality, but there was a resonance to them that Salter suspected Amelia Welbourne would not find particularly comforting.

"Humbling, wasn't it, Constable?" said Laraby as they made their way back between the rows of white stakes. "You stand before that sea, and you think, it's been doing this forever. You wonder what difference a policeman can make, when you see the timelessness of it all."

It had not been the comment Salter was expecting. She had been waiting to hear Laraby banging on about being blown halfway to Wales, and brass monkeys with missing parts. Instead, here he was philosophizing about one police officer's place in the grand scheme of things.

"Why Oakes, sir?" she asked. Had they missed something, Salter and Danny Maik and the rest, something that had pointed Laraby toward the celebrity photographer? With Jejeune, such questions were par for the course. But ever since he'd been here, DI Laraby had a knack for making you feel like you were all on the same page, all part of the same investigation. For him to hone in on a suspect out of the blue like this seemed out of character somehow.

"Robin Oakes lied to Sergeant Maik and me, Constable. And when somebody lies to a police officer, it's because they are guilty of something. Now perhaps it's just me, but I can't think of many things I'm going to be willing to lie about at the expense of giving myself an alibi for the time of a murder."

"Welbourne seems to genuinely believe he'd never be involved in anything like this."

"I'm sure she does. But it's all very well issuing blanket assurances based on somebody's family tree. Me, I'm a touch harder to convince. These people are not racehorses, Constable. Their bloodlines make no difference to me."

Laraby paused at the car and took one last look back across the fields, the wind making his eyes water. The distant grey shape of Amelia Welbourne was still making her way slowly along the coastal path.

"Hard to believe that forest was lying there all that time under the sea, isn't it, Constable?"

Salter knew what he meant: An entire forest, lying for millennia just offshore. And no one knew. No secret was too big to hide, if you chose the right place to conceal it.

15

Marvin Laraby stood at the front of the incident room, surveying all before him with an air of calm self-assurance. There was a lot to like about Laraby's approach to life. You got the sense of a man who had taken the occasional look in the mirror and come to terms with what he had seen. Maik had once heard DCS Shepherd, who seemed to have an Americanism for every occasion, describe someone as being comfortable in his own skin, and the phrase seemed to suit Laraby particularly well. Of course, it helped that there was something to feel comfortable about. They were making progress — in Laraby's view, anyway, if not quite as much, perhaps, in anybody else's.

They were listening to the reports from the teams that had been checking Dawes's contacts. Since it had been agreed that the break-in had been committed by someone who had visited Dawes's home previously, a random attack had been discounted. But the accountant's limited social circle meant the detectives had been able to approach things systematically until, one by one, the acquaintances of Erin Dawes were definitively eliminated as suspects. The number of people who had the opportunity to kill Erin Dawes, let alone motive and means, was dwindling with every new report.

Laraby nodded contentedly as the last of the teams reported their conclusions. "Okay, listen people, this is good work. Stellar. Well done, everyone."

The general stirring had an unmistakable undertone. Laraby's praise seemed to linger in the air all the longer because the group was not accustomed to hearing it. Shepherd eased herself up from her post by the doorway. Such was the wave of good feeling Laraby's input had created, it seemed almost churlish to dwell on the negatives in the investigation. But motive was going to be key, and to this point, as far as Shepherd could tell, they were nowhere near establishing one. There seemed to be little doubt now that it had been Dawes's plan all along to embezzle the IV League funds. One hundred and fifty thousand pounds had been withdrawn from the group account two days before the investment deadline. Now the money was nowhere to be found. But that was where the logical side of things fell off a cliff. First, no one could come up with a good reason, or even a moderately bad one, for why Dawes would have stayed around so long, when it was unquestionably just a matter of time before her crime was discovered. And neither Shepherd nor the rest of the Saltmarsh Serious Crimes squad had needed any big-time Charlie from The Smoke, even one who seemed to be morphing into a decent bloke before their very eyes, to point out that, if somebody had taken your money and hidden it, killing them was not the way you went about getting it back. As motives went, Welbourne's and Moncrieff's were about as weak as they came. The problem was, they were not just the best ones the investigating officers had at the moment, they were the only ones.

"I don't suppose there was anything in her safe that might lead us to where that money is?" Shepherd asked.

Laraby's expression suggested what he thought the likelihood of that might be. "I mean, I get that she didn't go to the same upper-crust universities as the rest of the IV League set, ma'am, but expecting her to keep incriminating details like that around the house is not giving her much credit. That money is racking up double digit interest somewhere a lot warmer than north Norfolk, and the details will be stored on a cloud server somewhere we can't get at them." Laraby turned to Maik. "That said, I haven't seen an inventory of the safe's contents yet. Think you could get me a copy, Sergeant?"

Maik pulled out his phone and murmured into it. "Nobody seems to have one to hand," he said. "It'll take them a couple of minutes to locate one. They'll run it up to us as soon as they do."

"Nothing on the mug yet?" Laraby made it a personal inquiry to Maik, but the sergeant simply shook his head.

"Erm, I looked into that bird plaque," said Salter to fill the awkward void. "Apparently, it is accurate, after all. The bird is a Golden Oriole. They're rare enough in these parts, but they have been seen in Norfolk on the odd occasion."

She looked as though she might be regretting bringing up the idea in the first place, but Laraby was having none of that. "Worth a try, though, Constable, just the same," he said, nodding. "Nothing wrong with following your heart once in a while. Now, what do we know about this other member of the IV League. Gerald Moncrieff?"

"He's made a small fortune by turning part of his property into a shooting estate, apparently. He does have a couple of hunting-related citations in the past." Salter handed Laraby a sheet of paper. "And, we have a car like Moncrieff's on CCTV moving toward Dawes's cottage late afternoon on the day she died," said Salter. "No sign of it returning. The thing is, it's a pretty popular model, a BMW X5."

"Right in our window, though. And I can't imagine a peaceful little village like Saltmarsh is exactly a hotbed of vehicular activity after the lights go down." He looked at Maik. "We should make him our first stop this morning."

"The financial checks didn't throw up any surprises," said Salter. "Oakes's finances tend to wobble a bit, but he is an artist type, after all, and you know what they're like with money. But he seems to have a fan, some billionaire in America who's an avid collector of his work, so he's doing all right at the moment. The other two are as solid as a rock. That's not to say they aren't going to miss fifty grand, but it's not going to send either of them into the poorhouse, either."

"I thought the landed gentry were all on their uppers," said Laraby, "donating their properties to the National Trust left, right, and centre to avoid paying all those inheritance taxes and such."

"It's true that many families have had to give up their properties. But the IV League members have all managed to stay on their ancestral estates, albeit in what they call "reduced circumstances." Like Oakes, for example. He lives in that gatehouse, now that the original manor house has gone. But the prestige is still there. These days, a couple of hundred acres and a granddad who'd been a local magistrate is enough to get you a mention in *Burke's Landed Gentry*."

"*Reduced circumstances*," repeated Laraby with heavy sarcasm. "Get me a tissue, will you, somebody. I'm starting to well up here with the tragedy of it all."

DCS Shepherd stirred. "The press will obviously be looking to play up the societal angle on this one, Inspector. Working-class accountant inveigles herself with the rural aristocracy and then embezzles from them." She looked at Laraby frankly. "We won't be going anywhere near that with our inquiries, I take it? I wouldn't like to think this case is going to turn into A Tale of Two Classes."

Laraby stretched his neck a little, as if trying to free it from the confines of his collar. "I don't generally conduct my investigations for the convenience of the media, ma'am." He gave his broad shoulders an easy shrug. "But I'll keep it in mind."

"Anybody else on our radar?"

"The doctor, Amendal," said Salter. "He's got some temper on him. I don't quite know why, but it sounds like that land of Oakes's was very important to his work. I doubt he took the news that he wasn't getting it too well."

Laraby shook his head slightly. "He's just a young man in a hurry." He smiled at the room. "I was a bit like that once. Thought I knew it all, and got a bit testy when I couldn't get the world to listen to me. We can have a look at him, if you like, but I doubt we're going to find any malicious intent there."

"The broker, Connor James. There's something not quite right there." Maik's sudden contribution from the side of the room, after so much measured silence, caused Laraby to snap his head around. "He's worked with a lot of high-profile clients in the past — footballers, recording industry types. You'd think there'd be wall-to-wall pictures of him with them, especially on a boat where he does all his meeting and greeting."

"Why? Because he's some unsophisticated yokel who suddenly finds himself moving in their circles? Come on, Danny."

"Because it's part of the package," said Maik evenly. "Look who I know, look who trusts me with their business dealings." Maik paused, but when it became clear nobody else was going to say it for him, he added the final piece himself. "Plus, James lost money on this deal himself. Quite a bit, if those option yields are as high as expected. And unlike Moncrieff or Welbourne, he had no reason to wait and see if his money was ever coming back again. He was never going to see those profits whether Dawes was dead or alive."

Laraby considered the idea for a moment before nodding. "Fair enough. I don't see it myself, but we can have another chat with Mr. James, if you like." He paused. "I've been having a think myself, as it happens. These arguments Oakes is reported to have had with Dawes. There's only two things that cause that kind of open hostility between a man and a woman: money and sex."

"And since Oakes wasn't contributing any money to the Picaflor project ..." said Salter.

"We know Oakes has a reputation in this area," said Laraby. "We also know Dawes wasn't the type to stand for any nonsense. My guess would be an advance that was rejected. The Robin Oakeses of the world have been bending the hired help over the parlour tables for generations. They don't get to hear the word *no* very often. I imagine it came as something of a shock."

"There's no evidence of an affair, is there?" asked Shepherd. "No stash of secret love notes tucked away among the papers in her safe?"

The reference reminded them they were still waiting for the inventory. Maik dialed again. He seemed to tense slightly as he listened to the person on the other end of the line, causing everyone else in the room to sink into silence as they watched him. He stayed on the line a moment longer and then murmured an indistinct comment before shutting off his phone. He turned to address the room. "The safe hasn't been opened yet. They've been waiting for authorization."

It was significant that no one had come to inform Danny about this in person, as protocol might have required. But looking at his expression now, it was easy to understand why. Volunteers for that sort of mission would have been few and far between.

Shepherd's face, too, had taken on a dangerously dark hue, and her tone matched it. "What the hell have they been playing at down there? I want to know who's responsible for this, Sergeant Maik. Names on my desk by the end of the day."

Around the room, people looked at one another in a mild state of panic, afraid their names might somehow end up on Maik's list. Only Laraby remained calm. He looked first at Shepherd, and then at the rest of the group.

"Listen, I'm going to put my hand up to this one. New bloke, just in, needs a proctologist to find his head for him the first few days. I think we can all see how something like this could have happened." Even when he switched gears, there was reasonableness to his tone that kept them on his side. "Still and all, people, this is a murder inquiry we're dealing with here, a proper, big-time crime." He slapped the backs of his fingers into the palm of his other hand. "So let's take it seriously from now on, shall we? We follow up to make sure everything's been done. Agreed?" He looked at Maik. "You've given them the go-ahead to open the safe, I take it?"

Maik nodded.

Laraby turned to Shepherd. "I think we can assume it'll be a priority now."

The assembled officers gathered their belongings as Laraby declared the morning briefing to be at an end. And if DCS Shepherd wasn't entirely over her anger at the debacle with the safe, she could still recognize that in stepping into the firing line for them, DI Laraby had once again done his reputation with the rest of the detective contingent at Saltmarsh Constabulary no harm at all.

16

The distant wail of a howler monkey drifted across the rainforest canopy on the still morning air. Almost as if in answer came the sweet *dios te de* of a troupe of Chestnut-mandibled Toucans, perched in the snags of a distant banyan tree. From his position at the top of the observation tower, Jejeune trained his bins on the birds, marvelling at their top-heavy, multicoloured bills as they flashed in the bright light. He looked out over the green sea of treetops, stretching as far as the eye could see. The variety of species here was astounding — fruiting trees, *Podocarpus*, figs, palms, broad-leafed evergreens. *Dios te de* — God gives to you. *Indeed*, thought Jejeune.

The sound of boots trudging up the wooden steps forewarned him that his solitary survey of this exotic wonderland was over.

"Toucans in the bare tree over there," said Jejeune as Traz emerged onto the deck. "Chestnut-mandibled."

His friend raised his bins, smiling as he watched the birds preening and posing. "Velvet-fronted Euphonia, too. Same tree, seven o'clock."

Jejeune followed the directions. "Something else just dropped in behind it," he said animatedly. "Black and blue, warbler-size."

"Black-faced Dacnis," said Traz. "Stunning."

The men traded sightings for some minutes, issuing directions and calling out identifications as the treetops came to life with movement. Sometimes, a bird perched for perfect looks, contentedly preening itself or basking in the warming morning air. Other times, the men received only the briefest of glances as a bird flitted in and away again; a quivering branch the only evidence of its visit.

Here, high above the forest floor, looking out over a vast, unbroken plain of green, with its rich profusion of birdlife, of life itself, Jejeune knew he should let it go. His brother hadn't intended for anyone to die. Domenic was sure of that. But four people had, and Damian was to blame. Just as Armando said, and Damian had himself even admitted. And yet ... who were these guides Armando had spoken of who felt shame when they should only have felt sadness, guilt instead of sorrow? Armando himself? Or someone else? — An expert on hummingbirds, perhaps? A phenomenon, even?

"Yesterday morning, when they were talking about Mariel, what did they say, specifically?"

Traz shrugged. "That they wished she was the leader this time. Nothing against Armando, but, you know, you get used to a guide's style, what they mean by 'close,' or 'three o'clock,' or 'the big tree.' They also said she never missed a hummingbird ID. Ever."

"Do they know why she stopped guiding?"

"No, but they let it go when Armando approached. It's not exactly the height of etiquette to talk about how great one trip leader was when you're on a tour with another."

Jejeune inclined his head to acknowledge the truth of Traz's statement. The sound of footsteps on the ladder ended their conversation; though Jejeune wasn't sure he had anywhere to take it anyway.

"Thea," said Traz, peering down through the slats that formed the floor of the platform. "Remember, you don't know anything about any book."

Thea had selected clothes that fit just a little more snugly today, and Jejeune noted a hint of makeup that hadn't been present yesterday. She stood beside the men as they briefed her on what was in view. She added her own contributions, quickly establishing that she remembered much of what she had learned birding with her father.

A familiar call had them all spinning as a pair of Blue-and-yellow Macaws came into view, flying low and fast over the treetops. Jejeune's heart soared at the sight of the birds speeding over the sun-dappled forest, wingtips almost touching, as if they were holding hands.

"I'm sorry we left you behind on the trail yesterday," Thea said to Jejeune, when the birds had disappeared from view. "I had been hoping to talk to you about your work. I find police investigations fascinating. How do you go about honing in on a suspect, for example? What you look for, that kind of thing?"

Jejeune paused to scan the canopy for movement before answering. "There's a few things," he conceded. "There are predictors of behaviour, for example, in some situations."

"Really?" She leaned in closer. She was on the verge of being rewarded with a view behind the curtain; an offer few people could resist.

Above them, a kettle of Black Vultures inscribed a series of graceful, effortless passes on a cloudless blue canvas. Jejeune checked them carefully, in case a King Vulture was among them. When he lowered his bins, he saw that Traz and Thea had been doing the same.

"We were talking about criminal behaviour," she reminded him. "Predictors."

"There is one type of activity in particular that can be a predictor of predatory intentions," conceded Jejeune. "Not the act itself, of course, but it's often used as a gateway to escalate things to another level."

Beside him, Traz stirred uneasily. Domenic was normally deeply reluctant to talk about his work. It seemed inconceivable he was interested in Thea, given how much he cared for Lindy. But there was an undeniable flirtatiousness about the way he was using the secrets of his profession to draw the woman in.

"A gateway?" repeated Thea. She leaned forward again, her eyes shining with interest.

"Gift-giving," announced Jejeune. "Obviously, the gift could be just a simple act of generosity. But if so, there would likely be no further reference to it. But a man giving a woman a gift, especially a relative stranger, and then trying to use it as a gateway to a more intimate situation." Jejeune shook his head sagely. "I'd always advise extreme caution in a situation like that." He leaned back, breaking the seal of intimacy. "Of course, there's no science to this. It's just a few casual observations."

"Fascinating," said Thea. She picked up her bins. "I should be heading back. I need to see my father before he disappears into his work for the day. But maybe we can chat again at lunch. You too, Traz. See you later?"

"Sure," he said, forcing a smile that wasn't really in him. "Later."

The sound of her departing footsteps had barely died away before Traz turned to his friend. "That was low, man," he said, shaking his head gravely. "Lower than Lowlie McLow."

"You gave her a book you had already given to me," pointed out Jejeune reasonably. "What do you call that?"

"Courtship. Which, by the way, would undoubtedly already be over if I wasn't working under this handicap."

"What handicap?"

"This rotten, clumsy English language of yours. If I could romance Thea in Spanish, the two of us would already be riding off into the sunset by now, leaving Armando circling the rotting carcass of his desires like the scavenging *chulo* he is."

Jejeune burst out laughing at Traz's sudden foray into purple prose, and even Traz couldn't keep a straight face for long.

"Hear that?" Traz said suddenly. "Cicadas. The heat's coming. The birding's all but done for the time being." He stepped aside and let Jejeune go ahead, placing a gentle hand on his friend's shoulder. "I tell you what, why don't you go ahead of me down these steep and unstable steps, Inspector Jejeune."

It seemed an impossible task. Jejeune and Traz had been owling before, many times, and the detective suspected the Spanish group had, too. But surely, none of them had ever faced a prospect as daunting as tracking an owl in such a vast expanse of wilderness. They had taken a thirty-minute Jeep ride up into the hills, tires slipping on the loose gravel of the steep tracks, coating the bushes with a fine patina of dust as they passed. A fugitive moon had made a brief appearance when they arrived on the ridge, bathing the treeline in its milky glow. But it had now disappeared behind a bank of dense cloud, leaving behind a deep, intense darkness that settled all around them as they gathered for their night hike.

Armando distributed flashlights, one for each two people, advising the group to play them at their feet, not too far in front. "Make sure both of you can see the trail two steps ahead when you are in single file. And stay on the path. Night snakes are here, fer-de-lance. Scorpions, too."

The group set off cautiously, the frail flashlight beams seeming to hold them in this world, almost, preventing them from slipping off into the dark abyss that waited on either side of the path. The soft chorus of insects was broken only by the occasional chirruping of a frog or rustle of a falling leaf.

They had been walking for a long time, and Jejeune had secretly given up hope of success when he heard a call. Armando froze, halting the group in its tracks. He said something in Spanish. "Crested Owl, close," breathed Thea from behind Jejeune. "He's asking if it's okay for him to use a tape to call it. The others said yes."

Jejeune and Traz murmured their assent. Night was the owl's natural time to be active, to patrol for food. Another bird calling to contest a territory would not cause it undue stress.

The bird responded to the taped calls, and Armando inched forward before finally stopping beneath a large kapok tree. He played his flashlight up into the branches, and suddenly, staring down at them, was the menacing cat-like face of a Crested Owl. One by one, the group handed off their flashlights to put their bins on the bird and to receive in return the unsettling dead-eyed stare of the formidable night hunter.

Tracking the bird in the dark had been an amazing feat, and Armando graciously accepted the high-fives offered him by the delighted group members. "This was a good bird, but it took us a long time to find him. We should go back now. The Jeeps will be waiting for us."

Once they were moving again, Armando did not retrace their steps along the path, but veered toward the ridge instead. He stopped and pointed to a narrow walkway of half-round bamboo slats fastened precariously to a rock wall.

"The Jeeps will meet us on the other side of this bridge," he said. "It is safe, but narrow, and the railing is broken in some places. I will escort each person in turn and then come back for the next one. The footing in places is tricky, so watch where I place my feet and do the same. If we stay close to the rock wall, there will be no problem."

One member of the group played their light over the bridge. The slats looked slick, and the broken rail leaned out drunkenly over the ravine that plunged down the side of the rock face.

"Remember, slowly and carefully. Close to the rock wall. You will be fine."

"Armando." The voice was Jejeune's. "My flashlight is not working."

The guide took it from Jejeune and tried it, tapping it gently against his palm when it refused to turn on. Eventually, he gave up. "Okay, he said, pocketing the broken light. "You go last. I will bring a flashlight back with me when I come for you after everyone else has gone over."

"I'll stay until the end, too," said Traz.

"As you wish," said Armando easily. "Thea, you come with me first."

The party watched in silence as the twin lights trailed through the darkness over the ravine and eventually disappeared at the far end. One by one, Armando led the party over and returned, until only Traz and Jejeune remained on their side of the bridge. The two men stood unmoving, the darkness like a shroud around them. It was quiet now, not even the sounds of insects reached them. The empty silence seemed to ring in their ears.

"That flashlight is not the same one I had earlier," said Jejeune quietly. "The other one had a notch in the handle. I handed it off to someone so I could get my bins on the Crested Owl."

"Who handed it to you again afterward? Was it Armando?"

"I don't know. It was dark. It could have been."

They saw the unsteady trail of a flashlight bouncing toward them as Armando returned over the narrow bridge. He extended a hand toward Jejeune.

"Here is your light, Inspector," he said as he stepped onto the ground again. "Stay exactly here. I advise you not to move around too much. The fer-de-lance, they like this leaf litter."

"He can come with us. We can both go with you together," said Traz.

"No." Armando was firm. "You may slip, miss your footing. We will do it one by one. You first."

He turned and stepped onto the bridge again, playing his flashlight on the smooth bamboo slats. "Walk at my pace, in my footsteps. Exactly."

As Armando stepped onto the bridge, Jejeune felt Traz's gentle shove in the small of his back urging him forward. Jejeune silently stepped onto the bridge behind Armando and followed the guide's slow, deliberate steps. Traz could hear Armando's low murmurings of reassurance floating back on the quiet night air, but he knew Jejeune would not answer until they had reached the far side.

Traz heard the guide's raised voice in the darkness, telling him the men had crossed safely. "You think this is a joke, Inspector? This is a serious situation. Dangerous, still. You must do as I say out here. Always. *Muy importante. Muy!*" The rest of Armando's rant dissipated into the still night air. He sounded so angry it crossed Traz's mind that he might be inclined to leave him to make his own way across the bridge in the darkness. But with Jejeune now safely on the far side, he knew his friend wouldn't allow that to happen, and in time the thin light of Armando's flashlight appeared as he approached, sullen and silent, to guide Traz across.

Armando chose a different Jeep from Traz and Jejeune for the ride back, and once he had counted off everyone at the lodge, he disappeared into his room without speaking to either of them.

"He'll get over it," said Traz, watching him walk away. "Or not. Either way, there was no way I was letting him leave you as last man up there, JJ. Just you and him crossing that bridge? And no witnesses?" Traz shook his head, and said it again. "No way."

17

Along the lane, the leafless trees stood like silent sentinels; totems marking the place where life had so recently been, and was now gone. A low sky hung over the farmlands on each side of the road, the flat light robbing the landscape of its contours. Single blocks of colour, browns and beiges, greys and blacks, swept away to the horizon on either side of the car. It would make a nice composition for one of Robin Oakes's photographs, thought Danny Maik incongruously. A black-and-white.

Laraby also seemed to find plenty in the landscape to hold his attention, so Maik turned up the music slightly. "Don't Leave Me This Way" wasn't a choice Maik could have seen himself making under normal circumstances, but Laraby's mention of Thelma Houston had started an ear worm the sergeant hadn't been able to shake. And besides, Danny consoled himself that Henry E. Davis's scintillating bass lines would not have been out of place in any Motown era.

"Brings back a few memories, I can tell you," said Laraby. "Me and the wife dancing to this. Donna Summer," he said suddenly, "she was another one. Was she Motown as well?"

Maik's wrists thickened as he tightened his grip on the steering wheel. When Special Forces had spent all that money training him to kill with his bare hands, they had probably not envisioned visiting detective inspectors being among his victims.

"No, sir. She was something else. Any thoughts on that other group you were trying to remember?"

Laraby shook his head. "No, but they were massive for a time. Bit of an odd name, I seem to remember that much."

The appearance of their destination on the crest of the hill prevented Maik from proposing any new candidates. The entrance to Moncrieff's estate was littered with signs advising that it was private property, and warning against trespassing, but Maik didn't have much time to consider obeying them. Laraby's gloved finger pointed directly ahead, and Danny drove between the imposing stone pillars without stopping.

"Never gets old for me, that bit," said Laraby with a smile.

It was hard to gauge Gerald Moncrieff's actual build, but the bulky outdoor jacket he was wearing gave the man standing on the steps beside the gravel forecourt a formidable presence. He had the dark jowls of a man who needs to shave frequently, and piercing, deep-set eyes. His protruding jaw and his unwelcoming scowl did nothing to make his appearance any more accommodating. Nor did the two black dogs flanking him. Maik had always considered Labradors to be a friendly breed, but these two looked like they had inherited their owner's sour disposition.

Laraby got out of the Mini as soon as the wheels had stopped rolling and marched across the gravel toward Moncrieff. At his approach, the estate owner had drawn his *Dealing with the Domestics* expression from his narrow repertoire and put it on. He was standing on the lowest step of a stone staircase that led up to an impressive double-winged manor house in red brick. It was a building of the type that by its mere presence suggested it had been around a long time. Laraby stopped before him and, despite the one step difference in height, squared up to the other man as if he might be looking forward to this encounter. Neither of the dogs moved a muscle.

Moncrieff jutted his chin out toward Laraby. "Police?"

The detective introduced himself and the approaching Sergeant Maik. Moncrieff nodded shortly to himself, as if impressed with his own deductive skills. "Come to tell me how you're going to get my money back?"

"No." Laraby's flat answer hung in the air uncomfortably. Maik had already seen the DI in action with Robin Oakes, and the relationship with someone else he would consider a member of the rural aristocracy didn't seem to be getting off to any better start.

"We're making inquiries into the death of Erin Dawes," said Maik reasonably.

Moncrieff shrugged aggressively. "Much the same thing then, as I understand it." He made no move to invite them inside his house, or to step down, so they stayed in the same position, the two detectives at the foot of the imposing stone staircase, Moncrieff hovering above them, the dogs at his side, stock-still and impassive.

"Can you tell us in what capacity you knew the victim?" asked Maik. It never hurt to establish a baseline for truthfulness with a question to which you already knew the answer.

"She was part of my investment group," said Moncrieff. "She wasn't the sort that normally moves in our circles, but she'd done a bit of accounting for us all at one time or another."

Laraby continued to stare at Moncrieff, albeit with a faintly incredulous smile on his face, such as a man might have watching a freak show at the fun fair.

"Can't say I ever cared for her particularly."

"Why's that, then?" asked Laraby. "A bit uppity, was she? Didn't always remember her place?"

"Had a bit of a chip on her shoulder, as a matter of fact. Seemed to resent the fact that the fates had decreed some of us would always have a little bit more than she had." He stared hard at Laraby. "In retrospect, we all needed our heads examining, I suppose, trusting our money to a person like that."

"An accountant, you mean?" asked Laraby in an innocent tone that Danny Maik was already learning was not to be taken at face value. Moncrieff was not taken in by it either.

"Look, Inspector, I'm sorry if it goes against your touching socialist sensibilities, but the fact remains there was only one person of her ilk in our group, and she's the one who pinched my bloody money. Those are the facts, as simply as one can state them."

"I understand you weren't particularly keen on the investment," said Laraby, unfazed by the man's bluntness. "Not a fan of drone technology, I hear?"

"Not much, no. I don't hold with all this erosion of our civil liberties, invading our spaces, spying on our doings." Moncrieff turned to Maik, as if perhaps he'd found a decent person he could at least talk to. "An Englishman is entitled to a bit of privacy on his own land, one would have thought."

"Especially if he's not obeying the law," said Laraby, smiling pleasantly. "You've got a record, Mr. Moncrieff, hunting out of season."

Moncrieff exploded in exasperation, rousing the dogs slightly. "Good God, man. You're bringing that up now? It was years ago. I got an early start on a nye of pheasants one year, that's all."

"No, sir, it's not all. A gamekeeper of yours poisoned a couple of birds of prey, too. Buzzards, I believe they were."

"Nothing to do with me," said Moncrieff sharply. "I let the man go as soon as I found out."

"Hardly surprising, putting your government farm subsidy in jeopardy like that."

A small hiccup of discomfort rose within Maik. Laraby seemed to have an agenda beyond the inquiries, one the sergeant wasn't privy to. Maik was used to this kind of feeling watching Jejeune work, and he didn't like it any more now than he did all those other times. But whatever Laraby was up to, his clear intention to antagonize Moncrieff was threatening to derail the interview. Maik didn't particularly fancy coming back here again to stand in the cold at the foot of a staircase being stared at by a pair of black dogs, just to go over all the things they had failed to ask this time around.

"You knew about the plan to use the land between yours and Amelia Welbourne's as a test strip for the project?" he asked.

"Whole thing seemed like a monumental waste of good shooting land, as far as I'm concerned. I've often told Amelia we should combine forces, buy that land off Oakes and link our two properties." He looked out over the distant forest tract, as if imagining the prospect. "Be a formidable force, a Moncrieff/Welbourne partnership."

Whatever its merits, Maik noted that Amelia Welbourne would receive second billing.

"But that was never likely to happen once that Amendal chap starting banging on about reforesting it. She's an admirable woman, Amelia, determined, intelligent, but she does rather tend to get the old worship mat out when she finds somebody who might help save her damned trees."

Something caught the attention of the dogs and they stirred, padding restlessly and twisting around on the step. Moncrieff looked out over the fields. He shifted his position slightly on the step and the gesture settled the dogs immediately. It was an impressive piece of silent command.

"When did you learn your money had gone? That the investment had not been made?" asked Laraby.

"When everybody else did, two days ago."

"So after you'd handed over the cash, you never requested to see any of the investment documents."

"Clearly not," said Moncrieff irritably. "All I was after was a quick turnaround. Throw a few bob at this thing, and as soon as it starts to shoot up a bit, get out. I tend not to concern myself with the *whys* and *wherefores* of my investments. That's what I pay my bloody accountant for."

"Who in this case was Erin Dawes." There might have been more subtle ways to point out Moncrieff's naiveté, but Laraby didn't seem particularly keen to spare the man's feelings.

"Where were you when Ms. Dawes was killed, Mr. Moncrieff? That would be Saturday night."

"Where I usually am, in my study, with a good book, halfway through a bottle of The Macallan," he said in a tone that suggested he understood the need for the question, even if he didn't particularly care for it.

"Alone? No witnesses, then? Only a car like yours was captured on CCTV in the village, quite near the victim's house."

"Like mine?" Moncrieff's already low voice dropped a further intimidating level. "I presume you can't see the number plates in this CCTV footage of yours, or you'd know it wasn't mine. Not altogether effective, is it, this surveillance nonsense you lot rely so much on these days?" Moncrieff raised his eyebrows in a way that even Maik found irritating.

Given Laraby's performance so far, the sergeant expected his DI to be bristling. But Laraby apparently wasn't rising to the bait. "Funny you should mention that," he said pleasantly. "It appears those plates were covered in mud. Illegible. That's an offence, you know. If I find out who was driving that car, I can nick him."

"Or her."

"Or him." Laraby returned Moncrieff's stare, unblinking.

"What's this all about, Inspector?" asked the other man in a mocking tone. "Not bullying at school. You don't strike me as the type who'd put up with that. A scholarship, I would guess.

To a place your parents couldn't quite afford. Always the one in the shabby blazer, were you? Always the one looked down upon, thought of as being not quite up to the mark? I've seen it all before, you see. Same thing with Erin Dawes. This resentment, this railing on about class and privilege and inequality. Only it's always about something else, really, isn't it? Well, I can tell you this. If it's designed to make me feel guilty, it isn't going to work. My family's been on this land for centuries, and I'm not going anywhere."

"So if we need to speak to you again, we'll know exactly where to find you, won't we?" said Laraby brightly.

He began to make his way to the car, and Maik followed. Both men paused as Moncrieff called after them. "I'd advise you to call ahead before you come out here again."

Laraby turned. "Really? Why's that, then?"

"I do a spot of shooting at this time of the year. I wouldn't want anyone to get hurt."

"Anyone else, you mean."

"Yes, Inspector, anyone else. Good day to you."

And having dismissed the men as abruptly as a left-wing agenda, Moncrieff marched up the steps to his house, dogs at heel, and went inside.

18

"I didn't know anybody still used those things."

The comment startled Lindy from her reading, but when she looked up, DCS Shepherd was smiling, so Lindy would be able to discern her own fondness for books. Shepherd looked around. "You've found a cosy little spot for yourself, I must say."

Lindy had chosen a wooden table tucked into a corner of the tiny Saltmarsh Library. Through the window behind her, a cloud-laden sky hovered over the library's tiny garden, shrunken into dormancy by the cold weather. But the interior of the stone building was being warmed by a hearty brazier set in the middle of the room, flickering orange light along the racks of books that stretched away in all directions.

"It's one of the things I enjoy most about village life, just running into people like this," said Shepherd.

Lindy couldn't ever remember running into Domenic's boss before, but Saltmarsh was the kind of place where you did see most people eventually, in one capacity or another.

"The internet was down at home, so I came to use the wifi here," said Lindy. "But one thing I still refuse to do is read poetry on a screen. It deserves better."

"Reading poetry in front of a fire on a Thursday morning."

Shepherd shook her head. "There aren't many things that would make me rethink my career choice, but …"

The comment took Lindy by surprise. She did not have Shepherd down as a poetry lover. Little insights like this, into those you thought you knew, were one of the constant joys Lindy found in her encounters with people. Perhaps Domenic's uncanny ability to see beneath a person's surface meant there were fewer surprises like this for him, and therefore less to enjoy in being around other people.

"I don't blame you indulging yourself in a little guilty pleasure like this. I imagine you must be enjoying having a bit of breathing space, not having those men under your feet. So who have you chosen?" Shepherd turned her head to look at the spine of the book Lindy was holding. "Poe?" she asked with amazement.

"*The Raven*."

Shepherd pulled a face. "I might have known."

"It's your bloke's fault," said Lindy lightly. "Eric's decided we should do a feature tracing the connection between Dickens, Poe, and Gaugin."

Shepherd was interested enough to take a seat opposite Lindy at the small table. "Is there one?"

"Apparently." Lindy touched the assortment of books splayed out on the desk. "Dickens took a pet raven to the U.S. and showed it to Poe when they met. Poe scholars are pretty much agreed that the bird was the inspiration for the poem. A few years later, *The Raven* was one of the poems read aloud at Gaugin's farewell dinner when he left for Tahiti. And what bird appears in Gaugin's painting *Nevermore*?"

"Ravens." Shepherd shook her head slightly. "Hard to see the attraction, personally. To me, it's like the spectre of death flying overhead whenever they pass."

"Dom loves them," said Lindy. "He voted for it to be Canada's national bird."

Shepherd raised her eyebrows. "They vote on such things over there?"

"It's called democracy," said Lindy, "a little thing they learned from us, apparently."

"Did it win?"

Lindy shook her head. "It was something called a Gray Jay. At least they didn't choose the Canada Goose. I think Dom would've renounced his citizenship."

Lindy found her thoughts drifting back to their previous conversation at the Malvern Tea Rooms. She eyed Shepherd carefully across the book-strewn table. "I wonder if he knows just how much he's dominated our conversation since he's been away."

"I imagine he'd be delighted. It's a sign we're missing him." Shepherd let her comment linger for a moment. "Marvin Laraby. You said you knew the name. Anything I should know about between him and Domenic?"

"Nothing that isn't already in the files," said Lindy cautiously. "A personality clash, Dom called it. I could see it. Laraby wouldn't be the first senior officer who's found working with Dom a bit intimidating. It's not that he's trying to be clever all the time. He just bloody well *is*!"

Lindy seemed to remember who she was talking to and stopped suddenly. But Shepherd merely offered a soft half-smile. "You're right, I suspect we both have the same issue, me professionally and you personally. We both found Mr. Right, we just didn't know his first name —"

"… was going to be 'Always.'" Lindy chimed in, the two women finishing the saying together.

Lindy sighed. "I just wonder sometimes if he appreciates how frustrating it is to be around somebody who seems to know so much about so much."

"I'm not sure Domenic even knows what frustration is. He's about as sanguine as any person I've ever known."

Lindy smiled. "I think in terms of frustration, Dom is what the medical profession would call a carrier."

Shepherd rewarded the comment with a generous smile of her own. "We've still not heard anything from him at the station, by the way, which we take to mean whatever he's up to over there in Colombia, things are going well." Shepherd rose to her feet. "Well, I suppose I'd better leave you to your reading. After all, any discussion Eric has about birds while he's at work is one less we have to have when he comes home." She gave Lindy a wan grin. "I'm hoping this rush of enthusiasm will burn itself out sooner or later or at least settle into something a bit less obsessive."

"It's possible," said Lindy in the same tone she might have used if Shepherd had suggested the little thing called democracy might one day result in a Green Party government. "The birding getting a bit much, is it?"

Shepherd tilted her head to one side slightly. It was a coquettish gesture that should have looked ludicrous on her, but somehow didn't. "I wouldn't say that, exactly."

"But inexactly?"

"I just feel guilty sometimes, that I'm not more involved. I mean, I just don't know if I should go with him on his trips."

"That depends, I suppose," said Lindy, "on whether there is anything about sitting around for hours in a drafty hide, bored out of your mind, that you'd find unappealing."

Shepherd smiled. She liked Lindy, even if she suspected that Jejeune's girlfriend was behind most of his obstinate moments. Domenic Jejeune was for the most part a passive individual. Opposition to Shepherd's new initiatives, when they came, often had the tang of another person's arguments, and on more than one occasion she had felt the words she was hearing from Jejeune were more or less verbatim as his girlfriend had suggested he should deliver them.

She turned to leave. "I really must get on," she said. "Say hello to Domenic for me, the next time you talk to him."

Lindy spent a long time staring after Shepherd, even when the DCS had disappeared from view. Perhaps it was already there, even then, in the back of her mind, but it wasn't until she'd packed everything up and left the library that she was able to grasp it fully. She walked toward her car and stopped dead in her tracks. She felt the flush of anger rising within her, and barely made it into the driver's seat before the dam of pent up emotions burst forth.

"Cretin," she seethed, pounding on the steering wheel in her frustration, until the horn gave a tiny blast. She sat for a moment letting the waves of anger wash over her before getting out of the car again, not trusting herself to drive in this condition. She marched back and forth in the car park, hardly noticing the frigid air. She wandered over to the back of the parking area and leaned on a low railing that looked out over a small pond. A thin rime of white frost had claimed its edges, but there was still a little open water in the middle. Good for the birds, she thought absently. Dom would be pleased. Dom. She bunched her fists and pressed them to her skull in frustration. *Oh, Lindy, Lindy, how could you have been so stupid? How could you have not been watching, waiting for Shepherd to ask, so that when she did, you wouldn't just walk right into it and serve it up to her on a plate?*

Those *men* under your feet. *Men.* And Lindy had just let it go like some halfwit who had never heard of the difference between the singular and plural forms of Jejeunes. Because that was what Shepherd was talking about — Domenic and his brother. Lindy had confirmed Damian's presence in Saltmarsh for Shepherd, and allowed her to segue straight over to Domenic's trip to Colombia without even a whimper of protest. So Colleen Shepherd had just stopped in, had she? Just as she was driving past perhaps?

Only she hadn't seen Lindy's car in the library car park. It would have to have been this one, the loaner she had cadged from the repair shop this morning, while hers was in getting a winter tune-up. One more piece of evidence, if Lindy wasn't already long past needing it, that the encounter with Shepherd hadn't just been a happy accident.

She pushed herself back from the railing and began walking again. She had the feeling that someone was watching her antics, probably from one of the library windows overlooking the car park, but she was too angry to care. *You had to know Shepherd would be prowling*, she told herself as she tried to walk off her frustration. *You had to know she would want to confirm, finally, that Damian had been here, in north Norfolk; that he and Domenic had spent time together.* The inference now was clear. Domenic was in touch with his brother. And that meant he had been lying to Shepherd, deceiving her all along. Lindy had to phone Dom. He needed to know. Perhaps it wasn't too late, if he got on the phone to Shepherd and made a clean breast of everything. True, Domenic had gone to Colombia to try to unravel the truth about his brother's situation, but there was no crime in that. The only link between the two brothers was that list, the endemic hummingbirds of Colombia, and who could tell what significance that would hold, if any?

Perhaps she should approach Shepherd herself, call her, chase after her now, even, and tell her Domenic didn't know where his brother was, that it was she, Lindy, who had been in touch with him. Because the truth, the razor-thin, borderline truth was, of course, that Domenic *was* innocent in all this. He didn't know where his brother was. Even if Shepherd didn't believe her, it might introduce that element of doubt, one that could make the difference. She was aware she would be admitting her own guilt to all sorts of crimes, probably some she wasn't even aware of. But she would be willing to do it, if it would help, if it would keep Domenic free from Shepherd's incorrect assumptions.

Her face and ears were beginning to tingle with the cold. She realized she was standing still and she hurried back to the car now, turning on the engine to get some heat around her. She didn't know what to do, what the answers were. And that meant calling Domenic, *Mr. Always Right*. Dom would be able to tell her what needed to be done. Evening, his time, he had said. The best chance of reaching him, when the day's hikes were over and he was back at the lodge. It would mean waiting a few hours. But Lindy had plenty to occupy her mind until then.

19

Dawn was just breaking over Las Tangaras Reserve when Jejeune poured his cup of coffee from the urn on the tailgate of the Jeep. From the surrounding vegetation came the first tentative bird calls — doves, thrushes, wrens — as if they were trying out the morning air for its suitability to carry their messages. Above the trees, the sky was still lightening, but even this early, the air held a humidity that seemed to hang over the forest like a blanket. The T-shirt Jejeune had rinsed out and left on the balcony last night was just as damp when he picked it up this morning, possibly even slightly more so.

He was tired, and he knew the rest of the group was, too. They had risen early this morning to drive up here to the entrance to the tanager habitat, but they had not had much sleep. The party had arrived at the lodge in darkness last night, weary after the drive from Paujil. As they were rocking through the dusty Colombian countryside, Armando had come back along the bus to where Jejeune was sitting alone, Traz preferring the free seat next to Thea. The guide had come to discuss his outburst the previous evening, but it was an explanation, more than an apology. "I am responsible for your safety," he said in conclusion. "It is important that my people follow my instructions. Always."

Jejeune was pretty sure Traz would bristle at the thought of being one of Armando's "people." But the guide's tone was soft and reasonable, and Jejeune rewarded it with an understanding smile.

"Of the other business," said Armando, dropping his voice, "on the trail. Nobody thinks your brother is a bad man, Inspector. I did not wish to imply this." Armando nodded to acknowledge a truth. "Sure, there was resentment he was given such a high-paying assignment. Some said your brother was not skilled enough for this task; it should have been a guide from our country who took this rich foreigner to find the last five endemic hummingbirds, somebody who knew the birds better, knew our culture better. But what your brother did, staying with the man until the emergency services could reach him, this earned everyone's respect. The Karijona were already sick. Your brother must have known he would be arrested by the authorities for what he had done, but he would not leave that man alone."

Jejeune had continued looking out at the passing scenery as Armando spoke, but the guide placed his hand on Jejeune's arm now, and the detective looked at him. "It tells me your brother is a good person, Inspector, a good person to whom a bad thing happened. Nothing more."

The rest of the group was milling around the Jeeps, picking at the array of sandwiches and fruit splayed out on the tailgates, but Jejeune was off to the side slightly, staring up into the canopy. He sensed someone at his elbow. "This is what it's all about," said Traz, "being here to watch the rainforest come alive like this." Despite the early hour and the bone-jarring ride they had just concluded, Traz was as immaculately turned out as ever; his hair neatly combed and his clothes clean and pressed. He was holding a wrapped breakfast *arepa* in one hand.

Almost as they watched, the last of the darkness seemed to lift like a veil from the treetops, and gentle sunshine began to settle over the clearing. The bird calls increased, in both number and volume, and soon the air was alive with a hundred different songs.

A small bird dropped into view, bouncing on a philodendron leaf. "Blue-grey Tanager," said Traz, setting his bins on the bird with one hand, holding the *arepa* down by his side with the other. Jejeune smiled. He had almost forgotten that, in addition to his almost legendary neatness, Traz was also the best one-handed birder he had ever known.

Other birds began to emerge from the forest cover to start feeding. Many fell into the category Traz called neck-breakers, working the branches and leaves high up in the canopy overhead. Others, though, proved more accommodating, coming in to the palm fronds and low shrubs around the clearing, popping out occasionally for eye-bursting views. Everywhere there were excited calls as someone in the group got on a spectacular tanager. *Glistening-green, Beryl-spangled, Purplish-mantled.* The identification parade was led by Armando, but Traz proved almost as adept, particularly with the higher birds, pointing out a steady procession of species as they flitted through the canopy. Jejeune spent the better part of an hour spinning from sighting to sighting, for once, it seemed, missing nothing.

"What an amazing … flock," said Traz, during a rare lull. "It's not *flock*, though, surely. A group of tanagers?"

Jejeune shrugged. "A palette?"

Traz gave an easy smile and pointed to a Bay-headed Tanager that had dropped into the lower branches to feed. "Hard to argue when you look at that. A palette of tanagers," he said thoughtfully. "Yeah, I could live with that."

Armando approached. "Good, yes?" He wore a broad smile. Everyone in the group had managed excellent views of the birds, and he was happy. "You are ready to go on to the upper hummingbird feeders? It's a long walk, but we can bird on the way."

Traz and Jejeune took the long, gradual ascent at an easy pace, chatting along the way. Jejeune began to sweat slightly as the heat and humidity built, but his friend seemed unaffected. He had acquired the easy, rolling gait of people who lived in hot climates, and he seemed at home in the conditions.

All along the trail, Traz spotted birds and pointed them out before Jejeune had even detected their presence. Once, their skills had been comparable. It had even been Jejeune and his brother who introduced Traz to birding. Now here he was, his birding skills far ahead of the detective's. Jejeune mentioned it; his tone suggesting his comment about his envy was not entirely a joke.

"Come on, JJ," said Traz easily, "you found an Azure-winged Magpie in the U.K. A first record, no less. That's going to take some beating."

"I didn't find it," said Jejeune quickly. "I was just with others who did."

"That's not what the record says. Yours was the name they put on it. And you know why? Because they needed the sighting validated by someone people would trust. Who better than a detective who was being seen on TV most nights?" Traz shook his head. "In any meaningful sense, that sighting's yours, JJ. Cop yourself some credit."

They climbed the steps to the elevated seating area by the hummingbird feeders, but even before they took their seats, Jejeune was pointing. "Is that what I think it is?"

Traz snapped up his bins as a hummingbird zipped into view, its body three inches of glittering emerald, its tail a further four of deep, luxuriant purple.

"Violet-tailed Sylph," confirmed Traz. "What a stunning bird."

Armando and the rest of the group had already arrived, and the guide was standing by one of the feeders now. He beckoned

Thea forward from her seat. "Come, stand like this and spread your hands over the base of the feeder." He stood behind her and pressed in closely, wrapping his arms around her from behind, to demonstrate how she should hold her hands.

"What kind of showboat guiding is this?" murmured Traz to his friend. "This clown ought to be in Vegas."

"Thea seems to be enjoying it," said Jejeune mischievously. "I'm sure he's just trying to give her the best birding experience he can."

"Yeah. Right. You gotta stop seeing the best in people, JJ. You're a cop, for God's sake, I'd have thought you'd have figured this out already. I'm telling you, I don't trust this guy. And neither should you."

As Armando backed away from Thea, a Velvet-purple Coronet hovered for a moment before settling delicately on her hand and drinking from the feeder.

"Oh," Thea drew in a small breath. "It's like having a feather on your hand, except I can feel its tiny nails." She watched the hummingbird fly off and then looked at Armando, her eyes glistening with delight. "That was amazing. Thank you so much," she said gratefully. Traz got up suddenly. "I'm going to look for a Gold-ringed Tanager. You know, one of the target species for this area that Circus Boy hasn't managed to find for us yet. You coming?"

Jejeune looked across to where a man was sitting alone. "Maybe later," said Jejeune. He stood up and walked over to sit next to Carl Walden.

"Wonderful," said Walden. "Just sitting in one spot, letting the birds come to us, for a change. So much of what we do on these trips comes down to 'bird-seeing,' it's nice to have the time to do a bit of actual watching. I take it you're enjoying the day so far?"

"Are you asking as a fellow birder?" said Jejeune pleasantly, "or as a shareholder in Mas Aves?"

Walden didn't take his eyes off the birds as they flew in and out, but he did allow himself a sheepish grin. "Okay, I admit I am here to babysit you. Nobody knew if you spoke Spanish, so we thought, if you had any questions ..." He turned to Jejeune now. "I didn't tell you at our first meeting because I didn't want it to seem like the company had drafted me in to keep tabs on you. Plus, I didn't want to make Thea a part of it. She asked to come along, but she didn't know about any of this."

Jejeune nodded, watching the tiny birds as they sliced the air with their rapier-like passes. "So how does a psychologist from Tucson become an investor in a Colombian bird tour company?" A light seemed to go on behind his eyes. "Mariel."

Walden nodded. "As she began to come to terms with her condition, we talked a lot about how she might use her new abilities. She'd always loved watching birds, and now she could see them like no one else. No sighting was too brief, no flight too fast. Colombia was just beginning to open up for birding, and guiding seemed like the perfect job for her. I invested in Mas Aves the day she joined them."

A Booted Racket-tail zoomed in to perch on a feeder near the men, a tiny reminder of the incredible beauty and diversity the natural world could produce. "Birding sounds like a perfect match for her skills," said Jejeune.

Walden nodded. "And for a while, it was. Word got around. No one can guarantee a sighting on a bird tour, but Mariel was the next best thing. Hummers especially, if you wanted one, the endemics, the rarities, Mariel was who you went to. She even looked the part. She wore a glittering headband and jewelled earrings and a sequined top with red flowers. The birds would fly right up to her. It was amazing."

"So why did she stop?"

Walden leaned forward, the light dancing off his gold-rimmed glasses. "Neither Mariel nor I ever thought of her abilities as a gift, Inspector. The constant bombardment of her senses was overwhelming. The birds, the butterflies, even the movement of the leaves in the wind: she would get terrible headaches, migraines that would last for days. Perhaps, for people with Mariel's condition, there is such a thing as too much beauty."

An Empress Brilliant perched in the shade of a nearby tree and the older man gave Jejeune the time to enjoy the humming-bird. Not until it had flown off did he speak again.

"I've actually been looking to divest myself of my holdings in Mas Aves for a while. Not because Mariel is no longer a part of it. The company is on solid ground now, well established. It's time to turn ownership over to Colombians."

"Your daughter is a Colombian national, isn't she?"

"Thea isn't interested in being a part of the company. Nor is her mother. Besides, sometimes it's best to make a clean break with the past. Don't you agree?"

Jejeune was quiet. It might have been in agreement with Walden, but as the older man had already discovered, with Inspector Jejeune, you could never quite tell.

20

Marvin Laraby displayed admirable dexterity in carrying four drinks back from the bar. It helped that one of them was a bottle of mineral water. It attracted a considerable amount of attention as he distributed the other three drinks around the table; a pint of Greene King for Maik, a vodka tonic for Salter, and a glass of Chardonnay for DCS Shepherd.

Laraby made a show of looking around the interior of The Boatman's Arms as he took his seat. He nodded appreciatively at the nautical brasses hanging on the white stucco walls and the broad black oak beams that criss-crossed the ceiling. "Even got a good fire going for us. A proper country pub on a cold winter's night. I don't know about you, but I can think of worse places to be just now."

He twisted off the top of his bottle and took a sip from the mineral water. "What?" he asked the faces gazing at him. "I can't see any reason why you can't have a nice night down the pub without drinking alcohol."

"I'm sorry, you've lost me," said Salter, enjoying their little inside joke.

"Should be some dark tale of woe attached, shouldn't there? A battle with the demon drink?" Laraby gave them a grin. "Truth is, I just don't like the taste of beer. Never have."

"Nor the hard stuff?" asked Salter.

"I think if you have to work that hard to swallow something, you probably shouldn't bother. And wine," he nodded to Shepherd's glass, "just overpriced fruit juice, really, isn't it? No, water is about all I drink, other than the odd cup of tea." He waved his bottle by the neck. "And the only reason I order this bottled stuff is because I got fed up of people asking me if I felt sick every time I asked for a glass of water."

There was a relaxed atmosphere round the table, of the kind Maik hadn't experienced in quite a while. The safe in Dawes's cottage had yielded nothing of value beyond paperwork for the options purchases, which proved to be forgeries. Though none of the other investors had shown much interest in the administrative side of their investment, Dawes had undoubtedly had the certificates made up in case they ever asked to see them. The discovery of the documents brought them no closer to a motive for Dawes's murder, and a resolution to the case did not yet have that comforting feeling of inevitability about it, but no one round the table doubted they were making progress. Their breakthrough, Laraby insisted, would come about through policing by procedure, simple but effective. In a results-based business like theirs, nobody was going to mind how they got there, just so long as they did, in the end.

Laraby took a long drink of his water and winced as a middle-aged woman in leather trousers launched into an off-key rendering of *I Will Survive* on the karaoke stage.

Salter turned to him. "You think this is bad, you should count yourself lucky Tony's not up there. We once heard him do 'The Lion Sleeps Tonight,' didn't we? All four parts of the harmony himself at the same time. I was laughing so hard, I thought I was going to throw up."

"Tony? That would be this Constable Holland, the one off on compassionate leave?"

"Yeah, you'd like him, wouldn't he, Sarge? Bit of a wild streak, but he's got a good heart. The death of his girlfriend has really shaken him up, as you might expect. But in the old days he used to love a night down the pub like this."

"The old days? You haven't done pub nights recently, then?"

"We come out with DCI Jejeune now and again," said Salter, "but I always get the impression he'd rather be off somewhere else."

She bit her lip at the indiscretion and flashed a look at Shepherd, who was sipping her wine impassively. Maik, as usual, watched from the sidelines. Laraby seemed to have a rare ability to draw little truths like this out of people. It was a handy skill for a police detective, but Maik would have preferred it if Laraby had restricted his talents to eking out secrets from the criminal classes.

"Did he come out much when he was at the Met?" asked Shepherd with what sounded like studied casualness.

"Once or twice, but as the constable says, I don't think his heart was ever really in it. The IT lads used to call him the mathematical zero; took up a place but didn't add any value. I thought that was a bit harsh, but there was an element of truth to it, I suppose."

"Must be quite a change of pace for you out here," said Maik, who counted talking about absent superiors among his least favourite pastimes.

"It is, Danny, and that's a fact. But you know what I like most about being up here. It's a chance to do a bit of proper policing. Down The Smoke it's all about the next case, solve this one as fast as you can, then move on. There are about one million crimes a year in London on average, and well over thirty thousand police officers to deal with them. But here, you have a chance to connect with a case, remember why you're doing your job, why you joined the police force in the first place. I'd forgotten what that part of being a copper was like, to be honest."

"Any more thoughts on our suspects?" asked Shepherd. Like Maik, she had noticed the relaxed atmosphere that had long been absent from the unit. But she was aware, too, that under the proper circumstances, a lot of good police work could be done within the confines of a nice warm pub.

"I'm pretty good at this," said Laraby without a hint of irony. "I've been doing it a long time." He tapped the nozzle of his water bottle against his pursed lips and then wagged it at them. "And I'm telling you now, Robin Oakes is our 'doer' on this one, ladies and gentlemen. I don't know why yet, or how, but it's him all right."

"So do we need to bother getting any actual evidence, then, or do you think the CPS will settle for your word?" Salter kept it playful, giving it a bit extra, with wide-eyed wonder and over-done awe.

Laraby turned to Maik and smiled. "I like this one, Danny. More nerve than Indiana Jones, our constable." He turned to Salter. "You show that kind of brass at that sergeant's exam and you'll be a shoo-in."

Maik and Shepherd exchanged a glance, and Salter looked abashed. Shepherd not hearing about this before was fair enough; the higher ranks were often the last to know about the career aspirations of the junior classes. But Danny? Until now, the role as Salter's confidant had been almost exclusively his. Before Holland's most recent girlfriend, his interests had mostly been fixed on finding the next ride for his bedroom carousel; a role Salter had already notified him in no uncertain terms that she wouldn't be filling. Jejeune was, simply put, off in a world of his own most of the time. So almost by default, Danny Maik had become used to hearing Salter's news first. But perhaps Laraby had just been closest at hand this time.

"I said I was thinking about it, that's all." It was the second time Laraby had caused Salter to blush like this, but for some reason, she didn't seem to mind as much as before.

"To answer your question, Constable," said Laraby, "we shall indeed gather our evidence. I'm just saying, when it's all said and done, it will turn out to be Robin Oakes. You mark my words."

"Are you ever wrong?" asked Salter, having recovered her composure. There was no hostility in her inquiry, but the sarcasm had gone.

Laraby nodded. "Now and again. But not this time."

On the stage, the act had concluded to a response it would be generous to call applause. A corpulent man with a crew-cut and thick glasses stood up and announced he'd be doing a song by "some Canadian bloke called Pat Travers. It's called 'Boom, Boom (Out Go the Lights).' That's the bit you all shout out when I get to the chorus, after I sing *When I get her in my sights*? Got it?"

Maik looked like he could hardly wait.

Laraby drained the last of his mineral water and crushed the plastic bottle between his hands. "Well, I'd better be getting back to the House of the Dead Fowl. I'm telling you, once I leave that B&B, the only place I'll ever want to see dead birds again is in a KFC."

"You can't eat that rubbish," said Salter. "You ought to come over to dinner with Max and me on Saturday. Have a decent meal."

For the second time in a few moments, DCS Shepherd and Sergeant Maik exchanged significant glances. Even Salter herself looked like she was wondering where exactly the invitation had come from. But Laraby was not about to allow the moment to pass.

"To a bloke living in the land of Chinese takeaways and late-night baltis, you have no idea how good an invitation like that sounds."

"It's a deal, then," said Salter, looking slightly trapped. "You can come too, Danny, if you like. And you, ma'am, unless you have something else to do."

They both did, and agreed with regrets that it would have to be another time for them.

The karaoke act had reached the chorus, with the man inviting the audience to let him know what would happen when he got his baby in his sights: *Boom, boom, out go the lights.*

The officers declined his invitation. They stood up and left the table, pausing in the pub's small hallway to don their heavy coats. They had walked the short distance to The Boatman's Arms, but Laraby would need a ride to his B&B. Salter's statement that it was on her way suggested she wouldn't be going home by any of the routes Danny knew, but he made no comment. Behind them, the singer was giving it everything now, as the song reached fever pitch. *If I get her in my sights …*

The explosion rocked the front of the building, the shockwave tearing the pub door open and allowing the bitter night air to pour in. Among the shouts and cries from inside, Maik was able to make out the most important thing; no one had been hurt. There had been no flying debris, no glasses broken. The four police officers had been the closest to the door, and they, too, were okay, protected from the blast by the solid, centuries-old stone walls of The Boatman's Arms. Everyone seemed to realize the fact at the same time, and their next reaction was also in unison. They rushed out into the cold winter air and began sprinting along the high street in the direction of the orange ball of flame burning brightly against the dark night sky.

21

Lindy had been standing at the sink in the office kitchen, eating cold rice pudding straight from the can. She smiled, thinking about the last time Dom caught her eating like this. He had marched her away, arms on shoulders and unceremoniously dumped her in a chair at the kitchen table to wait while he prepared her a proper meal. The salad had been limp and drenched in dressing, and there were black flakes in the reheated ravioli, where he had let the sauce burn. But he had made his point. No matter how busy she claimed to be, he didn't want her eating like a convict on the run. She swilled off her spoon and rinsed out the can before dropping it in the recycling bin beneath the sink. Convenience was another argument for eating like this, as well as avoiding the washing up.

She looked out at the darkened offices beyond the kitchen, the tiny desk lamp and the glow from her laptop the only lights. She didn't mind being here on her own late at night. It could be a very productive time, even if it wasn't exactly her choice. But the internet connection to the cottage was supposed to be up and running by tomorrow, so she could finally work from the comfort of her own home again.

She hadn't phoned Dom. She had spent the evening see-sawing her way through her emotions; one minute reassuring herself that no real damage had been done, the next convinced she was the author of a catastrophe from which Dom's career would likely never recover. In the end, a late-night walk along the cliffside path near their cottage had resolved her conflict. Domenic, not to put too fine a point on it, was pretty bloody brilliant at what he did. And that, in the end, would be the one factor that would outweigh everything else. Shepherd, she was sure, wouldn't want to lose the best detective she and the Saltmarsh Constabulary had ever had, ever would have. Whatever other emotions Shepherd might be feeling at the moment, that underlying truth wouldn't go away. After all, Shepherd must have already known, by any reasonable definition of the word, that Damian had been here in north Norfolk. All Lindy had really done was to confirm it for her. The DCS, too, could have little doubt as to the real reason for Jejeune's trip to Colombia. She was, as Lindy had pointed out to Domenic, a very astute person. But when he returned, he could finally tell her everything. Any lingering feelings of resentment Shepherd might be harbouring would surely take second place to the idea that Dom was back now, ready to be Domenic again, perhaps even more so, more locked in and focused, with the distraction of his brother's dilemma finally behind him.

So she hadn't called Domenic. She had walked back to the cottage and settled into the living room with her chilled hands wrapped around a mug of hot tea. She would let him get to the bottom of whatever it was he went over there to sort out, and see as many toucans and hummingbirds and whatever else he could while he was doing it. And if she was still occasionally sideswiped by a wave of guilt so strong it almost made her nauseous, well that was just her penance, for her stupidity and for letting her guard down.

Lindy was leaning in the doorway of the kitchen, idly contemplating the wall beside her desk, as she considered these thoughts. So she saw it happen. The orange-red flash snaking up the outside of the window, the slow-motion swelling of the plaster before it splintered into a thousand pieces and sent shattered fragments of brick hurtling in all directions, including hers. And then, only then, the deafening sound, the terrible rip-roaring blast, and the shockwave that knocked her off her feet and sent her flying back into the kitchen.

Nobody was giving out medals, so it didn't matter that Salter arrived first. But by the time the others reached the site of the explosion, she had already identified the building.

"It's the magazine offices," she told Laraby as he approached. From the high street, the building's facade looked untouched. But along the side, where the building ran down a narrow lane, the wall was blackened and scorched. A gaping hole, about the size of a double doorway, had been torn through the brickwork, and it was possible to see into the offices, where a thick cloud of pale dust hung suspended, as if in shock itself. Everywhere, small fires were gathering strength, fed by the icy air. Flames crackled, igniting the exposed wall studs and devouring the window frames.

Through the flames, Laraby could see the confetti of papers still spiralling around inside the offices. "It's all dark in there," he said. "It looks empty, thank God. Gas leak, you think?"

Shepherd shook her head. "I don't smell anything. But whatever it is, we can't rule out the possibility of a second explosion." She turned to Salter. "There may even be the danger of structural collapse. Let's get this entire area cordoned off. I want everybody back a safe distance." She looked around. "Where's Maik?"

He approached them at a run. "One car in the car park round the back," he said. "I don't recognize it but …"

But why park there when, during the winter in Saltmarsh, you could park right outside any place you wanted to.

"Oh my God," said Shepherd. "There could be somebody inside."

Maik was halfway to the gap in the wall already.

Danny heard the distant howl of a fire engine as it rushed to the scene.

From the opening in the wall behind him, Shepherd called out to him. "The first hint of problems, Sergeant, I want you out of there! These flames are getting worse. The fire crew is almost here. We can let them handle it."

Even with the piercing beam of his police light, the dust and the darkness made it virtually impossible for Maik to see where he was going. He stumbled over some rubble on the floor and pitched to one side. In the darkness, his hand found a desktop and he steadied himself. Patches of plaster dripped from the exposed roof beams, and from all around him came the sounds of heaving and creaking, as if the injured building was rocking back on itself to take stock of its new state. Maik was almost at the far side of the room, where a darker space indicated another doorway, when his foot nudged something that moved. There was a low groan and Maik crouched down, still unable to see what it was but knowing anyway. "I'm a police officer," he said gently. "There has been an explosion. Are you able to move?"

He heard a mumbled response, but he felt a hand reach out and grab his forearm.

"Was there anyone else in here with you?"

The voice was low and frail. But certain. "Just me."

A call came from outside. Maik heard the soft rush of air build like a gasp, and the sudden hiss as a new bank of flames ignited, this time inside the office. He spun around to see the fire taking hold, sucking in the air from outside to build in intensity, licking the inside walls, searching out the exposed wooden beams above.

"The fire crew is here, Sergeant Maik. Come out and let them get in there. Now."

"One survivor, ma'am," he called back over the roar of the flames. "Injuries unknown. Better get a stretcher. I'm going to try to get us both to the front door."

And then he heard it. The one thing that went to the root of all his fears, ever since he had realized which building this was. The voice was still weak, still feeble. But the word was clear.

"Danny?"

22

Jejeune sat on the steps of the lodge, watching evening creep into the valley. The thermals had drawn up ragged patches of cloud into peaks, and the dying sun set them ablaze, turning the horizon into a cityscape of orange and red. As the last of the light faded, Jejeune watched a Yellow-headed Caracara quarter the valley in a series of slow, graceful glides, each pass a marvel of ballet-like precision as its wingtips rippled on the updrafts. The beauty of the scene still found a place in Jejeune's heart, as troubled as it was.

Traz came to sit on the steps beside him. From somewhere below, the comforting sound of the fast-flowing river jangled through the still evening air. Jejeune indicated some scars near the summit of a high range of hills on the far side of the valley, where the trees had been clear-cut. "Think those are old marijuana plots?"

Traz shook his head. "They were always small, less than one hectare. Otherwise they could be spotted from the air and bombed. No, Armando was telling the Spanish group that those are where they're taking out invasive trees, Mexican Pines. They want to replant the area with native species." Traz shook his head gravely. "It is a good plan, but I'm not sure they'll be able to pull it off. We tried something similar in St. Lucia. Felling trees is one thing, but setting up the infrastructure to support a large-scale planting operation in a remote area like that will be very difficult."

"Armando said they were paying Damian three hundred US a day, Traz, to lead that tour."

"He's a good guide, JJ. He's spent a lot of time in this part of the world. He knows what he's doing. Okay, granted it's a lot of money, a hell of a lot of money, if we're being honest, but if they were in a bind ..."

"They told him they thought he couldn't do it, couldn't find Graumann those five endemic hummers."

"You're kidding, right?" asked Traz. "He couldn't learn the habitats, songs, and behaviour of five target species? Hell, even our guide *Don Juan de Colibries* could probably manage that."

Jejeune shook his head. "Not entirely the point, though, is it?"

No. It wasn't. Traz had been friends with the brothers for a long time and he recognized the truth. For the right amount of money, Damian would do a lot of things. Ignoring some arbitrary park licensing system would definitely be among them. But the bigger issue was with somebody questioning his skills. It would have ensured Damian would accept the assignment, whatever the odds, whatever the hardships and risks. Because that combination, money and misgivings, was about as guaranteed to motivate Domenic Jejeune's brother to take on a challenge as anything Traz could think of.

He looked across at his friend, staring now into the twilight nothingness that hung over the valley. Domenic had accepted it, he realized. He had finally come to terms with the idea that it was Damian's fault. His brother was responsible for the crime that took the lives of four innocent Karijona natives. Guilty. As charged. And convicted in absentia — in the court of popular opinion, if not yet by the Colombian authorities.

"So what happens now?"

Jejeune sighed, grateful for the years of friendship that allowed him to confide in a way he may not have with anyone else. "I'm just tired, Traz. I'm tired of fighting the truth, looking to find holes in a story that doesn't have any. I've spent months peeling back the edges of this thing, peering into every corner to see if I can find anything that gets Damian off the hook. There's nothing to find."

"Then just enjoy the birding. Today was a fabulous day. Tomorrow will be better, or as good, or maybe not quite. Or maybe it will be a complete washout. What the hell does it matter? You're here, JJ, you might as well enjoy the rest of the trip."

Jejeune nodded absently until a thought came to him. "Did you ever see that Gold-ringed Tanager you went to find?"

Traz gave his head a short shake. "Maybe heard it a couple of times. It's not going on my trip list though. Looks like Armando will have to record a dip on that one for this tour. Not going to do much for his rep, missing one of the major target species, is it? You coming for supper?"

"Maybe later. You go on ahead."

Out over the valley, night had completed its descent, and an insidious inky darkness had settled around the camp. Constellations filled the black velvet dome above, like the skeletons of long-dead sky dinosaurs. Jejeune sat in silence, thinking, until the soft burr of the phone in his pocket startled him back to the present. He reached for it without checking the caller ID. He assumed it would be Lindy, so the man's voice surprised him for a second, until he recognized the familiar gruff tone.

"Sergeant Maik? Everything all right?"

There was a pause from the other end of the line, a heartbeat of silence that gave Jejeune his answer. "What is it, Sergeant?"

"It's Lindy, sir, Miss Hey. She asked me to call you." Maik had thought about the phrasing a long time before he dialled.

Let him know first she was okay, she was coherent, she was making decisions.

"Why would she do that?" Jejeune found that he had stood up, though he couldn't remember doing so. His hand was gripping the phone tightly. "Is she okay?"

"She's in hospital, sir. It's just for observation. I went with her in the ambulance myself, and she was talking to me the entire way. She was conscious and alert, but they just want to watch her overnight, and as soon as they're satisfied everything's okay, they'll release her."

No timeline, no guarantees, noted Jejeune. But this was still vintage Danny Maik, giving Jejeune the outcome, the part he would want to know about, first. The details could wait.

"What happened?"

"An explosion at the magazine's offices. Lindy was inside at the time."

"But she's okay? Not hurt?" Jejeune was pacing like a caged animal. His chest felt tight, as if he couldn't draw enough breath into it.

"She's put me on my oath to tell you she's not injured, and that she's ... all right." *Fine* wasn't a word Maik used, but it would have been the way Lindy delivered it to him, Jejeune knew. "I only got the okay from her to make this call on the understanding that I made sure you knew that, sir."

Jejeune looked around numbly. The surrounding darkness pressed in like prison walls. "Tell her I'm coming home, would you, Sergeant? I can't get a flight until the morning. Our time. I can be there by ..." His mind fogged, unable to compute the time difference between where he was now and where he so desperately wanted to be, needed to be. He ran a hand through his hair in exasperation, confused, unsure, directionless.

"Lindy said not, sir." Maik paused, as if deciding whether he really wanted to deliver his next line. "She said to tell you she was *ordering* you not to come back." *And now I have*, his tone seemed to say, *so it's up to you two to work out the rules of engagement from here on in.*

Jejeune managed a half-laugh, a frail gasp of relief. "That sounds like her. Please tell her I'll think about it. I'll call her tomorrow, as soon as I can." The pause was almost undetectable, but Maik was ready for it. He was expecting what came next. "The explosion, do we know what caused it?"

"It could be a gas leak. We've found no signs of anything suspicious."

But Maik was on shakier ground with the incident details. Or rather, Jejeune was sharper, less numbed by shock now and picking things up. If it could be a gas leak, it could be something else. And how long would it take before you had investigated the scene of an explosion thoroughly enough to definitively declare there was nothing suspicious about it? Certainly longer than they had been looking.

"I'd appreciate it if you could keep me informed," said Jejeune, trying to make it sound like professional curiosity, but falling some way short.

"Will do, sir."

Was there still a slight hesitation in Maik's voice? "Anything else, Sergeant?"

The pause lasted one more beat. Now there was no doubt. "Do you know Robin Oakes, sir, the bird photographer out this way?"

"No, I don't think so."

"You've never met him, or had any dealings with him?"

"Not that I know of. Is he saying I have?"

"No. But when Inspector Laraby and I interviewed him as a person of interest in the Erin Dawes case, he made a point of asking about you. Twice."

Jejeune took a leaf out of Maik's book and paused himself, just for a moment.

"Inspector Laraby noticed, I take it?"

"It wasn't the sort of inquiry you could have missed," said Maik flatly. "Anyway, it was just something I wanted to clear up."

Maik sounded as if he regretted bringing it up, especially when he knew the DCI had so much more on his mind at the moment. Not to worry, though. He had no doubt Jejeune wouldn't be dwelling on it after they hung up. Thoughts of his girlfriend lying in a hospital bed thousands of miles away would see to that.

23

Danny Maik was quiet on the drive out to Oakham. Everyone had signed off on the explosion as an accident, an unhappy coming together of a box of abandoned chemicals and an errant cigarette butt. But Danny wouldn't mind giving it a bit more thought. He might have to let it go for now, though. He had other things to contend with, like this single figure walking across Robin Oakes's land, carrying what looked like a gun bag. Marvin Laraby, sitting in the passenger seat next to Danny, had noticed it, too, and signalled the sergeant to pull over, just in case it hadn't already occurred to him. Maik slowed the Mini to a stop and grabbed a pair of binoculars from under the driver's seat.

Through a screen of bare trees Maik could see the figure striding purposefully across the barren fields, silhouetted against the white sky. Maik tracked Robin Oakes as he approached the haphazard jigsaw puzzle of ruins that had once been his family's home. Oakes stopped and looked around before sloughing the bag off his shoulder and crouching beside it.

"Looks like he's out to do a bit of photography," he told Laraby, still watching as Oakes withdrew a large tripod from the bag and began assembling it.

"As good a place as any to have our chat," said Laraby. "At least those walls might provide a bit of a break from these winds. Come on, Sergeant, a nice bracing walk in the north Norfolk air. Do us both the world of good." He opened the door and started off across the frost-rimed fields, leaving Maik to trudge along dutifully in his footsteps.

As they approached the ruins across the open field, the detectives were able to better appreciate the former magnificence of the old manor house. In addition to the maze of low walls, one of two larger remnants of the old building still survived. A couple of buttressed corners stood steadfastly against the keening winds, while nearer to Oakes, fragments of a chimney soared above the remains of a once-imposing fireplace.

Laraby and Maik carefully picked their way over the rubble gathered around the base of the walls. Oakes looked up from his camera as he heard their footsteps.

"DCI Jejeune is not back from his trip yet? I presumed he would have taken over this investigation by now," he said.

"See that, Sergeant?" asked Laraby over his shoulder. "Detective Chief Inspector Jejeune's star power carries some weight even among other celebrities. You've got quite the fan yourself, I understand — an American billionaire, no less. Likes your stuff, does he, this bloke?"

Oakes inclined his head. "He has an eye."

Even with two, Maik couldn't see how Oakes could possibly make enough from his photography to manage the upkeep of this estate. But then, these so-called musicians of today were hardly what Danny would call talented, and they were making amounts that would have made the old Motown stars' eyes water. If you could sell a picture of an owl for five hundred quid these days, who knew what you could get for some commissioned work from a billionaire.

"There's a picture on my wall at The Birder's Roost B and B," said Laraby. "A bunch of Dotterels. Would that be one of yours? Only there's a fairly hefty price tag on the bottom of it."

"I believe they do have some of my work there. Although I think you'll find it's not a bunch of Dotterels. It's a trip."

"A trip of Dotterels?" Laraby looked first at Oakes and then at Maik as if suspecting he was part of some elaborate joke. Maik looked as if he wished for all the world he could say he was. But he knew better.

"You've got a significant following among the local environmental groups, I understand," said the inspector. "Your pictures of birds seem to have caught their attention particularly."

Oakes shrugged easily. "One tries."

"Who's this *Juan*?" asked Laraby, so deadpan you couldn't really be sure whether he'd misunderstood or not. But neither man chose to pursue it. "It got me to wondering," continued Laraby, "this interest you seem to have in Detective Chief Inspector Jejeune. Is he a mate of yours? I imagine you photographers are pretty tight with the birders. They find 'em and you photograph 'em. Is that how it goes?"

"I don't believe the inspector and I have ever met," said Oakes evenly, "though I am aware of his interest in birds. He found an Azure-winged Magpie some years ago. That sort of thing gets noticed in birding communities."

Laraby looked around, past the ruined walls to the flat, featureless land beyond. "I have to say, I can't see much here worth taking pictures of. A few old walls, a few empty fields. What is it about this spot that that makes it worth coming out here on a cold day like this to snap a few photos, I wonder?"

Oakes shook his head in what might have been pity. "Really, Inspector? The play of light on these weathered surfaces is lost on you, the lichens tracing their way across the bleached stone? Even the pockets of shadow in the crevices, or the remains of the walls themselves, set against the backdrop of this stark, barren landscape. None of this seems worthy of capturing? I have to say, I find this place very evocative. The bleakness, the sense of loss. It's a fitting metaphor for winter in this part of the world."

Oakes raised his camera to his eye and tested a couple of settings. "Is there something else you wanted to ask me?"

"As a matter of fact there is. When we spoke to you last, you seemed to believe the Picaflor deal was still on," said Laraby carefully. "But it must have been obvious nothing was happening on your land."

"I'm rarely at this property these days. I spend a fair amount of time in the United States. And besides, I had no idea what sort of timeline we were dealing with. For all I knew, there were months of preparations to go through before Amendal began his trials. I simply expected to come home one day and find a squadron of drones flying across my land."

Maik turned up his collar and eased back slightly into the meagre shelter of the wall they were standing beside. But despite the raw winds reddening his cheeks and making his eyes water slightly, DI Laraby seemed to be enjoying himself.

"You said before you had no reason to kill Erin Dawes. But it seems you've lost out on a fairly lucrative options holding with the investment not going through."

Oakes lowered the camera and looked at Laraby directly, giving him the full benefit of his handsome, playboy features. "Beyond some vague possibility that Picaflor stocks might rise in value at some point, I lost precisely nothing by the deal not going through, Inspector. I'd have thought both Gerald Moncrieff and Amelia Welbourne had stronger motives. Assuming, of course, you've already eliminated Dr. Amendal himself from your inquiries."

Maik couldn't help himself. "Amendal? What's he got to do with this?"

"He was furious at Erin's continuing delays. He claimed every day the deal did not go through was one day further his trials fell behind."

"When you say furious," asked Maik, "did you ever hear him threaten Ms. Dawes?"

"Not in person, but the tone of those phone messages he left…. Would you call them threats? I don't know, but from what I understand they were hardly friendly inquiries."

"We've checked her phone messages," said Laraby curtly. "There was nothing from Dr. Amendal."

"Not on her home phone. He called the IV League number. It's a separate line we set up." He looked at the men quizzically. "You don't know about this?"

He gave them the number and Maik dialed it. A female voice recording identified the line as the IV League's number and made the standard request for the caller's details.

"I'm afraid I don't know the code for retrieving messages," said Oakes, in answer to Maik's expectant look. "I imagine that might be something the phone company could help you with?"

"Or you could tell us what the messages said yourself?" Laraby accompanied the words with a smile. But it wasn't a friendly one.

"I never heard them, I'm afraid. But I do know Erin was upset by them. She said Amendal was growing increasingly hostile. Borderline harassment, she called it, and somewhat abusive. I did think of calling him about it myself to give him a piece of my mind. I mean, Erin and I didn't always see eye to eye, but bullying a person like that, it's just not on, is it?"

"You didn't call," confirmed Maik.

"Erin said she would take care of matters and everything would be resolved."

Laraby looked like a man whose day wasn't turning out quite as he had planned. "On the night Erin Dawes was murdered, as you remember things, you were up at the gatehouse. Alone."

"I was."

"Looking at photographs, you said."

"Correct."

"Of what?"

"Of birds, actually. Barn Owls. As I told you, they roost here, in the chimney remains, mostly." He began to dismantle his tripod and pack up his photography equipment. "Not getting the contrasts I need at the moment," he explained. "Perhaps I'll give it a try later. I hear there's a storm coming. I might get some nice atmospheric cloud cover."

Maik watched the careful way Oakes put away his equipment, a series of precise actions performed almost mechanically. It was the work of a man with a love of order, a methodical mind, a planner. Laraby seemed to be watching him, too. "This photography you do," he said, as Oakes snugged a lens into his bag. "I don't suppose you ever took any pictures of Erin Dawes? In dodgy poses, for example?"

Oakes looked up at him from his crouched position. "Not my thing, Inspector. I might be able to put you in touch with somebody who deals in that area, though, if you'd like a few more prints for your collection."

Laraby rewarded the comment with the thinnest of smiles. Maik had wondered at the time if perhaps Laraby had missed the upward flickering of Oakes's eyes again when he'd claimed to be in the gatehouse looking at the bird photographs, but the DI's parting remarks suggested he'd seen them after all.

"Thank you for your time, Mr. Oakes. I'm sure we'll meet again soon. I have a feeling I'm going to come across more evidence about who killed Erin Dawes any day now, and when I do, I'm going to make sure you're one of the very first people I share it with."

24

The appearance of DCS Shepherd in the doorway at the start of the morning briefing had become a rarity during the last few weeks; part of an ongoing effort, at least as far as Maik could tell, to stay as far away from Inspector Jejeune as possible. That she had showed up for the second consecutive briefing under Laraby's tenure told Maik a lot.

"Now, as you all know, I like to stay out of the way as much as I can." Maik's eyes grew wide at the comment. Perspective was a strange thing, but he doubted anyone would be willing to offer a different one. Besides, even if Shepherd's declaration was ostensibly directed to the group at large, there was really only one person in the room she needed to reassure. Her next statement seemed to acknowledge as much. "For the record, I'm happy with progress on this case. I just want to make sure you're aware you'll have support at the senior levels, regardless of where this goes."

To the upper reaches of Saltmarsh society, she meant. If an outsider like Laraby wanted to go around questioning the rural aristocracy of north Norfolk, it was going to be okay with her. Laraby spread his arms expansively. "I'm sure my team appreciate the vote of confidence, Superintendent. We are looking to bring this case to a speedy conclusion, for everybody's sake, but we'll do our best to ruffle as few feathers as possible." He gave the DCS an accommodating smile and Shepherd offered one of her own to acknowledge the comment.

She looked across to Maik. "Have you heard if Lindy Hey has been released from hospital?"

"She's got a couple of minor cuts and bruises, but she said she'll probably feel like going back to work by tomorrow. Wherever that is, of course. I understand the magazine's looking for temporary premises."

Shepherd nodded. "Keep me informed. I'll pop over to see how she's doing as soon as I can. Domenic's not coming back early, I understand?"

Laraby's head swivelled around at this information. "Must be some important birds he's seeing out there," he said. "I'd have been on the first plane home."

"There certainly appears to be something keeping him in Colombia." Shepherd seemed to realize she had spoken aloud and hurriedly indicated to Laraby to begin the briefing.

"Right, let's have a quick run-through, shall we? Sergeant, anything on the Connor James angle you were so keen to have a look at?"

Maik, who had farmed it off to Salter, looked at the constable expectantly and she scrolled through her tablet. "Nothing to suggest any criminal activity, but that photograph by Oakes is not the first item he's sent over to the gallery recently. There's been a steady stream of items, mostly from his flat in London: paintings, sculpture, all on consignment. They definitely all belong to James; he's providing original purchase receipts for everything, and the items all have solid provenance, so, as I say, nothing illegal seems to be going on."

Maik pointed in the direction of the information. "He's selling up. That's what the boat reminds me of, a place that's been staged for sale. See if *The Big Deal* is on the market, Constable."

"Selling a few items is not suspicious activity, Sergeant," said Laraby reasonably. "Not even a boat. Nor is failing to report it to the police. It might explain why that boat's still in the water so late in the season, though. If he can flog it quickly, the buyer might still be able to sail it away."

Salter's fingers hovered over the keypad. But Danny didn't rescind his request. If Laraby noticed, he made no comment.

"What about those messages from Dr. Amendal?" Shepherd asked Laraby. "Has anyone had a chance to listen to them?"

Laraby wagged his finger between himself and Maik. "We did, this morning. A bit of aggro, but nothing in the nature of a specific threat. Amendal was miffed, rightly, that the IV League seemed to be playing games. He made it crystal clear that any delay would mean they'd have to begin tests on a site other than Oakham, and this would mean extra work for him."

As Laraby shrugged his shoulders, Maik did his best to hide a look of surprise. "A *mountain* of extra work" was how he remembered Amendal phrasing it. And *miffed* would hardly be the term he'd choose for the string of invective the young scientist had unleashed into the IV League's answering machine. There seemed to be an escalation, too, as the deadline for the investment drew closer. Amendal didn't strike Danny as the type of person who would act on his anger to the extent of murdering somebody. But then, he hadn't struck Danny as the type of person who would leave such vitriol on an answering machine in the first place.

"I'll be having a word with him about his telephone manner," said Laraby, "especially to a woman, but beyond that …"

"So you *are* going to pay him another visit?" confirmed Shepherd from the doorway.

Whether Laraby had been intending to or not, it was clear now that he would be.

"I've been promised you'll be getting those DNA results from the cup in the kitchen any time now," she said. "We got voluntary swabs from everyone to compare the result to?"

"Except for Moncrieff," said Laraby. "He refused point blank."

Salter peered at her tablet. "I don't see a consent form from Connor James here, either." She looked up inquiringly at Laraby.

"I never got around to asking him," he said cagily. "If there's no match when the results come back, I'll request a sample. My guess, though, is that it isn't going to be necessary."

"You suspect Moncrieff?" Shepherd's tone was wary. The path might be heading where she suspected, but it didn't mean she liked it.

But Laraby shook his head. "I know there's a lot of inbreeding in these upper class types, but I don't think even Gerald Moncrieff would be stupid enough to draw attention to himself like that, if he was guilty. Much easier to make up some story that he had been there before. Cover yourself that way." He looked at them all. "That sample is going to belong to Oakes. I'd put money on it, if I had any."

Their silence was its own request for elaboration. "I think Oakes and Dawes were in a relationship. My guess is she put a stop to it, perhaps because she was tired of seeing that dopey playboy grin of his, perhaps because she was planning to do a runner with the IV League cash. Either way, he goes round there to talk her back into his bed. They have a nice cup of tea, but she refuses to co-operate. Must have been a bit of a blow to his ego, I imagine, especially from a commoner like Dawes. The old red mist comes down and he kills her."

The silence persisted, but it wasn't disapproval; it was the sound of police officers considering a scenario. They were back in Jejeune country, and nobody was feeling particularly comfortable about it. Deductions based on patterns they didn't see, supporting evidence a mere afterthought. Laraby gave them a heartbeat or two and then continued. "It's the pillow. There was a heavy statue, that bird one, right to hand. A panic killing, someone who breaks in to find her sitting there, that would have been the weapon of choice. But a pillow? It's how you'd kill someone you once had feelings for, or possibly still did."

From the doorway, Shepherd drew a small breath. "We'll see," she said, "but remember, Inspector, this is about a person taking the life of another person. Classes, and titles and stations in life aren't going to be a part of it. Clear?"

"You're preaching to the choir here, ma'am," said Laraby. "You'll never find a person keener to make sure rank and privilege don't affect the outcome of a case. As far as I'm concerned, the law's the same for all of us, and anybody who breaks it needs to pay the same price."

Maik recognized it wasn't exactly the message Shepherd had been sending, and he suspected Laraby knew it, too. But the DI simply clapped his hands together to get the group's attention one last time. "Right, we've got a few new angles to explore, a few more gaps to fill in, so let's get to it. Good work again, everybody. Well done all round."

The meeting broke up with the usual low murmurings and gathering up of materials. The drab, über-functional decor of the Incident Room made it a place few people wanted to linger any longer than absolutely necessary, and within a few minutes only Shepherd and Maik remained. Shepherd left her gaze on the DI for a long moment as he disappeared down the corridor. When she turned around, Maik was staring at her from across the room.

"I know, Sergeant. I know. But a lot of people aren't too keen on the aristocracy. I can't say I have much time for them myself, truth be told."

Maik didn't answer, but Shepherd had not expected he would. She knew Maik was no more comfortable than she was when somebody brought any kind of pre-held convictions to an investigation — social, political, or otherwise. It was too easy to slip into the trap of seeing all the evidence through the prism of your own prejudices, of making things fit, selecting the convenient interpretation. If you tried hard enough, you could usually find evidence to support your points, but that didn't mean they were necessarily right. That's why police forces generally liked to let the evidence tell them who the guilty party was. It was a bit more dependable than relying on personal preferences.

She crossed the room and sat in one of the chairs opposite Maik, folding one leg across her other knee so a nylon-clad shin faced directly at him. This was a different DCS to the one he had seen around here recently. Her ongoing troubles with DCI Jejeune had seemed to be taking a toll on her. She had become more withdrawn, less self-assured. It had winnowed its way into her physical presence, too. Colleen Shepherd was a person who took pride in her appearance, and a crisp, well-dressed look had been the norm for a long time. But to Maik's eye, the standards had been allowed to slip a little recently. Now the polish was back, the hair and makeup immaculate, the neat, professional business suit with the silk blouse undone that one extra button. Whatever had caused this resurgence, the DCS Shepherd of old had returned. And that was good news for everyone, even if it almost certainly meant an uptick in the number of supportive visits to the Incident Room briefings.

A young constable who'd been subbing in for the desk sergeant during the recent staff shortages appeared in the doorway behind Shepherd.

"You need me?" she asked, half rising in anticipation.

"I was looking for DI Laraby. He asked to be informed as soon as we received anything back on the DNA off that cup found at Erin Dawes's cottage."

"He's just left."

The constable hesitated slightly, his eyes flicking uncertainly from Shepherd to Maik and back again.

"I think you can assume the information will be safe with us," said Maik patiently. "Is the person in the system?"

"Not in the criminal database, but amongst the voluntary donors. The DNA is from Robin Oakes."

Shepherd raised a manicured eyebrow in Maik's direction. "As I remember," she said with more than a hint of irony, "he even said he'd put money on it."

"If he had any," said Maik.

25

A breeze drifted through the vegetation, stirring the palm fronds and setting the leaves of the wild coffee plants aflutter. Jejeune and Traz were sitting on the banks of a stream, directly across from a small waterfall that traced its way over the rock face in a series of silvery trails. Only the sounds of the forest came to them: the wind in the treetops, the soft coo of White-tipped Doves, the steady, rhythmic ticking of cicadas. In the deep woods around them, shards of light filtered through the canopy and fell in tiny bright patches among the vegetation, but here in the open, the waters danced in the vibrant tropical light pouring down from the blue sky overhead.

Jejeune flicked a pebble into the water in front of him, watching the circles spread until they were swallowed up by the gentle churning beneath the waterfall. He flicked in another small stone, the tiny splash like a wound in the skin of the calm water, instantly healed. *If only*, he thought.

"Green-fronted Lancebill." Traz pointed as the colourful bird danced in and out of the sparkling waters like a tiny fragment of wind-blown ribbon. He raised his bins and tracked its erratic flight until it disappeared from view. It was a good bird, a prize any hummingbird seeker would covet, and Traz allowed himself a contented smile. Jejeune appeared to have barely noticed it.

"I should be there with her," he said, as if continuing an earlier conversation, although he had not spoken since the two friends sat down.

"I'm fine, Dom," Lindy had told him, "really. It was just an old oil drum with a bunch of chemicals somebody had fly-tipped in the alley. Some kid probably chucked a ciggie away and that was all it took. The last thing I remember is seeing these towers of flame, like cathedral spires, outside the window, and then bam, I'm on the kitchen floor with a plaster dust facial, and Eric has a new side entrance to the office. And then Danny Maik is calling me *ma'am* and lifting me up as if I were a rag doll. And that's about it."

Except that wasn't "about it." There was a thready quality to Lindy's voice when she spoke about the incident that made Domenic wince. And there had been something else, too, throbbing behind their breezy, let's-pretend-everything-is-normal conversation. Lindy had a secret, something she had wanted to tell him but in the end had decided not to. But before he could press her, or find some other way to approach it, she had pleaded tiredness and stayed on the line only long enough to secure a promise from him that he wouldn't cut short his trip.

"I believe you asked her if she wanted you to come home, did you not?" said Traz. "And her reply was…?"

"That she'd be so angry with me if I did, she wouldn't even come to the airport to pick me up."

"There you are then. Lindy's a lot tougher than you give her credit for, JJ." Traz thought for a moment. "It's good, though, how much you care about each other. It must be nice to have something like that. Who knows, perhaps I could still have something similar with Thea, if you stop turning me into Traz the Ripper." He smiled. "Listen. You want to let Lindy know you're thinking about her, why don't you FedEx her a gift?"

Jejeune gave it some thought. "She loves magic realism. I could send her a Gabriel Garcia Marquez novel from here, his homeland."

"Yeah. Because nothing tells a woman she's in your thoughts quite like a book titled *Love in the Time of Cholera*." Traz shook his head sagely. "Take it from me, my friend, you send her a Marquez book, you'd better make it *One Hundred Years of Solitude*, cause that's likely what you'll be looking at when you get home."

"What do you suggest, then?"

"Simple. What's the one combination no woman can resist?"

Jejeune shrugged. "I don't know. Chocolate shoes?"

Traz pointed at Jejeune and nodded. "Okay, the other one. Baskets and candles, man. I'm telling you. Think about it. How many of each does Lindy have around the house right now?"

"To the nearest hundred?"

Traz slapped his thigh. "There you go, then. You get her a nice handcrafted Colombian basket, stick a few candles in it, and she'll feel better in no time. Trust me on this, my friend. I'm telling you, when it comes to gifts for women, I'm never wrong."

"I'll think about it," Jejeune told him.

For a few minutes the men sat in silence, shoulder to shoulder, the quiet hiss of the rainforest ringing in their ears.

"I saw it, Traz," said Jejeune quietly, "in the sky that evening. The fire Lindy was trapped in. Cathedrals of flames, that's how she described them. That's what I saw."

Traz shook his head slowly. "Every day our brains are bombarded with a constant stream of images, ideas, sounds. We never dwell on most of them, but occasionally someone says something, or does something, or shows you something, and that tiny fragment snags on some past memory, and you think, *Hey, I'm supernatural*. There's nothing going on here in the rainforest, JJ. No magical realism, no mysterious, mystical happenings. Lindy tells you she saw flames. You saw a flame-coloured sunset. You put one and one together and got three. Lancebill's back," he said suddenly.

This time Jejeune was moved to track the bird through his bins as it made its quicksilver forays beneath the tumbling waters, its aquamarine tail coverts flashing in the sunlight. He watched the bird until it tired of its water games and sped off into the forest once again, leaving nothing but a memory.

"You know what I'm wondering? Who got Graumann the rest?"

Traz drew his eyes away from the waterfall and looked at his friend.

"There are fourteen endemic hummingbird species in Colombia. Damian's job was to find Graumann five — the last five endemic hummingbirds. That's what Armando said. So any guesses who got him the other nine?"

"You can't know that for sure, Dom. Besides, what sense does that make? If Mariel had already led him to nine, why quit there. Think about some of the birds she'd already found for him. The Santa Marta Sabrewing, a hummingbird that even some of the local guides think is a myth. And the Blue-bearded Helmetcrest. It's a three-day horseback ride up a mountain, camping out overnight in single-digit temperatures, to reach the *Espeletia* fields where that bird lives. Does that sound to you like somebody who's going to bail halfway through the job?"

"No. It doesn't." Jejeune paused as if weighing his next words carefully. "And that's why I need to talk to Damian. I need to find out what happened before he arrived on the scene."

Somewhere deep in the forest, the plaintive, falling whistle of a Black-throated Trogon reminded them there were other lives going on, other hearts beating in this world.

Traz shook his head slowly. "You can't, JJ."

"I know it'll compromise what you and Lindy have been trying to do. I understand that. You've been trying to protect me, and I appreciate it. But it's gone beyond that now. This is important. I have to speak to him."

Traz looked at his friend, fixing him with his gaze. "You don't get it, do you? He won't talk to you, JJ. You think this whole ridiculous charade is Lindy's idea? These are Damian's rules. If anyone tells you how to contact him, he goes dark and that's the last we'll ever hear from him. He knows you're here in Colombia looking into it all. He can't help that. But he won't allow you to put your career at risk by contacting him. Not again."

Domenic didn't argue. He knew what Traz was telling him was the truth. Even if Domenic could convince him to give up Damian's contact details, his brother would never allow him to get close enough to risk being arrested for aiding and abetting a fugitive.

"What's this all about anyway, JJ? Five birds, fourteen, what's the difference?"

"Have you got that book with you, your copy of the second edition?" Jejeune asked.

Traz fished it out of his pocket and handed it over wordlessly. He sat in silence, watching the waterfall, but the lancebill did not return. Momentary chances. Blink and you missed them. The story of birding; the story of life. Domenic riffled from page to page through one section of the guide: Hummingbirds. He closed the book decisively; a man who'd just confirmed something he already knew.

"People were already saying Damian wasn't up to this task. You've known him a long time, Traz. How would he react to something like that?"

"He'd set out to prove them wrong. Damian would want to jam it right in their face as quickly as he could."

"Four of the birds Graumann was after are within a day's drive of the Bogota area, in pretty accessible areas. So why go for the Chiribiquete Emerald first? You have a chance to get four of the five birds on the list within a couple of days of taking over. It was a situation tailor-made for Damian to prove his doubters wrong. Instead, he heads straight for the hardest target, the one with the greatest chance of failure, the most difficult access."

Across the valley beyond the clearing, vast tracts of forest covered the land in every direction, dappled green and shimmering in the afternoon heat. From here, the forest looked pristine, untouched, unexplored. How many hundreds of birds were out there? How many thousands?

"I can't help you talk to Damian," Traz said finally. "But that doesn't mean I can't help you."

26

A low sun struggled over the horizon, bringing with it a flat Nordic light from the east. The fields on either side of the road looked parched, as if the cold had sucked all the colour from the vegetation and left only dry bones behind. The grasses moved in the wind like the white flames of some ghostly prairie fire. The sunshine hadn't made any noticeable difference to the temperature, but it made the crisp coldness of the air more invigorating, somehow; a welcome respite from the overcast greyness that had enveloped the coastal lands for the past few days.

The sunshine, though, hadn't made it inside Maik's Mini. It had been clear from Laraby's grudging greeting as he got in that he thought today's trip was a waste of time. Amendal had left some nasty messages for a woman who had later been murdered. It needed clearing up. But Maik knew the DI's suspicions were setting like concrete around Robin Oakes now, and anything that took him away from the task of proving the man's guilt was going to be seen as nothing more than an irritating distraction.

Maik turned up the music against the silence from the passenger seat. A thought struck him. "It wasn't this group you were trying to remember, was it? Smokey Robinson and The Miracles? They had a long string of hits."

Laraby turned from the window to reject the suggestion with a thoughtful expression. "No. This other group was pretty big, though. There was about half a dozen of them, I remember that."

Maik fell silent again. *Six?* It was a big number for a Motown group. He should have been able to pinpoint it easily. He felt frustrated at not being able to come up with the answer, but he gave up racking his brain as the large white dome hove into view.

Once inside, Maik was struck by the absence of noise. There were a number of drones aloft, a couple flying in formation, others at various altitudes, all seemingly very much on a prescribed flight pattern. But the only sound was a faint hum, one that built slightly and then receded as an individual drone flew past. He thought back, and realized now he had never heard the approach of the other drone, the one that had almost struck him, until it was right next to his head. The thought made him look around cautiously, but all the airborne machines were safely manoeuvring over the grid-wired interior.

"I can give you about ten," said Amendal looking at his phone as he approached them along the perimeter track. "We've got some important routes to program today."

"I find it helps if we don't set a time limit on these things," said Laraby pleasantly. He had been indulgent with Amendal before, willing to make allowances for his youthful zeal. But he wasn't about to let him take any liberties.

"We have some questions for you about a series of phone messages you left for Erin Dawes in the days leading up to the investment deadline."

Amendal didn't say anything. He merely swept a lock of his unruly dark hair back from his forehead. Whether this look of calm unconcern was the man's normal way of reacting to unwelcome news, Maik didn't know. But he suspected they were about to find out.

"It wouldn't be too great a stretch to interpret your messages as threats, Dr. Amendal. Threats to a person who is now dead."

"I wouldn't call them threats," said Amendal, his eyes flashing behind his large lenses. "I told her to stop faffing about and transfer the money they had agreed to invest, that's all. And to get me that agreement for the land."

"You said every day's delay set your project back that much further?"

"With the trees bare and the vegetation dying back, winter is the perfect time for an aerial survey like ours. But it's a big undertaking and we needed to have the terrain survey complete and the 3-D models all generated before we could plan our spring planting program. So yes, every day was vital."

"Mind if I have a look at your phone, sir?" Laraby held out his hand. "I'll try not to delete any sensitive data."

Amendal handed over the phone. "I wouldn't worry about that. There are three layers of encrypted security on it. It would take an army of hackers weeks to get in. Look," he said, turning to Maik, "it was a couple of irate calls. Okay, I may have been a bit over the top, but there was a lot at stake. I have a chance to make a real difference here, but that opportunity is not going to last forever. I don't want to wake up one day and find I'm nearly thirty and no longer relevant. Besides, I was in the middle of a run of very long nights. Sleep deprivation doesn't do much for your decision-making skills."

"What's its effect on your impulse control?" asked Laraby without looking up from the phone.

"Oh, come on, behave yourself," said Amendal, flapping a hand in frustration. "You can't think I had anything to do with this. It was weeks ago that I made those calls."

Laraby handed the phone back and pulled a face. "That's a lot of security for a phone, sir. Anybody would think you've got something to hide on there. Besides records of phone calls to Ms. Dawes, I mean."

"Oh, there's plenty to hide. Intel-raids are the next great crime wave, Inspector. You are aware, I suppose, that the take from cyber-crimes already nets more revenue than the global drug trade. Picaflor is going to be a vastly profitable enterprise when it hits the market. People would be willing to pay a lot of money for the algorithms on that phone."

"In your call to Ms. Dawes," said Maik, "you kept asking her if she was *serious*, whether she was *really interested*."

Laraby looked up sharply. Sergeant Maik had been studying somebody's techniques, apparently, listening to the messages behind the words, the hidden cadences. The DI's expression suggested he wasn't any more enamoured of this approach now than he had been on the previous occasions he'd come across it.

"That was the whole problem," said Amendal, hunching forward intensely, chopping the air in front of him with both hands simultaneously. "I just got the impression that the IV League were stalling, all of a sudden."

"Why was this particular piece of land so important?" asked Laraby.

Amendal drew in a breath and composed himself. "How long have you got? The land between Sylvan Ridge and Moncrieff's Wood checked just about every box on my criteria for a test site. To knit together existing fragments of forest by replanting the gaps, we need genetically appropriate seed stocks. To preserve the integrity of the ecosystem we are trying to recreate, the seed has to come from plants already on or near the site. The oldest trees will almost certainly have the greatest genetic diversity; ancient woods, say ones mentioned in the Domesday Book, like these, are about as good as it gets."

Amendal paused and looked at the detectives quizzically. Maik half-expected him to ask if he was going too fast, but for once even he could keep up. Laraby also looked like he was having no trouble with anything the young man had covered so far. Perhaps the DI, too, had spent enough time standing here like this, as scientists explained concepts to a certain other detective they both knew.

"In addition to all that, the Welbourne family has allowed a number of studies of Sylvan Ridge going back decades. We have data on the soil matrix, water supplies, fungi, and microbial life up there. And if that wasn't enough, the Oakham Manor tract has exactly the kind of topographical challenges we needed to test out our equipment, and, of course, this wonderful four-seasons-a-day Norfolk climate. As I say, all in all, just about the perfect package."

"A lot to lose, then," said Laraby thoughtfully. "It sounds like the land was more important than the money the IV League was going to invest."

"Finding investors was no problem. I didn't need to hire that idiot James for that. There were people lining up to get in on this project. The land was the key. That's why I particularly needed him to get the IV League investment. And in that, of course, he failed. Spectacularly."

Laraby and Maik looked at each other. Based on the way he dealt with Dawes's failure to meet his expectations, Amendal didn't strike either of them as the kind of person who would keep that sort of disappointment to himself.

"But you've managed to press on?" Laraby's inquiry had the air of a man simply trying to clear up a puzzling detail.

"We had to divide our data gathering into a series of separate experiments." Amandal waved a slender hand at the vast indoor soil beds behind him. "Then some poor sod had to come up with a set of algorithms to stitch all this disparate data together, while compensating for variances in each category's data-gathering parameters."

"It sounds like a lot of work."

"Ya think?" said Amendal sarcastically. "Two weeks of twenty-hour days, Inspector. But eventually, I got it done. Other than a couple of weeks' worth of caffeine pills, we're not out anything at all," he paused, "if that's where you're going with all this."

"But you didn't know at the time you were leaving abusive messages on Erin Dawes's answering machine that you would be able to compensate for the loss of Oakes's land."

"No, I didn't. Oxford weren't offering courses in clairvoyance when I was there. Look, losing the Oakham property could have spelled the end of this project. It should have. A lot of people thought it would be impossible to make the adjustments we needed, given the time we had. I have to admit, when I first realized we hadn't secured that land, I was one of them. To set up an indoor system like this, to write the algorithms," Amendal shook his head, "I didn't think it could be done."

There was something about the open, unchecked way Amendal was barrelling into motives that Maik found disconcerting. For a bright man, the scientist didn't seem to appreciate that admitting to additional reasons for wanting to take vengeance on Erin Dawes wasn't much of a way to convince someone you hadn't taken it.

27

L indy stared out at the olive-green water, moving like a restless animal in the confines of the harbour walls. In some ways, it seemed like only moments since she had been here with Colleen Shepherd and her ever-so-casual inquiries about Domenic. But in others, it may as well have been a lifetime ago, so much had changed. As for the last time she had been here with Dom, Lindy couldn't even bring her mind round to the question; it seemed as if it belonged to a different life altogether, some parallel universe; remote, unattached, floating somewhere out there in the cloud-dappled sky.

There was a loud crash from the café's kitchen, and Lindy flinched, physically jolting in her seat and twisting toward the door. Angry voices brought her back to this time, this place, the arguing drowning out the echo of the metal pot hitting the tiled floor. When she reached for her tea, she found her hand shaking so much that she had to set the mug down again. She waited, pressing her hands together tightly in her lap.

She was still in the same pose when Shepherd walked to the table. She slid her hands down casually to her sides and then brought them up again, resting her elbows on the table, setting her chin on her clasped hands, just in case.

"How are you feeling?" asked Shepherd as she sat. "It will take a few days ... at least. You should think about seeing someone. I could give you some names, if you like."

Lindy looked out at the dark, uneasy water. No matter how much it churned, how much it roiled and seethed, in the end it always settled again and became calm. With time.

"Thanks. I hear you've been asking a lot of questions of the other reporters. Is it my turn now?" The question was as clear a signal as possible that Lindy wanted to move on from the subject of her mental health.

Shepherd pursed her lips. "Our investigations lead us to believe this is exactly what it appears to be; an accident caused by flammable chemicals ignited by a chance spark. However, we put a bit more into it because it was the offices of a news magazine, home of a high-profile journo, as a matter of fact." Shepherd allowed herself a small smile. "So what about it, Lindy? You haven't written anything to upset anyone lately, have you? No editorials espousing the claims of the Canada Goose as Canada's national bird, for example?"

"If I had, I think we both know who'd be number one on your suspect list. What about you? Have you made a decision yet?"

"I'm sorry?"

"Eric's gift."

"Oh. I ended up buying him a stuffed duck online. A Lesser Scaup. Apparently, a lot of the birders out here believe it's the rarity most likely to show up next in Norfolk. Eric desperately wants to be the first to see one, so I've made his wishes come true." She shook her head. "Honestly, I think I'm becoming as mad as he is."

"He'll love it," said Lindy, genuinely. "But you do realize he'll take it to work and put it on his desk? We'll all have to stare into the thing's beady little eyes every time he calls us into his office to tell us what a crap job we're doing."

"You're welcome," said Shepherd, smiling again. But the banter was never going to last very long, as strained and as forced as it was. It was Shepherd's turn to look out the window for a moment. "I was a bit surprised he didn't come back," she said to the glass. "Everything all right out there?"

"I asked him not to. Told him, actually. He's been looking forward to this trip, and he needed a break."

"Lindy," Shepherd said softly, "Colombia, it's where his brother ran into all that trouble."

"Maybe. Yes." She found herself unable to deny it, the fight gone from her. She felt weak, hollow, as if the blast had blown away her insides and left only a shell — fragile, brittle, unable to withstand any scrutiny at all.

"If he's there to offer assistance his brother, Lindy, it's a criminal offence. I won't be able to help him."

Lindy shook her head. She felt dizzy, her thoughts blurring into a mist of uncertainty and confusion. "No, he doesn't know where his brother is. Not anymore. He went there to see it for himself, to come to terms with it all. We didn't discuss it much. He spent most of the last week studying the birds he might see. So many double-barrelled names. Shrike-vireos, chat-tyrants, nightingale-thrushes. And so many that seem to like ants. Antpittas, antwrens, antbirds. I mean, are there really that many ants in Colombia? I'm surprised they have any room for the people." She was rambling, but Shepherd was sitting still, not intervening, just listening.

"The thing is, Lindy, if he does manage to reconcile himself to it, the terrible thing that happened out there, do you think it will make any difference to how he feels about being here in north Norfolk?"

Lindy had recovered, and was distressed at having found herself so far out of control. But she stared at Shepherd now, wide-eyed, uncomprehending.

"The trouble with his brother was what brought him to the U.K. in the first place. In fact, *drove* him here might be a better way of putting it. If that issue is no longer hanging over him, I wonder if his need to be here would disappear, too. Of course, we've loved having Domenic, but nothing lasts forever in a policing career. We must all prepare for the day when somebody moves up. Or on."

"What? No, Dom loves it here. The birds, the wind, the seas … the birds. No, Colleen, DCS Shepherd, no, he'd never dream of leaving. He loves it here. The police work," she added lamely.

Shepherd looked at Lindy for a long time. "I feel so sorry for him sometimes," she said. "He's so talented, so successful, but it never seems to be enough for him, somehow." The DCS weighed her thoughts for a moment. "I suppose the truth is, success doesn't really test you. Only failures can show you where your limits lie. And he has experienced so few failures in his career. Except the one, of course. Do you think that's what this is about, Lindy? In part? Do you think trying to help his brother is an attempt at redemption for what happened to that boy? When he rescued the Home Secretary's daughter?"

Lindy had never considered this. Another great big flashing sign that she had quite simply failed to see. Where had she been for so long? On the circuit, yukking it up with her friends, that's where, while Domenic was wrestling with his twin demons all on his own. She felt embarrassed, humiliated, that someone else had to point it out to her that there might be another reason, perhaps one Dom didn't even recognize himself, that was driving him on to solve the unsolvable, to acquit his brother of a crime even he had confessed to.

Shepherd gathered her bag suddenly and stood up. "I should be going. Take care of yourself, Lindy. I mean it, you look tired. You should get some rest. And please do call me if you want those names." She changed her tone to signal another topic, a lighter one this time. "Oh, did I mention that Eric wants me to go up to Strumpshaw Fen to see the murmuration of Starlings?"

"It really is a magnificent sight," said Lindy, summoning every last vestige of energy she possessed to rally back to the world of normal. "Dom says there are upwards of eight thousand birds there some nights, though I'm not sure how he knows. I can't imagine anybody being barmy enough to count them all. Well, I suppose a birder might," she added with a weak smile that seemed to drain her of all her remaining strength.

Shepherd waved goodbye and Lindy stared after her, unblinking, until she had seen the DCS get in her car, fasten her seat belt, and drive away. Only then did she allow herself to drag her eyes away. She stared around the empty interior of the Malvern Tea Rooms. Outside, the waves continued their tortured ballet, writhing and churning, crashing and falling. Except one. In her imagination, it didn't crest, didn't break. It kept coming, a spume-flecked, brown-white wall of water that grew until it filled the entire plate glass window, smashing through it and sending glittering fragments of glass hurtling toward her.

She took a deep breath. Her heart was racing and her skin was damp with sweat.

Normal. How long before she was normal again? Did she even know what normal was anymore? Lindy looked out, taking in the stark, bleak beauty of the coastline beyond the harbour. She loved it here. Tears started to her eyes at the thought of ever leaving. She raised her hand angrily and brushed the palm against her cheek. She gathered her bag. Lindy was determined not to weep in public, but if she was going to break down, it certainly wasn't going to be in some poxy little café where they couldn't even get their apostrophes right.

28

This was wilder country than any they had been in so far. Ahead of them profusions of ferns and wild ginger spilled over the edge of the narrow, muddy path. On either side, deep tangles of bracken and palm leaves formed screens, behind which ranks of densely packed trees receded into darkness. Epiphytes dripped from the tree limbs, every pocket of light, every space, it seemed, had been exploited, taken up by some form of vegetation. And over it all, the humidity clung to the air, sapping the energy of the two men as they made their slow progress along the path.

The tour had entered a stage where the initial enthusiasm of seeing new species had worn off, and people were choosing to expend their energy carefully in the draining tropical heat. Many had chosen to spend the afternoon lazily engaged in activities around the lodge, writing journals or performing running repairs on equipment and clothing. Others lounged around flipping through guidebooks, correlating lists, checking and re-checking identification marks in the field guides. Armando had offered to lead a walk for anyone who was interested, and a few had taken him up on his offer. Others, like Jejeune and Traz, had gone on leisurely hikes of their own along the trails surrounding the lodge. But they would all be encountering the same thing, a sultry stillness settling over the forest; the torpor of an ecosystem dealing with a tropical day in Titi National Park.

"You ever wonder how we ended up where we are, JJ?" asked Traz as they trudged along the path. "You some big-time police detective half a world away, and me the one who ended up making a living from birding? I don't think either of us saw that coming."

Jejeune said nothing.

"It's a gift, isn't it, this detective thing of yours?"

Jejeune turned to search Traz's face for sarcasm, but found none.

"You wouldn't come all the way to Colombia just to reconcile yourself to what had happened. There's a reason for the things you do. You were always like that. You knew from the start that there was something not quite right about all of this."

The clumsy crashing of a pair of Greater Anis in the undergrowth had both men turning simultaneously, but as soon as they had identified the large black birds, they lowered their bins. Jejeune waited for Traz to continue. He had started along a path, but he had not reached his destination yet.

"The word was, there was some big bonus at stake, like maybe a thousand dollars per bird, if Mas Aves could get Graumann all fourteen endemic hummers. Mariel had started the tour and found him nine. But for some reason, right after they checked off the Glittering Starfrontlet in Urrao, she announced she was quitting."

The word was. Damian's phrasing. Traz had spoken to Jejeune's brother, but to ask was to invite more secrecy, more evasion. And they were past that now. All of them.

"They returned to Bogota, where Graumann was told to wait in the hotel. Two days later, Damian arrived to take over the hunt for the five endemics left on the list."

Jejeune nodded silently. The list Lindy had given him; the ones he had stared at on the coastal path in that watery-eyed mixture of wonder and bewilderment that seemed like ten life-times ago. Four birds in the Bogota area and the Chiribiquete Emerald, deep in the Amazonas region. Karijonas country, where people had died and Damian's life had come apart at the seams; and Domenic's, for a time, had fallen apart along with it.

They heard footsteps on the path behind them and turned to find Thea.

"You didn't go with Armando, then?" asked Traz, tucking away the men's conversation neatly.

Thea shook her head. "On a day like today, it's more about backlit views of the underside of some bird in the canopy that I'm never going to identify unless Armando tells me. It's okay if you're into list-building." She shrugged. "I'm not." She pointed along the path. "Besides, there are other things to see."

A large morpho butterfly came flitting into view along the path. They watched its dancing, puppet-string flight as it approached, the rainbow-blue of its wings glittering in the patches of sunlight. It settled on the edge of a muddy puddle to drink from it, driving off a smaller heliconia butterfly that had been resting there. Even amongst the gentlest things, thought Jejeune, the rules of life played out.

"That woman your father was telling us about at Casa de Colibries, the one who could identify individual hummingbirds, did you know her yourself?" Although Jejeune's question may have sounded casual, Traz realized it was anything but.

"Mariel? I met her once or twice when my father was treating her. She seemed nice, a little frail perhaps. Fractured, damaged in some way. Many of my father's patients are like this." She seemed disinclined to say more, and Jejeune was prepared to let the subject drop until Traz intervened.

"Her last name; Huaque. It's not Spanish, is it?"

"Indigenous, I think."

"Karijona?" asked Jejeune, stirring slightly.

Thea looked at him carefully. "I never asked. In Colombia, it is not always wise to inquire too deeply about a person's past. It's enough that they are prepared to be a part of the country's present, whatever they may have been in a past life." She gave them one of her smiles. "It's pretty quiet here," she said. "I'm not sure there'll be much bird activity in this heat. I'm going to head back to the lodge and take a nice cool shower. See you at dinner, maybe?"

They watched her go, her step light and energetic despite the gluey mud tugging at her boots.

"Something we said?" asked Jejeune.

"A lot of people have secrets they'd like to keep in this country, JJ. Maybe they were part of something they'd rather not admit to, back when. Asking too much about somebody's background just makes people nervous, that's all."

The men watched a trail of leaf-cutter ants threading its way across the path, their leaf-segment burdens moving like self-propelled emeralds. They tracked the line until it disappeared into the foliage on the far side of the path.

"I just don't understand why Mariel would quit, if she was so close to that bonus," said Traz.

"Perhaps she wasn't up to the trip. You heard Thea. She was frail. A trek into Chiribiquete is taxing enough for a person in good health. A hard drive from Bogota, a boat into the park, and then a three-day hike into the Serranía de Chiribiquete mountains."

"Maybe," said Traz. "Still, it's strange no one seems to know where she went afterward. I even risked a little Spanish on one of the group. Nobody ever saw or heard from her again once she quit guiding."

Traz's hesitation was so slight others might have missed it. But he and Jejeune had known each other for too long.

"What else, Traz?"

"It's nothing."

"What?"

"Mariel. In the trip notes she left for Damian when he took over, she warned him not to go to Chiribiquete. She said she foresaw deaths, many deaths. I know what I said about magic not existing here, JJ, but this woman is starting to give me the creeps. And I've never even met her."

The campfire glowed orange against the surrounding darkness, its intensity contrasting with the pale yellow lights strung across the verandah of the lodge behind them. Around the edge of the fire, the group was gathered in small knots, murmuring quietly to each other or staring silently into the flames. On the far side, near the edge of the circle of light, Armando and Carl Walden stood in earnest conversation. The firelight flickered on their faces, hollowing out eye sockets and cheekbones into skeletal masks. It was strange, thought Jejeune, that even from this distance he could tell they were speaking a different language. He couldn't have identified it as Spanish, though he knew it would be, but there was something in the cadences, perhaps even the ebb and flow of intensities, that separated it from a conversation in English.

Traz approached and sat beside Jejeune on the ground, handing him an opened bottle of beer and sipping on his own. His eyes seemed to shine in the firelight. Perhaps this was not his first Club Colombia of the night. The fire crackled slightly and gave a soft rush as a glowing fragment collapsed within its core. The flames guttered, dancing higher, sending fingers of light out over the clearing. The men stared into the fire, transported to somewhere else.

"Memories, eh?"

Jejeune nodded and raised the bottle to his lips. "I can't even remember what we used to talk about around a campfire back in those days."

"Damian, probably," Traz paused, "about whatever trouble he had got himself into, and how we were going to get him out of it. We've been doing this a long time, JJ." He gave Domenic a strange, knowing look. He seemed about to say something else, but he saw Thea approaching and fell silent. She crouched beside Jejeune. "Apparently, there's a problem with the accommodations for tonight. The room you two were supposed to take has a broken water pipe. There are two other rooms, one here, one at a farmhouse about ten minutes away. Each has only one bed."

She looked from Traz to Jejeune. In the firelight, her skin glistened with an orange glow and her pupils took on a tawny, tiger-like intensity. Traz seemed unable to take his eyes off her.

"The room here is really basic," she continued. "No fan, slatted windows. For somebody not used to these humid conditions, it could be a long night. They are wondering if it might be best for the inspector to go to the farmhouse."

She offered an uncertain smile. The daughter of an American, thought Jejeune, sent to broker a deal with the two Canadians, to deliver the *This is South America, after all* argument. From the far side of the fire, Armando and Walden watched, waiting to see how the men would react to the news that the accommodations weren't going to be as advertised; to this apology that wasn't an apology.

"You can stay here as long as you like, Inspector," said Thea. "Whenever you're ready, I'll run you over there by bike."

Jejeune's easy smile reassured her there would be no problem. She stood and returned to deliver the good news to Armando and her father, treating Traz to a smile as she left. The men on the far side of the fire seemed to relax, having picked up on Jejeune's reaction. They drifted away slightly, into the shadows, to await Thea's return and her confirmation.

"Did it look to you like Armando might have something else on his mind when he was staring over here?" asked Traz.

"Like the thought that you'd be alone in a room now, with Thea only a few doors down, you mean?"

Traz smiled, as if he hadn't considered that possibility. He stood up and began to make his way toward her. "I'll tell her you're ready to go now, shall I? We've got an early start in the morning. You need to get some rest."

Jejeune called after him. "Traz, what was it you were going to tell me, before Thea came over?"

Traz flapped a dismissive hand toward him without turning. "It'll keep," he called over his shoulder. "See you at breakfast."

29

Dinner had gone well. Better than well, in fact. Despite spending most of the day cursing herself for extending the invitation in the first place, Lauren Salter had found herself quietly anticipating Marvin Laraby's visit as the time drew near. Now the only thing to worry about was Max. Some police officers couldn't seem to tell the difference between a three-year-old and a thirteen-year-old when it came to dealing with kids. Not unless they had a few of their own. She had no idea if Laraby did. Worse still were the ones who saw it as their duty to open a young boy's eyes to the terrible realities life had in store. Salter wouldn't have considered herself an overly protective mother, but once Max had crossed the threshold of innocence, she knew there would be no bringing him back. She would take as many more nights of cuddles and stories and shared experiences as she could before she was prepared to let him go off into the world. So the second DI Laraby veered toward the seamier side of their profession, she'd be ready to call it a night.

But he hadn't. He managed to strike that perfect tone that some adults seem able to find with children, and answered Max's questions with gravitas and sincerity. If Salter paid particularly close attention, it was because she expected she might be dealing with follow-up questions from Max later, and it would be important to know the context that had raised them.

"Here's one you can impress your teacher with on Monday," Laraby said to Max as Salter distributed the dinner plates. "Did you know that when the Metropolitan Police Force was first established in London it was illegal for them to investigate a crime?"

"That's ridiculous," said Max. Salter knew he had just acquired the word and she was surprised to see he felt comfortable enough to use it with a stranger.

"The job of the police was public order, to stop fights and such. Police officers were actually forbidden by law from looking into anyone's private affairs, so you couldn't try to find out anything that might help tell if they'd been involved in a crime. Can you imagine? Your mom would be out of a job. She'd have to start working as a fashion model instead."

Salter's look toward Laraby as she sat at the table wasn't lost on Max, but he had other lines of inquiry to pursue.

"Is it hard to catch criminals?" he asked, sliding his carrots to the side of his plate with a bravado that suggested he wasn't expecting his mom to make a scene about *vegetables* in front of the company.

"Sometimes. But the thing to remember is that most criminals are not very clever." Laraby leaned forward to add a confidential note to his response. "To tell you the truth, Max, in my experience, if brains were dynamite, most criminals wouldn't have enough to blow their hats off."

Max laughed and Salter smiled dutifully, even if she wasn't so sure about the truth of Laraby's statement. Criminal cunning might not get you a nice piece of rolled-up paper from a university, but it let some people hide their crimes from the police for a very long time. Surely there was some kind of intelligence in that. She took the conversation off in other directions, to avoid it becoming an interrogation. Max's school life featured strongly, but the two adults managed to exchange a couple of points of view, too.

As Salter returned the dinner plates to the kitchen, Max's downward look took Laraby's eyes to the floor also. He bent and picked up the kitten in one hand, raising it to eye level, exactly as he had done in Erin Dawes's cottage. It had filled out a little since then, but it still fit comfortably in Laraby's large hand. He twisted the kitten slightly to bring its face around to meet his own. "A good home?" He made a show of looking around the small, neat living room. "You could do worse, pal. Got a name for him yet?" he asked Max.

"Mom calls him Laraby."

There was a sound of dishes crashing in the kitchen. It was a long time before Salter emerged again. She looked composed as she carried in the dish containing her homemade Duke of Norfolk's pudding, and offered them both a small smile as she set it down. But the smile had a brittle quality to it, as if the slightest tremor might break it into a thousand pieces. Neither her son nor her guest decided to test it.

"Hands?" asked Laraby, rising. "Cat hairs," he explained.

Salter directed him toward the bathroom and he made it as far as the doorway before turning. "Oh, I nearly forgot, I've got a spare ticket for Norwich's match next Saturday. If either of you can think of anybody who'd like it, let me know, would you? Be a shame to go and sit there all by myself. This way?" he confirmed, before disappearing around the corner. His timing was excellent, as it happened, because it seemed as if Max had something urgent he wanted to discuss with his mother in private.

Salter recognized that she was approaching, very cautiously, something important. If she'd begun the evening observing

Laraby from a cool distance, she had gradually been drawn in, little by little, as the DI exhibited various facets of his character, some surprising, some enlightening, all admirable. There was his engaging way with Max, whom he addressed in the same confiding adult tone her father used with the boy. His answer to Max's earnest question, for example.

"Do you like being a detective?"

Laraby had given the question some serious thought.

"Not always. But the thing is, Max, it matters. And that's important. The law is there to make things fair for people. Otherwise, the powerful people would just set the rules. And we couldn't have that, could we? You know what they used to call the slave classes in the early times, Max? *Live money.* The rich didn't even think of them as real people."

Having tried it out successfully once earlier in the evening, Max went to his new default response. "That's ridiculous."

"I couldn't agree more. When somebody killed somebody else back in the olden days, they paid a fine; the amount depended on how much value the other person's life was judged to be worth. Now, I ask you, is that a society you'd like to live in?"

Max looked uncertain about the word *society*, but he understood the tenor of the question well enough to give the required answer. He shook his head.

"Me neither. So, I see being a detective as being about making sure everybody gets treated the same. No exceptions. Nobody gets off just because they've got a bit more money, or a fancier house. You do something wrong, you get punished the same as anybody else. Sound fair? 'Course it does!"

There was his easy self-confidence, too. He was a bright man, a good copper, and if he didn't need to keep reminding people of the fact, he wasn't about to pretend it wasn't true either. But mostly, he was just good company. He seemed free of the angst that plagued so many of the people Salter knew these days. If

Laraby had any inner demons, he knew how to keep them hidden. When you invited Marvin Laraby to dinner, what you got was a man who came prepared to eat your food, take an interest in your points of view, and enjoy your hospitality. As the evening progressed, Lauren Salter found herself trying without success to remember when she had enjoyed an evening more.

Max had made mild protests when his mother told him it was time for bed. She hadn't heard this before, and she recognized it as one more sign, if she needed any, that her son had also enjoyed the company of their guest.

When she returned, Laraby was just finishing off the last of his mineral water. He handed the glass to her. "I should be going."

"Back to the station?"

"Me? No. I never understood this idea of poring over records until all hours," he said. "If the answers are in the paperwork, they'll still be there when you go in again the next morning. No, I'll get back and get settled in for the night, and think about what a lovely evening it's been. Good food, good conversation." He paused. "Good company." Laraby shrugged on his topcoat but held up a hand as Salter moved toward the coat rack for her own. "I wouldn't think of it. Besides, you've had a couple of glasses of wine. I'll get a minicab."

Salter dialled, waiting patiently for the pickup. Five minutes, they said. She found herself wanting it to be longer. The two of them stood in an awkward silence in the small hallway. Laraby looked at her seriously. "I'd like to do this again. Perhaps just you and me next time? We could go out for a bite to eat. Somewhere nice, if you think you can find a babysitter."

"That's what grandads are for." Salter didn't trust herself with any other response just now. "Can I ask you something … personal?"

Laraby stood more still. But he didn't ease away from her. "If you like."

"Your marriage. What happened?"

Laraby thought about it for a moment, head down slightly, the way he seemed to do with serious questions. "Is it important?"

"It could be. To me. To us."

Laraby's eyes widened slightly, but he still hadn't backed away. Not a half-step, not a sway, not even a shimmer of movement. The lights of a car lit up the living-room curtains. It was a time for avoiding distractions, so neither of them bothered to announce the minicab's arrival.

"I'll tell you what happened. Domenic Jejeune happened."

Laraby was outside before Salter could even draw breath again. By the time her mind had stopped reeling, the rear lights of the minicab had long since disappeared into the cold, dark night.

30

"Harpy Eagle. A report of a nest on the other side of the reserve. Quickly, Inspector. We need to get there before first light. The others have already gone on ahead."

Jejeune had already been awake when Thea's urgent knock had come at his door; his troubled sleep broken by a spiralling kaleidoscope of images and imaginings. But the banging had still startled him, coming as it did a full two hours before their scheduled breakfast time, and so insistent. He dressed rapidly while Thea waited outside his room, issuing terse messages through the door. "We need to take the bike, so bring only your pack and your bins. You can leave everything else until we return."

Jejeune emerged from his room into a dark night already heavy with the building humidity. Daylight was still not even a suggestion in the sky, and the quiet stillness that hung over the forest told him they were approaching the envelope, that sliver of time when the nocturnal creatures were retreating to their lairs while the dawn predators were still yet to emerge. He climbed on the back of the bike and held on as Thea throttled away from the clearing at high speed.

They weren't able to maintain the pace for long. As they drove deeper into the forest, the uneven trail began to rise, slightly but steadily, and Thea spent much of her time easing the front wheel around the large rocks that loomed in the headlight.

"There have been reports of a Harpy in these parts before, but until a ranger located the nest, we had no way of finding one. This might be the best chance you will ever have to see this bird, Inspector, but we must be there before it leaves for its morning hunt. If we miss it, we have no idea how long it will be before it returns."

Jejeune tapped Thea's ribs lightly to let her know he had heard her remarks and acknowledged the truth of them. A Harpy Eagle, the monkey hunter: the bird had been beyond his wildest hopes for this trip. Its immense power and secretive ways made it a creature of almost mythical status; a prize few birders would ever get to see. The excitement was beginning to build within him, and he knew the discomfort of a dusty bike ride on a long, uphill track would fade into insignificance the moment he set eyes on the bird.

They had been riding for about twenty minutes when they crested a small rise. Thea slid the bike to a stop and switched off the light. All around them, the darkness was total. Without the light, they could not see a hand before their faces. She switched on a small flashlight and played it across the ground in front of them, picking up a small trail that disappeared into the vege-tation. "On foot from here, around to the other side of the hill. Not far, maybe ten minutes. The others will be waiting for us. They have a scope."

She motioned for Domenic to lead, and he set off, following the faint white trail painted by the light shining from behind him. Insects darted in an out of the beam, their buzzes and trills gradually becoming audible as his ears recovered from the thrum of the bike's now silent engine.

They had managed a good pace, picking out a series of trails through the vegetation, the occasional scuffing of a boot on a tree root the only disturbance to the rhythm of two sets of foot-falls padding over the soft leaf cover. Only the metronomic click of nighttime insects accompanied them. The steady swishing of the vegetation as they brushed past suggested the trail was getting narrower, but Thea's beam was unwaveringly fixed on the track ahead of them, so there was no way of knowing for sure. Jejeune thought they were under the canopy most of the time. Once or twice the air stirred about him, or a small breeze, in a way that made him think they had emerged into a clearing. But soon the air would close in again, warm and still, without even a breath of movement to stir the leaves. The night felt heavy, close, and Jejeune was sweating slightly as they walked.

"Would this be a lifer for you, too?" he asked over his shoulder.

"Yes." Thea also sounded a little breathless, anxious even. But conversation was difficult at their pace, and Jejeune was not inclined to slow up. The prize on offer was too important.

They had been travelling for so long, daylight would surely only be a few minutes away by the time they joined the others, thought Jejeune. He felt the surge of excitement again at the possibility of seeing this magnificent bird. He wondered if Traz had ever seen a Harpy before. He tried to remember if they had ever talked about it. He couldn't recall, but it didn't matter. A sighting of a Harpy Eagle wasn't something you would get blasé about. His friend would be as charged up as Jejeune at the prospect that awaited them, whether he had seen one before or not.

Thea seemed to be falling back slightly, the light from her flashlight barely reaching in front of Jejeune now. He turned to see if she needed any help, but all he could see was a shadowy outline behind the beam.

Domenic Jejeune took only two more steps, but it was two too many. He knew, a heartbeat before it happened. He felt the spongy undergrowth give way, a little more than usual. He felt his foot travelling deeper, continuing down. He knew, but it was too late. By then, his entire weight had already come forward and his other foot had followed through and found nothingness. He fell through the opening with an explosion of rushing earth and debris and twigs. Leaf litter confettied around him, spiralling in the air, and a cascade of dirt and branches rained in on him as he hurtled down through the darkness.

Jejeune didn't know how long he had been unconscious. The sky above the pit was light now, and the day's warmth was already beginning to saturate the air around him. He was dazed, and he felt weak, as if the strength had been wrung out of him. He rolled to his side, but as he tried to stand, his left ankle gave way and he collapsed in agony. He dragged himself to the side of the pit and rested his back against the smooth dirt of the wall, gingerly touching his leg to test for pain. A sprain from the fall, but not a break. *The fall.* He looked around, confused. The floor of the pit was littered with twigs and leaves, and he found his hair and clothes were, too. A poacher's pit — one large enough and deep enough for wild boar, or deer even. The amount of debris that had fallen in after him suggested the opening had been well covered by vegetation. Even in daylight, it would have been unlikely he would have spotted it. He waited silently for a moment, listening to the forest. He felt tired. He could feel the weariness tugging on his consciousness, threatening to drag him under. He fought it off, knowing he needed to listen for Thea's calls. But only the sounds of the forest filled the morning air, the clicks and trills of insects and the dawn chorus of birds already building.

Jejeune fumbled for his pack and his fingers closed around his water bottle. But he could tell, even before he pried open the lid. It had been full when he left the lodge. He remembered filling it the night before, as was his habit every night on this trip. Now it was empty. And then he realized. Through the confusion, and the throbbing in his head, and the weariness, the truth came to him. He had been in here long enough for anyone who was looking to have found him. So there would be no calls from Thea. She would not be coming to help him. Nor would anybody else.

When he awoke again, it was hot, stiflingly, overwhelmingly hot. From the far side of the pit there was a rank odour of rotting flesh. A large bird of some kind, a guan, perhaps, or even a currasow? It was impossible to tell now; just a mass of matted feathers and dark, dried flesh. A victim of the forest's harsh justice? Or bait perhaps, left to draw a foraging predator into this trap.

How long would a trapped animal survive in here, he wondered. He knew no creature would be able to last long in these conditions without water. Already, it was a craving for him, his tongue thick, his lips dry. He reached for the sides of the pit to ease himself up to a standing position again. The lip of the pit was too high to reach. His fingers carefully searched the smooth walls for footholds. He knew dark spaces were the haunts of many dangers in the rainforest. Scorpions and tarantulas lurked in such places, waiting out the heat of the day, but still ready to strike at anything that came their way. But he found no crevices, no niches that would give him any purchase to climb. His ankle was throbbing, and the effort of standing was more than he could manage, so he slumped back against the wall and carefully stretched his leg out in front of him to ease the pain. He tipped his head back, feeling the cold earth of the wall against his scalp, and gazed up. With the sun climbing ever higher in the sky even the shade from the corners of the pit was shrinking away little by little. Soon, there would be no escape from the relentless heat. He looked at the fetid mass of feathers and desiccated flesh on the far side of the pit. One day. Perhaps two? But surely no more.

31

It was a crisp morning, the air cool and clean, the pale blue sky open and high. Off to the east, a watery sun was pouring its light into the stands of trees, and their shadows climbed the boundary wall of Oakham Manor like dark vines. Maik and Laraby were in the Mini, and when they eventually arrived at the stone archway leading to Robin Oakes's property, they expected to find a parked police cruiser. The officers had instructions not to enter. Yet. The car's back seat would have been empty on the way to the property. Maik and Laraby expected it would be occupied when it left.

Laraby was in high spirits, and with good reason. It wasn't every day you arrived at the station, fresh from your full English, with an extra slice of fried bread, to find the answer to your prayers sitting in the reception area.

"Young lady would like a word, sir." The desk sergeant had smiled at the woman, and her father seated beside her, to show them there was no disrespect intended. The young lady looked nervous, like an animal that had been captured and wasn't sure what was going to happen to her. Laraby had seen a hundred like her, a witness who had maybe seen something, *but, you know, it might not mean anything, so I'm sorry if I'm wasting your time.* He gave them both a broad smile and kept his gaze on them as he said, "Then I think it's tea for three in my office, Sergeant, if you wouldn't mind." He ushered them ahead of him with his hand. "Why don't we go on through."

Only it hadn't been a waste of his time. Even before the soft knock announcing the arrival of the tea, Laraby had surmised that much. He took the opportunity to invite Danny Maik into his office; the one with Domenic Jejeune's name on the door, and asked the woman casually to repeat her statement. Softly, softly, in case she picked up on how significant it was, and started to enter the land of make-believe just to please them.

Laraby had his back to them, gathering the tea from the tray. "This is Gillian Forsyth, Sergeant. She's just got back from a holiday in Malta. All right for some, eh? The thing is, the night before she left, Miss Forsyth had a nasty incident happen to her. She didn't report it at the time, being keen to get away on her hols and all. But now she's back, and she's been hearing on the news about this shocking business with Ms. Dawes. So she thought she'd better come in and have a chat." Laraby turned, a cup and saucer in each hand, and passed them out. "So you were saying this was around five o'clock, just about twilight. And the street lights were on?"

"Yes," said the young woman confidently. "And all the lights in the cottages, too."

"But not that one," her father said. "She remembers that distinctly."

"Yes, sir," said Laraby reasonably. "But your daughter is going to need to tell us all this herself. Just the way it is, I'm afraid." There was no room for compromise in the smile he gave to the man. "Why don't you just run over it again for the sergeant, Miss Forsyth, as far as you'd got with me, and we'll pick it up from there?"

So she did. She told Danny how she'd been walking along the lane that night when a man had burst from the cottage, the one with no lights — a sidelong look at her father — and run into her. At her, actually, knocking her down and giving her a nasty bang on the back of her head when she hit the lamppost.

It was a better account this time, as Laraby had suspected it would be. She'd left out the minor details, the weather, her reasons for being there at that time, and such. Now the account was clean and clear, like a bright, shiny diamond.

"Interesting, eh, Sergeant? How's your tea, by the way, Miss Forsyth? Can I call you Gillian? Enough milk?"

"I understand it was getting dark," said Maik, "and that it must have been a bit frightening, to say the least, to have this man running toward you like that, but did you get any sense of him? His build? His size?"

"As a matter of fact, she thinks she did. Sorry ..." Mr. Forsyth looked down into his tea, to avoid Laraby's admonishing stare.

Maik and Laraby tried their most benign looks out on Gillian Forsyth. This, if it came off, was treasure. But it couldn't be rushed, cajoled, suggested. It needed to come from the witness's memory banks pure and unblemished. It would never be like this again. With every subsequent retelling something would change, a detail, an embellishment, an uncertainty.

"Tallish. His build was hard to tell. He was wearing a brown leather jacket, the kind with a corduroy collar. A cap, too, but I think his hair was longish. The thing I did notice, though, was the moustache. The ends twirled up a bit, like a villain in those old films, only perhaps not that, you know ..." She twirled the ends of an imaginary moustache with her fingers. "And he had a goatee."

Maik was impressed with Laraby's response. He knew the DI wouldn't be able to get them out of the room fast enough, but he was the model of professional courtesy as he eased them toward an officer who could take the woman's statement down on paper. The *ish*es wouldn't be his favourite part, *tallish*, *long-ish*, but the rest was more than enough to satisfy him.

Beside them, along the boundary wall to Oakham, the bare branches of the trees criss-crossed the sky like netting. Strands of wispy white cloud had begun to drift across the pale blue background, high and distant. Under such a great, wide sky, everything in the landscape appeared smaller, diminished.

"Oh, I remembered who that group was, by the way."

Maik looked over in anticipation.

"The Village People."

The wheels of the Mini had returned from the grass verge to the road surface by the time Danny looked over again. He saw Laraby with a mischievous grin on his face and his arms raised, palms upward. "Altogether now, Sergeant. *It's fun to stay at the ...*"

A genuine smile spread across Maik's stony features. And why not? They had an eyewitness identification of a murder suspect, Laraby was turning out to be not bad company, and, for once, the sun was shining. It came as something of a shock, but Danny realized he was enjoying himself.

There was a metallic spangle of light far up ahead; some bit of metal off the cruiser, reflecting in the flat morning light. Or perhaps not. It seemed to be moving toward them in erratic spurts, wavering from side to side, dancing on the air. Maik realized what it was, just as Laraby raised his hand to point. They had both seen enough of them recently. But there was no time to avoid it. The drone hurtled toward the windscreen of the Mini and smashed into it with a juddering force, shattering the glass into a spiderweb of cracks. Maik's involuntary flinch took the Mini off the road for the second time in as many minutes. Only this time it didn't come back. The small wheels found the boundary ditch, and the car somersaulted over the wall, bouncing off its roof. The front end catapulted viciously downward and slammed into the trunk of a massive oak tree with a force that sent a shudder throughout the forest. By the time the trees had come to rest, inside the car, there was no movement at all.

It was as if the crash had shocked the world into inertia. Apart from the hiss of steam from the Mini's ravaged radiator, the only sound was the tick of hot metal. Danny regained consciousness to find Laraby slumped over beside him. He squirmed around to free up an arm and stretched it out so he could lay a finger on the carotid artery of the inert form beside him. The sudden tap on the driver's side window startled him. Danny reached across to open it.

"Danny. You okay?" the man asked, gasping for breath. As crew chief of the Saltmarsh Emergency Services Team, Tom Cavendish had worked with the police on many occasions. He had recognized the Mini as Maik's and sprinted the last hundred metres to the crash site.

"I'm okay. The DI's out. Strong pulse, though. No blood that I can see."

"Let's get you out of there, and we can get one of our lads in to help remove the DI."

But that didn't make much sense to Maik, and a Danny Maik who'd just been catapulted twenty metres off the road and brought to a sudden stop by an oak tree wasn't a man to argue with. He was here, in the car, he was able, and he would help with the transfer of the DI from the Mini.

Two other rescuers were working on the passenger door of the car, but the impact had twisted the frame. It took the additional force of Maik reaching across the still-unconscious form of Marvin Laraby and pushing from the inside before the door finally gave way and swung open. Maik unclicked the seat belt and eased the slumping torso of the DI toward the rescuers. There was a sound like a groan as they twisted Laraby's body slightly to drag his legs clear, but by the time they had loaded the DI onto the gurney and wheeled it away, Maik had still seen no signs of consciousness.

Once he had managed to unfurl himself from the driver's seat, Danny himself proved more unsteady than he thought, reeling slightly and resting against the dented bodywork of the Mini. He was led off toward the road by one of the rescuers. Whether it was part of the plan or not, he was not given the opportunity to look further into the damage to his car.

He looked out toward the dappled edges of the glade, where the crisp white light filtered through the tree trunks. "It was a drone," he said. "Black. About half a metre across. Have our lads look around for it, will you?"

Simultaneously, calls came from either side of the search perimeter, and each officer supporting one of Danny's arms moved off in a different direction, leaving him swaying uneasily in a clearing a few metres from the wreckage. He hoped the calls meant they'd found the drone, even if the two separate directions suggested it had disintegrated on impact. With luck, there would at least be enough left of one piece to identify a serial number. Right about now, Danny Maik was thinking he would be extremely interested to know who that drone belonged to.

32

Jejeune's life had left him sometime on the second morning, as the sun increased in its devastating, terrifying intensity and the heat settled like steam in the bottom of the pit. He had made it through the night, with its respite of soft, warm air that seemed like a gift from the gods, but now, whatever was left — this faint, thready pulse of existence — wasn't life anymore; it was just hanging on.

Jejeune no longer had the strength even to drag his shirt across his face to keep the sun's rays out of his eyes. He had tried once, long ago, lifetimes, it seemed, to make a shelter, taking off his shirt and propping it on his shoes, to keep the worst of the sun off his head. But his body had become red and burned and blistered as he lay there, too weak to move, and when the shirt had fallen away, he had left it where it was, as useless and flaccid as he had become himself.

He had used a lot of energy in the night, too much. A procession of delirious dreams had come to him, coalescing in a single moment of clarity through the haze. *Hayes*. He had realized Lindy was in danger, and also that he could not help her, could never help her. He would die here and she would be unprotected, unaware. He couldn't save her. That thought disturbed him even more than the prospect of his own death. If he could have made tears he would have wept them, in frustration, in sorrow for Lindy.

A faint shadow seemed to cross his eyes, but it was too late for him now. He had accepted he would die. It would come soon, to release him from this terrible, searing pain of thirst. It would take him away to coolness, to shade, to water droplets. In his mind, one touched his cheek now, burning with his coolness, but he was too weak even to dream, to imagine any more. He lay on his back and let the relentless sun beat down from high in a clear, cloudless sky to finish its task.

The word drifted down to him. *Drink*. It was the cruelest of jokes; his greatest desire in life and he was being taunted by his mind. But not his mind, something external, above.

"JJ, the bottle. Drink!"

Jejeune's eyes fluttered open, but he could make out only the burning white light of the sun.

"JJ, the bottle. It's beside you. Drink. I'm going to look for something to get you out."

But he couldn't. His one wish in the world and he couldn't move, not even for water. He closed his eyes again.

Fire was burning his ankle, and from somewhere in a dark tunnel of awareness, Jejeune recognized it as pain. From the top of the pit, Traz was throwing large clumps of hard-packed mud to rouse his friend.

"JJ, you have to drink, man, I can't get down to you. The bottle is there beside you."

Jejeune scrabbled around with his fingers and touched the cold, wet plastic, but he couldn't close his fingers around it and his hand flopped to his side with the effort.

Traz watched in horror as Jejeune's touch set the bottle rolling away the six inches that may as well have been six metres. As he stood at the edge of the pit, looking down, Traz's options divided before him as cleanly as if they had been cleaved by a blade. Find a way to get some water into his friend's mouth. Or stay up here and watch him die.

Up close like this, the liana Traz had hacked from the undergrowth seemed disturbingly thin as he tied it around the tree trunk. But it was strong. He gave it a fierce tug and it held, its sinewy tendrils biting into the bark on the tree.

At first he had looked around the small clearing, frantically considering anything that he might be able to use to push the bottle back to where his friend could grasp it. But the pit was deep, and he knew he could never manoeuvre a limb long enough and sturdy enough, even if he had somehow found a way to hack one free from a tree. He had thought of sprinting back to the Jeep, which he had left far down the trail, but in his panicked state, he could think of nothing in the vehicle that could be of help — a jack, a spare tire, a can of gasoline. Besides, leaving his friend now was out of the question. It was a twenty-minute return trip to the Jeep, minimum, and in Jejeune's present state, Traz doubted his friend could survive that long in the heat and sun. In the end, he had decided on the liana, severing a length of the pliable brown vine by pounding it with a sharp rock. The test he had just performed reassured him a little, but still, he hesitated. He didn't need it to be strong enough for him to go swinging through the treetops, but if it broke under his weight as he climbed down, he knew that two people would die in the bottom of this pit. Still, he was out of options. Drawing a breath, he tossed the end of the vine into the pit.

He grabbed it tightly, twisting it over the sleeves of his shirt and gingerly began to lower himself down. His feet could find no purchase on the packed, smoothed soil of the pit sides and he dangled for a moment, twirling as he slid and kicked and scrabbled for a foothold. He let go finally and fell the remaining distance onto the floor of the pit. He landed on his back, the breath knocked from him slightly, and stared up in horror. The vine had kinked around something on the surface; a root, or a rock and it now dangled a couple of metres above the pit floor. Even if he could reach it, there was surely no way he could get enough purchase to pull himself back up out of the pit. Certainly, in his present state, his friend stood no chance of managing it. Not alone.

Traz rolled to his feet and crossed to his friend, grabbing the bottle and cradling Jejeune's head as he dribbled the water onto the parched, cracked lips.

"Just a little. We can't waste it. This is all I have."

But Jejeune grabbed at it with a desperate strength and tried to force it into this throat until Traz wrestled it away from him. "Easy," he said. "Let's get you out, and we'll find some water up there." He helped Jejeune to his feet, but even with an arm draped across Traz's shoulder, his friend seemed unable to bear weight on his leg. Traz took a quick look down and saw the mass of blueish-purple swelling. He lowered Jejeune gently to the ground again.

"We need to get you out of here, JJ. The heat's coming. It's going to be … not good down here." He raised Jejeune again and propped the rag-doll form against the wall. "Okay, on my shoulders, using the wall for balance. You stand on your good leg and you grab the vine. Listen to me." Jejeune's head had slumped forward. Traz wasn't even sure he was conscious, but when he crouched, there was movement and Jejeune raised his head slightly. "I'll boost you as far as I can, but you've got to do some of this yourself, JJ. That last half metre or so, that's all going to be up to you. You understand?"

Traz crouched and half-lifted Jejeune onto his back, using the wall to steady them both. He cajoled his friend up onto one knee, even as the other leg dangled uselessly by Traz's side.

Jejeune was still not fully upright when, with a supreme effort, Traz straightened and teetered and screamed at his friend to grab onto the vine that dangled above them. Jejeune did, holding it in both hands, even as he swayed on his friend's back.

"Up now, JJ, use the vine to pull yourself up. Wrap it around your wrists, tightly. Pull yourself up onto my shoulders." The sweat was pouring down Traz's temples, stinging his eyes and blurring his vision. But he couldn't wipe it away. His friend's balance was so precarious, if Traz withdrew even one supporting hand, he knew Jejeune would keel over sideways and fall.

Jejeune seemed confused about what he needed to do, and Traz repeated his instructions in a constant stream; *grab on, climb, pull*. Eventually, from his crouched position, Traz felt the slightest relief as the vine took some of Jejeune's weight, and as he straightened, he could feel his friend ascending. He cupped one hand under the sole of Jejeune's strong foot, pushing and holding and balancing until his arms trembled with the effort. The final half-metre beckoned. Would Jejeune's strength hold? Would the vine?

Afterward, neither man could have said where the effort came from. Perhaps the faint breeze at the top drew Jejeune there, so cool after the stifling heat of the pit. But Jejeune hauled himself up somehow, scrambling his knees against the wall in the final assault until he crested the rim and collapsed motionless at the top, his wounded leg still dangling over the emptiness of the pit.

Traz reeled back and slumped to the ground, his face and body streaming with sweat. He felt spent. Beside him, the water bottle held barely enough for a mouthful, but he took only half, the warm plastic taste doing little to relieve his thirst. It was not until he looked up again that he realized the vine was nowhere in sight.

Jejeune had dragged it up with him as he had squirmed his way from the pit, and it was now beneath his inert form. He knew Jejeune could not stay like that for long. The sun was beating down on the path, and his friend was still dangerously dehydrated and probably suffering from heatstroke. If Traz didn't get him to water and shade, soon, Jejeune might still die on this trail.

He called up desperately, screaming his friend's name. For a long moment there was no movement. And then Jejeune rolled slightly to his side and the vine slithered from beneath him and dangled down into the pit once again.

It took Traz three tries to secure a hold on the vine. He knew he wouldn't have had enough left in him for a fourth. He got enough of the vine to wrap it around his arm and swing toward the wall, where he found the faintest of footholds to take the pressure as he secured his grip. Walking his feet up the wall, he laboriously hauled himself up, scrabbling over the final stretch to make a desperate grab for the edge.

Despite his fatigue, Traz hauled his sweat-soaked body upright. First he dragged Jejeune to the edge of the path, where the vegetation gave some small pockets of shadow to shelter him from the sun's rays. Then he took the water bottle and stumbled in a clumsy half-run to a nearby creek, where he drank like a cheat before running the full bottle back to Jejeune, pouring half of the cold, clear liquid over his friend's shirt in an effort to get the fluid into him. But there were bigger problems to deal with: Jejeune's breathing was shallow and his face was scarlet. Traz shouldered him once more and helped him to the creek, where he lay his friend in the cold water, submerged to his neck, while he ran down to the Jeep. Even now, he couldn't drive it all the way up the trail. He was forced to stop fifty metres shy of the creek by a combination of large rocks and deep ruts. Any farther and he'd either snap an axle or get to a point where he couldn't turn around.

Jejeune wasn't as red when Traz returned to help him from the stream, but he wasn't shivering either, as a man who had been immersed in the cold water for that long should have been. By the time Traz loaded Jejeune into the back of the Jeep beneath the ragged canvas top, his friend's pupils were rolling around unsteadily and his breathing was coming in erratic snatches. As Traz reached over to set a blanket beneath Jejeune's head in preparation for the rugged journey ahead, the detective breathed the faintest of words. Traz heard them but they made no sense.

"Call Maik. Ask. Ray Hayes. Not Lindy."

Within seconds, Traz was bouncing the Jeep down the trail, his precious cargo stowed in the back. Safe. For now.

33

Maik was first in the next morning, clean-shaven and wearing a neatly pressed shirt and tie. By the time the first of the other detectives rolled in, the lights in the Incident Room were burning brightly against the darkness beyond the windows and the kettle was ready to dispense its first cup of tea. It was an old copper's way of showing he was suffering no ill effects from the events of the day before. A few bumps and bruises, perhaps, a sore spot or two when he had rolled out of bed this morning, but otherwise fit and ready to go. It was an important point to make. All day yesterday, Danny had studiously avoided mentioning that he'd been knocked out in the crash. DCS Shepherd had recently implemented what she called a Concussion Protocol. Danny suspected it was most likely an import from America, but Shepherd's version had her officers on twenty-four hours enforced leave after any incident in which they had been rendered unconscious. Laraby, who hadn't fully come to until the ambulance was almost at the hospital, was on bed rest at home for the day. Danny knew he was okay himself. He'd been injured enough times to know the difference, and the cause of his own head-ache wasn't some phantom brain shake. It was a bloody big dent in the window stanchion of the Mini, one that had left a sizeable bruise on his forehead. Besides, he very much wanted to be involved in this morning's suspect interview.

DCS Shepherd sat in the interview room next to Danny Maik, her face a mask of repressed anger. Across the narrow table from them, Robin Oakes's solicitor was making a point of staring at the left side of her client's face. Oakes himself seemed oblivious to the red welt on his cheek and the bruising that was beginning to form around it.

"I am sitting in for DI Laraby," Shepherd told the two people opposite her, "but I am also in charge of internal discipline at this station, so I'm going to recuse myself from interviewing your client personally."

Oakes held up a hand. "I won't be pressing charges, Superintendent. Emotions were running high. Two of your men had just been injured; though, you must understand, I wasn't aware of this at the time the uniformed officers came to arrest me. I may have been somewhat dismissive."

"Nevertheless, I can assure you both, I'll be holding a full investigation." From the set of her jaw and her dangerously controlled tone, Maik was in no doubt that Shepherd would. He suspected the careers of the arresting officers would be unlikely to survive her inquiry. Though they were both good lads at heart, Maik wouldn't be much moved to intercede on their behalf either. At the very least, their actions could have compromised the case against a prime suspect in a murder.

"My client trusts his show of good faith can be reciprocated and this matter can be resolved quickly."

Maik wasn't sure how long it would take, but he was fairly certain it was going to be resolved, if not perhaps in the way the solicitor had in mind. She wasn't one they had seen at the station before. Along with her expensive outfit and immaculate grooming, she had brought an air of assured competence. It was the kind of representation money can buy. Contrary to the old adage, Maik had always believed good help wasn't hard to find. You just had to be prepared to pay for it. She had introduced herself brusquely, some double-barrelled name that Maik had missed. It wasn't like him, and it troubled him a little. Still, he was certain DCS Shepherd had caught it, despite the distraction of Oakes's facial injury.

That the solicitor had advised Oakes not to exploit the assault surprised Danny somewhat. Interviews, and prosecutions, were contests for advantage. To relinquish such a strong position so easily was either very careless or very calculating. However, the sergeant recognized that, despite the solicitor's assurance of good faith, the DCS would want to stay as far away from the actual questioning of Robin Oakes as possible. It would be up to him to lead the way. Only if it came to a decision would Shepherd want to weigh in.

"Your phone has operating software for a drone, Mr. Oakes?" said Maik pleasantly. "Do you own one?"

"Yes."

"Where is it now? Only our officers have been unable to find it in your home."

"I'm not sure." Oakes shrugged and slid a look toward his solicitor.

"I'm curious as to why you'd own one," said Maik. In fact, he had a fairly good idea, but he'd learned a thing or two from Inspector Jejeune about interview techniques, and chief among them was to let the suspect give you the answers, rather than supplying them yourself and asking for confirmation.

"All the IV League members were given one by the Picaflor project, a means of getting us to understand just what sort of hardware we would be investing in. They were quite rudimentary prototypes. None of the proprietary software was loaded onto any of them, of course."

"If you've been unable to find this drone, then clearly you have no evidence that the equipment which caused this dreadful accident yesterday belonged to my client," pointed out the solicitor. "And I would remind you that my client was not informed that he was being detained in connection with this incident, anyway."

Both she and her client were taking an approach to all this that was jarringly out of place. Robin Oakes had been arrested on suspicion of murder, and here was his solicitor reminding them of the fact, urging them to get on with it almost. Danny looked across at Shepherd as if he might know what it signalled, but if the DCS recognized the signs, she wasn't prepared to show it.

"We have an eyewitness who can place your client at the scene of a murder," said Maik flatly.

"Your witness is mistaken," said Oakes forcefully. "I wasn't there."

The solicitor reached forward to place a gentle hand of restraint on her client's forearm. "As I understand it, your eyewitness has given a description of a person in the street outside the cottage, nothing more. Furthermore, I don't believe any formal identification of my client has been made. I think we all know there's no basis for holding my client until there has. He has pressing business that he needs to attend to. We are requesting he be released on his own recognizance."

"Local business?"

Neither Oakes nor his solicitor answered. America, then. That would be where Oakes's pressing business lay. Could they really be requesting that he be allowed to leave the country with the evidence in a murder inquiry stacking up against him like this? Like the rest of the interview to this point, it seemed to make no sense.

"Where were you, Mr. Oakes, on the night Erin Dawes was murdered?"

"At home, looking at photographs."

It was the third time Maik had seen Oakes's eyes move upward like this when he gave them this answer. Whether it was just a touch of frayed nerves from the accident, he didn't know, but this time the man's performance exasperated Maik. If you were going to lie, at least put a bit of effort into it. He reached over to the recorder.

"Interview terminated at 13:36." He clicked the stop button. "Given that a senior police officer has been injured in what we consider to be a related incident, I'll be applying for special dispensation to hold your client for a further twenty-four hours," Maik told the solicitor, wishing he could recall her name to add formality to his statement. "The DCS here can advise you as to whether I'm likely to be granted it, but my guess is that I will." He leaned forward across the interview table and addressed Oakes directly. "In the meantime, I'll be setting up a formal witness identification. And a positive identification from that will give us enough to hold you until you go to trial for the murder of Erin Dawes, Mr. Oakes. The DCS and I are going to leave now, but we'll give you a second before I send the officer in to escort you to the cells, just so your solicitor can confirm that we're within our rights to do all of this."

Shepherd sat very still. Maik's breach of protocol was so out of keeping with his character, she was wondering if there had been more impact from the accident than Danny was letting on. Maybe it had been a mistake to let him stay around. She should have insisted he took the day off, like Laraby.

Maik waited, exuding a patience no one else in the room shared. With the slightest of movements, Oakes rocked back and his solicitor leaned in. Behind the man's raised hand, they conferred for a moment before Oakes leaned forward again and resumed his upright posture.

"You'll find the drone in the back of my car, beneath my photo equipment," he said. "It wasn't my device that hit your car yesterday."

Maik waited for the rest of the explanation. Now the stone-walling was over, the facts could come pouring out. Maik knew they would be in Oakes's favour. Whatever was coming, it would be designed to help the man to avoid the charges he was facing. This, whatever it was, had been behind his calmness, and his solicitor's assurance, during the interview.

"I was at home on the night Erin Dawes died," said Oakes. Despite the fact that he had taken a breath to prepare himself, his voice was wavering and uncertain. "But not in the gatehouse. I was out at the ruins."

"At night? Doing what, sir?"

"I was flying the drone. I have been spending the past few weeks trying to acclimate the Barn Owls to having the drone fly beside them as they hunt. The photographic opportunities it would present are fantastic."

"My client is aware that in admitting to this activity, he is confessing to committing a crime under section 18 of the Wildlife and Countryside Act, 1981," said the solicitor. "He is prepared to accept the charges, and the considerable public fallout that will no doubt accompany them."

Maik was puzzled, and it took him a moment to recover himself. Beside him, Shepherd stirred uneasily. The interview was going sideways, and wherever it ended up, she had a feeling they were not going to be in the position she had hoped when they had first entered the room.

"Is that the reason you were interested in investing in the drone technology in the first place?"

"No, not at all. To be honest, it sounds like a genuinely important project. I'd have been quite prepared to provide the land anyway."

"You have proof that you were there at that time, I take it."

Maik waited while Oakes and his solicitor conferred again behind the man's raised hand.

"Actually, I don't. Only my word, I'm afraid." Oakes's playboy smile couldn't have been more out of place at a funeral.

Maik was stunned. Even Shepherd shifted again, though she offered no contribution.

"None at all?" It was all Maik could do to stop himself from offering a few suggestions of his own — time-stamped photographs, GPS data from Oakes's phone. He looked at the solicitor significantly. Surely she could see her client's position. But she looked as cool and unperturbed as before, smoothing her skirt with two hands and flicking her head slightly so a cascade of light rippled down her dark hair.

The silence ticked by as Danny considered the new information.

"Clearly, there is not enough to consider freeing your client, Ms. … ma'am," said Danny awkwardly. "We'll make the application, as I stated, and set up the eyewitness identification. Until that time, your client will remain in custody." He looked across to see if Shepherd had anything further to add, but she stood and, after offering the minimum courtesies, left the room without any further comment. Oakes's solicitor followed suit and a uniformed constable came in to lead Oakes back to his cell.

Danny remained in the room for a long time. It had been a troubling interview. Not only had Oakes passed on an opportunity to bring charges of assault, he had readily admitted to a crime that was guaranteed to bring a public outcry, not to mention a damaging blow to a lucrative career. Maik doubted he would sell another photograph of a bird, at least in these parts, for a very long time. And for what, when none of it did anything to prove he was innocent? Surely, even if Oakes could convince himself that this self-sacrifice was going to be enough to deflect charges of murder, his high-priced solicitor would have a more pragmatic view. Maik had no doubt Oakes had used the drones to track Barn Owls, as he said, but he could offer no evidence of any kind that he was doing it the night Erin Dawes was murdered. Oakes had been identified at the scene, leaving the cottage. And for the life of him, Danny couldn't see how an unsubstantiated claim of involvement in a minor offence was going to be any defence against that.

34

"Well you don't look as much like beef jerky as when I brought you in, so I suppose that's a good sign."

Despite his light tone, the relief in Traz's face was evident as he saw the person he knew as his friend staring back at him.

The two-room clinic was a single-storey breeze-block structure facing onto the only road through the small town. The buzz of passing traffic entered through the open windows in a constant stream, and a lazy fan did little to distribute the dusty air in the reception area. The interior of the clinic was clean, but the decor was wilting under the tropical heat and patches of damp showed through the plaster on the walls. Jejeune was in one of the two beds in the room at the back. The starched white linens were dazzling in the sunlight that flooded in through the window and the floor glistened with polish. If the staff could do nothing about the condition of the building, they were determined to ensure the things within their care were well maintained.

There were bright lights behind Traz's head, and Jejeune raised an arm to shield his eyes from them. He realized he was not wearing a shirt about the same time he realized he had a plastic tube trailing from his arm.

"They're rehydrating you. They think you should be okay, but they're going to watch you for a while." Traz drew up a rickety wooden chair and sat next to the bed. "They were worried about the heatstroke, but your bloodwork came back okay, so it looks like there's been no internal damage."

Even in his drowsy state, Jejeune realized this was surely due to his friend getting him immersed in cold water so soon after the rescue. He scooted himself up on his elbows so he could see Traz more clearly.

"Thanks," he said simply.

"For what? It's all my fault." He lowered his voice slightly. The receptionist in the next room had spoken to him only in Spanish, but Traz was pretty sure the nurse who had treated Jejeune would know some English. She was also in the other room at the moment, but Traz was taking no chances. "I found Mariel's address. Armando left his laptop open and I searched the past trip reports. I knew he would have them, as reference for this tour. They must have thought it was you who'd searched."

"How did they find out?" asked Jejeune.

Traz shook his head. "I accessed the files before we went to dinner that night. The internet connection was going in and out. It was down when I searched, but it must have come back on when Armando returned later, and Dropbox alerted him that the files had been accessed." He banged his forehead with the palm of his hand. "There's a word in Spanish: *idiota*."

Despite his discomfort, Jejeune managed a smile. "Lindy would say it's the inevitable result of artificial intelligence meeting genuine stupidity."

"It's no joke, JJ. You could have died because of me."

"I'm alive because of you. As a way of making amends, I'll take that."

"You said something," Traz told him, "when I was loading you into the Jeep. About a call, a mic, a haze, and not to tell Lindy? That last part I got, but the rest didn't make sense."

But it did to Jejeune now, as it came flooding back; the shaven-headed man with the tattoos up his neck who'd come dancing into the detective's mind in his delirium, taunting him with his threats to Lindy.

"Ray Hayes," he said softly. "And *Maik*, not *mic*. Danny Maik, my sergeant. I have to call him." Jejeune hiked himself up on one elbow again. "Is my phone around?"

Traz shook his head. "No signal in here, and I'm betting there is no way they're letting you use the land line for an international call."

"Can you call him for me, Traz? Now? Today? It's important. Sergeant Danny Maik." Jejeune gave him the number. "Ask him to make inquiries about Ray Hayes. But discreetly. Not through the official police records. Tell him that part is vital. Will you do that?"

Jejeune's intensity burned brightly, perhaps in spite of his frailty, perhaps because of it. Either way, Traz was left in no doubt as to the importance of the request. He agreed to take care of it as soon as he found a signal outside.

The nurse came in and carefully checked the dressings on Jejeune's wrists. There were deep red welts where the lariat-like vine had bitten in as he was hauling himself out of the pit.

Traz made a comment to the nurse, who gave Jejeune a strange look before replying to his friend. After a short conversation, she departed, apparently satisfied with her work, if not with Jejeune himself.

"I told her you were into bondage," said Traz flatly. "We agreed that, while neither of us understand it ourselves, it's your business."

Jejeune managed a weak smile. "You're aware of the condition called *mythomania*, also known as compulsive lying disorder? I come across it every now and then in my line of work." He fixed Traz with a serious look. "How did you know what had happened to me?"

"At first light, we boarded Jeeps for Monteria. Thea, her father, and you weren't around, so I assumed you were all coming in a separate vehicle. When we got to Monteria, I asked about you and Armando said he'd been told you had to return home early — an emergency. It sounded wrong, but I thought, you know, something to do with Lindy maybe? If you'd received a call late at night, it was a possibility. Until I started unpacking at the lodge and found this." He fished in the top pocket of his shirt. It was a black wallet containing Jejeune's passport. "I have the same wallet. I must have picked yours up by mistake. Which I suppose means my own passport is at the bottom of a ravine somewhere in Titi National Park by now, with the rest of your stuff." He paused. "I got back to Titi as fast as I could."

"I still can't understand how you knew to come to that part of the trail to find me," said Jejeune.

"Ah, you know," said Traz, tilting his head casually. "There was only one road up into the hills from the farmhouse. You didn't have to be Jim Rockford to figure it out. At the end, there was one good trail into the forest. I thought even someone of your Bambi-like innocence might get suspicious if someone started leading you through pristine rainforest on a trek in the middle of the night."

"Unless she had a weapon."

"The forest is the best weapon you can have, if you use it properly." Traz looked up at Jejeune. "*She*? Thea?" Sadness flickered across his features. "She knew that pit was there, JJ. This was no accident. What did she tell you she was taking you to see, anyway?"

"Harpy Eagle."

Traz nodded. "Elevation's right. We were on the edge of its range." He pulled a face. "It's possible. It's clever, though. You might not make that trek for a Baudo Guan, but nobody's going to turn down the chance for a Harpy. That's the holy grail bird down here."

Jejeune's mind went back to the trail, to virtually the last thought he had before falling. "Have you ever seen one?"

Traz nodded. "Once, in Panama. A guide was showing me a howler monkey in the top of a tree when a Harpy swept in and took it. Imagine, a full-grown howler, plucked just like that. Even from our distance, I heard a sound like a gunshot. I thought someone was firing at it. Know what it was? The monkey's skull, popping like a pea pod in the eagle's talons." Traz looked up at Jejeune, something sad and haunted behind his eyes. "It stayed with me a long time, that sound. One minute a living thing is sitting in the treetops, just looking around, the next …. I couldn't stop thinking about it, the move from life to death, how sudden, how final."

Jejeune felt the slight pressure as Traz squeezed his hand in an unconscious gesture that would have embarrassed them both. Traz recovered himself and came back to the present. "Yeah," he said, nodding, "I would have gone with her on the promise of a Harpy, too." He thought for a moment longer. "Now that you're awake, I suppose I'd better go and get the cops. They can come here to take your statement."

"No," said Jejeune, sitting slightly more upright.

"This is not the Wild West, JJ. They have laws here, too, you know. You were the victim of a serious crime," hissed Traz, lowering his voice. "You can't brush this off, or pretend it didn't happen. You have to tell them Thea Walden tried to kill you."

"Did she? Or did I just wander off and get lost in the forest? I was unconscious. Maybe she tried to find me. Maybe she went to organize a search party. At the moment, we have no proof at all of any wrongdoing."

"What about Armando's story that you'd gone home?"

"You can hardly expect a tour company to tell the group one of the party members is missing, maybe dead. They'll say they just didn't want to alarm the rest of the group. My bet is they'll have alerted the authorities. If Thea happened to get a little confused about which part of the forest we were in, you could hunt around forever up there and never find anybody. I'm just saying, if they have been clever enough to plan this, they'll already have come up with a story that covers them."

The nurse came back in the room and began making up the bed next to them. Traz lowered his voice again, but turned it into a discrete murmur, rather than the whisper that might have attracted the nurse's attention. "None of this makes any sense. Nobody would want to … do what she tried to, just because you were looking into your brother's case. He's as guilty as he always was. He took Graumann to Chiribiquete. He was denied a permit and he went anyway. Graumann infected the Karijona and they died. However Mariel is involved, it's not going to change those facts, is it?"

"No," said Jejeune slowly, "not those facts." But if Traz had been looking at his friend instead of the interesting way the nurse was leaning over the bed, he might have seen in his eyes a light that suggested that something *had* changed.

"We need to see Mariel, Traz. Right away." Jejeune leaned forward slightly, but sank back on the pillow with the effort. The nurse looked over, but Traz held up a hand to indicate everything was okay.

"You're here for another twelve hours. After that, maybe we'll talk."

"She could be in danger."

"So could you, if you don't get properly rehydrated." Traz handed him his iPod. "Here. I was going to load some Justin Bieber on there for you, but I didn't know how much morphine you were on."

Jejeune smiled and closed his eyes. "Twelve hours? You'll come back and we can go? It's important."

"Most things are, when you're lying in a hospital bed. Get some rest."

Traz was already at the door when Jejeune's weak voice reached him. "Traz. Make that call to Danny Maik for me, would you? Now?"

But Jejeune didn't hear Traz's answer. He was already asleep by the time his friend assured him that he would.

35

Maik hadn't wasted much time after the interview, getting a car from the pool and heading down to the marina. Connor James was on his hands and knees scrubbing a section of the deck below the topsail that Maik wouldn't have thought was particularly susceptible to dirt. He looked up at the sergeant's approach. He seemed surprised to see Maik, and hesitated a moment before abandoning his cleaning with the enthusiasm of a man who didn't have a lot of practice at it, and didn't particularly want much more.

"Sergeant. Fancy a can of sugar water? I know how important it is that you lads keep your wits sharp."

It would have been hard to find offence in James's upbeat banter, and Maik was in an indulgent mood. "Mine are about as sharp as they're going to get," he said. "I will take a cup of tea, though."

The men went below, where there was more evidence of cleaning and tidying. A couple of half-filled cardboard boxes stood near the stairwell, and it looked to Maik as if a few more artifacts had gone since the last time he was here. He wondered whether he'd find them if he went to the gallery in Norwich.

"You're doing a lot of work on this boat." Maik left the comment dangling as he watched James's body for any signs of tension, a slight shuffling of the feet perhaps, or a shimmy of discomfort. There were none. But then, standing stock still was a form of response, too.

"Time for a change," said James. "I'm putting her on the market."

As Constable Salter had already told him. Maik nodded. One chance, one truth. So far, James was still on the right side of doubt.

"Leaving Saltmarsh?"

"Maybe. Just passing by, were you? Today?" If James had noticed the bruise on the sergeant's forehead, he'd done a good job of showing no interest in it.

"Inquiries, as a matter of fact." Maik offered a flat smile. "When did you know the IV League options had not been exercised?"

"When the deadline passed. Amendal was straight on the blower. None too pleased, neither. He'd spent weeks researching the properties of that plot, in preparation. He said more than once that it was ideal. The perfect place to run his tests, he said."

Maik nodded as if it was exactly what he had expected to hear. "So you contacted Ms. Dawes?"

"Tried to. Left a few voicemails, got a couple of emails back." He smiled. "You know a relationship is on the outs when you're leaving heartfelt messages on somebody's answering machine and getting cease-and-desist emails in return."

"Did you tell any of the other IV League investors the deadline had been missed?"

James shook his head slowly. "No, my instructions were to deal with Dawes. She was quite clear about that."

Maik seemed to hesitate for a moment. "Er, that tea?"

"Oh, right." James turned to the countertop and began to prepare the tea with the precision of a surgeon. "Somebody told me you collect old Motown records, Sergeant," he said over his shoulder.

"Who might that have been?"

"Can't remember, to tell the truth." Maik saw James's head nod forward approvingly. "Good money in the nostalgia market. Lots of collectors. What did that Frank Wilson record go for a few years back? Twenty was it?"

"*Do I Love You (Indeed I Do)*? It was closer to twenty-five, I believe. How do you know about that? A Motown man yourself, are you?"

James turned and presented Maik with a mug of tea. "Not particularly. But it's my business to know what investments make sense. And twenty-five thousand dollars for a seven-inch piece of vinyl sounds like it'd be an investment worth having a part of."

"That was a one-off," said Maik. "That record is the most sought-after pressing there is for Motown collectors. I don't think you could call that representative of the market."

There was a loud noise as James opened a can of pop. Maik hadn't seen him open the fridge, but he hadn't noticed any cans on the counter either. "If somebody's willing to buy it, and somebody's willing to sell it, I'd say that's representative enough for me." He looked at Maik frankly over the top of his pop can. "If you're interested, I could find out who bought it. Perhaps they'd be willing to let it go. Tell you what. I'd even waive half my normal fee if you decide you want it."

Maik's smile suggested he would pass. He took a casual sip of his tea. "I understand the potential investors were all given drones by the Picaflor project."

"That's right. They wanted them to have some understanding of the technology, make it all a bit less *sci-fi* to them. I got one myself, as a matter of fact." James set down his can and lifted one of the calfskin-clad benches. He fished around in the storage space for a moment and emerged with a box, which he sent Maik's way with a soft, underhand toss. "Here you go. It's the prototype for the survey drone, not the one they'll use for planting."

"And you're sure everybody got one?"

"Handed 'em out myself. Why?"

"We didn't find one at Erin Dawes's house," said Maik.

"She probably threw it out. They aren't a lot of bottle, to be honest. They were discards. The cameras weren't up to scratch; the resolution's not sharp enough for accurate survey work."

Maik turned the machine over in his hands. It was impossible to tell if it was the same model that had hit the Mini the previous day. He supposed it could have been. He had managed only the most fleeting of glances, but the one that hit the windscreen seemed bigger. But perhaps that was just the perspective you got when something like this was hurtling toward you at top speed.

"I'd like to take this, to assist us with a case, if you don't mind."

"You can keep it. I've got no use for it now, have I? That drone has flown." He gave a lopsided smile. "Let's call it a bribe."

"Let's not," said Maik, making no attempt to match the other man's cheeky grin.

A skein of geese flew over the boat, honking loudly. James looked up, despite being unable to see them. He seemed to be listened to the strange, nasally calls as the birds disappeared along the coastline. A wistful smile crossed his lips. "I'll miss this place," he said. "A man has a chance to think out here, remember what's important." He took a swig from his can. "Easy to forget that at times."

"How did Josh Amendal react when he knew you'd failed to deliver his investors? And his land?"

James gave a soft, knowing smile. "Ah, you heard about that, did you?"

"I heard he pulled no punches about what he thought of you as an investment broker. He's got a wide circle of influential friends. It can't be good for business."

"What? No. In this game, your reputation is your last deal. Get a couple of juicy ones under my belt and I'm back in the saddle again. There's always a market for a good investment product. Personal feelings don't come into it."

He hadn't denied Maik's claim, though, the sergeant noted.

"The trouble is, as I see it, at the moment your last deal is the one that didn't get made, the one everybody Amendal speaks to is getting to hear about."

James spread his arms out indulgently, pop can in one hand. "Listen, he's just a kid. He's gone a bit over the top with his criticism, but I understand. Really I do. After all, he's got a point. I'm paid to deliver, and I didn't. It could have cost him the entire project."

"What about Erin Dawes? How were your feelings toward her?"

Maik had tried ambiguity; leaving the question open to interpretation, in the hope that James might tell him something he hadn't asked. It was a technique he had seen his absent DCI use to good effect in the past. The problem was, a clever person could always misinterpret the question to their own advantage, as James did now.

"Like I said before, nice enough. A bit wounded, though, I'd say, like maybe some dastardly cad done her over one time and she couldn't quite bring herself to get over it." He gave it some thought. "Interesting project, I suppose, for the right person. But I don't do restorations, buildings, or women. Best leave jobs like that to the experts, eh?" he said with a wink.

Maik seemed to consider the answer for a long time. "When I asked you last time, you said *these days*," he said. "You're Connor James these days. What does that mean?"

"Means I used to be James Connor when I was growing up. But I couldn't even get in through the servant's entrance of a place like Sylvan Ridge as plain old Jamie Connor, could I? So I switched my names around, added a touch of the old Bohemian to my lifestyle, and presto. Now people like the IV League can't get enough of me. Funny old world, innit?"

Danny lifted the mug to his lips but it slipped somehow. He batted it into the air, but was unable to catch it and it fell to the deck with a loud clatter.

"I'll cancel that audition with the Cirque de Soleil, then, shall I?" said James with a broad grin.

"Sorry about that. All over your nice clean floor, too. If you give me a cloth, I'll wipe it up."

"It's okay, I was going to mop down here today anyway."

Maik picked up the mug and looked at it. "Good job it didn't break."

"Them things? They're indestructible. Ideal for the boating life. Not exactly the place for your best china, top deck in choppy waters."

"At least let me wash it out for you." Maik crossed to the sink and swilled the mug before replacing it in the rack above. "Any idea where you'll be heading when you leave Saltmarsh?" he asked, his back still to James. "Be staying in Norfolk, will you?"

"Hard to say. There're opportunities everywhere if only you're willing to go out and grab them. Look at Asia, for example. There's an entire continent of people out there that thinks rhino horn and seahorses can cure impotence. Can you imagine, in this day and age? Get in amongst that lot, and it'd be a licence to print money for an unscrupulous man. That's my trouble, see." James put his hand on his chest as Maik turned around. "A bit too honest for my own good, sometimes, a victim of my own integrity, you might say. Because the truth of the matter is, in this game, the good guys don't just finish last, they're lucky to finish at all. Was there anything else, Sergeant? Only I've got to get on, if you don't mind."

"No, sir. There's nothing else. Good day."

Back on the boat ramp, Maik thought about the last time he had been here. DI Laraby and James had seemed to get on particularly well. It was strange the boat owner hadn't asked where Laraby was. In fact, he hadn't mentioned him at all.

36

The narrow entrance greeted them as they crested the top of the hill, though if they had not been looking for it, the surrounding vegetation would have swallowed it from view as soon as they had passed. Traz pulled the Jeep to a stop at the top of the dusty driveway, beneath an ancient wrought iron archway. He pointed to the rusted gothic script. "I'd say we're in the right place."

It took Jejeune a few seconds to make out the name: PICAFLOR.

"Spanish for *hummingbird*," said Traz.

"I thought it was *colibries*."

"Gray Jay/Whiskyjack, Great Skua/Bonxie," said Traz with a shrug. He slipped the Jeep in gear again and eased the vehicle along the dusty, rut-filled track that passed as Picaflor's driveway. It ended at a small garden, from which a narrow path weaved its way between rows of vegetables and vines before disappearing behind a large hedge of bougainvillea.

Traz parked the Jeep and the two men followed the path, emerging at a sight that froze them where they stood. The land sloped away dramatically into a valley, and stretching out across it the massive mounds of the Sierra Madre mountain range receded in a series of slow, rolling waves toward the horizon.

The valley, and even the lower reaches of the mountains them-selves, was swathed in a blanket of pale, translucent cloud that took on an ethereal quality in the afternoon light. Far out beyond the mountains, a distant glint of amber showed them where the land met the sea in the sunshine of Santa Marta. It was like standing on the edge of the Earth, looking out over other worlds. Domenic Jejeune didn't know what it was that had driven Mariel Huaqua to seek her hermitage out here, but it was clear what had convinced her to stay.

It was some moments before either man could drag his gaze away from the vista, but when they did they saw a small wooden hut huddled in the dense vegetation behind them. Tucked in at the far end of the bougainvillea hedge, the back wall of the building was pressed into a niche that had been hacked out of the steep hillside. The front and side porches were open and painted by the bright sunlight shining over the ridgeline. In an old armchair at the far end of the porch sat Mariel.

Jejeune wasn't sure he had ever formed a mental picture of Mariel Huaqua, but it was obvious the woman was nothing like Traz had imagined her to be. Jejeune's friend actually faltered, as if he might take a step back, before fixing on a smile and calling out a greeting in Spanish.

Mariel made no move to rise, but waved the men toward her, nodding her head slowly as if their appearance had confirmed some long-told prophecy. She was short and small-boned, but she held herself upright even as she sat in her chair. There was no sign that age, or life, had bowed her. Her hair was completely grey, hanging down long and straight over her plain linen dress, but otherwise her age could have been anywhere between thirty and double that. Her body could have belonged to any num-ber of women they had seen since they had been in Colombia. But Mariel Huaqua's face would have been unmistakable any-where. The skin was so smooth it appeared flawless. It was free of blemishes of any kind, as far as Jejeune could see, and there were no signs of wrinkles or sagging flesh anywhere. Deep-set within her face were eyes of the palest grey the detective had ever seen.

The woman stared at the men, unspeaking, for a long time. Her eyes seemed drawn to Jejeune in particular. She seemed to be searching his features for something. If she found it, her expression gave no sign. She said something in Spanish and made a gesture with her hand.

"She's asked us to have a seat," said Traz. "She said she's been expecting you."

The men rounded the porch rail and settled in rickety wicker chairs on either side of a small table. Mariel's own chair, an old, stuffing-spewing armchair covered in blankets, sat on the other side of the table, resting against the railing. Hanging from the porch roof were a series of five hummingbird feeders; there were no birds at any of them.

Mariel said something and smiled.

"She says we should have been here five minutes ago. The feeders were alive with birds."

"Where have I heard that before?" asked Jejeune, managing an ironic smile. Now he was here, he was filled with the same kind of uncertainty that had plagued him when he first arrived in Colombia. What was it that he expected this woman, this place, this time, to be able to offer him? He didn't know now, as he didn't know then. But he had already found some of his answers. Perhaps Mariel could provide him with the rest.

Without speaking, the woman rose and disappeared into the hut. It gave Traz a chance to catch Jejeune's eye and gesture at the porch. Along the railing, Mariel had arranged a series of small glass jars, each holding a tiny unlit candle. At the base of the railing was a row of woven wicker baskets bearing indigenous patterns. Traz wagged his finger from the candles to the baskets. "Never wrong," he mouthed.

Mariel returned and handed the men paper cups filled with a murky brown liquid. Traz passed on her message. "It's her homemade blackberry wine. She wants to propose a toast."

Mariel settled in her chair and raised her own cup. "*Hermano Pakisusu.*"

Traz spluttered his drink and laughed so hard there were tears in his eyes. Mariel laughed with him. It was a strange sound, a light, musical thing, like rain falling through a wind chime. Jejeune waited until Traz was ready to translate, but it wasn't with patience.

"To the brother of the bearded bush pig," said Traz. "It doesn't quite roll of the tongue like *JJ*, but I might start using it anyway."

Jejeune looked startled. "Brother? And what did she mean by she'd been expecting me? How does she know who I am?" He half rose in his alarm, but Mariel patted him back into his seat with a tiny hand. She leaned forward, speaking rapidly to Traz with an intensity that she had not used before. When she had finished, she leaned back in her armchair and smiled at Jejeune once more.

"She says not to worry," said Traz, "magical realism is for storybooks. You have the same bone structure as your brother. And she's right, with that beard you have growing, you do look a little like Damian. *Pakisusu* is what the indigenous people down south call the white-lipped peccary — the bearded bush pig. The local people don't have facial hair, so Damian's beard made an impact on them."

Jejeune was silent for a long time. Mariel's reminder that Damian knew the Karijona people from previous visits wounded the detective. Damian had never referred to it, but Domenic could imagine how much worse it must have made things for his brother to know he had brought a community he had spent time with so much pain and sorrow.

Traz stirred as a bird made a lightning foray from a nearby papaya tree onto one of the feeders.

"Above you, JJ, quick. There it is."

Jejeune snapped a glance up and caught sight of the bird as it danced between feeders. A second bird joined it, repeatedly jousting with the first, trying to drive it away from the nectar tube. The tiny green bodies of the two birds glittered in the sunlight, and as they twisted and spun, the watching men were treated to occasional flashes of the pure blue throats. Eventually the first bird retired to the cover of the nearby vegetation, and after a brief victory sip, the other bird spun off in a tight loop and disappeared over the roof of the hut.

"Santa Marta Sabrewing," announced Traz. "Lifer. Could hardly ask for better views either. Excellent." He turned to pass on his pleasure to Mariel. She replied with a smile and a short comment of her own.

"She calls them her little ones. She says she used to ask them why they must fight, when there is plenty for all. But she says this is nature. When you have something, somebody else will try to take it from you."

The history of the world, in a single statement, thought Jejeune sadly. How much of his life had been dedicated to unravelling variations on that same theme. He sipped his wine and made a face.

"She seems quite proud of it," said Traz in a conversational tone meant to disguise the import of his words. "She is obviously expecting you to like it."

Jejeune steeled himself for another sip. He smiled and raised the paper cup appreciatively in the woman's direction. She smoothed her drab dress. *She used to wear bright colours*, thought the detective.

"Is this where you found the Santa Marta Sabrewing for Alex Graumann?" Jejeune asked Mariel directly, knowing Traz would supply the translation. His friend listened to Mariel's answer while Jejeune watched her face carefully. There was no need. Mariel

Huaqua would not lie. He was sure of it. She would tell him only the truth. It was up to him to ask the questions, to unlock the secrets. But if he did, he knew he would receive his answers.

"She didn't live here then," said Traz, "but she played here as a child and knew of it as a place where they could be found. They come in to the bromeliads and the papaya flowers. She says they have always come here. No one ever disturbs them."

Mariel was sipping thoughtfully from her cup, staring out over the valley. Traz murmured a comment and she responded in a low voice, as if there might be something else on her mind. The light was beginning to fade over the distant mountains, and the clouds had taken on the colour of peaches. The faintest of breezes stirred the bushes at the side of the cabin and the shadows on the porch were inching longer. Evening was readying its approach over the valley and Jejeune could sense the change. He eased his leg out in front of him. The aching in his ankle was constant, but it became worse if he stayed in one spot for too long. Another time, he might have even struggled to his feet, just to stretch. But he was ready now, and he would not risk fracturing the atmosphere.

When he spoke to Traz, it was in a voice so low and soft even hummingbirds would not have stirred. "Ask her if she could have found all fourteen birds for Graumann, if she hadn't stopped."

Traz set down his paper cup first. Perhaps he thought these soft gestures with his hands would help. Mariel stirred slightly, like a forest creature sensing something on the breeze. She moved her tiny shoulders slightly, and turned her pale grey eyes on Jejeune even as she answered Traz in Spanish.

"I can only find the ones that choose to show themselves to me."

"But you know where to find them, don't you, Mariel? All of them."

It was almost as if she didn't need Traz's translation. She kept her eyes on Jejeune, seeming barely to pay attention to his friend. *Are you going to ask me?* her look said. *Are you afraid of the answer, Hermano Pakisusu?*

And then Traz had it, the secret that danced like a humming-bird on the electricity between his friend and this woman. Only he didn't have it. "Have you ever seen the Chiribiquete Emerald, Mariel?" he asked, in Spanish, then in English.

Still Mariel stared at Jejeune, her eyes deep seas of grey, endless and timeless. "No. I have never seen this bird."

Traz slumped back, disappointed.

"But you did go to search for it, didn't you?" Even before Traz finished delivering Jejeune's question, the detective saw the light fade from Mariel's eyes. And he knew he had his answer. The one he had come all the way from north Norfolk to find. Here in this tiny hummingbird garden on the side of a mountain, he had found the truth.

Mariel had started to cry. Small round teardrops like tiny pearls ran down her smooth cheeks. But she smiled through them and reached over to press her palm gently to Jejeune's cheek. The ice-cold touch of her hand was startling.

"She says she is grateful for your wisdom," said Traz. "Your question has set her free."

37

Interior design had long been a mystery to Danny Maik, but even he found Laraby's room at The Birder's Roost disquieting. Despite the eerie presence of two stuffed shorebirds in a glass case on a corner shelf, the Dotterel Suite was as forlornly impersonal as any room he had been in for a long time. There were no homely touches, nothing at all, in fact, to relieve the ruthless functionality of the furniture and furnishings. It made the recent contributions of Constable Salter all the more conspicuous.

On the dresser, a basket with a red ribbon around it held a couple of magazines, while on the small occasional table, a wooden bowl held a better variety of fruit than you could reasonably expect to find in Saltmarsh in the middle of winter. On the narrow window ledge, Maik saw a card made of brown construction paper. The cover was a crayon drawing of sunshine and a house. The note inside was simple and to the point: *I hope you get well by saturday love MAX.*

Laraby watched Maik as he read the card. "I might get other cards, but none will ever have a more sincere message," he said, smiling.

"Saturday?"

"I'm taking the lad to the match."

"Ah." Maik replaced the card gently. "Everything okay?" Maik wasn't asking about the DI's health. By his count, Laraby had about half a day left on his enforced leave. Judging by his expression when Maik had entered the room, it was going to be at least half a day too long.

"I'm going mad here, Danny. Things are so bad, I'd even be willing to listen to some of that disco music of yours, if you've brought any with you. I'm hoping you've at least brought me some good news about Oakes. Like he's confessed, for example."

"Not to the murder."

"To what, then?"

Maik told him.

Laraby stared wide-eyed. "Flying a drone around some owl? He expects us do him for that? Over a murder?" Laraby was incredulous. "He knows we have an eyewitness? And he's still maintaining he wasn't at Dawes's cottage that night?"

Laraby looked around as if searching for a place to offer the sergeant to sit. But there was only one chair in the room, an ancient wooden thing with an assortment of clothes and papers sitting on the seat. In the end, Laraby gave up. The sergeant looked comfortable enough on his feet anyway.

"So he offered no proof he was there on the Saturday night? He just told us, and we're supposed to believe it? The word of a decent chap, and all that?"

"It was almost as if he felt he didn't need to provide an alibi."

Something in the way Maik said it had Laraby looking at him. The DI didn't ask, but he didn't say anything else, either. Maik looked outside. A bank of low cloud sat menacingly over the fields to the east. He considered mentioning them, just as a way of deflecting Laraby's intense gaze. But he had started now, and Danny Maik was a person who made sure he finished things whenever he could.

"James has form. It didn't come up in our searches for Connor James, but when we ran them again for James Connor, there it was. A couple of ASBOs for disorderly conduct, but there was a domestic on there, too, and an assault with a deadly weapon. No convictions, but it shows he knows his way around the violent side of things."

Laraby sat down on the edge of the bed and rubbed his face with his hands. But it was not distress, merely contemplation. "We never escape our past, do we, Danny? No matter how hard we try, how far we run, it's always with us. Change our name, change our appearance, it makes no difference. It's a part of us, and we're doomed to carry it with us, wherever we go." He shook his head. 'No, Danny. It's Oakes. We've got his DNA at the scene and an eyewitness who can put him there at the time of the murder. He's our killer. I can feel it."

Maik perched on the edge of the window ledge and twisted slightly to look out the window. A listlessness seemed to lay over the landscape, as if it was exhausted by its struggles to withstand the cold and the winds. Maik was silent for so long, Laraby wondered if there was something the sergeant wasn't telling him. Bad news, perhaps. "The girl, Forsyth, no last-minute doubts about what she saw? Not suddenly remembered her assailant had a second head, nothing like that?"

From his window ledge perch, Maik shook his head. "She's not wavering on her statement at all. There's little doubt she's going to select Oakes from that line-up."

"Then it's all over, regardless of what he claims about harassing some helpless bird. I suppose that clears up one mystery. All this interest in DCI Jejeune. *Where is he? When's he coming back?* He was looking to unload this drivel on him, hoping to get a sympathetic hearing from a fellow member of the birder brotherhood."

"Oakes is more of a photographer. I'm not sure they consider themselves as part of the same group."

"'Course they do, all part of the same old boy network, always looking out for each other, sticking together, protecting one another's interests. Must have come as a bit of a shock when us two came up to question him instead, eh?"

It had grown darker in the room. Maik's own bulk blocking off half the window wasn't helping, but the clouds were gathering outside, hunkering low, smothering the light from the sky. Maik stood up, careful not to disturb Max's card. He walked over to the shelf where the Dotterels stared out from their glass prison. "Just the two of you? Going to the match?"

Laraby nodded. "His mom's off at a class on drone surveillance. She seems very keen on all this business, I must say. Still, she's a bright woman, so it's understandable she'd be interested in broadening her horizons."

He looked out the window, at the frost-hardened fields stretching out beneath the cloud cover toward the faint dark smudge of hedgerows in the distance.

"It's not our game, is it Danny," he said quietly, "all this drones and cyber criminals and offices on your cellphone? We're more comfortable doing things the old way, you and me, kicking a few arses, taking a few names. What we want is a place to sit and watch the changing world slide on by, leaving us alone to do our job the way we want to do it, the way we know it should be done." He looked at Maik. "There are worse places than Saltmarsh to do that."

"Ever come across anyone named Ray Hayes?" If Maik's slow wandering around the room was a way of taking attention away from his question, it didn't prevent Laraby from tracking him with his eyes. There weren't many places in the tiny room you could have hidden anything, the significance of an inquiry included.

"Ray Hayes? Now there's a blast from the past. A real piece of work, Mr. Hayes. There are some villains who don't really understand why they do things, and then there's some who just can't help themselves. But few enjoy it as much as Hayes. He used to like to let his victims know he was coming for them. Give 'em a couple of warnings first, just to terrorize them a bit. I haven't thought about him for a long time, I'm happy to say, now that he's safely inside."

"Your doing?" Maik found something interesting in the display case, the birds' plumage, perhaps. He leaned in for a closer look as Laraby continued talking to his back.

"Me and your DCI. We did him on a murder. He blew most of a woman's house into the neighbour's garden, with her still inside it. I let Sergeant Jejeune interview Hayes when we brought him in. It was the first time I'd ever seen him in action." He nodded his head at the memory. "Old Ray was in his element at first. He saw it as a meeting of the minds, communing with a fellow intellectual. Hayes was clever, you see. The TV would have you think we're dealing with Rhodes Scholars all the time, but clever villains don't come my way all that often. Hayes was an exception. He enjoyed being the brightest one in the room, and Jejeune let him think he was, at first. But it wasn't too long before he had Hayes contradicting himself left, right, and centre." He shook his head. "It didn't go down well. Hayes didn't take too kindly to some jumped-up sergeant with a funny accent showing him up every time he opened his mouth." A thought seemed to come to Laraby suddenly. "Why are we talking about Ray Hayes anyway?"

Why, indeed? Up until a few minutes ago, Danny had no idea. But he did now. A man from Jejeune's past, with a history of setting explosions.

"Just a name that came up," said Danny. He turned and came to the window again. Outside, the light was all but gone, the clouds so low it was as if they were sagging with the effort of holding up the sky. "I was thinking, if that Barn Owl's a regular around the ruins, there might be one or two of the local birders who'd gone out to see it on Saturday. They could tell us if Oakes was there or not."

"Perhaps we could get the DCS's boyfriend to ask around. He's a birder, isn't he? Another one of Jejeune's mates? He and the DCI are all part of some cliquey birding club, I suppose. It's a wonder you haven't joined them yourself, Danny. Give your career prospects a bit of a boost with the Super."

"I'm not sure birding would be much of a positive with the DCS these days. I don't think her partner's interest in it has brought them any closer."

"Is that a fact?"

Maik regarded the inspector carefully. He wondered what it was about him that encouraged these indiscretions. Whatever magic Laraby managed to weave with his questions, if criminals in the interview room found it as hard to keep their mouths shut as Danny, he could well understand why Laraby's closure rate was as high as it was.

38

Night descended over Picaflor with the stealth of a hunting animal, inching into the valley below and consuming the mountains as the pink-tinged clouds faded into the darkness. Mariel lit the candles along the porch rail. Fireflies danced in the distance and the steady trill of night insects began to fill the still, warm air around them.

Mariel had not cried aloud. She had let the tears fall freely from her cheeks as the two men sat in silence beside her. But the tears had stopped after a while, and she had started to speak, slowly and earnestly. At first, Traz had tried to translate on the fly, but Jejeune had stopped him. Nothing should interrupt Mariel's words, escaping from her now, after being held inside for so long. Freed from the need to pause, she poured out the details in rapid-fire Spanish now, barely halting for breath. It was as if she wanted to purge herself of these memories, to cleanse herself of them, every detail, every deceit. But Jejeune knew Traz would forget none of it. The intensity of Mariel's delivery would etch her account on his soul. He knew his friend would remember it all, every phrase, every word.

Jejeune had no idea how long they sat there with the flickering candlelight dancing across Mariel's face as she leaned forward to emphasize a point or rocked back into the shadows as a sad memory visited her. His ankle began to throb, but he dared not move, unwilling to disturb Mariel, or her narrative, or even the soft night air itself. So he sat, listening to the cadences of her voice, the rise and fall of a language he did not understand, though he already knew the meaning of her words.

Only when she had finished, rid herself of her burden, did Mariel stop talking. She sat in silence for many minutes, sunk back in the armchair, her memories wrapped around her in the darkness like a shawl. The flames from the candles guttered slightly in the evening air, reflecting off her flawless, shiny skin. The insects continued their trills; the faintest of breezes shuffled the leaves of the bougainvillea. But nobody spoke.

And then Mariel stood. "Food," she announced, disappearing into the hut. By the light of the candles, Traz began to tell Jejeune Mariel's story. He used her words exactly, her phrasing, her inflections. It was as if he had become a vessel to deliver the story only. Jejeune did not interrupt him.

"At first I thought it was *soroche*, altitude sickness. We had just returned from finding the Blue-bearded Helmetcrest, and it was a hard trip. *Dios mio*, three days on horseback up to the Espeletia fields. We camped and it was cold at night, very cold. When we came down, Graumann was shivering and sweating in turns. We came here, for the Santa Marta Sabrewing and the Blossomcrown. He seemed to recover, but by Urrao I knew he was ill again. He was sleeping later and later each day. To see other birds, this would have been a problem, but hummingbirds love the sun. They feed all the time; morning, noon, evening."

It was unnecessary information, facts Jejeune already knew, and delivering it seemed to snap Traz back into the present. He began telling the story as a narrator.

"She called the company from Urrao. They said to continue. Graumann was paying them a lot of money. She never did find out how much, but they promised her more for herself if she carried on. She told them she thought Graumann should go back to Bogota first, to get some medical treatment. By now she could sense his sickness, smell it in him."

Traz paused and looked at Jejeune. "The way she said it, JJ, I believe her."

Jejeune simply nodded, though whether his friend could see the gesture in the low light of the candles he didn't know. Traz continued anyway. "After a day of rest in Urrao, Graumann seemed to rally. He told her he was okay, but that he wanted to go to Chiribiquete next. It was going to be the hardest part of the trip, and he wanted to get it over with. They went by Jeep and canoe. It took them four days. But Graumann was getting weaker all the time. In the park, they met a family of Karijona. They said the river was high and the mud along the banks was hard to walk through. She asked them if they had any traditional medicine that might help Graumann, but as soon as they looked at him, they told her he would die if he tried to make the trip. The Karijona went with her in the canoe and helped her to get him back to where she had left the Jeep. When Mariel and Graumann arrived back in Bogota, she called the company to tell them what had happened. The next day somebody called her at the hotel and told her if anybody asked, she was to say she had quit in Urrao. They said not to tell anyone she had been to Chiribiquete, or she would be in trouble. They told her to leave the man in the hotel room and they would send someone to help him. She wrote up some trip notes and left them in the room. She never saw Graumann, or anybody from the company, again."

Jejeune struggled up from the chair and hobbled along the porch. He looked out over the hillside. Only an occasional speck of light disturbed the darkness in the valley, a tiny hint of human habitation, all but swallowed up by the surrounding blackness. Far below, a thin trail of lights traced the Santa Marta coastline, but beyond, all was black space, the vast empty nothingness of the ocean. A flash of lightning lit up the sky in the distance, but it was so far off no sound reached them. A wave of fatigue washed over him, and he felt unsteady suddenly, as if something that had been supporting him had been removed. He reached out shakily for the porch railing until Traz appeared at his side and guided him gently back to his chair.

Through the open doorway of the hut they could hear the sounds of food being prepared. A smell of warm rice and beans drifted out, and Jejeune realized he was hungry. He couldn't remember the last time he had eaten. He was surprised that Traz, who observed mealtimes with an almost religious devotion, hadn't mentioned it. Mariel appeared at the doorway with two plates for them. She handed them out and returned for her own. They ate, balancing the plates on their knees and swilling down the food with blackberry wine.

"The person Mariel spoke to at the office, who told her what to do," said Jejeune, "could it have been someone who wasn't a native Spanish speaker?" He recoiled from his own question slightly, uncomfortable at leading a witness like this. But Mariel didn't understand — you spoke Spanish or you did not. This person, this *hombre*, Jejeune heard, spoke Spanish.

The three sat in silence, eating quietly, hunched over their plates. Not until she had finished her food did Mariel speak again. It was a softer statement now, less emphatic, more tinged with sorrow.

"She didn't hear about the Karijona deaths for a few weeks," Traz relayed, "and when she did, she heard that Damian had caused them. She heard he'd confessed. She believed it for a while. But then she stopped believing it." Traz paused. "She says she has known the truth for a long time."

The truth. The evidence that exonerated his brother, the evidence Jejeune had always known would exist, somehow, even when he had no reason to believe it. No one had ever been able to verify exact dates for the deaths of the Karijona, but it was days, at most, after Damian's contact with them. And now, here it was, evidence of earlier contact with the same source of infection. Testified to. Admitted. Witnessed. The dates of Mariel's visit, he knew, would be an exact match for the incubation period for bacterial meningococcal meningitis when he researched it.

Traz set his plate down on the floor beside his chair and looked at his friend. "You know what you have to do, JJ," he said, his voice even and soft. "Let's take care of it now, then we can get you back to the hotel room. You need to rest."

Jejeune shook his head. "She won't do it."

"She has no choice. She committed a crime your brother has been charged with. Maybe they'll go easy on her. Nobody's saying it was deliberate. But she has to admit to it. It's the right thing to do, the human thing."

The human thing. So often acting like a human being was upheld as a positive, but in Jejeune's world, human beings were capable of the worst kinds of depravity. That was acting like a human being, too. What about asking Mariel, this frail, sad, simple woman, to sacrifice her home in this paradise, to swap it for a life in a prison cell? Was that, too, the human thing to do?

Traz spoke to Mariel slowly, deliberately, without urgency or insistence. He listened to her answer, nodding to acknowledge it, nothing more.

"I told her she has to come with us to the police, to tell them the truth about what happened. But she says if she does, the authorities will take this place away from her. And for what? Damian has already confessed to the crime."

"She's right," said Jejeune quietly. "Damian did all the things he's accused of, going to Chiribiquete despite being denied a licence, taking a man with a communicable illness, contacting the Karijona."

"But Graumann was already sick when *she* took him there. She could sense it."

"Unless she's a medical professional, her opinion would carry no weight. The man declared himself fit to travel. Even when the illness reaches the stage where it's going to be fatal, it still may not manifest itself fully. She can't have known for sure what was causing his sickness at that time."

"It introduces an element of doubt, surely. Maybe enough for them to clear Damian, or at least reduce the charges. You have to convince her, Dom. You have to try. Despite all you've done for him, you owe it to Damian."

"No," said Jejeune simply. "Tell her she doesn't have to testify. But tell her she must not stay here. Mas Aves think it was me who found her address on that computer. If they find out I was rescued from that pit, they're going to assume I came looking for her. Mariel's the only one who could tell me, or the authorities, what really happened."

"She's already said she will refuse to testify."

"Mas Aves may not want to take her word for that. If she stays here she could be in danger, Traz. It's not safe for her to be up here all alone. How much cash to do you have on you?"

"None. It's back at the hotel room."

Jejeune eased his leg out straight and fished uncomfortably into his pocket for a moment, drawing out some crumpled bills.

"There's a few thousand pesos there, maybe a hundred dollars. Tell her to take it and go somewhere safe. Just for a few days. Once Mas Aves know I have the whole story, it will be too late to try to silence her."

Traz looked at Jejeune incredulously. "She's your brother's only hope for justice, JJ. And you want to give her money so she can go into hiding?"

But he didn't sound angry. And there was a strange understanding in his face when he looked at Jejeune again. "You don't do much for my love life, but I can think of worse things than being your friend."

39

Maik was watching from the window in Jejeune's office as the new Jaguar XF swept into the car park. Even though it was cold, the window was open a crack, just as DCI Jejeune liked it. Through it, Maik could hear the various noises of approval as Salter and Shepherd came down the steps to greet DI Laraby.

"Got to have something to run around in for a few days, haven't I, now that Sergeant Maik's Mini is out of commission? I thought I'd treat myself. Besides, I've got a very important appointment to keep on Saturday."

He looked knowingly at Salter, and from his vantage point, Maik saw the exchange register with Shepherd. She would mis-interpret the situation, he knew, but the signals she would get would be accurate anyway.

There had been a shift in the landscape at Saltmarsh Station during Laraby's absence. It was as if his injuries in the line of duty had earned him a place among them now. DCS Shepherd was regarding him with that same look of solicitous concern she bestowed on the rest of her team at such times.

"And you're sure you're okay to return to work? We do value your contributions, but —"

"But you don't want me stumbling around all fuzzy-headed and confused. Any more than usual, anyway," he said with a grin. "It'll take more than a conk on the old noggin to put me out of action. The MO has given me the all-clear. I have to say, though, whoever came up with that Concussion Protocol has got the right idea. You can't be too careful with head injuries."

Maik was pretty sure it had come up in conversation just whose initiative the Concussion Protocol was. But perhaps it had just slipped Laraby's mind, a minor effect of that conk on the old noggin. Shepherd wasn't about to point out whose idea it was, but she hadn't missed the comment. She returned to the building with a satisfied smile, leaving Salter alone with Laraby. Maik couldn't hear their murmured exchange and withdrew from the window, not wanting to be a part of it. But it would have been hard to miss the radiant smile Salter was showing Laraby upon his return. Or the message it conveyed.

Maik was still in Jejeune's office when Laraby entered. The sergeant seemed to have something important to say, but the way he was studying a Saltmarsh skyline he must have seen a thousand times was a clue that he wasn't going to come right out with it yet.

"Another cold one out there, Sergeant. I'll bet this place sees some punishing temperatures when the storms come in off the sea."

The weather wasn't one of Maik's favourite topics, but it would do for now.

"Sometimes, it seems like it's colder out here on the clear days. I've been out there in bright sunshine when the air is so cold it takes your breath away."

Laraby nodded and moved to take a seat behind the desk. *Jejeune's chair,* thought Maik. *In Jejeune's office.*

"I saw an impressive example of high-end legal talent in the waiting room as I came in. Oakes's brief, I take it, here for the formal ID?"

Maik confirmed that it was.

"Good. As soon as we get that, he's ours. With Oakes's life-style, flitting off to America and back all the time, I can't see a judge granting bail." He nodded to himself. "It'll give us time to come up with a motive. We'll start with a relationship gone south and work backward from there."

From the window, a stream of pale light painted a trail across the hardwood floor to the desk, and to Laraby behind it. Maik looked at the DI. "The cup left in the kitchen, the one with Oakes's DNA on it, James has a set of them in the galley on *The Big Deal*," he said. "But there are only five. It seems like an odd number."

Laraby eased the chair back from the desk slightly and thought for a moment. "James blames Dawes for ruining his reputation. But if he's going to kill her, he needs to pin it on someone. When Oakes goes round to the boat to pick up his drone, James offers him tea and saves the cup to plant it later?" He looked up at Maik. "Is that where we're going with this, Danny? Or did Oakes pinch the cup off James when he was there? Took it as payment for that photo he gave him, per-haps?" He gave Maik a smile, to let him know he was joking, and switched direction so abruptly it took Maik a second to realize the question was directed to him.

"Was it DCI Jejeune who asked about Ray Hayes?"

Maik froze at the window. The answer would tell Laraby that he'd been in touch with Jejeune. He wasn't one for babbling explanations of his conduct, but the inference was clear; Danny had been providing progress reports to the DCI while he was away. And perhaps he had, if not quite in the way Laraby would have understood it.

He turned to face the DI, who had pushed himself farther away from the desk, letting the wheels of the chair roll him where they would. He sat now with his hands folded in his lap — a man with forever at his disposal — to wait for the truth.

"He didn't say why," said Maik.

"No, but I think we both know, don't we? That explosion." Laraby shook his head. "I've been giving it some thought since you brought his name up. It wasn't Hayes. That explosion was against the wall directly alongside the desk of that girl, what's her name … Lindy? If she'd have been sitting there, she'd have been killed outright." For the second time in as many moments, Laraby shook his head. "That's not Hayes's style. I told you, he likes to stalk them first, let them know he's coming. That woman he killed, a week before it happened, her car had caught fire inside her garage. They put it down to a spark off a worn battery cable. Then a propane tank went off in her garden shed. Faulty seal. She knew it was Hayes. He'd told her he'd be coming for her after they broke up. She couldn't eat, couldn't sleep. She pleaded with the investigating officers to listen to her." Laraby fell silent for a moment, gazing at some inner landscape that he seemed reluctant to visit. There was a long beat of silence before he spoke again. "But you know how it is, we were busy with other cases, and she was a bit hysterical to begin with, so …." It took some effort, but Laraby brought himself back to the present. "There'd been no previous incidents with this Lindy, had there?"

"There's none on file." Jejeune had never mentioned any either, and Maik was pretty sure something like that would've made it into the DCI's pre-departure briefing.

Laraby smiled a little, as if he had been watching for something in Maik, and had perhaps seen it. "Can I ask you something? Do you ever wonder why DCI Jejeune never mentions me?" From his low-slung position in Jejeune's chair,

Laraby raised his eyebrows as he looked at Maik. "His mentor, the one who showed him the ropes. You must have wondered about it, a smart copper like you. Oh, don't worry," he said, as Maik stirred uneasily and cast a glance at the door, "I won't be roping you into our little drama. But you've worked with me. Any reason you can see why you and I couldn't get along?"

"No."

Laraby's question was a reasonable one. It deserved an honest answer, and Maik had no reason to avoid giving one. So why did it feel like any answer he could have given the DI would have been wrong?

"I value loyalty, Danny. A lot." Laraby leaned forward a little, striving for sincerity. It was an incongruous arrangement for such a conversation, thought Danny fleetingly, the DI sitting in a chair in the centre of the room and Danny standing half an office away. There was an awkwardness about it that didn't seem right. "If you had been asked to look into Ray Hayes, I wouldn't have any problem with that. I can tell you he's wrong. Hayes didn't have anything to do with this. It's an accident, just as it appears to be. But it's his girl, and I understand. If he wanted you to have a poke around, it wouldn't change my opinion of you. You're still an officer I'd be happy to have on my staff. All I'd ask is that you come to me directly. Let me know what you're up to. That's all."

Any comment Maik was going to offer was stilled by a hesitant knock on the door and Constable Salter poking her head around without waiting for an answer. The sunshine smiles from the car park had disappeared. She looked like she would rather not be here. Laraby stood up. He made no move to approach her, but he slid his hands into his trouser pockets and straightened his back.

"I'm not going to like this, am I?" he asked with a thin smile.

"No."

Laraby waited. Pauses for dramatic effect were part of Salter's repertoire, but Maik recognized this as the real thing: hesitation.

"There's been a development, sir. Some kids found a bag on the riverbank, snagged on an overhanging branch. There was a set of clothes inside. A cap and a leather jacket. The cap has some makeup on it. We're checking now, but we're pretty sure it's Gillian Forsyth's. As far as they can tell, both items are brand new. No signs of wear at all."

Laraby looked at Maik. "Bought for the purpose, then?"

The tension in the room was palpable, but Maik could tell Salter wasn't finished. From his slowly forming look of concern, Laraby had come to the same conclusion.

"There was something else in the bag, too. A false moustache and beard — a goatee like Robin Oakes's."

Laraby considered the information for a long time.

"Any prints, Constable?" asked Maik.

Salter nodded. "A lot on the clothes; the kids showed the stuff to their teachers, their parents. The thing is, we've eliminated all those, and there's still one set left. On the jacket."

"Just one?"

Salter's silence answered Laraby.

"Even with all my years of experience, I couldn't tell you who that set of prints belongs to, Constable Salter," he said quietly. "But I can tell you who it doesn't. It's not Robin Oakes, is it?"

"No, sir. Not him." Something in the way she said it revealed the truth. Even before Maik had formed the words of the question, he knew the answer. And Laraby did, too.

"Positive ID?"

Salter nodded. "One hundred percent. The prints belong to Connor James."

40

If there was a sense of casual decay in Bogota's old quarter, it was not accompanied by hopelessness. In the glimpses of former glories afforded Domenic Jejeune as he walked past the once-magnificent structures, there was a certain stateliness to the decline. There seemed to be an inevitability to it all, as if the gradual slipping away of the old buildings was part of some natural order. In Colombia, so much of the new was being built on top of the old; it was as if the country's history was nurturing the growth of the coming era.

Jejeune had taken this early-morning stroll around the near-deserted streets surrounding the hotel as a way of combatting his restlessness, but his ankle was starting to throb again, and it was time to return to his room. With each passing hour, his conviction grew that his appeal to the Colombian Attorney General would be declined. He had spent an afternoon in a small air-conditioned office some-where deep in the bowels of the Colombian Ministry of Justice and Law. The prevailing sentiment seemed to be that any special consideration to which his rank may have entitled him had been used up in securing this video conference. His cache of goodwill was empty now, and his case would be considered on its merits only.

He had painstakingly gone through his explanation with the representative of the AG's office; the desire of a dying man to see the fourteen Colombian endemic hummingbirds, the offer of a bonus a sign that money was no longer his major consideration; rather, time was.

"Although Mariel Huaqua had told Mas Aves that Graumann was very sick, they had no reason to suspect his illness was contagious. He'd travelled with Mariel Huaqua and she showed no signs of infection. But she had spent a lot of time in cities, in hospitals. She has a modern-world immune system and had likely been vaccinated against many diseases. But the company did know Graumann was too sick to travel, and that whatever he was suffering from, he shouldn't have been allowed to come into contact with the Karijona. They knew if they revealed to Damian that Graumann had been forced to return from Chiribiquete once because of illness, my brother would not have taken him the second time. So they made up the story that Mariel had quit in Urrao and told Graumann to stay silent about his previous trip."

But Jejeune had always known that the word of a man desperate enough to come to Colombia in an effort to exonerate his brother would not be enough. The glitchy quality of the video feed gave the movements of the head on the screen a robotic feel. The representative's English was equally mechanical.

"But there is no one willing to verify this earlier visit to Chiribiquete? The Karijona who you claim came into contact with this man are dead, as is Graumann himself. And this guide, Mariel Huaqua, she has not come forward to support this version of events." Though the pixilated face betrayed no expression, the voice sounded surprised, perhaps even a little affronted, that Jejeune would come without such proof. "You must understand, Inspector, it is not that I doubt your word, but this case has gained national attention. There are questions which touch the government's duty of care to its indigenous peoples. To turn this into a matter about one man's desire to see a rare bird ..." Two grainy hands appeared at the sides of the screen. "However, this decision is not mine. I will relay your position to the relevant authorities for their consideration. You will be contacted with their decision in due course."

Jejeune watched the slowly disappearing screen for a moment after the man had signed off, wondering whether his hopes, too, were doomed to fade into nothingness.

As he approached the hotel, he saw a yellow taxi idling at the curb. Traz was waiting for him in the lobby. "I thought we could take a trip out to Casa de Colibries again. We can grab breakfast in La Calera on the way. I'd like another shot at seeing the Sword-billed."

Jejeune smiled. It was probably true, although the way Traz was fervently over-selling the idea suggested he was just looking to avoid another day of lounging around the hotel lobby, waiting for *due course* to produce an answer from the Justice Department that Jejeune was increasingly certain was going to be negative.

As they took their place at a small table in the courtyard, Traz looked around anxiously.

"They won't be coming," Jejeune assured him. "My guess is the Waldens left the country as soon as you disappeared from the tour. They must have suspected you were going to try to find me. Carl Walden, at least, would have been on the first plane out. Thea wouldn't have wanted her father around to answer questions if you decided to go to the police."

Traz had pieced together most of what Jejeune suspected, but there were still small gaps, pockets of darkness on to which the DCI had shone no light. It wasn't as if either of them had the appetite to discuss matters much. Their conversations had dwelled more and more in the past recently; their reminiscences of college days and early birding trips a refuge from what they had experienced together recently.

"One of the constants in my conversation with the deputy attorney general's representative was the idea that a foreigner was responsible for this tragedy among the Karijona. Indigenous rights issues are still a delicate topic for the Colombian authorities. They have to be seen to be protecting groups like the Karijona. As far as the Colombian prosecutors are concerned, having a foreigner to indict for the deaths was a big plus, politically."

Traz nodded. "Walden's an American. Maybe a different foreigner would fit the bill just as well if they decided to let Damian off the hook?"

"I'm sure that's the way Thea saw it. I'm not convinced they'd be so eager to consider a man with a Colombian wife and daughter a foreigner in that sense, but she wasn't going to take any chances. Whatever her father knew about the Mas Aves involvement ..." The detective's pause left Traz in no doubt what Jejeune believed, "Walden's American passport would put him directly in the firing line if the charges against Damian were ever dropped."

The same waitress as before brought them coffee, setting the tray down with a demure smile. The men looked around as they sipped from the tiny cups. Sunlight dappled the courtyard just as before, and full sun fell on the banks of fuschia and passiflora against the wall. Despite this, the courtyard seemed devoid of birds. Traz commented on it, and Jejeune pointed up to the sky. "There's always *chulos*," he said.

"Black Vultures, JJ. They deserve some respect."

Jejeune was surprised by the earnestness of his friend's response. He watched as the large black birds soared effortlessly on the thermals, their extended wingtips gently filtering the winds. "Not many people would agree with you. Vultures are probably the most reviled family of birds in the world."

Traz moved his shoulders easily. "All I'm saying is they have their place, just like all the other birds. How's your coffee?"

Jejeune had acquired a taste for shade-grown Colombian coffee. He could not imagine himself drinking any other kind now, even when he returned home. Lindy would roll her eyes at the prospect of tracking it down in the Saltmarsh area. But he knew she would find some, and both this country's economy and its songbirds would benefit, however slightly.

"It may not work out how you'd like, JJ, but you got what you came for," said Traz quietly. "You cleared Damian. Maybe not in the eyes of the law, but in yours. And in Damian's, too. Besides, it's not over yet."

Jejeune was quiet. "They can create enough doubt to acquit, if that's what they decide they want to do. They can look at the incubation period for bacterial meningococcal meningitis and see it matches up with the dates I gave them."

"You didn't tell them?"

"They need to come to it themselves. If they need a reason to find Damian not guilty, they won't want it to be one I brought them. People are always willing to fight harder to validate evidence they discover for themselves."

"And if they don't?"

Jejeune didn't answer. Instead, he stared past Traz, over his shoulder. His expression made Traz turn round so quickly he almost tipped over his chair.

"Your brother is a good man," said Mariel. "He has kindness in his heart. He cannot be punished for this."

She was wearing a red sequined top that flashed with irridescence. Across her brow was an embroidered multicoloured headband. Violet beaded earrings dangled from her tiny ears.

As she approached the table, the dazzling sunlight danced across her scarlet top like flames.

There was a tiny scream from the edge of the courtyard, and the waitress ran across to Mariel, embracing her tightly. They talked animatedly for a moment, the waitress brushing tears from the corners of her eyes. As she left, Mariel sat with the men, smiling at them.

"This is a place of healing," she said. "A place of much magic."

Jejeune was nodding his agreement even before Traz finished translating.

The waitress returned with Mariel's coffee and a plate of dulche de leche muffins. Jejeune eased the plate closer to Mariel and himself. Traz was one of the most well-mannered men he had ever known, but with these treats, the detective knew he could take no chances.

Mariel pointed to a small passiflora bush almost at Traz's elbow. "Ah, your bird comes," she told him. A Sword-billed Hummingbird danced into view, its bill as long as the glittering green body that shimmered every time it banked and caught the light.

"Worth the wait," said Traz, barely breathing the words. He drew his eyes away long enough to see Jejeune watching the bird too. His friend's shining eyes and soft smile matched his own.

The garden seemed alive with other birds now, too. Woodstars and Violetears darted from the cover of nearby bushes and snatched drinks from the dangling flowers before retreating to roost once more in amongst the shady branches.

"You brought the birds with you, Mariel," Jejeune told her. "Until you came we were reduced to watching these." He indicated the vultures above. Even without translation, Mariel seemed to understand. She watched the vultures for a moment, speaking to Traz without taking her eyes off them.

"She says they wait for their prey to cross the line between life and death," said Traz. "It is the thinnest line of all."

Mariel's eyes were drawn to the scarred hillsides around La Calera. "Life. Death. Birds. Forests. Once, trees covered these hillsides," she said. "Where can the birds go, if we take away their homes? The forest has a heart, and it is breaking."

They sat for a long time, saying nothing, sipping their coffees and eating their muffins. The late-morning sun was inching higher, but it lacked its fire today. It was a warm, benevolent thing, a healer for Jejeune's red skin, rather than a tormentor. Birds flew around their heads, so close they could hear the faint buzz of the wings and the tiny chips and tics as they passed. *Healing.* Jejeune doubted he could have found any place on earth so tranquil, so soothing, on this soft tropical morning.

Mariel finished her coffee and stood up. A flurry of birds departed from the flowers behind her, where they had been feeding. She looked out at the land again, at the huge swaths of denuded hillsides. "The native people believe the forest will one day be saved by hummingbirds," she told Traz, knowing he would pass on her words. "*Colibries con cuatro alas.* They will come to replant the forests and restore them to health." She nodded to herself, sighing, and said something else.

"She will go to the authorities now. She will tell them what she knows." Traz said something to her, and she replied. "I told her she was doing a good thing. She said it was you who did the good thing. She wishes you and your brother peace."

Mariel reached out and touched Jejeune's cheek, as she had that night on her porch. Her hand was warm now.

Jejeune smiled his thanks as she stood up, and the two men watched the tiny form of Mariel Huaqua walk out of their lives.

"*Colibries con cuatro alas,* she said. What does that mean?" asked Jejeune.

"Hummingbirds with four wings." The Sword-billed Hummingbird approached again, and the two men watched it,

holding, hovering, then finally reversing away from the passiflora flower in a masterpiece of precision flying. Traz shrugged.
"Who knows? This is a place of much magic, JJ, where birds can
fly backward and upside down. Look at this one, a bill longer
than its body, perfectly formed to feed off certain flowers. I
wouldn't want to say anything is impossible here."

He watched the bird fly away. "*My bird*, she called it. Did
you tell her we'd missed the Sword-billed when we came here
before?"

Jejeune shook his head slowly. "I don't think so. I don't know.
We talked about a lot of things that night, Traz. We were both
tired. Perhaps one of us said something."

He lapsed into thought. *Perhaps.* But as far as Jejeune was
aware, they hadn't told anyone they were coming here today.
Maybe Traz had mentioned it to the hotel receptionist, offering
her his special smile, as he was waiting for Jejeune to return
from his morning walk. But Jejeune would have imagined his
friend had better things to discuss with the girl than their destination for the morning.

He looked at Traz now, taking in the magical surround-
ings of Casa de Colibries as it basked in the soft shadows
and the warm tropical light. After a moment's reflection, he
decided not to ask.

41

The water was as still as Danny Maik could remember seeing it. Reflections of the dry yellow grasses along the bank lay motionless on the silvery sheen of the river's surface. Over the fields on the far side, a watery sun hung in the sky. Beneath it, nothing moved.

It was a watching brief; not one of Maik's favourite activities, but part of the job from time to time. Laraby had understandably wanted to handle the arrest of James himself, and he had taken a couple of uniforms with him. If there was a surprise, it was that DCS Shepherd had gone along with them, leaving Maik and Salter to watch the towpath next to the river. If James spotted the arrest team moving in and decided to make a run for it, this is the way he would come.

Next to him, in the driver's seat, Salter sat deep in thought.

"I don't believe I ever thanked you," said Maik. "For shoving me out of the way of that drone."

It was obvious that it was difficult for him to revisit the memory, not for the incident, but for what had happened immediately afterwards, when he had struck her.

Salter touched her top lip reflexively now, though there was no visible wound. She gave him a small smile. "It's what we do, isn't it, watch each other's backs, look out for the ones we care about?" She turned away slightly. "That road widening they're doing around Fakenham, once it's done I reckon you could do the drive from here to King's Lynn in about forty minutes, even in rush hour."

Maik nodded. "Likely, though I don't know why you would want to."

"I've been thinking about this sergeant's exam. If I passed, it would mean I'd have to change stations. Unless you've got any plans for early retirement?"

"Not voluntary ones," said Maik, matching the jokey tone, even if he could detect the other tenor behind it.

"I wouldn't want Max to have to change schools, so either King's Lynn Constabulary or Norwich Central would be my best options."

"Sounds like you've been considering this for a while." Maik's delivery didn't suggest what he thought about this.

"I've been here more than fifteen years, Sarge. Even killers get shorter sentences than that," she said. "I think it might be time for a change — personal and professional."

The response might have encouraged another person to follow up, but she knew Danny wouldn't. *Even now, Danny, when I'm telling you I'm going. Even now, as I'm telling you I have to try to find my happiness with someone else, a detective inspector who might ask. Who might care about me.*

"Well," said Maik, inclining his head, "as long as you were sure you were doing it for the right reasons."

"Thanks," she said, more tersely than she intended. She looked at him now, staring out the window at the barren, lifeless fields. She had given him one last chance, and Danny had failed to grasp it. As he always did.

"Can I ask you something? Do you ever wonder why DI Laraby and Inspector Jejeune fell out?" Even Salter seemed uncertain as to where the question had come from. Was this about Jejeune, or Laraby? Perhaps she wasn't really sure herself.

Maik continued to look out at the still, silent water. He thought it might be to do with notions of entitlement and privilege, somehow. The way the establishment rallied around the DCI, held him as one of their own, as Laraby seemed to imagine the aristocratic classes did with each other. But Danny Maik was reluctant enough to share any sort of speculation about superior officers. Casual thoughts like these would never see the light of day.

"Of all the men you know, who would you say is the least likely to have an affair with a married woman?"

Maik's expression suggested it wasn't a question he had struggled with much recently. But Salter wasn't one for non sequiturs. A nice steady progression in linear thought was the constable's forte. Except she couldn't possibly be connecting this idea to her earlier question, could she?

Before Maik could come up with an answer himself, or get one from Salter, his phone rang. It was Shepherd. "He's coming your way, Sergeant. He'll be appearing in view any second."

Maik didn't think so. Even at a good clip it was going to take James at least a minute to get here. He and Salter would be well prepared by then. But then he saw it, just as Shepherd spoke again: *The Big Deal*, coming around the bend in the river, gathering speed.

"He was casting off just as we pulled up," Shepherd told him, breathing hard into her phone as she ran back to the car. "You need to find a way to stop him, Sergeant. If he gets to open water, he'll be gone before we can get a search team out here."

Maik didn't bother replying. He was already out of the car, sprinting along the towpath. Salter was right behind him.

It was the only chance he would have. The high iron bridge spanning the river just beyond the next curve. James was already manoeuvring the boat to the centre of the waterway, where clearance beneath the bridge would be highest. Even as Maik began mounting the steps up to the bridge, he could see the water moving, the silky surface lifting over ripples pushed out from the bow of the boat as it carved its way through the water. At the base of the steps, Salter waited, uncertain. Was he intending to call out to James from the bridge? What good would that do? Danny had a fairly good line in intimidation, but she could hardly see a fleeing murder suspect being cowed enough to heave to because of it.

Farther along the bank, she saw two cars bounce out of a narrow laneway and spin onto the towpath. They were heading toward them at high speed, Laraby's Jag in the lead, the uniforms following in their patrol car. Salter looked back out to the water. *The Big Deal* was almost at the bridge; Danny was still a few metres from the apex. She heard him bellow to James. She could see the faint smudge of a human in the wheelhouse. And she could see he was not going to stop. The boat ploughed on, the waves from its wake like white furrows on the metallic surface of the water. The uniforms piled out of the car as soon as it stopped and took the bridge steps two at a time, the pounding of their boots on the metal ringing through the air. The bow of the boat disappeared beneath the bridge just as Danny got to the top. He swivelled to watch for it appearing behind him, and in one motion vaulted onto the guardrail.

"Danny, no!" yelled Salter in horror.

Shepherd appeared beside her. "He can't be…. Sergeant, stop!" But he didn't.

A second later and Maik would have hit the rear rail of the boat, but he had timed his jump perfectly, landing squarely on the rear deck, and even softening the landing with bent knees, just as he'd been taught on those courses all those years ago. James spun around at the sound, letting go of the wheel in his shock. Maik was taking a second to recover, breathing heavily. He started forward, steadily, purposefully, and James ran from the wheelhouse and edged along the side of the cabin. When Maik arrived on the bow deck, he found James facing him, his back pressed against the polished chrome of the rail. The unmanned boat was continuing its relentless path, a grey-brown chevron of water churning from its bow. James looked at Maik and half turned; his hands on the rail.

"If I had to go in there after anybody," said Danny evenly, "I wouldn't be best pleased. I'd make sure I'd let them know that, too, after I caught them." His breathing had returned to normal now, but his adrenalin was still high and it gave his tone an unmistakable edge. "So what you're going to do now is get back behind the wheel of this boat and take us in to where those police officers are waiting for us on the bank."

Maik had acquired that perfect pitch over the years that left no room for debate.

DCS Colleen Shepherd, too, had a way of making her true feelings known even when she was forced to obscure them in official-speak. On an operational level, the department's response was obviously to strongly disapprove of such dangerous approaches as Maik's. But as she stood in the little huddle that had gathered to meet the returning boat, Shepherd wasn't going to let that get in the way of her appreciation for his efforts.

"It hardly bears thinking about how much it would have cost to get a helicopter and a team of pursuit boats out along these waterways, not to mention the extra manpower." She looked at Maik over the top of her glasses. "Any way you look at it, you've undoubtedly saved the police department a few thousand pounds, so on that score at least, I suppose it's job well done."

Maik nodded his thanks. After the flurry of excitement, calm had returned to the riverbank. There were still no signs of life in the surrounding fields, but weak sunshine had broken through and a soft golden light covered the landscape. The officers that had gathered around Maik knew better than to make a fuss, and instead turned their attentions to discussing the next steps now that James had been placed under arrest. The broker had made a point of declaring his innocence as soon as Laraby had finished reading him his rights.

"Other than that, I'm saying nothing to you lot. No offence, but I'll let my lawyer talk for me." But he had offered no resistance as he was eased into the back of the patrol car.

Laraby rejoined the group now with a broad smile. "Nice job by everybody," he said. "But especially you." He placed a hand on Maik's shoulder, rocking him gently a couple of times. "I'm sure the DCS has already told you it's not the way we'd encourage senior investigators go about doing things," he slid a sidelong glance at Shepherd, "but, let's face it, Danny. You were bloody magnificent. The way you went over the top of that bridge, it was like watching one of those actions heroes."

"I thought Super Mario wore overalls," said Salter, earning a laugh from the others.

"Seriously, well done, Danny," said Laraby sincerely. "I mean it. Brilliant."

He patted the sergeant on the back again. It was a lot of physical contact for Danny Maik, thought Salter. But for once the sergeant didn't seem to mind.

Liquid reflections shimmered on the water surface beside the small group. Laraby looked into them for a moment and became suddenly earnest. "Most likely. I'll be leaving it to Sergeant Maik to handle things from here on in …" Again, the look was to Shepherd. "Don't get me wrong, this was a team collar in every sense. But I think he's earned it."

No one disagreed, even if it seemed to Salter that there might be more to it than that. Acknowledging James's guilt meant Laraby had to concede that his little class war with Oakes was over. As hard as it might be for him to watch the fall of a man who had dragged himself up from working-class background, the DI was going to have to accept that Robin Oakes and all the rest of those rural aristos he held in such contempt were in the clear on this one. And that might just be easier for DI Marvin Laraby to do from a distance.

"So, what do you say, Danny?" asked Laraby heartily. "Ready to see this one through to the end?"

Maik shrugged modestly. "Please yourself."

Laraby managed one final glance at DCS Shepherd. "I just have."

42

"Sergeant," said Jejeune, "I can barely hear you. Wait while I try to find a stronger signal."

Traz had retired to a discreet distance after handing Jejeune his phone. He pointed now to a spot near the hotel lobby's revolving glass doors where he'd had success finding a stronger signal before. He hadn't recognized the number when it displayed, but the gravelly English voice had been unmistakable.

"You closed the case?" asked Jejeune, putting a finger in one ear against the traffic noise coming from the street outside.

"A man named Connor James. He's not saying much, but we've got all the physical evidence we need."

"So you're satisfied?" It was their code. Was there anything troubling Maik, any pieces that didn't fit?

"More than I was," admitted Maik. "I can't say I was ever particularly taken with our first choice."

"Robin Oakes?"

The first part of Maik's reply disappeared in a burst of static, but he was still speaking when the signal returned. "… flying a drone around a Barn Owl, trying to acclimatize the bird to it so he could follow it and get some pictures from above while it was hunting."

Jejeune's grip tightened on Traz's phone. "I hope he's been reported to the authorities. I can text you a number, if you like."

"No evidence, I'm afraid, other than his word. Now James is in custody, I doubt Oakes will be keen on repeating what he told us. Your own trip going okay, sir?"

It was Maik telling Jejeune the affairs of Saltmarsh Constabulary were no longer a topic for discussion, at least, not until he returned. He wasn't sure how much the sergeant knew about the real reason for his visit to Colombia. Jejeune had taken great care to exclude him from as many of the details as he could. He prized Maik's loyalty greatly, and would not knowingly put him in a situation where he would have to make a difficult decision, if questions were asked in an official capacity. But some level of openness was called for now.

"There's a chance things could be resolved." His mind went to the grainy, disembodied image he had spoken to via the Justice Department's video screen. How long, now, would it take for the *relevant authorities* to reach a decision? He tried to imagine how he would react if Mariel came to offer a confession, especially one with such profound ramifications. Would he listen, dispassionately, and hear the sheer, unguarded honesty that would convince him of the truth of her statement? Or would he be distracted, instead, by her appearance, her smooth skin and long grey hair? By her glittering outfit, and her thready philosophy, and her talk of hummingbirds with four wings and a forest with a broken heart? His eyes caught the strangeness of the scene outside — the bright sunshine, the busyness of the human traffic along the street, the frenetic activity of a Bogota afternoon. He realized it must be late in the U.K., and with a jolt of awareness he realized Maik would not have called at this hour just to update him on their progress in the case. Or to inquire about his.

"Anything else, Sergeant?" he asked guardedly.

Maik had gone quiet, realizing Jejeune was on the right wavelength now. "You asked to be kept informed, sir," he said, reaching for his formal tone.

Jejeune's stillness seemed to reach across the miles. From the glass-fronted lobby of a Bogota hotel to the quietness of a deserted Saltmarsh Police Station, where only a desk lamp kept Danny Maik from the darkness, nothing moved.

"Informed?"

"About Ray Hayes."

Traz was up and moving, approaching Jejeune across the lobby, reading the alarm in his friend's face, sensing trouble.

"He's out."

The bright lights of El Dorado International Airport shone down on the bustling activity beneath them with the relentlessness of the Colombian sun. Now that his first flush of panic was over, Jejeune had come to terms with his concern, knowing he could do nothing more. He had booked his flight and made it to the airport. The departures board assured him the plane would be leaving on time. Beside him, Traz stood with his hands in his pockets, looking as well groomed as always, despite their frantic drive through Bogota's rush hour traffic.

With nothing to do but clear customs, it was time to reassure his friend that he was settled, back in control and ready to accept he was helpless to affect matters until his flight landed in the U.K. Lightness was the key.

"You have to promise me you won't try to hook up with Thea again after I'm gone," he said.

Traz was ready to meet him on this safe ground, where the demons of emotion might not venture. "The woman tried to kill my best friend. In some cultures, that's considered a bad omen. No," he said, with a theatrical sigh, "I fear it's all over between us. Still, as they say in those romantic movies, at least we'll always have ... parrots."

"I think that might be *Paris*," said Jejeune, rewarding his friend's efforts with a smile. Through the large windows of the airport, the detective saw a pair of Black Vultures circling lazily against the blue sky. "Your friends," he told Traz, pointing.

Traz smiled, but there was sincerity in his eyes when he looked back at Jejeune. "I just think we should give them a little respect. They're important ..."

He stopped short. And then Jejeune knew. It was not phantom tracks in the mud that had led Traz to him in the forest that day, not magic realism, or the supernatural sleuthing powers of Jim Rockford. It had been these, the *chulos*, painting his position on the ground with their dark crosses as they circled, waiting for Jejeune to cross the line between life and death; the thinnest line of all.

He looked back to see his friend choking back emotion at the memory. They both bore scars from this trip, he realized. They had been through so many things together. It was hard to know how to thank someone who had done so much for Jejeune's family, even before they had ever come to Colombia.

"They are going to fast track your new passport, I take it?" asked Jejeune.

"A couple of days. I'll be fine hanging out at the hotel. I could use a little down time."

"Besides, the St. Lucia authorities should know the procedure by now. This isn't the first time you've lost a passport, is it, Traz? You reported one missing, along with your driver's licence and a credit card, about a week after Damian made it safely away from St. Lucia and back into Canada."

Traz stared at Jejeune, not smiling, not doing anything. "It's not a good idea to check up on your friends, JJ, not unless you're prepared to deal with what you find. That's your flight they're calling. You'd better get going. Say hi to Lindy for me. She's going to love that basket and candle set. Trust me. I'm never wrong."

"Damian was never the best at saying thank you, so just in case, I'll say it for him. Thank you. Traz. For everything." Jejeune extended his hand. "It's been, you know …"

Traz nodded. "Yeah, me too."

43

From the air, London looked like a sepia photograph. A tapestry of monochromatic slabs fanned out across the land, robbed of their light by the bank of low cloud that hovered over the city. From this height the river was a shiny grey cord, weaving its way between the blocks on either side.

Jejeune had spent most of the flight thinking about Lindy. Only now as the pilot banked the plane for approach and the colourless landscape of London tilted into view did he think about the country he had just left. Bright sunshine had accompanied his take-off, and in order to round onto their flightpath out over the ocean, the plane had performed a slow curl over the Sierra Madres. Jejeune had looked down over the wooded hillsides and the vast, pristine valleys between the peaks. So much wilderness. Would it be preserved, or would it one day look like this, a grey wasteland of human sprawl? Or would the answer lie, as in most conflicts between conservation and development, in some compromise between the two, vaguely unsatisfying to either party, perhaps, but the best one could hope for in a world where humans and nature were forever destined to collide.

Danny Maik was waiting at the arrivals gate when Jejeune emerged. He had a spare jacket over his arm. "It's been cold here," he said. "And I wasn't sure how much time you'd had to look at the weather reports."

Jejeune took it with gratitude and slipped it on over his light sweater. The two men walked to the car park, engaging in only the lightest of conversation. There were many things they needed to discuss, but none of them were suitable for a busy airport terminal.

Jejeune stopped in surprise as they approached the vehicle. Jejeune's Range Rover, nicknamed The Beast by Lindy, sat in the parking space, shining from a fresh wash.

"Lindy was kind enough to lend it to me a couple of days ago. I hope you don't mind."

"Where's the Mini? Having the speakers repaired?"

Maik gave a dutiful smile. The volume at which Maik played his Motown songs when the men travelled together was a constant source of comment from the DCI. "I'm having some work done on it."

It was typical of the men's relationship that neither would mention their recent traumatic experiences to the other. They were events in each man's life, neither of which affected any case they were working on. What need was there to bother the other person with the details?

Maik extended a set of keys, but Jejeune refused. "You'd better drive. I didn't get much sleep on the flight, and anyway, I'm not sure my ankle could handle the clutch."

Maik nodded and climbed behind the wheel as Jejeune went round to the passenger side. "How do you like it?" asked Jejeune, as Maik manoeuvred the vehicle toward the parking exit.

"Reminds me of the three-tonner I once drove in the army," he said. But whether that was a good thing or not, Jejeune wasn't able to tell.

They waited until they were on the motorway, slowly inching their way around the periphery of Britain's capital, before they ventured into the territory they needed to visit.

"Miss Hey ... Lindy, she's busy with her appearances, I suppose?" Maik's tone was innocuous, but his meaning was clear enough.

"I haven't told her I'm coming home yet. I wanted to talk to you first."

"About Hayes?"

Jejeune was quiet for a moment, his eyes watching the slow crawl of traffic around them. "Hayes wants his victims to know he's coming for them. He builds up to it. In the past he's always given two warnings. The first you could write off as an accident; the second removes most of the doubt. The moment we show him we think the explosion could have been something more than an accident, he'll move again. Any police presence, a protection detail, anything like that would tell Hayes we're on to him. It would almost certainly increase the danger to Lindy."

Maik had gone very quiet. His hands were still as they gripped the steering wheel and he was staring straight ahead. "It's not been much," he said, "driving by your place on my way home. Not stopping in, mind. And a uniform strolling past the magazine's new offices a couple of times a day. They've moved into a shopfront on the high street temporarily. There's a bakery nearby. It's not a stretch that the lad would be popping out for a custard tart now and then."

"Since?" Jejeune's voice was tight with tension.

"My chat with DI Laraby. A few days."

Jejeune rubbed his forehead. He was tired. The Range Rover had a formidable heating system and Maik had it set on high, probably to protect his DCI's tropically-tempered bones from the cold English weather. But the warmth was dragging him toward sleep and making his mind swirl. How could he be ungrateful to his sergeant for caring so much about Lindy that he had put her in danger?

"We need to find Hayes." It was a vapid statement, unnecessary. But it was all he could muster at the moment.

"There's no sign of him," said Maik. "But I've kept the inquiries informal to this point. We could use official channels, but …"

But the chances of keeping their inquiries off Hayes's radar went down a lot. Jejeune looked out at the traffic again. In the next lane, a yellow truck was now one vehicle ahead of them. It had been more or less beside them since they had entered the motorway's slow crawl. All this time, all this distance, and being in different lanes had made no difference at all to either one's progress.

"You won't need to drive past the cottage on your way home anymore," he said thoughtfully, "and if you tell your uniformed officer to lay off the custard tarts for a while, it will break the pattern. If Hayes has been watching for a reaction, he might think we've decided to write the explosion off as an accident after all. He will come again anyway, but it might give us a little time."

Maik inched the Range Rover ahead, concentrating on the traffic. The heat and the silence in the car began drawing Jejeune toward sleep again. He laid his head against the window, feeling the coolness against his scalp. He wanted to sleep, needed to, but he knew if he succumbed now, his internal clock would be out of sync for that much longer. And he needed to be fully turned around as soon as possible. With Ray Hayes now back in his life, time was a luxury Domenic Jejeune no longer had.

He cranked the window down slightly, letting in a thin sliver of cold air. "Why don't you put on some music, Sergeant? Something upbeat."

Maik didn't need to be asked twice. Laraby's introduction of Thelma Houston to his thinking had given Danny licence to expand his horizons a little. Even if the Isley Brothers weren't with Motown when they recorded "Who's that Lady?" the band was at least a child of the studios. And if the DCI wanted something upbeat to keep him awake, then Ernie Isley peeling the paint off the studio walls with his guitar work was just the ticket.

Jejeune stirred to life, as Maik had suspected he might.

"See lots of birds over there?" asked the sergeant.

"Plenty. You?"

The two didn't share standing jokes, but Maik's exaggerated aversion to birding was probably as close as they came.

"I did see the Barn Owl on Oakes's property, presumably the same bird he was trying to film with that drone."

"I still have trouble believing anybody who professes to care about wildlife could bring themselves to do that."

"From what I've read online, there is some evidence that birds of prey have become habituated to the presence of drones."

Even in his sleepy state, Jejeune managed a look of contempt that suggested Oakes would not have received quite the sympathetic hearing that Laraby had predicted.

Jejeune thought for a long time. "Can I ask, what was it that had you looking at Oakes originally for the murder?"

"For me, it was because he lied about being at home at the time of the murder. We know why now, but back then all we had was his eyes telling us he wasn't where he said he was."

"And for DI Laraby?"

"I think it was probably his family's listing in *Burke's Landed Gentry*."

Jejeune smiled. Maik had a nice line in irony when he chose to use it.

"Are you any closer to a motive for Connor James?"

It was conversation more than professional curiosity, Maik realized. But if he wanted to give his honest, unguarded opinion to anyone about this case, there would probably never be a better opportunity than in the middle of this slow-moving traffic with an uninvolved detective of Jejeune's abilities sitting beside him.

"There are a couple of contenders. Dr. Amendal is the one who ruined his reputation, but it was Dawes's fault the investment wasn't made. Ultimately, she's the one responsible for his loss of standing in the investment community. On the other hand, when the earnings statement came out, he found out exactly how much she had cost him. You don't have to be in James's company very long to understand how much money means to him." Maik moved his big shoulders slightly. "Some combination of the two?"

"But he still claims he's innocent?"

Maik nodded. "And he does it well."

"He's a salesman," said Jejeune. "It's his job to be convincing. What is he saying about why he tried to escape? It's not the action of an innocent man."

"He said he intended to come back in on his own terms, with proper legal representation. Negotiating from a position of strength, he called it." Maik looked across at Jejeune. "He grew up in a rough neighbourhood — inner city. He says as far as he's concerned, once the police have got someone in their sights, they stop looking for anybody else."

Jejeune pulled on his bottom lip and stared thoughtfully through the windscreen.

"I worked those estates when I was first with the Met," he said. "The kids didn't often get the benefit of the doubt. The officers at the Met don't like to lose. A few of them were known to get impatient, waiting for proof to show up."

Danny waved a car over from another lane, though this one was moving no faster. "I looked into James's previous arrests," he said. "If somebody was inventing evidence, there's no suggestion they were trying to pin the crimes on the wrong person."

But Maik was still unsure. Jejeune could tell. There was something that wasn't fitting for him. And Jejeune knew his sergeant well enough to understand that if it was troubling Danny, he would probably have some doubts of his own.

"Nothing wrong with the evidence in this case, is there?"

Maik moved his shoulders again. "No one else's fingerprints are on the leather jacket. And the cup in the cottage with

Oakes's DNA comes from James's boat. He claims he knows nothing about it, but it didn't get there by itself."

Jejeune was quiet. Two pieces of evidence, a cup and a disguise. Both attempts to point the police toward Oakes, but they did it in different ways. It was as if two different forces were at work. But fatigue was starting to take over again, and he couldn't bring his mind to concentrate on whatever it was that was bothering him. The traffic started to move more freely and before long the Range Rover was easing along at a steady clip. The gentle rocking and the low hush of the tires on the road surface became a lullaby for Jejeune, and despite his efforts, he slid into a deep sleep.

Maik raised the passenger window, but he left the low music on. It was probably three hours to Saltmarsh, and he wasn't expecting to have any other company on the trip. He took a brief look across at the sleeping DCI. He had brought his quick mind to the case, filtering information, sorting clues, asking all the right questions with an evident active interest. But the one topic he hadn't asked about during the entire conversation was how the investigation had been conducted. Of the techniques and operating procedures and working theories of his one-time boss, DI Marvin Laraby, Jejeune had not made a single mention.

44

Shepherd and Laraby were sitting in a quiet corner of The Boatman's Arms. From her vantage point, she could see the lobby, where the whitewashed wall displayed a fresh-looking gouge in the shape of the door handle. She wondered if it had happened the night of the explosion, when the impact of the blast had sent the door bursting inward. Her eyes drifted around the room. She had no doubt that many of this crowd were in the pub that night, but the comforting normality of their daily ritual in here seemed to have airbrushed the incident from their minds already. She found it reassuring, and yet, at the same time, faintly troubling that Saltmarsh could settle so quickly on its axis again after such a traumatic event and continue as if it had been entirely unaffected by it.

On the noticeboard behind them was a poster advertising an upcoming karaoke night.

"I suppose if I was to make this my local, I'd have to get up to speed on my singing," said Laraby, nodding at the poster. "It seems to be a mandatory requirement in here. You know what I've just noticed, as well? There's no TV."

Shepherd took a sip of her wine. "Nor will there ever be as long as Jackie Tatlow is the proprietor. People come in here at lunchtime to enjoy a quiet drink, not follow the stock market or the latest failings of the Whitehall crowd."

Laraby watched a man in a tweed jacket approach the bar. The barman greeted him with a friendly smile while the man on a stool beside him reached down and ruffled the ears of the man's aging English pointer, greeting the dog even before its master.

Laraby smiled. "That's not something you see much of in London anymore."

The DCS smiled at the comment. "If bringing a dog into a pub is the biggest difference you've noticed between here and London, you haven't been paying attention."

Laraby took a drink from his water bottle. "I'm not going to pretend it didn't take a bit of getting used to, being up here," he said, "but there's a lot to like — this countryside, the wide open spaces. I was standing on the coast just the other day, as a matter of fact, watching the surf pounding in on the rocks." He leaned back again, making a point of looking around the pub. "You might think it's a strange thing to say, but murder seems worse here, somehow, in a quiet, decent, honest little place like this. It makes you want to try harder to preserve this way of life, to put all the pieces back in place, so people can get on with their lives again, safe, unafraid." He tipped his head back a little, breaking the mood, and took another swig from his bottle, holding it by the neck and waving it around slightly afterward. "Aah, ignore me ..." he said with a broad smile, "it's just the water talking."

The low murmur of conversation around them seemed to amplify Shepherd's silence.

"I've been made aware of a request for the station to be informed if anyone knows the whereabouts of a man called Ray Hayes." She stared at Laraby, eyebrows raised.

"An old collar of mine," said Laraby easily. "He got released recently. I should have been informed, but it never happened. They had no idea where to find me. Typical bureaucratic cock-up."

Shepherd shook her head. "What's the collective noun for bureaucrats, I wonder? A *lobotomy* would be my suggestion. So nothing for me to worry about then?"

"Not a thing. Just my curiosity, that's all."

Shepherd held up her wine, the glass reflecting an amber glow from the room's wall lamps. The pointer had settled peacefully beneath his owner's bar stool, and the ambient noise of the lunchtime crowd didn't seem to be disturbing its rest in the least. Beside her, a fire crackled in the grate. She had a glass of good Chardonnay in her hand. And now she got to tell the man opposite her he would be getting the reward his work deserved. She'd had worse lunch hours.

"It wasn't just for a bottle of fizzy water that I brought you here," said Shepherd. "You'll have already heard, I'm sure, that a DCI position is coming up at Minton. As is often the case, they've come to the Detective Chief Supers to see if we have any recommendations." She paused and looked at him. "I have."

Laraby hung his head slightly, in what might have been humility. "I would be honoured to be put up for it, of course, but I'm sure there'll be other candidates. I'd be surprised if Minton wasn't looking for an up-and-comer, some high-flier to bring over a bit of that outside-the-box thinking. You know, the kind you've been such a big proponent of here in Saltmarsh. I don't know if you realize it, DCS Shepherd, but some of the innovations you've put in place here, they've not gone unnoticed."

Shepherd looked at Laraby steadily. "Then, presumably, that should mean a recommendation from me would carry considerable weight," she said evenly. "I suppose what I'm telling you is that the position would be yours, if you're interested." She sipped her wine again. "I understand that you'd need to give it some thought. It's a big step. And a new area like Minton, it would be quite a change from the Met, I suppose."

Laraby inclined his head to acknowledge the point. "The thing is, people think the City is all blokes swilling pink gin and calling each other *my dear chap*, but it's not all as sophisticated and refined as they might imagine. There's a lot of grit and grime down there." He smiled and took another sip of his water. "Listen to me, carrying on as if you lot up here still think London is broken up into Monopoly colours, and any street with four houses on it gets a hotel. You must get a bit sick of know-it-alls swanning up from The Smoke and treating you as if you've never seen electric lighting before."

"We get used to it," said Shepherd with a smile. But she didn't deny it. Behind him, she watched as the pub's owner rounded the bar and set down a steel bowl of water beside the dog.

"On the house. I mean his drink, not yours," he said, pointing to the man on the stool.

"Perhaps you should have asked for yours in a bowl instead of a bottle," Shepherd told Laraby. She became serious. "The Dawes case. You know the CPS is saying that for all the evidence pointing to Connor James, they're not entirely convinced about the motive."

Laraby nodded. "With respect, ma'am, that's because they don't come from his world. They don't understand how hard he worked to get inside their circle, having to put up with their airs and graces, always being seen, if we're being honest, as nothing more than some raggedy-arsed chancer who could make them a few quid."

"Like Dawes herself, you mean? You think that's what James found so hard to accept? That she was from the same background, that she must have known how hard it was for him to get where he was, and yet she was still willing to destroy it all for him by stealing the IV League's funds?"

"He'd spent the better part of his life building up to where he was. Now he'd arrived, those were the sorts of contacts that would have set him up for life. She took all that away from him."

"It would help if we could get James to say all this himself. I understand he's no closer to confessing."

Laraby shook his head. "He's been around the circuit. He knows it's up to us to prove his guilt beyond reasonable doubt."

"And can we?"

"Already have, as far as I'm concerned. But if the CPS wants more, we'll get it for them. There will be something in amongst the evidence we've already collected — a witness statement, a report, something that will be enough to convince them." He set his water bottle down on the table and leaned forward a little. "I've been thinking. Now that DCI Jejeune is back, I imagine he'll be having a bit of trouble adjusting to the idea of sitting this one out. I'm not saying we need to have him cover what we already know, but we could get him sifting through the evidence again, just to check we haven't missed anything. Contrary to the rumours, I'm not perfect."

Shepherd leaned toward Laraby, as if it was very important she understood this point clearly. "Are you saying you'd welcome his involvement?"

Laraby shrugged easily. "We need to get the right result, and that means putting personal differences aside."

Across the room, the barman set a steaming steak pie in front of the man in the tweed jacket. The dog stirred slightly, as if expecting that the occasional piece might find its way down to him. Shepherd suspected the dog might be right.

"This business between you and DCI Jejeune," she said, without taking her eyes off the dog. "It stems from the case involving the Home Secretary's daughter, doesn't it?"

"In a way." Laraby picked up his water bottle and took a long drink before returning it to the table. "We were investigating the death of a young lad on an inner city estate when the call came in about that case. Understandably, they were looking for recruits to be seconded to the detail; high-profile case like that, you wouldn't have expected otherwise. I felt we were getting close to a breakthrough on our own case, and I argued we should see it through first." He shrugged. "I like to finish what I've started. It's just the way I was brought up. But Sergeant Jejeune, as he was then, he couldn't get away fast enough. I suppose he always thought he was destined for greater things. And let's face it, he was right. Once he'd volunteered, it was inevitable that, as his immediate supervisor, I would get drafted to go along and keep an eye on him." Laraby looked around, as if unsure whether to deliver the next sentence. In the end, he gave his shoulders another easy roll. "I'm not saying he didn't care about the lad on the estate. He just seemed to care more about the Home Secretary's daughter. It just never really sat right with me, that's all, and things between us went downhill from there."

Shepherd seemed to consider the information for a long time. She looked at her watch. "We should be getting back."

But instead of rising, Laraby eased back in his seat and slid his hands into his trouser pockets, puffing out his chest slightly. "Listen, if you think Minton could use my services, modest as they may be, I'd be delighted to accept. The only thing I would request is that I get to stay on here and see this Erin Dawes case through to the end. As I say, I like to finish what I start."

"Oh, I think we can arrange that," said Shepherd, draining her wine. As she stood up, she looked around the pub again. Its history was etched into its walls, the uneven floors, the long wooden bar shiny with elbow polish. Despite all the force's emphasis on modernity and progress, there was a lot to be said for traditional values, too.

45

Lindy had declined the invitation to go up to the Deputy Consul's office with Domenic. Instead, she had remained seated on the brown leather couch in the cavernous marble atrium, flicking listlessly through the messages on her phone, in clear violation of the sign on the wall of a circled cellphone with a red diagonal line drawn through its heart. The security guard had made one half-hearted approach, but Lindy had stopped him in his tracks with one of her special smiles and he had retreated to his post, from where he continued to cast the occasional furtive glance in her direction.

The echo of Domenic's awkward shuffle down the wide marble staircase reached her long before he came into view. He gave her a tight smile, but said nothing as he waited for her to tuck away her phone and stand up. They walked across the lobby's harlequin-patterned tiles and waited wordlessly, side by side, until the security guard buzzed the door open for them.

When they got outside, she turned to him. "Well?"

"No decision. Mariel Huaqua is considered an unreliable witness, though nobody seems willing to say why exactly. The government is considering her testimony, but on its own it may not be enough."

The wind swirled Lindy's hair around her head as she turned to look at him. "On its own? What else is there?"

Jejeune was silent for a long time. "Nothing. There is nothing else. Their decision to reopen the investigation or stay the charges against Damian depends entirely on whether they choose to accept Mariel's account."

From their position on the top step of the Colombian consulate building, they could see the busy traffic on Sloane Street heading down toward Knightsbridge. It was the lower tier of the scene Jejeune had seen from the window of Carmela Rojas's office. He realized her office must be directly above the portico of this door. She would be at the window now, he imagined, watching for his departure. He resisted the temptation to look up at the window.

Lindy touched his arm. "It's okay, Dom. You did everything you could. Everything it was possible to do. You proved your brother's innocence."

"Unless the Colombians agree to withdraw the charges, nothing changes. He'll still be a fugitive under an international warrant."

"That doesn't matter, not to Damian. Surely you must understand that? It was never about the warrant. It was the guilt he wanted to be free from. You did that for him, Domenic. You took away his responsibility for killing four people. He's a free man now, whether the Colombians withdraw the charges or not."

Jejeune shook his head. "He deserves more than that. All he's guilty of is failing to secure a permit to enter a national park. That shouldn't be a life sentence. For anybody."

Lindy let it drop. The truth was, there was much more at stake. They both knew Damian would never contact Domenic again as long as he remained a fugitive. He had almost cost his brother his career once, and no matter how deep his gratitude that his conscience had been cleared, he wouldn't put Domenic at risk again.

They descended the steps and began walking in the direction of Hyde Park. The destination had been a favourite of theirs when they first met. It was warmer then, and the lime trees lining the pathways had provided a glorious canopy of leaves to shelter them from the sun. Perhaps neither of them had thought much about the future during those strolls, but for Lindy, these days, her thoughts were of little else.

They walked among the bundled-up early Christmas shoppers and bought shade-grown Colombian coffees at a small specialty café. They entered the park and followed a gravel path down to a bench by the water.

"I've had Danny's jacket cleaned, so you can give it back to him when you see him next."

"His jacket?"

"The one he brought to the airport for you. There were one or two marks on it, but it's come out looking like new."

"He brought me a jacket," said Jejeune slowly, speaking almost to himself, like someone trying to remember something. He stared at the lake, lost in thought.

Lindy had experienced Jejeune's distance before, been a *victim* of it, she might have said. But previously it had been work-related, as Jejeune had retreated into a shell to consider some aspect of a case, wheedle out some connection, or interpret some piece of evidence. This was different. There was an edginess about him that had been interposing itself between them since he had returned from Colombia. She had thought it was tied in to the decision hanging over Damian's fate, but it was here now, hovering as darkly over them as ever, despite the Colombian embassy fading into the distance behind them.

"We haven't been here for years, Dom. I'd say it's highly unlikely anybody familiar is going to show up."

Jejeune looked puzzled.

"You've been staring at everybody that's passed us. Are you expecting to see someone you know?"

"Sorry, just the policeman on duty, I guess. Ever vigilant." He tried a faux dramatic gesture, one of a number of ways of dissembling that he wasn't very good at.

It was part of a pattern Lindy had noticed since he had appeared unannounced at the front door of the cottage a couple of days ago. His hug had been long and lingering, and she had no doubts about its sincerity. Her own feelings, too, swamped any fears her mind had been trying to taunt her with. Dom was here again. She felt like a missing part of her had been replaced and she felt a wholeness and balance she had not known since it was ripped from her by the explosion.

But almost as soon as Dom had set his bag down in the foyer, the other little things began manifesting themselves. He had sat opposite her in their living room, asking her again and again if she was okay. No ill effects after the explosion. Never mind that it was he whose skin looked like it had been through a blast furnace and who was hobbling around with a pronounced limp. At one point he had even leaned forward and taken her face between his hands, tenderly brushing away her hair so he could peer directly into her eyes. "I'm so sorry I couldn't be here. Are you sure you're okay now?"

"You know that scientific experimentation has largely dispelled that idea," she told him in a flippant way, to rob the moment of its awkward intensity. "This business about being able to tell if a person is lying by watching which way their eyes move; sound in theory, apparently, but not supported by the research. At all."

She had drawn her head away gently, unnerved by both his guilt and his concern. And besides, even if she did have the faintest suspicions she wasn't one hundred percent right yet, there was little point in telling Dom about it. There was nothing he could do about her continued flinching at loud noises and bolting wide-awake from a dead sleep every once in a while.

Only time would heal those scars. Time and settling back into a nice steady routine with work and Dom — well, once the madness of the Christmas season had passed, that is.

But Domenic's concern had continued, even if it had exhibited itself in slightly less hands-on ways. There was the sudden need to have surveillance cameras at the cottage, for example; selected, purchased, and installed in the time it normally took him to get around to considering an idea. And this business of having her drive him everywhere? Fair enough, he was hardly in a position to drive, given his wonky ankle. But didn't the police have drivers for situations like this? At times, it was almost as if he was trying to find reasons to have her constantly in his orbit, and as lovely as it was that he wanted to spend so much time with her after his long trip, she did have a life of her own to be getting on with.

They walked a bit more, then sat down side by side on a bench near The Serpentine, Dom stretching his leg out gratefully as he sank into the seat. They sipped their coffees in silence for a while, watching the hardy ducks etch wakes like frost patterns on the silvery surface of the water.

"I thought you'd talk about it more," said Lindy, cupping her hands around the warm coffee cup and lifting it to her lips.

Dom drew his glance away from the ducks.

"Colombia, the trip, the birds. I thought I'd be drowning by now in a sea of ant-blackbirds and warbling trogons and bronzy-fronted sabrebills. But you haven't said very much about it at all."

"You're welcome," said Domenic. But then, as if acknowledging his attempt at evasion was unlikely to satisfy a Lindy as serious and focused as this, he dropped the smile and turned to look at the water again. "There are a few things going on."

Lindy sighed in exasperation. "Damian, you mean? Yes, I had noticed."

"More than that. I don't think Erin Dawes's murder has been solved."

"I'm not sure Saltmarsh Constabulary would agree. They do already have somebody in custody, you know." The realization hit Lindy like an electric current. "Bloody hell, Dom, you think they've got the wrong person? Again? Shepherd will go ballistic. The press wasn't overly understanding the first time they got it wrong, when they had to release Oakes. I can only imagine how she's going to take the news that she has to stand in front of them a second time to deliver the same apologetic speech. So who did do it?"

"I'm not sure. If this was an impulse killing, a spur-of-the-moment rage, I might just about be able to accept James, but this murder took a long time to plan. And that means a long time to think about it." Jejeune shook his head slowly, his eyes still on the water in front of him. "All James had worked for, all the years he had put in, making his high society connections and celebrity contacts. It's a lot to throw away, especially when you've had time to consider your actions."

"The physical evidence is pretty conclusive, as I understand it."

"Yes," said Jejeune, nodding. But somehow he seemed to suggest even that was a problem.

Lindy watched the ducks for a long time, her body still, following the energetic forays of the birds with her eyes only. "I don't think 'a person or persons unknown' is quite going to fill the bill for Colleen Shepherd on this one, Dom. If you expect her to release James, you'd better be able to offer up somebody she can present in his place."

But even now, Lindy wasn't sure she had entirely uncovered the secrets Domenic Jejeune had been carrying around with him since his return from Colombia. Because hard as she was trying, she couldn't see why Jejeune's misgivings about the identity of Erin Dawes's killer would have him scrutinizing every face that passed by for the fifteen minutes they had been sitting on this bench. Or, even worse, from her perspective, trying to hide from her the fact that he was doing it.

46

"Somebody said you looked the worse for wear. Suntan cream at a premium over there in Colombia, was it?"

Jejeune was standing before Colleen Shepherd's desk as the DCS cast a critical eye over him. It had taken many days after his rescue for the skin on Jejeune's face to heal, and there was still a faint redness on his forehead and cheekbones.

"And what's the matter with your leg?"

"Ankle ligaments. It'll take a couple of weeks to heal."

"So that's the reason your trip ended early? Too difficult to trek over those jungle trails after your injury?"

Jejeune didn't correct her.

"But it had all gone well up to that point, I take it? You'd found everything you went to find?"

Jejeune shifted his weight slightly. "Most of it."

Shepherd wasn't sure whether she'd managed to hide her disappointment from him, but she realized she didn't care. Despite Jejeune's legendary caginess, this time she had been hoping for something from him. An acknowledgement of his true motives? Of his feelings? A complete opening of his heart to her? She wasn't sure, but whatever she had wanted, she realized she would never receive it from her DCI. If he could not confide in her now, as wounded, as damaged, as vulnerable as he must have been, he never would. The thought saddened her immensely, but at the same time, something within her changed. A new resolve slipped into place, a hardening of her feelings.

"I suppose your condition is why it's taken you so long to come in. I expected to see you the day you arrived, to be honest." She looked at him frankly, but Jejeune couldn't decide if there was any message there or not. "I hear you've been down in London. Anything I should know about? Not being promoted, are you, whisked away from us to pastures new?" Her eyes suggested she was going to wait for an answer before continuing.

"I went with Lindy," he said casually. "It was nothing to do with police business." Jejeune left it at that. As he always did. The facts, bereft of any extraneous details, as if he didn't dare trust anyone with those.

"So nothing to do with this man Hayes, then? Despite what you seem to think, I'm not a complete fool, Domenic. I note, for example, that you were part of the arrest team. Did the Prison Service inform you he was being released?"

"No."

But his face showed that he knew about it. His eyes were darting slightly as he tried to bring his expression under control.

Jejeune was torn. For once, he would have been willing to confide in Shepherd. She deserved it. But the way Hayes operated made it impossible. Perhaps if he could resolve the situation quickly it would not be too late to come back, to open up, to chat about things and try to get them back to where they had once been.

Shepherd waited until it was clear that he was not going to say anything more.

"Right, so I have your personal assurance that you and Mr. Hayes have not crossed paths since he got out." She nodded briefly and pulled a set of papers toward her. "Well, as a service to that poor long-suffering girl of yours, I suppose I'd better find you something to do around here. Though I've no idea where I'm going to put you. After all, you're still not officially back until Monday."

Jejeune didn't point out that there was an office down the hallway with his name on the door. Shepherd hadn't forgotten.

"How is Lindy, by the way? She looked a bit shaky the last time I saw her. You'll need to watch her for a few weeks, Domenic. Closely, I mean. She's been through quite an ordeal." The contrast between the softness in Shepherd's tone when she spoke about Lindy and the clipped brusqueness she had been using with him was impossible to miss.

"I plan on staying close for the next little while," said Jejeune. "You were saying you thought you could find me something here?"

"Possibly. But first we need to discuss why Gerald Moncrieff is calling me to find out exactly who is in charge of the investigation of the Erin Dawes case."

Fired from the space between her eyebrows and the top of her gold-rimmed glasses, Shepherd's eyes were like lasers.

"I asked him for permission to visit Moncrieff's Wood."

"What on earth for?"

"I wanted to see the land that Picaflor had intended to connect to Oakham. But Moncrieff refused to grant me access."

"As well he might. You are not a part of this case, Domenic. It has been solved without you. If you'd like a minor role in the wrap-up, I have one for you, but there's to be no more of this, do you understand?"

Though she was rarely willing to take Jejeune's silence for acquiescence, there was something in his expression this time that seemed to satisfy her. "I'd like you to review the evidence for anything that may help the CPS make its case against Connor James. Anything you find should go directly to DI Laraby."

It was the first time the name had come up, and it sat there between them now like an unclaimed package.

"I'm not sure that is going to work," said Jejeune dubiously.

"If you're suggesting DI Laraby might have a problem with this arrangement, then I should tell you he's the one who requested to have you take on this assignment."

Jejeune was quiet for a moment. "Are we sure there *is* evidence to prove James's guilt?"

It took Shepherd a moment before she felt she could trust herself with a measured response. "We have our man, Domenic. I'm aware that you and DI Laraby have had your differences, but he's fit in quite nicely here during your absence, and I have to say he's done excellent work on this case. I won't have you undermining it because of some personal vendetta."

"There was no reason for him to wait so long before killing Dawes. James would have known his reputation was ruined as soon as the options were not exercised. That's when he would have been angriest, when he could see it all falling apart. But the thinking is, he didn't act then. He took all that emotion, that rage, and stored it away."

Shepherd was furious. *How dare he come in here taking apart their case like this?*

"Even after his career is in a tailspin, and he's started selling his possessions to cover his losses, he still doesn't act. Instead, he takes the time and trouble to make himself feel worse by reading an earnings statement, and only then does he go to kill Erin Dawes? With respect, I don't see how you can consider Connor James a viable suspect at all."

No, Chief Inspector Domenic bloody Jejeune. With no respect. With no respect at all.

"We have evidence, physical and circumstantial, that puts him there, that's why," she shouted in frustration. What was it Lindy had called him, *a carrier*? It had all seemed so light and funny back then, in the comfortable confines of that snug little library, with Domenic Jejeune half a world away and absolutely no threat to this investigation. With a start, she realized she had just articulated to herself the feeling that had been floating around her consciousness these last few days. It was an ice-water shock to her system to now be able to recognize her sentiments for what they were. Things had been better at the station when Jejeune was not here.

She found it hard to meet his eyes, as if she was ashamed of her own thoughts. Jejeune's look did little to ease her discomfort. How dare he? Jejeune was the one coming in here with secrets — about his brother, about Hayes, about Laraby even. How dare he look at her quizzically like that, as if she had betrayed him with these secret thoughts of hers? She gave him one more chance.

"Do you have anything else to you wanted to discuss, Domenic?"

Jejeune hesitated. He knew if he left this office without confiding in her, their relationship would likely never recover. But there was nothing he could do about it.

Shepherd seemed to have reached a point where all her anger, all her frustration had gone. Another tone took over now, one Jejeune didn't recognize. "It occurs to me that you must have had some time to think in Colombia, all that sitting around in the jungle, with nothing to do but wait for birds to come by. It must have given you a fair bit of time for reflection, a chance to re-evaluate where you are in certain things — your life, your relationship, your career."

She paused and looked at Domenic to see if he was going to take up the running. But she had never really expected that he would. Even if he had come to conclusions about things in the steamy rainforests of South America, he was hardly the sharing type. The social media sites were not designed for the Domenic Jejeunes of the world. "If I could be of help in any of that," she said, "I'd be more than willing to give you my thoughts."

The brisk, businesslike approach from the earlier part of their meeting returned, informing her actions, her looks, her words. "Right, then your remit is clear. You can work on this case until it is resolved. After that, we'll see where the land lies with regards to future duties. In the meantime, you are to have no further contact with any of the principals in this case. That's a direct order, Domenic, I'd be grateful if you'd take it as such. Please close the door on your way out."

47

Normally, it was Jejeune proffering an arm to Lindy when they picked their way across any uneven terrain his birding ventures took them on. But he said he was concerned about going over on his weak ankle again on the rock-hard ruts of the field. It had happened a couple of times since his return from Colombia, and apart from the excruciating pain, they were both aware each new impact on his damaged ligaments put the healing process back that much further. So Domenic had already accepted Lindy's forearm on a couple of occasions. To her credit, she went for neither comedy nor the studied solicitousness of sympathy, but rather extended her arm wordlessly as the more rugged patches of land appeared in front of them.

Which was not to say she was necessarily happy about the arrangement; already she'd cancelled two interviews because they conflicted with Dom's needs for transportation. Okay, she pretended to herself that the interviews were becoming a nuisance now, and she really was genuinely uncomfortable talking about her own success. But that was hardly the point. They were part of her life at the moment, and they were being put on hold, *it* was being put on hold, because Dom insisted on having her drive him everywhere. No, she decided, she wasn't having it. If Domenic wanted to go somewhere from now on, he would have to ask the Saltmarsh Constabulary to supply a driver. And if he was reluctant to do that, as he so clearly seemed to be, then he could just bloody well stay at home. She had things to do.

They paused for a moment as the rolling fields of Robin Oakes's land opened out before them; a beige expanse of emptiness that stretched down to the ruined walls of the manor house. Lindy and Domenic stood together looking at the sweep of the barren, desolate land between the patches of trees on either side, Moncrieff's Wood and Sylvan Ridge. The bare branches of the trees reached to the sky like a congregation of the penitent. But their prayers did nothing to still the punishing winds that strafed the ridge.

The sound of a chainsaw ripped through the silence, startling them both. They saw a shape moving between the dark trunks of Sylvan Ridge and they heard the deceptive soft crush of a falling tree. Amelia Welbourne noticed them and began walking in their direction, swinging the chainsaw at her side. She had curiously broad shoulders for her slender build, and it struck Jejeune that, from a distance, or perhaps in low light, it would be easy to mistake her for a man.

"It's tragic," she said, shaking her head sadly as she approached. "First the elms, and now those old things." She pointed a gloved hand in the direction of the fallen tree. "It makes you wonder what's going to be left of the English forest as we once knew it in a few years. Did you know it's said a squirrel could have once crossed this island from the west coast of Wales to the Wash without ever touching the ground. To look at our forest cover now ..." She shook her head again. "It's heartbreaking."

"That stand looks pretty healthy to me," said Lindy.

"Felling them is preventative, but I can assure you, it is necessary. Chalara ash dieback is a fungus that will kill them all if it's allowed to spread. Sadly, you have to be ruthless now and again for the greater good." She looked at Lindy carefully. "You're that journalist, aren't you? I've read your articles."

Lindy waited uncomfortably to see if Welbourne intended to add anything. Perhaps this was as close as the landed gentry came to a compliment. Or criticism. Welbourne turned toward Jejeune.

"Come to view the scene of the crime, have you?" she asked him.

Lindy looked puzzled, but the man standing at her side understood. "This was the site earmarked for Picaflor's reforestation experiments," he explained to Lindy.

"Experiments which are proving remarkably successful," said Welbourne, tossing her head slightly as if in defiance of the winds that swirled around her. "The entire area could have been one forest again, the two ancient fragments reunited for the first time in centuries. It would have been a magnificent thing to witness. Instead, that dream was sacrificed for one person's greed. That's the real crime here, Inspector, the opportunity that has been stolen from us all. That's the tragedy."

"A woman did die, Ms. Welbourne," Jejeune reminded her reasonably.

"Yes. Yes, she did." Welbourne hung her head slightly and gazed at the ground. "I'm sorry, forgive me. I suppose people consider even one human life is too high a price to pay to keep any dream alive."

A train of Jackdaws exploded noisily from somewhere among the ruins down below, churring and clammering as they wheeled around the white sky. Lindy watched their dark shapes as they spiralled up, but for once Jejeune's eyes didn't follow the birds. His stare stayed on the rubble-strewn ruins from which they had flown.

"Have you seen anyone on the property this morning?" he asked Welbourne.

"No. Robin is in town for a couple of days. He no longer has any staff on the estate, so there's no reason anyone else would be down there. I'm sure it's just a fox or something that's put those birds up." She turned to Lindy. "I didn't mean to sound callous about Erin Dawes's death. It's just that we were so close, so close to making at least some small amends for our centuries of awful, narrow-minded, wrong-headed approaches to our forests. Do you know how many intact patches of large forests are left on this planet, Miss Hey? Two — the Amazon and the Congo. Twenty percent of the world's forests are less than a football field's length away from a forest edge. I ask you, can you truly consider such a place to be wilderness? So you see now why the prospect of re-establishing a large tract of intact forest here was so important. And why the loss of such an opportunity is so tragic."

Dom had switched his gaze from the ruins and it was now fixed firmly on Welbourne. Something about her passion seemed to have triggered an instinct in him and he was watching her now, animal-like, his pupils barely flickering. Welbourne seemed unaware of the scrutiny. It was as if she had been waiting for someone to spill this all out to, as some kind of explanation, a justification almost. But for what? For feelings she harboured still about the value of one human life when measured against a regenerated ecosystem? Or for actions she had already taken, based upon those feelings?

As Dom and Lindy walked away from the ridge, it was his turn to be lost in silence. But he had been quiet on their way here, too, she now realized. It was just at the time she was too wrapped up in her own thoughts to notice. She felt ashamed of her selfishness. Of course she would drive him around. Anywhere he wanted to go. If Domenic had suddenly decided he couldn't do without her company, well then, her inconsequential little press interviews could wait. Her partner needed her, was relying on her. It was all the justification she required.

"So, are you any closer to discovering who killed Erin Dawes?"

Jejeune's eyes stayed on the ruins as they walked, but not even the Jackdaws were stirring now. "I think so."

"And you're convinced it wasn't Connor James."

"It wasn't James."

"What's wrong, Dom. You're not worried about Laraby getting the glory, not after all this time, surely? Isn't it more important the right person is brought to justice?"

He turned to her. The wind was tousling Lindy's hair again, and she reached up to bunch it in one hand.

"I think Colleen Shepherd is going to offer Laraby a position at Saltmarsh as soon as this case is resolved."

"And you can't see the two of you working together?" Lindy pulled a face. "I suppose you two will just have to try and bury the hatchet. Preferably not in each other."

"There is no DI position at Saltmarsh. Only a DCI. And there's only one of those."

Lindy had stopped walking, and when Jejeune looked back, her face was ashen. She looked so unsteady he was afraid she might fall. He returned and wrapped his arm awkwardly around her shoulders, drawing her in to him. She was shivering slightly despite her heavy coat.

"You can't tell him, Dom. You can't hand your position over to Laraby like that. You have to go to Shepherd yourself. Show her you're the clever one, show her Laraby's just the buffoon you always thought he was."

"No, I never thought that. And I don't think it would make any difference anyway. I think she's already made up her mind."

"Then don't tell them, for God's sake." Lindy was shouting now, her anger carrying to him over the winds. "Let him charge the wrong man, then show them he's wrong. Shepherd would never want him after that."

"I can't do that either, Lindy."

"They need you here, Dom. My God, without you to show them the way, this lot would give the Keystone Cops a run for their money." She was shaking her head now, fighting off thoughts she couldn't even voice. He looked at her, so weak and yet so strong, so desperate and yet so resolute.

"I can't, Dom. Not after all that's happened lately, the explosion, the, the …" she flapped a hand from the wrist. "I don't think I could face leaving here. Could you? Leave this place, this landscape, the birds?" She searched the skies frantically, but maddeningly she couldn't find a single bloody bird to make her argument for her. The skies were as empty as her soul.

"You need to get out of the cold. Let's go back to the car."

But Lindy stood for a long time, looking out over the empty fields of Oakham. Apart from the ruins of the manor house, it was a landscape that offered no shelter. Not from the elements. Nor from anything else. Domenic stood close by, not looking at the land, but at her. It occurred to him she had not asked him who the real killer was. Perhaps, to Lindy, it no longer mattered.

48

Jejeune climbed in the Range Rover's passenger seat and handed a brown paper bag to Maik. "Your jacket. The one you brought to the airport for me. Lindy had it dry cleaned."

Maik nodded his thanks and set it on the seat behind him. "She's not available to drive you today?"

"She's in Norwich for a meeting. Last minute."

Maik nodded approvingly. No prior notice of her agenda. Jejeune noticed Maik's expression, and raised the question with his eyebrows.

"There might be a lead on Hayes, sir. There's a report he's been seen in a village near Peterborough two days running. Around a church that's known to help out ex-cons, refugees, illegals, and the like."

A brief look of alarm passed over Jejeune's features. But Lindy was safe enough today, in a public location, in the company of others. Should they go to the church now? They had no evidence against Hayes, but perhaps if they took him off-guard by showing up unexpectedly, he might slip up, say something or do something that could lead to his arrest. But Hayes was clever. He wasn't prone to making mistakes, and if they got it wrong and alerted him that they were on to him without being able to hold him, he would be gone. No, Jejeune decided. He would want better odds than a spontaneous visit based on a possible sighting could offer. He would want confirmation that Hayes was staying at the church, at the very least, before he acted.

Maik seemed to read his mind. "I'm trying to get verification, I'll let you know as soon as I hear anything."

Jejeune gave him a small smile of appreciation. "Any chance we could take a run up to Oakham? I've not seen a Barn Owl for a long time. If that one's around the ruins, I wouldn't mind a look."

It wasn't like Jejeune to use a bird sighting for obfuscation. It was usually the other way round. But Maik though he'd better be sure, just in case. "Oakes won't be there, sir. He's informed us he'll be in London for a couple of days. Seems he wasn't sure whether the requirement to inform us of his travel plans was still in place, so he thought he'd err on the side of caution."

Jejeune nodded. "I know he's not there. Did he say why he went to London?"

"No. But I think it may have been to fire a high-priced solicitor." Maik waited. "So, Oakham still?"

Oakham still.

Jejeune stood in the shelter of the one remaining wall of the great hall, the main building that had once dominated the manor house complex. At the top of the wall, short sections of the upper storey survived, weathered stone punctuated by window openings that gazed like unseeing eyes over the surrounding fields. Above, Jejeune watched a bird circling over the ridge, effortlessly drifting on the high winds.

"Rare?" asked Maik.

"No, but it's not for the want of trying."

Maik looked puzzled.

"It's a Marsh Harrier. I was looking to see if I could make it a Rough-legged Buzzard."

Maik gave a short nod, as if he might understand, but both men realized he was fooling no one. "That owl doesn't seem to be around either." He looked at Jejeune. "Anything else we might want to be looking for out here?"

Signs of human habitation, thought Jejeune. But it was cold even now, under this empty blue sky, in the half-shelter of these walls. At night, the temperature would plunge and it would be punishing out here. Refuge in a church would be a better option.

"Do you know where Amendal met the IV League members to hand out their drones?"

"*The Big Deal.* James's boat."

Jejeune nodded, as if he might already know this information. "It would be interesting to find out what the weather was like that day." He looked across at Maik. "Don't you think?"

Maik sighed inwardly. Here they were again, back in the land of hidden queries and half-revealed thoughts. After the bright sunshine of Laraby's see-through procedures, it was like a veil of mist was descending on the investigation again. He knew the role Jejeune had been assigned in this case. What he didn't know was why the detective was suggesting Maik should find out about the weather that day when he could easily have done so himself.

A skein of long-necked birds flew in low and landed in the fields in the distance, and the two men watched as they started foraging amongst the wheat stubble. Pink-footed Geese, from the gathering at Snettisham, where Jejeune had taken Maik on a couple of occasions to see the roosts of tens of thousands. From somewhere, nowhere, the idea came to Maik on the keening winds that scoured the barren landscape.

"If we knew, sir, about the weather, do you imagine it would strengthen the case against James?"

Jejeune shook his head slowly. "No, Sergeant, I don't think it would."

And there it was, as clear as if Jejeune had drawn a chalk diagram on the walls of these ruined buildings. James was not the murderer. They had been led away from the truth by a trail of breadcrumbs. But the question all along was not where they were going, but who was leading them. And the only man who had thought to ask that question was standing right in front of him.

Jejeune's approach became clear now, too. Whether he needed it or not, Marvin Laraby would be unlikely to listen to advice from the DCI, of all people. But he might listen to Danny, if he was told in the right way. Only Danny had to know how they had gotten there. And not just for Laraby's sake. The prosecution, too, when the case was finally brought to trial, would need Maik to be able to walk them through it. Because for an investigating officer to admit he had simply been given the answers by somebody who wasn't working the case was never going to hold up in a court of law. So Jejeune was going to lead Danny Maik, and Danny, in turn, would lead Laraby.

"Sometimes the smallest of differences make the biggest impact, Sergeant. Like the DNA report on the bag of disguise items, for example. Did you read it?"

Maik had been with Jejeune long enough to know where the value lay in his questions.

"I was told about it. I didn't read it."

Jejeune nodded. "The report said the moustache had spirit gum on the back of it."

"It's what actors use to attach prosthetics to their face. It would have been suspicious if it didn't have any. But the report said it hadn't been possible to recover any DNA from it."

Jejeune shook his head. "No, Sergeant. The report said there was no DNA on there to recover."

Maik looked around the collapsed rubble, laying like so much melted wax around the bases of the walls of the old building. It was hard to envision the beauty and the splendour that had once existed here. Now there was nothing but the bare bones, the shell of this once-magnificent building, strewn all around them. It was what they did, thought Danny. They walked into the ruins of people's lives, Jejeune and him and the others, and tried to reconstruct pictures of the past, of how things were before everything began to fall apart.

It was what he would do now, and what Laraby would get credit for, and what Shepherd would admire. And meanwhile, the person who had unravelled it all would stand on the sidelines, watching the man drafted in to replace him, the man occupying his office, receive all the praise. The accolades wouldn't have meant anything to Jejeune himself, Maik knew, but watching someone who held you in such undisguised contempt collect the fruits of your labours, that would be hard for anybody to take.

"This business with Laraby, sir," said Maik, without taking his eyes off the ruins. "I wouldn't ask normally, but given the history between you …" Maik faltered awkwardly, and Jejeune saw this was difficult for him. Perhaps he would have even helped the sergeant out, if he could. But he had no idea where Maik was going with this.

"It sounds like getting on the wrong side of Ray Hayes is not a decision you should take lightly," said Maik finally. "I'd just want to be sure I was doing it for the right reasons."

Jejeune gave a short nod of understanding. "Our personal history, Laraby's and mine, doesn't come into this, Sergeant. Ray Hayes is a dangerous criminal who intends to do Lindy harm. You'd be doing it for the right reasons."

He knew he could have left it there. It would have been enough for Danny. He would have gone along with Jejeune now, whatever the cost. But he deserved more. The stakes were high, and he should have the whole picture.

"The case involving the Home Secretary's daughter," began Jejeune, speaking so quietly the winds threatened to snatch away the words, "Laraby didn't come out of it looking very good. In fact, he was disciplined, lucky to keep his job. There were people, powerful people, who wanted to see me promoted over his head." Jejeune looked uncomfortable. "They made it difficult to say no."

Maik said nothing. In the distance, the fields of wheat stubble stood empty now. He hadn't seen the geese leave. He wondered if Jejeune had.

"The whole situation — Laraby's humiliation, my promotion — it led to problems in his marriage. Not abuse," said Jejeune quickly, "nothing like that, but ... perhaps there were already problems." Jejeune seemed to consider this for a long time. "Perhaps not. In the end, his wife left him. She moved to Canada." Even he couldn't suppress a small smile at the irony. "So, did I break up Marvin Laraby's marriage, Sergeant? No, I didn't. But was I responsible for it breaking up?" Again, Jejeune seemed to weigh the question heavily in his mind. "Yes, in part, I suppose I was."

Maik pointed at a bank of gunmetal clouds rolling in low over the fields. "If that owl's got any sense, it's going to be staying where it is for the time being. Perhaps it's time we were on our way, sir. You all right on that leg over this section?"

"I'll see how I get on."

But he knew Maik would be there if he needed him. He always was.

49

The disappearing sun was laying trails of pale pink on the water. Though it was still only late afternoon, the temperature was starting to drop. There would be a hoar frost tonight, and in the morning these tiny, fragile blades of grass at their feet would be sheathed in white, brittle to the touch.

Despite the biting winds coming in off the water, Jejeune had been standing at the edge of the cliff for a long while. Lindy stood a couple of steps behind him, slightly off to one side. The setting sun was a show she enjoyed from this vantage point in all seasons, but she was not watching its gradual slide toward the horizon today. She was watching Domenic as he stood there, motionless, staring out over the sea. She knew what it signalled and her sadness was overwhelming. She felt as if something had broken inside her. She wasn't sure she was a complete person anymore. So much of her seemed to be missing. Domenic was drinking in the view, trying to draw it into his memory, to store it away, hoping he might be able conjour it up again sometime when the real thing was no longer available.

Their talk earlier, in the cottage, in front of the hearty fire burning in their hearth, had been nothing more than sifting through the ashes of another fire, one that had already burned itself out in their hearts some time before. Lindy had tried, as she always would; optimistic, irrepressible Lindy. But there had never been any possibility she would win this time.

"You know?" she had asked.

Is there any room for doubt? she was asking him, any uncertainty that might keep you silent until Laraby has processed the arrest of Connor James? But she already knew that answer. She had known it since the moment her world imploded on that wind-ravaged hilltop above Robin Oakes's property. Domenic was sure. And he would not stay silent. Perhaps she had hoped the magic of this place, the sunsets and the mesmerizing, endless motion of the seas, and the untracked, limitless trails of the coastline, might be enough to persuade him. But she knew in her heart it would not. Nothing would. Nothing could.

"So Laraby gets his revenge, finally."

Domenic had shaken his head, staring into the flames. "I don't think that's what this is about, not entirely. I think he really likes it here. And his interest in Lauren Salter seems genuine."

"But you can't deny he's going to get some satisfaction from taking your position away from you."

"No, I can't deny that."

One more try? Why not? What did she have to lose?

"You can still prevent this, Dom. You could let it happen. Let Laraby charge Connor James with the murder of Erin Dawes."

"Could I? Allow an injustice to take place, when I had the power to prevent it? Could I do that and still call myself a police officer? I'm not sure I could."

He had looked at her, and she knew it was the other consideration that would never permit him to withhold his findings, even if Lindy somehow found a way past the armour of his personal integrity. To put Saltmarsh Constabulary in the position of having to release a second suspect would do more than damage the reputation of the people he worked with. It could destroy the credibility of the investigation; make them look as if they were prepared to charge anyone and everyone out of desperation. It would do the defence counsel's work for them, making a case of reasonable doubt for whoever the CPS eventually prosecuted, before the first piece of evidence was even heard. Robin Oakes had already been charged and released. If Domenic allowed Marvin Laraby to now charge Connor James, before having to let him go free as well, the Crown Prosecution Service would likely never get a conviction in this case. A murderer would go free.

So Domenic would make sure Laraby arrested the true killer. He would even do it the right way, allowing Danny Maik to bring Laraby to the clues, so no one would see any flaws in the investigation procedure, no one might wonder from where this new insight of DI Laraby's had magically appeared. A murderer would be brought to justice, and Marvin Laraby would reap the rewards of a new position at Saltmarsh. And Domenic Jejeune would face the consequences of his choice. Lindy supposed she had always known he would.

Darkness had started to creep in at the edges of the landscape, and now that the sun had left the sky, Lindy was cold. But she didn't move. She would stand here for as long as he was here. Or anywhere, for that matter.

It was a few moments before Jejeune was able to tear himself away from the view, the sky, the sea.

"What will happen to us?" Her heart skipped a beat. She waited for the words with dread. *Home. Canada. Us?* None of them came.

Jejeune shrugged. "I'll be offered Minton. It will be up to me to accept. Or not. Us," he added hurriedly. "It will be up to *us* to decide."

Minton. The desolation of a brand new purpose-built bedroom community. Clean, convenient, soulless. And with it, the prospect of much more time away from each other, as Domenic was forced to go away on long-distance drives to see his birds now, possibly even overnighters, while she stayed closer to home to weave her journalistic magic for the good readers of Minton. She didn't know how long it would be before the arrangement became as unbearable to him as the prospect already was to her, but she knew it would, one day. And what then? Canada back on the radar suddenly? With Lindy in tow? Without? She stepped forward and intertwined her fingers with Jejeune's.

"So, Minton, then," she said, so brightly it sounded like a punch line. She couldn't even tell him how she truly felt about the prospect. He looked so crushed, so devastated to be leaving this place that he loved. She could not bear to make him feel worse. "We'll go there and make a fresh start, shall we? Turn 'em on their heads: Dom and Lindy, boy wonder copper and ace journo. Poor buggers, they'll never know what hit them."

"A new start," he said, with a bravery that almost brought her to tears. And yet, he would come back to life. She could see it in him, even now. He would survive this. *They* would survive this, as long as they were together.

"I think I've at least earned the right to know." Lindy was going to keep the bubbly side going, pressing down the darkness until she was alone and she could let it rise and have its freedom, tearing her apart until the next time she had to pretend to be happy for Dom.

Jejeune pulled away slightly to better look at her. "To know what?"

"Not what, *who*. Who is responsible for all this packing I've got to look forward to in the next few weeks? Who was wearing that disguise?"

Jejeune took one final look out over the sea, dark now, indistinguishable from the black mass of the night sky above it.

He turned to Lindy and offered her the faintest of smiles. "No one."

50

They were at the testing facility at first light. The Drone Zone the team was calling it, and if the pedant in Maik could have pointed out it was actually a series of separate zones, rather than one large one, the name had a nice ring to it. It would be a handy short form for an arrest report, too. If it was ever needed.

Laraby was waiting at the top of the metal steps, blowing into his cupped hands, when Maik pulled up in the Range Rover. He had his collar turned up against the cold, but he was still leaning into the doorway, trying to escape the worst of the winds. Apart from the gleaming rented Jaguar, Amendal's vehicle was the only other car parked outside the Drone Zone, so it was no surprise that it was the doctor himself who opened the door when they rang the bell.

"Not a lot of time today, gents," he said. "Big presentation in Norwich this afternoon. Progress report." The doctor had at least made some concession to the formality of the forthcoming occasion. He was wearing a white shirt with a collar and a dark red tie, worn with the knot about six inches below his throat. If neither item had ever seen a steam iron raised in anger, they were at least clean.

Laraby might have commented on the dangers of setting time limits on police interviews, as he had done on their last visit, but this time he had no idea how long things would take. Danny Maik had come up with the urgent need to visit, and as yet, he hadn't told his DI why.

"And will it be positive, this progress report you're giving?" asked Danny.

"Extremely. We're on the verge of a live trial of the first stage. It means we're streets ahead of any of our competitors."

"Really?" said Laraby. "Now that's interesting. I'd heard another company was running neck and neck with you now. I'd heard you gave up all the ground you had on the others when you had to go back and write those algorithms. All because you lost the chance to test on that property you wanted from the IV League."

He paused and stared at Amendal while Maik looked on with interest. He'd been intending to run the show today, setting the agenda he needed. But perhaps he'd underestimated Laraby's ability to get there by himself, after all. He was certainly asking some of the right questions.

"There's a lot of money at stake in this field, isn't there?" asked Laraby.

Amendal shook his head. "That's not why I'm doing it."

"Nevertheless, you are the principal stakeholder in Picaflor. You stand to make a tidy sum if the project ever becomes viable."

"It will," said Amendal with a certainty that had Maik regarding him carefully. "So yes, it's true. I'm likely to be worth a considerable amount of money in the next couple of years." He looked at his phone's time display and turned to them both. "Look, guys …" he said in a tone that was pleading for reason.

"Just a couple more questions, and we'll be on our way," said Maik evenly. Whether this was a concession to the time limit imposed by Amendal, Laraby couldn't say. But somehow, he doubted it.

"I just wanted to confirm, sir," began Maik, "the day you distributed the drones to the IV League members, they were all there, in person?"

Amendal nodded. "We were all on James's boat. Though …" He hesitated and tilted his head from side to side slightly. "Well, I'm not sure how accurate you guys have to be in your reports."

"Let's say *extremely* for now, shall we?" said Laraby, leaning forward with interest.

"Okay, strictly speaking, James distributed them. I took them in, five, in boxes, but I set them on the counter. James was the one who handed them out to each person."

Laraby looked at Amendal carefully, trying to judge whether he was serious or just trying to wind them up. He suspected Danny would be halfway to breaking this clown in two, having driven all the way out here to listen to this rubbish. But when he checked on his sergeant, Danny was smiling benignly, waiting to get on with things, ready to move on to the next question.

"And you'd say the mood was positive, would you? They all seemed in favour of the project, ready to invest?"

"Absolutely." Amendal nodded vehemently. "They were enthusiastic, engaged, asked a couple of really good questions." He checked himself in mid-flight. "Except that Moncrieff guy. But I got the impression it wasn't the project he was opposed to, or the investment. He just seemed to have a pretty negative take on technology as a whole, and drones in particular." Amendal raised his shoulders a touch. "You know the type, slumped over a half of brown ale in a pub, telling everybody how he doesn't 'get' smartphones or social media." Amendal shook his head, in apparent disbelief that such dinosaurs could continue to exist in the modern world.

"Do you remember what the weather was like that day?"

Laraby looked at Maik in astonishment, but Amendal fielded the question without hesitation. "As a matter of fact, I do. It was belting down with rain. I remember James made us all tea and we sat around inside the cabin and listened to it hammering on the deck above. It was quite cool, actually."

"Okay, sir," said Maik, folding away his notepad. "That will be all. Unless the DI has some questions?"

The DI didn't. Not for Amendal, at least.

He stopped on the metal steps outside the door to the Drone Zone and turned to Maik. "Why are we here, Sergeant?"

Maik shrugged his big shoulders easily. "Just a thought, sir. I was looking for an explanation as to how James's prints could have appeared on the coat, yet on nothing else in that disguise bag. If it had been nice weather, we might have been able to make a case that one of them, wearing gloves, could have just carried the jacket over their arm and given it to James to hang up when they got on the boat." He shrugged. "But it's hardly likely anyone would go unnoticed if they were carrying a coat in the middle of a downpour. Never mind, it was just an idea."

Laraby held up a hand. "Hang on a minute. That photo Oakes took over to James. What date was that?"

Maik made a production of looking in his notebook. "The ninth. It was a Tuesday."

"Come with me."

Amendal looked up in surprise as the two detectives entered. "Guys, I told you …"

"Have you got a record of local weather conditions in that office of yours?" asked Laraby, nodding at Amendal's phone.

"Of course."

"Tuesday the ninth of October?"

Amendal hit a couple of keys. "Sunshine, clear skies, eighteen degrees."

The men were outside again before their thanks had stopped ringing in the doctor's ears.

"So that's one piece of the evidence against James gone up in smoke," said Laraby as they descended the metal stairs to their cars. "Let's see what we can come up with on the rest."

"Sir, the beard in that bag. When we rechecked, the forensic report actually says there was no trace of DNA, not even the faintest sign."

"On a beard that somebody has had glued to their face? There's only one possible way there could be no DNA on there at all, surely? And you know what that means, Sergeant."

He did. And he had done for a while. Connor James wasn't guilty. And now they both knew who was.

Laraby stopped by the door of his Jag and turned to Maik. "We'll make the arrest tomorrow. I'll get going on processing James for release as soon as I get back to the station."

Maik moved uneasily. "We could go to make that arrest later on today, sir. There's still plenty of time."

"No, we need to get this right, Sergeant. I've got to make sure I've got all the answers before we move. Because something tells me DCS Shepherd is going to have more than a few questions. Tomorrow morning, bright and early."

Maik leaned on the Range Rover, watching the Jaguar disappear down the bumpy track that led to the main road. He was thinking about the news he had heard on the way over. Ray Hayes had been seen again. He knew, without a doubt, if DCI Jejeune was going after him at all, it would be tomorrow. Maik looked back at the vast white wall of the Drone Zone testing facility. Inside, Dr. Josh Amendal was working his miracles with technology. He was one of the brightest people Maik had ever come across. Perhaps he could help the sergeant with his problem. Perhaps Dr. Amendal could devise a way for Danny Maik to be in two places at the same time.

51

The sighting was twenty-four hours old, but it had a lot of good elements to it. The target was on foot and going about normal activities. He wasn't buying supplies for a trip, or hoarding dry foods for a long stay out of sight somewhere. He wasn't frequenting the kind of areas where a copper's inquiries might be met with only a sullen silence, or worse, outright disinformation. The man fitting the description of Ray Hayes was wandering the streets of Elvery with the air of someone who planned on staying there for a while. Both Jejeune and Maik would take that kind of sighting over one five minutes old that told them a suspect was on the run and desperate. Every time.

Maik eased the Range Rover into the parking space beside the small church and switched off the engine. Jejeune looked across at him. He felt as if he should say something to the sergeant; offer him one last chance not to be here, to be risking his career in this way. He knew Danny wasn't a man of second thoughts. He had committed to helping his DCI and he would do so now, until the end. But still, there was something in Jejeune that wanted to let the sergeant know, one last time, that the door was still open for him. It wasn't too late.

His eyes met Maik's, and he saw the faintest traces of an ironic grin on the sergeant's face.

"Nice day for it," said Maik, getting out of the car.

It was. A clear blue sky arced over the quiet village and the air was crisp and clean. There was a gentle, lilting backdrop of village noises, but otherwise nothing disturbed the peacefulness of the church grounds. Jejeune stood for a moment in the car park and looked at the tiny church sitting in the bright sunlight. He never felt more foreign than when he was confronted by these small manifestations of England's storied past. Parts of the nave of this church dated back to centuries before the first Europeans had set foot on his homeland; a stone structure built as a place of worship on this carefully selected site when his own country was still tree-clad and inhabited only by people whose temples of worship were the forests and the fields themselves.

He took a deep breath, drawing in a lungful of cool, fresh air. Like the sighting itself, the circumstances held promise. The priest was a known supporter of reformed criminals and second chancers, and the church had a reputation as a sanctuary for those who sought refuge from the world's hardships.

Maik had been leaning on the low metal railing, peering into the graveyard at the headstones, row upon row, lost in his own thoughts. He joined Jejeune and they made their way to the doors of the church. Neither man had any expectation that Hayes would be here at the moment, but the spot of the last-known sighting was as good a place as any to begin their search. And wait. Nevertheless, the side door and the front door were not in sight of each other, and it would be easy enough for someone to slip out undetected if both officers went in one of the doors together. Maik peeled away wordlessly to stand in the arched doorway of the side door. He could resume his contemplation of the graveyard from here, albeit from a distance.

Jejeune entered the front door of the church cautiously. The quiet inside wrapped itself around him, settling him to its peace. Along the aisle, the worn tiles were dappled with light, multicoloured swatches from the stained glass windows that lined the nave. *The past deeds of long-forgotten men,* he thought, *commemorated in light.* Who were they, these sheriffs and lords and magistrates, these protectors of society, these upholders of the law? Had they faced these same choices Jejeune was facing today? Perhaps they had. Perhaps everything came down to a choice between two options: to act or not to act. He had chosen to act today, to protect society, to uphold the law, even if it was not in a way DCS Colleen Shepherd or any police conduct review board might understand.

Jejeune had no idea what he might do when he saw Ray Hayes. The only thing he was sure about was that he would know. When he looked into Hayes's eyes, he would be able to tell, without any doubt, whether he was guilty. And Hayes would know something, too, from looking back into Jejeune's eyes. He would see exactly what lengths the detective was prepared to go to in order to protect the woman he loved. And then the rest would be up to Hayes.

At the far end of the church was a small altar, dressed in white, flanked by two elaborately carved oak screens. Delicate filigree work traced across their tops. Jejeune could see doors leading off either side of the altar space. The vestry would be one. The other, he didn't know. A priest was bending toward a low table off to one side, facing away from Jejeune. The echo of the detective's footsteps rolled around the vaulted ceiling, alerting the priest to his approach.

Jejeune stopped at the raised dais, observing the sacred boundary marked by the low wooden railing. "Good morning. My name is Domenic Jejeune. I'm a police inspector."

The priest inclined her head. "I am Reverend Jane. Welcome to St. Margaret's. I make it a point to know the police officers in the area. I don't believe you are one of them." She held him with steady blue eyes.

"I'm wondering if a stranger has been here recently, someone else not from this parish."

The priest had straightened but not approached, as you might to welcome a visitor. There was a hint of defensiveness in the way she held her arms, slightly tucked up against her sides, and a judicious set to her expression. It suggested you could expect a fair hearing from her, but there was self-righteousness, too, that would go some way to eliminating any recriminations about any decision she made.

Jejeune heard a faint creak from somewhere; just an old building warming its bones in the sun, perhaps? He let his eyes wander slowly across the chancel, but he could detect no movement, no strange shadows.

"The church attracts its share of visitors," said Reverend Jane. "As you can see, it's a remarkably well-preserved example of late-Norman ecclesiastical architecture." She moved easily across the altar dais, her robes of office flowing gracefully around her. She seemed perfectly suited to her role. But her smile could not conceal the truth. Hayes had been here, or if not him, someone else who had been seeking sanctuary from the authorities.

"A man by the name of Ray Hayes."

"A person does not need to give their name to enter the House of God, Inspector."

Again there was the whisper of a creaking noise from somewhere, but the priest appeared not to notice. Perhaps you got used to such noises if you spent your days in old buildings like this. Jane still had not descended from the dais. She had even taken a small step back toward the screen behind her when Jejeune had moved forward slightly.

"Why have you come here, Inspector?"

"You have a reputation for sheltering those who might have been in trouble with the law. This man is a convicted criminal."

"Do the guilty not deserve the chance at redemption? And where are they likely to find that chance, if not in a church?"

"I don't think Ray Hayes is interested in redemption, Reverend. I believe he was involved in an attempted murder in Saltmarsh a few days ago."

There was another creak, but this time a blur of movement to go with it. From a side chapel a man in a grey hoodie raced toward the altar, vaulting the low railing, heading for the vestry door. The priest raised both of her hands. "Not here!" she shouted. "You will not come up here!"

The man twisted and ran back to the railing, vaulting it again just as Jejeune reached him. The detective grabbed the man's hoodie and checked him sideways, driving him back into the railing. The delicate wooden structure gave way and collapsed under the weight of the two men, sending them sprawling to the floor of the altar dais. The other man was first to recover, but Jejeune lunged at him again, his shoulder catching the man in the chest, sending him flailing back into the altar. A silver chalice teetered and fell as the cloth slid off the table, the jangling echo bouncing off the stone walls of the church. The man rallied for one final push and burst past Jejeune, smashing him in the face with his forearm. Jejeune reeled, grasping desperately to get some purchase on the man's clothing, his hood, anything. His fingers closed on a sleeve, but his grip was weak and he was pulled off balance. His ankle gave way as he twisted around, and he fell, clutching it in agony as he watched the figure sprint along the aisle and disappear into the blaze of sunlight that flooded into the church as he smashed open the front doors.

"My sergeant. Side door," shouted Jejeune from the floor. The priest looked around wildly, at her broken church, her violated altar. But she ran to the side door, robes flowing, and dragged it open. Maik was startled, but even from his side-on view he could see his DCS lying on the floor in a sea of broken artifacts and wooden railings. He looked at the gaping doors at the end of the aisle, the white-light beams streaming in, but he knew he was too late. He chose his DCI over the suspect and hurried over to help him to his feet.

Reverend Jane was seated in a front pew, hunched forward, assessing the damage. She looked distraught, but resolute. "I don't know the person who attacked you, Inspector," she said quietly. "I had not seen him before the other day. I only knew he was in trouble. He asked for my help. It was my duty to give it." She moved toward the altar and retrieved the silver chalice, which was badly dented. She caressed it with her hand and set it back on the altar, even though the cloth was still on the floor. "It is a matter of devotion. Of loyalty. Not to this person, but to my faith. You may not understand this, though I suspect you were once a man of God, if you are not now."

Jejeune was leaning against Maik, using his broad shoulder like a crutch as he stood before the priest in the transept of the tiny church. Through the rose window over the altar, a ray of filtered light shone down on the desecrated chancel, its watery pink radiance lighting up the space like hope. *The sunlight of the present, filtered through the glories of the past,* thought Jejeune. He wondered what future lay in store for them. For him, who faced a move to a new place, a new challenge, a new life. And for Danny Maik, who may have destroyed his own career to support Jejeune in his search for Ray Hayes. He suspected he knew rather more about loyalty and devotion than Reverend Jane could have imagined.

He smiled with gratitude at the sergeant. Maik was surprised. He did not see the despair he had expected to find in Jejeune's face. Instead there was a strange contentment. He would not discover its cause until they were in the car driving home. But from the brief glance Domenic Jejeune had managed as he was grappling with the man, the DCI was as sure as he could be that it was not Ray Hayes.

52

During quiet hours, the Incident Room was the ideal place for a private chat. It offered good sightlines of approach along the only corridor, and the three other walls backed onto only the emptiness of the surrounding land. Laraby and Salter had spent a fair amount of time in this room together recently. Always the case had been at the centre of their discussions. But there had been time, too, for the occasional quiet word of a more personal nature.

This time, however, Salter was alone. The constable had been deep in thought when Shepherd wrenched the door open, and she started violently at the sound.

"Well, thank God somebody's here at least," said Shepherd, pacing around agitatedly. "There's a situation developing at Oakham and I need someone to co-ordinate with the arrest team."

"What kind of situation?" Something stirred in Salter. Laraby had been heading out to the Oakes property this morning.

"Robin Oakes has set some fallen trees ablaze across the entrance to his estate to prevent anyone from getting in. Fire Services are on their way, and we're looking at calling in a Tactical Response Unit. But with no one here to co-ordinate things, all I'm getting are fuzzy pictures and garbled messages. The TRU commander is on the phone every five minutes asking for a situation report. I have no idea whether to deploy them or not."

"Is Marvin all right?"

"Who's Marvin…? Oh, Laraby." A flash of comprehension lit the DCSs features for a second. "Yes, yes. He hasn't gone in yet. He found his way barred when he arrived to arrest him." Shepherd shook her head. "This could have been handled better. I told him he shouldn't have released James until after we had Oakes in custody. Letting James go when he did sent Oakes a clear signal that we had someone else in our sights."

Salter had stood, ready to leave, but she stepped back now, feeling behind her for a desk to lean against. "He went to arrest Oakes?"

"For God's sake, Constable, this is not a comprehension test," said Shepherd with exasperation. "Laraby now believes Oakes is guilty of Erin Dawes's murder. He came to me with a plausible theory this morning, and now Oakes's actions would seem to suggest he may be right. This business with the fire is a deliberate attempt to evade arrest." She paused to reign in some of her ire. Perhaps her new understanding of Salter's relationship with Laraby softened her tone. "Oakes is known to have firearms on that property, and I'm not having DI Laraby, or anyone else, going over the wall without at least some idea of what's going on."

"Couldn't Inspector Jejeune run things from here?"

"He *could*," said Shepherd, emphasizing the word heavily." Shepherd strode to the window and looked out, unseeing. "Specific instructions," she said as if to herself. "I gave him specific instructions to be here for just this sort of eventuality, to help out, to coordinate an arrest, if necessary. And instead I find he's off chasing bloody birds again." She spun around. "One of those Golden Oriole things. I suppose if Eric wasn't out of town, he'd be out there with him." She suddenly seemed to realize she'd spoken aloud and abruptly brought the topic back to business. "As you know, Oakes is well-connected in this community, Constable," she said, turning to pace across the room again. "He has powerful friends. If we are going to charge him with murder, I want our conduct throughout to have been exemplary. Instead, I've got this potential fiasco on my hands and DCI Jejeune is nowhere in sight. Nor is Danny Maik, come to that. Have you seen him? I can't find him anywhere either."

Salter felt alarm rise within her. "He isn't up at Oakham with Mar — DI Laraby?" It was bad enough that Laraby was up there at all. Without Danny Maik's reassuring presence beside him, the situation wasn't likely to get any safer.

"Possibly he is, but I've heard no mention of him in the reports." Shepherd raised her hands in frustration. "Who knows what the hell is going on up there?" She looked at Salter. "I need you to get on to Laraby right away. Talk to Fire Services, too — someone at the scene, not a dispatcher. If Tactical are going in, I want them to have the clearest picture possible when they arrive."

"A drone," said Salter suddenly. "That would give them a view inside the estate's walls."

"I've no idea if TRU have one, let alone anybody who could use it."

"I've still got the one James gave to the sergeant. It's in my car. I know how to use that one … a bit. I've been showing it to Max." She faltered slightly. "It's not evidence, as I understand it. I didn't think anybody would mind."

Shepherd waved away the apology dismissively and the suggestion along with it.

"I can't let you go out there, Constable. I've just told you, I need you here. There is no one else."

"But ma'am, it could help," Salter's tone was insistent. She was leaning forward, using her hands to enforce her point. "A flight over the property, even a single pass, it could tell us what Oakes is up to, track his location, movements, even."

"I'm sorry. I need you here."

But Salter wasn't letting this pass. She knew she was right, for professional reasons, let alone any personal ones that might be churning away at her insides. "Ma'am, Oakes must be desperate if he's set that fire. If he's armed, and our people go in there unprepared …"

An argument that DCS Shepherd's people could be in danger was always going to win. She nodded. But she still needed something for the record, just in case. "Anything that increases the chances of us bringing in Robin Oakes without further incident is worth the risk. For that reason, I'm prepared to sanction a one-time use of a civilian drone in this situation." She paused and looked at Salter significantly. "So I suggest you get over there as soon as possible."

The high, bare hedges flashed past in a blur as Salter's car hurtled along the narrow lanes. Okay, she was driving faster than she intended to, but she was in control. There was no need to panic. Marvin was outside Oakham, with orders not to enter. He wouldn't do anything foolish. He would wait. Once she had sent the drone over, they would have a better idea of what they were facing, and how to deal with it. At the moment, it was just a few burning trees. The word *barricade* had crackled across the radio waves a couple of times during her drive out here, but she was sure that was just to give TRU some idea of what they would be facing if and when they arrived. Nobody was suggesting this situation was out of hand; any shouting and cursing she could hear in the background was just the result of a few frayed nerves. Danny's presence would change all that. As soon as they located him and got him out there, he would be able to bring a calming influence to the proceedings. He would know that the best way to deal with a potential gun threat was measured, rational procedure. No need for any heroics.

So why was her foot pressing down on the accelerator again as if it had a mind of its own? Because Shepherd felt *this could have been handled better*, that's why. And more to the point, she had told Laraby so. And DI Marvin Laraby's response to that opinion was going to be anything but calm or rational or measured. At the very first opportunity, he was going to go onto that property and try to drag Robin Oakes out by the scruff of his neck, gun threat or no gun threat. This time, she didn't even try to constrain her defiant accelerator foot. In fact, she gave it a little extra nudge of her own.

By the time she skidded the Toyota to a stop at the stone arch of the Oakham gatehouse, there was enough uncontrolled mayhem to be called panic. An emergency responder standing on the road had trained a pair of binoculars on a tiny fragment of the driveway still visible through the wall of flames rising from the tree trunks across the archway. She had caught sight of a man making his way hurriedly toward the ruins of the manor house. He was carrying a daypack slung over one shoulder, she said, and in his other hand she had seen something that could have been a shotgun.

"He's a photographer," Laraby was saying to the woman as Salter approached. "Could it have been a tripod bag?"

The woman shook her head firmly. "There was no bag. I saw a glint of metal. My first thought was *shotgun*, and I didn't see anything else that changed my mind."

"Look," Laraby leaned forward slightly to read the woman's name badge, "Karen, all I'm saying is a gun call is not something you want to make unless you're absolutely certain."

In a heartbeat, her conviction seemed to evaporate. "It was only for a second," she said weakly. "It could have been something else."

It was the enormity of what she was reporting, Salter realized: an armed man, fleeing arrest. It meant a full-on response, tactical units, possibly the use of deadly force. It was a lot to roll into action on the maybe of one brief sighting.

"If you saw a gun, Karen, it's okay to say so," said Salter gently. Laraby looked around. He hadn't realized she had arrived.

The woman nodded again and drew a breath. "I saw a gun," she said.

Salter set down the drone she was carrying and pulled out her phone before Laraby even had time to ask what she was doing. When she explained, he nodded.

"Just a quick sweep, Lauren," he said. "See if we can pick him up. I'll take it from there."

"You can't go in," said Salter. "Not now the weapon has been confirmed. You have to let the TRU handle it. You have to."

"Just get this thing in the air. Once we know the score, we can make the calls we need to."

The drone lifted uncertainly, teetering as Salter fought with the controls on her phone for a moment. It lurched toward the stone wall, seeming destined to make contact, until it lifted suddenly and spun back in a short circle. It moved so slowly and deliberately in flight, Laraby wondered how one of these things could ever have done so much damage to Maik's windscreen.

One more lurching, stilted, hesitant test run saw Salter announce she was ready to go.

Laraby leaned over her shoulder, having trouble at first making out the grainy grey images. Salter tilted the screen of the phone to avoid the light, and the drone went with it, sailing left in a careening, uncontrolled dive. "Sorry," she breathed, recovering the drone and holding a steady course, concentrating on the screen, gripping the phone tightly in both hands, hugging it in to her slightly.

"There. Movement." If Laraby was pointing, gesturing either at the phone or the land itself, Salter made no move to look up. Her eyes were locked on the screen. But she had seen it, too. Movement across the field, heading toward the grey stone walls of the manor ruins. And she had seen, too, the long object in the man's hand, carried in that low-slung, respectful way no one ever carries anything but a firearm.

"He's going in to the higher walls. He must be looking for a place to hide."

Salter heard a shout, but she wasn't inclined to look up, not until the urgency of the voices ratcheted up a notch. She looked at the archway, where one side of the burning trees had been damped down just enough for someone to squeeze through, if they were foolhardy enough to try. She was about to look over her shoulder to see what Laraby thought when her eyes fell on the screen again. A shard of ice pierced her heart. Running across her screen, toward the manor ruins, was Laraby.

Salter was sick with fear, but she couldn't take her eyes off the phone. Now, more than ever, she had to keep watching.

Karen approached. She had a phone in her hand. "It's DI Laraby," she said. "He wants you to talk him toward Oakes."

Salter positioned the drone slightly in front of Laraby as he ran, and she could see he had his phone cupped to one ear. "Where, Lauren? Left or right? I can see a big piece of wall coming up in front of me. Which side is Oakes on?"

She had no time to argue with him, or tell him he shouldn't be there, that he needed to turn around and come back. And the presence of Karen next to her stopped her saying other things, too, things her heart would have wanted her to say. She gave the drone a forward boost, over the buttress Laraby was describing. She saw Oakes furtively making his way along a low wall about twenty metres farther into the ruins. "Right," she said. "Stay low as you go around. He won't have a shot. There's a large mound of rubble in the way."

Laraby slowed to a walk and made his way around the buttress, pressing himself tightly against the huge stone structure. Salter watched him ease his way around the corner and pause, looking for cover, looking for Oakes.

Karen leaned in. "TRU have arrived," she whispered.

Salter nodded at the phone, still not taking her eyes off the screen. "Tell him," she hissed.

Karen passed the update to Laraby.

Salter watched as he paused for a second at the news. "Which way, Lauren?"

Salter moved the drone back over the spot she had seen Oakes before. He was nowhere in sight. Panicking, she elevated the drone for a wider look. But there were overhangs and niches everywhere. If Oakes had been unaware he was being tracked by drone to start with, he would have certainly known the last time Salter took the machine in for a low pass. Now he had taken cover.

"I've lost him," she shouted in alarm. "Get out of there, Marvin. I can't see him anymore."

She saw Laraby press the phone in more closely to his ear, even look up at the drone.

"You have to come out. Now!"

It was like blindness. The loss of the visual signal was so sudden, so complete, it filled Salter's senses. She could think of nothing else, see nothing else. Her entire world existed only in that black four-inch void, her own ghostly reflection its only image now. "I've lost the view." The panic transcended the message. If Laraby heard her voice, he would know she was falling apart. Would it be enough to bring him back out to her?

The sound filled the world, stilling the air, rolling around in the silence of the frozen landscape. For a moment, no one stirred, the firefighters, the uniformed officers, the newly arrived tactical squad. And then someone called out the word, and everything began moving again at the same time, in horror, in fear, in chaos.

"Gunshot!"

53

Dark clouds hovered low over the rolling landscape beyond the window in DCS Shepherd's office. She had switched on the lights against the gloom, but the oppressive greyness of the late afternoon still gathered at the window. Another day, she may have drawn the blinds altogether, but she felt they needed whatever light they could get from outside, to lift the sombre mood that pervaded the office.

Maik stared straight ahead, unseeing. Salter looked down at her hands folded in her lap as if they were alien things, unrecognizable. Shepherd was speaking, as she had done for the past few moments, disjointed, fragmented thoughts, utterances to keep the silence at bay.

"The loss of any officer is difficult to deal with. We all know that. And I recognize that, in this case, there are special circumstances, attachments that were formed, that also have to be taken into consideration. I'm sure I don't have to tell you, I find this as difficult as you do. But we must continue to do our jobs. So please, let's do them. We'll have plenty of time for our own feelings when it's all wrapped up. She looked up at Maik. "Robin Oakes has confessed, I understand? To everything?"

Maik roused himself from his thoughts and cleared his throat. "Yes, ma'am. Oakes bought the jacket and moustache but never wore them. He took the coat to James's boat on a day when he didn't need to wear it, and got the fingerprints. The cap he wore, with a plastic liner, so he could get the girl's makeup on it when he charged into her. Putting the cap and jacket in the one bag like that, it never occurred to any of the investigating officers that the two items might not both have been together at Erin Dawes's cottage."

Shepherd nodded silently. If it was an error, it was one she would have made, too.

Maik was silent for a moment. He seemed to be having trouble keeping his mind on the topic at hand. But Shepherd understood. She was surprised he could be so coherent and focused as he was, given the circumstances. Salter had not said a word. She understood that, too.

"Sergeant," Shepherd prompted gently.

"Oh, yes, ma'am. Sorry. Oakes was counting on the girl reporting the assault. She would give her description, we would arrest Oakes, and then the disguise would be found. James's print, James's cup with Oakes's DNA on it, it would all point to him trying to frame Oakes. No one would believe Robin Oakes was trying to frame himself."

"The cup?"

"Taken from *The Big Deal* when Oakes went over to drop off a photograph. James is a single man who drinks pop. He probably never goes near those cups except when company comes. My bet is he had no idea one was missing."

Shepherd nodded again. So much for the *hows*. It was the *whys* that had her guessing. But before she could ask, there was a tap on the door.

"Come in," invited Shepherd. "There you are. I'll make a general announcement later, but I've already told Sergeant Maik and Constable Salter. As of now, the role of Saltmarsh's DCI is yours, Inspector Laraby."

Shepherd offered a warm smile as she delivered the news. Only those who knew her very well would have been able to detect whether there was anything preventing her from fully celebrating the moment.

Laraby's own smile struck just the right balance of gratitude and humility. His right hand was heavily bandaged where the barrel of Oakes's shotgun had burnt it when Laraby wrestled the weapon away from him. Maik accepted the upturned left hand proffered as a substitute and shook it perfunctorily. Salter declined to notice.

"I'm grateful for the opportunity. I'm aware that the outgoing DCI has left some big shoes to fill, but I have no doubt our success on this case is a sign of some very positive things to come for this crack team here in Saltmarsh."

"You're aware that Oakes has confessed, I take it? Sergeant Maik took care of that while you were being treated at the hospital."

"I popped down to pay my respects just before they took him away. He had the decency to let me know he wasn't trying to kill us with that drone." Laraby flashed Maik a grin, of sorts. "He apologizes for the damage to your car. He actually offered to pay for it." He shook his head. "I told you, they live in a different world, this lot. Even now, I don't think he has a clue how much trouble he's in. He probably thinks it's going to be like being blackballed at the club for a couple of months."

"We did finally get to the bottom of his motive, I take it?" Shepherd looked between Maik and Laraby.

"Dawes thought Oakes was just being his usual playboy self, arsing around and not taking the deal seriously, so that's what their arguments were about. Finally, when he realized he couldn't stall any longer, Oakes agreed to have the documents drawn up for the land lease. But he told her he wanted to be the one to hand over the cash, with the documents, just before midnight on the deadline."

"Why was he so reluctant to commit the land?"

Laraby, Salter, and Maik looked at one another. *How had this not reached Shepherd's desk already?*

"It wasn't his land, not anymore. It hasn't been for many years, apparently. After the fire, his father sold the entire estate, titles and everything, to an American billionaire, with the proviso that Oakes should be supported in his chosen profession and allowed to live in the gatehouse on the estate, provided he remained single. Oakes has been trading on his aristocratic status since he moved in to Oakham, but it's all been a sham."

Shepherd stared at them for a long time. "The taxes on the land itself must have been crippling, and yet a man with a cash flow that can best be described as erratic, and a propensity to go through money like water, never misses a payment. How the hell did we miss this?"

"The land had been in the same family for four hundred years, ma'am. It never occurred to anybody investigating the case to look into its ownership," said Maik.

It was the second time Maik had used a similar qualifier, and this time Salter was certain. Somebody who hadn't been investigating the case had come up with this. And the idea that the jacket had been handled by James, but only the cap had been at Erin Dawes's cottage. *Jejeune.* He had solved this case and given the solution to Laraby, most likely through Danny. She couldn't imagine why, but she knew she wasn't wrong. And coupled with what else she already knew, it gave her the whole picture. Or as much of it as she needed.

Shepherd's radar, for once, was off. She seemed to have missed Danny's references. She seemed unaware, too, of the underlying electricity that now existed in the room. Instead, she was concentrating on understanding all the nuances of the case.

"Why on earth would Oakes ever agree to the IV League deal in the first place, if he knew he could never commit the land?"

"He thought the owner would jump at the chance," said Laraby. "A billionaire with an eye for a deal, a quick twenty percent return on the options, with no cash outlay. Oakes thought it was a formality; get the signatures he needed, discreetly file the papers, and nobody need ever know that Oakes had neither property nor title any longer. He could continue his rural aristo playboy lifestyle just as before."

Shepherd was puzzled. "So, why did the real owner of Oakham refuse such a lucrative deal?"

"Drones," said Laraby. "It turns out the financier shares Gerald Moncrieff's feelings about them eroding our civil liberties. He refused, point blank, to have anything to do with the project. Oakes kept asking, of course, and kept delaying, hoping he would change his mind. But he never did, and by then it was too late to find anybody else to take up the options, certainly without revealing that Oakes didn't own the land himself. So he was forced to appear as if he was prepared to go through with the deal."

"Oakes did make a point of saying he never intended for anyone to die, ma'am," said Maik. "He told me that more than once. Apparently, he told Erin Dawes that he would sign the land over if she gave him the funds, so he could present the entire package at once. He photoshopped some options certificates to keep her happy. Then all he had to do was make sure he intercepted any irate calls James made to the IV League phone line, reply by email, and no one would be any the wiser. For a while."

"Oakes kept the money?" asked Shepherd.

Maik nodded. "He claims he did plan to return it — some of it anyway. He'd been led to believe that without the land at Oakham, the entire Picaflor project would collapse. If it did, the share values would plummet. He could have made arrangements for the others to receive whatever was still due to them and pocket the rest. But he didn't count on Amendal being able to rescue the project without the land. By all reasonable expectations, what Amendal achieved should have been impossible. But he saved the project, and when Picaflor's stock rose, instead of falling, Oakes knew both Welbourne and Moncrieff would want to cash out. Even if he could have found some way to pay back their investments, he knew Dawes would have wanted to stay invested in the company."

Shepherd nodded to herself. "Oakes had robbed her of a wonderful investment opportunity, likely using up most of her life savings, I would imagine. She would have seen to it that his life was ruined."

Laraby stepped in again. "He knew he would have to kill her to maintain his secret, but he left it as long as he could, until the Picaflor shareholders' report came out, when it would have become clear the IV League weren't invested in the company. It gave him time to set things up — the cup, the clothing, everything." The newly appointed DCI shook his head. "A billionaire financier with principles and a project director who turns out to be a mathematical miracle worker? If Oakes didn't have bad luck, he wouldn't have any luck at all." But he didn't sound sorry for him. "The business of the attempted murder charge, ma'am. I'd like to make sure it's included."

"Robin Oakes discharged a shotgun at a policeman, in my jurisdiction. I'm not of a mind to let that go unacknowledged, DCI Laraby."

Laraby nodded. "I'd just like to be sure he faces the justice he deserves."

"I'm sure we all want that. For everybody," said Salter in an outburst that had both Maik and Shepherd looking at her. "If you'll excuse me, I've got some things to do."

The others watched her leave in silence. But Laraby's were the only eyes that stayed on the door long after she had left.

54

Jejeune stood outside DCS Shepherd's office for a long time after the door closed behind him. It had been a short interview. He had known it was coming, but he offered no defence. The time for speaking up, for making his case, had already passed. All that had been left to him was to observe a silence that saved somebody else. Jejeune himself was beyond help.

"You were ordered to give this case your full support and you were off chasing birds. A senior member of the force is getting fired at with a shotgun, and you're trying to tick a Golden Oriole off your bloody life list, Domenic?"

Shepherd had been agitated by other things, too, he knew. She had just returned from the hospital after seeing Marvin Laraby. The reports that had been flying around the station when Jejeune arrived back from Elvery were even more fragmentary and contradictory than usual. It had been impossible to get a clear picture of what had happened up on the Oakham property. Laraby had been shot, or not. He was injured; he was okay. Oakes had been arrested, or he was on the run. In the end, Shepherd had raced to her car and sped to the hospital, where only the very worst of the news, or perhaps the best, could be confirmed.

She glowered at Jejeune now. She was angry at so many things, not least what she had to do, and she was ready to blame him for all of them.

"What a bloody mess," she said, gathering up the reports from her desk and holding them in her hands. For a moment, Jejeune thought she might throw them all up in the air, such was her mood. But she laid them down eventually, and even made a show of trying to sift through one or two of them.

"I can't even make out where Danny Maik was in all this. He's listed under Officers Present on DI Laraby's report, but there's no mention of him at all beyond that. We've got Salter flying that drone all over the place, Laraby's off chasing over rubble and getting shot at like Captain Courageous, and Maik is ... where? Recording it all on his phone, in case he ever starts a Youtube page? I'd have thought he'd have been front and centre in the pursuit. This was exactly his kind of thing." A thought seemed to strike her and she looked up at Jejeune with a horrified expression on her face. "Oh, please God, Domenic, don't tell me he was out there chasing birds with you."

"Hardly likely, is it?" said Jejeune, not quite trusting his eyes to carry the message. "I understand it was a chaotic scene out there. I imagine it must have been virtually impossible to keep track of the movements of all the personnel at the site."

It wasn't Jejeune's comment that made Shepherd look up at him. It was the flat, deadpan delivery that triggered an alarm. She looked at him carefully, and he could see her wrestling with the decision. Pursue it and risk losing a good officer? Or let it go?

She lifted a sheet of paper from the desk. "I've made a formal recommendation that DI Laraby be promoted to DCI," she said. "He's been offered the posting here." It was clear that she had intended to deliver this information honestly and respectfully, looking directly at Jejeune, as frankly as she could. But her eyes never quite made it, sliding away to the refuge of the paper once again. "You'll be offered Minton. They're delighted, naturally, and you'll get only the very best of references from me. They are only interested in your policing skills, after all. Of course, the decision to accept or not is entirely yours, but I can tell you quite categorically that there is no position open at this station for you."

Jejeune said nothing. He had known the consequences of his decision. He had known it would end like this. Had he expected something different, some uncharacteristic act of magnanimity from Laraby, or a flash of insight from Shepherd that might have changed his fate? He wasn't sure.

"Please don't try to talk me out of this, Domenic," she said. "It was a difficult enough decision as it is. I'm sure you'll agree, in time, if not just now, that it's the best thing for all of us. The service will continue to value your unique talents, and your career will continue to soar. Though you may not believe it at the moment, I'll watch your progress with no little pride."

Was she asking for something from him? Some small show of understanding? Of absolution? Jejeune didn't know. But he had no emotions left in him, no desire, no wishes, no interest. He was numbed, now, by the reality of his situation, but he had his consolation, too.

It hadn't been Ray Hayes in that church. The explosion at Lindy's offices had been an accident after all. Hayes had been a product of a fevered dream, delirium brought on by heatstroke, but never anything tangible. All he had ever really had was a vague description from Lindy of some shaven-headed man with tattoos on his neck, a description that could have fit a thousand men. Other than that, what? An unusual explosion, the presence of Marvin Laraby, and a name from their mutual past. All sewn up, neatly tailored by Jejeune's imagination, swirling from illness, from tropical heat, from the strange magical realism of Colombia, and the ongoing uncertainty over Damian's fate, into one neat package that never existed. Ray Hayes had not been in Saltmarsh. And Lindy was safe.

Shepherd watched her outgoing DCI carefully. He was calmer than he should have been. As sanguine as he was, she knew he loved this place, this adopted north Norfolk home of his. He should be devastated. But he wasn't.

"I can understand this is all quite a shock for you. If you'd like a few moments to compose yourself, we can finish this up later."

"I'm fine, thank you." said Jejeune.

Fine? she thought. Why? Because Saltmarsh was just another roadside stop on your journey? "Fine" because then you can pretend being here has meant nothing to you at all. How dare you, Domenic Jejeune? How bloody dare you?

But Shepherd could see there would be no further comments coming from the man standing before her. "Very well, then. Let's try to make the handover as painless as possible for everyone concerned. You and Laraby are both good professionals and I expect you to conduct yourselves as such." She looked up. "Have you even seen or spoken to him since you've been back? I had hoped you might be able to resolve your differences while you were both here."

"No chance," said Jejeune.

Shepherd gave a small smile. *You were always so clever, Domenic. Always managed to hit that perfect pitch of ambiguity, so nobody knew quite what you meant, or what you were thinking, or feeling.*

"Very well. I intend to start processing the paperwork for the transfer as soon as possible. You can have the week to get yourself sorted. Anything else, DCI Jejeune?"

"No," he said. "I don't think there is."

Danny Maik was waiting outside the door to Jejeune's office when his superior officer arrived.

"He was clever," he said.

Jejeune nodded. "Yes, he was."

"But he knew you'd be clever, too."

Jejeune said nothing.

"He knew you'd look at the arguments. He knew you wouldn't settle for the obvious. But if they weren't about money, and they weren't about sex, there was really only one other thing Robin Oakes and Erin Dawes could have been arguing about: the land."

"Anyone in there?" Jejeune indicated the door to the office, the door that still bore his name. Maik shook his head and the two men entered.

"That was the only part I didn't quite understand," said Maik, as soon as they were in the room together and the door was closed behind them. "Why Oakes went to all the rigamarole of setting up the disguise, the planting of the evidence. But he knew you'd look into the land ownership, and he knew you'd find out he didn't own it. Then you'd have your motive — the only one that made sense."

Jejeune was walking a fine line between giving Maik his attention and sorting through things in the drawer of his desk. So far he was managing his balancing act, but it was a close thing. Maik paused for a moment to see if his outgoing DCI might spare him the ordeal of having to monologue the entire meeting. But he could understand why he wouldn't. Jejeune had a few other things on his mind at the moment.

"With you so firmly locked onto him, Oakes was going to need somebody else for you to look at. Enter Connor James. But even there, he was going to have to be clever. Don't frame him, but make it look like he was framing you, instead. Only leave just enough clues for a good detective," Maik paused and looked at Jejeune, "a very good detective, to follow." The sergeant shook his head. "Like I said, he was clever."

Jejeune paused in his drawer search and looked up at Maik. "Detective Chief Inspector Laraby is getting a good man, Sergeant. I understand it's not in your nature, but it might not hurt to remind him of it every once in a while." He offered Maik a thin smile.

"Even the business with the Barn Owls was part of his plan, wasn't it, sir? Directed at you."

"Yes, I think it was."

"The rest of us, we might have just shrugged it off as a bit of naughtiness by an over-zealous photographer. But he knew you'd go after him; pursue him to the fullest extent of the law, no leniency, no tolerance. To some, it might have looked like an over-reaction. It might even look like it was affecting your judgment, continuing to look at him for Erin Dawes's murder in the face of all this mounting evidence pointing to Connor James. It would have made a lot of people think twice about why you had Robin Oakes so firmly in your sights."

Jejeune replied with silence. He closed the drawer gently and looked at his sergeant. *A lot of people, perhaps, but not all. You wouldn't have questioned my approach, would you?*

"And to think, DI Laraby said clever criminals don't come his way very often," said Maik eventually, giving his head a small shake. "I think we could say Robin Oakes is the exception. Of course, Oakes's problem was, he was expecting somebody as clever as he was to be investigating the case. But he didn't get you, did he? He got Inspector Laraby. And me. So he had to give us those eyes all the time, make sure we knew he was lying, so he could lead us by our noses right where he wanted us to go, toward Barn Owls and away from land ownership."

"Marvin Laraby is a very good detective, Sergeant."

"Is he?"

"Yes. He is. Just don't …" Jejeune stopped suddenly. "He's a very good detective."

He took a small book from a shelf behind him and tossed it Maik's way. The sergeant caught it deftly with one hand. It was a guide to the birds of Norfolk. "In case you ever need it," said Jejeune. "For a case, I mean. You never know."

Maik tapped the book against his fingertips and nodded slightly. "You never know. I'll leave you to it then, sir. I'm sure you've got a lot of things to do." He looked at Jejeune. "I don't get over to Minton very often, but it's not that far. I could be there in a hurry, if ever there was a need."

"Thank you, Sergeant. I'll keep it in mind."

Maik had his big, calloused hand on the door handle before he turned around. "If you can manage it, sir, try to make a point of popping in before you go. I'd like the chance to say goodbye."

55

L araby took off his jacket and slung it over the back of one of the beige Formica chairs in the cafeteria. "So," he said brightly, "it looks like we've got a lot to talk about."

Rather than meet his expectant gaze, Salter looked around the room. She had always hated this place, with its functional furniture and insipid decorating scheme, and it's buzzing, sickly-yellow fluorescent lights. It was a room to kill appetites, of any kind; an oppressive windowless space designed, it had always seemed to her, to drain the joy out of any experience.

"It'll be a bit of a change of pace for everybody after what they've been used to recently. But at least DCI Jejeune's landed on his feet. Off to bigger and better things, just how he likes it."

"Does he?" Salter was still having trouble meeting Laraby's eyes. "It wasn't his decision, though, was it? I mean, I heard DCS Shepherd say she'd decided it was best for all concerned." She finally found a way to look at him, her eyes unwavering now, searching his.

Laraby shrugged easily. "I suppose we all knew he'd come unstuck because of this birding business one day. I don't say it was Shepherd's only consideration, but I'm sure it made a difficult decision a bit easier."

"Golden Oriole. That was the bird he went after, wasn't it? I wonder if he saw it."

"I'm not sure." Laraby was guarded now, some of the sunshine gone from his attitude.

Salter shook her head. "No, he wouldn't have. I talked to a local birder, a woman named Carrie Pritchard. She told me that the likelihood of a Golden Oriole showing up in north Norfolk this late in the year would be, let's see, how did she put it, "*somewhat beyond the bounds of probability*," which I think is birder-speak for *not happening*. She also said, if one had shown up, the rare bird lines would have lit up like Christmas trees. But they didn't. Utter silence."

Salter's eyes had dropped down to the stained, worn tabletop momentarily, but now they flashed up again and caught Laraby in their twin beams. "There never was a Golden Oriole. You created an alert, and then you sent it to Jejeune's laptop so you could show Shepherd. And then you deleted it before he returned. But did you know the police can retrieve deleted messages, Marvin? Has the technology reached that far, down The Smoke?"

Her anger was rising now, in her voice and her colour, flushing her cheeks red. But not the same blush he had found so attractive earlier, far from that. Very far indeed.

"It's called giving yourself an edge, Lauren. It's what we have to do. Not the chosen ones, not the ones who've been touched by the golden hand. You'd never expect them to stoop to anything as low as that," Laraby said sarcastically. "But the rest of us, the ones who've got to put themselves out there every day and make our own good fortune, we need that little boost sometimes. So a little white lie, padding an expense form, a bit of career sabotage for a rival, it's all fair game when you aren't part of the privileged set. I wouldn't expect Jejeune to understand any of this, but you should."

She shook her head slightly in what might have been some kind of admiration. "And you made sure Danny was with him, because you knew he would never betray Danny Maik, so he couldn't reveal to Shepherd where he'd been. Even using the one topic, birding, that was likely to find even less tolerance with Shepherd than being disobeyed." She nodded. "You want to stitch somebody up, it doesn't come much better than that."

"Look," said Laraby defensively, "regardless of whether he went birding or to find some bloke who likes setting off explosives, it was his choice to go. He was told to stay and mind the shop and he went. He showed where his priorities lay, as he always does. With himself, his own interests, his own agendas, not those of the police service."

"He was trying to save the woman he loved, Marvin. And you used that, you took advantage of it." She shook her head. "I could have forgiven a lot of things, but not that, not using someone's love as a weakness to be exploited."

"Look, why don't you call your dad and ask him to babysit Max tonight. He likes Davy. It'll be good for both of them. We can go out and have a nice meal and talk about all this."

But Salter continued as if she hadn't been listening. "Max's father can be a nice bloke in some ways. Thoughtful, attentive, he's never missed a birthday or anniversary. But he can be a devious, manipulative bastard at times." She looked directly at Laraby, as if to be sure he would get the message. "I can't have that for Max, not again. He needs a man around who can show him that decency and integrity mean something. That it's not okay to shove somebody under the bus just because you resent their success."

"He's not who you think he is, Lauren. Ask him about that case with the young lad on the estate, the case he abandoned to go chasing after the Home Secretary's daughter. Ask him about that one time, why don't you?" Laraby took a breath and reined himself in. "Lauren, please. Call your dad, get him to take Max for a few hours. Let's talk."

Salter shook her head, ignoring his plea. "She'll figure it out at some point, you know. Shepherd. She'll mention it to Eric when he gets back, and he'll tell her there never was a Golden Oriole alert. But it won't matter by then. You'll be here and Jejeune will be in Minton, and it will be too late to put things right. But it's not too late now, Marvin, not yet. I really wish it could have worked out. Truly, I do. But it didn't, and it can't now."

"It can."

"No, it can't. Because you're going to tell the DCS that you'll be taking Minton instead."

"Now, wait a minute, let's think this through. This is not just my future we're talking about here, Lauren, it's yours, too. Ours. Even Max's."

"Because if you don't," she continued as if Laraby hadn't spoken, "first thing tomorrow I'll be telling DCS Shepherd all I know about Golden Orioles. It's not much, but I'm betting neither job offer is going to be on the table by the time I'm finished."

She sat resolutely, staring at him. She had wondered how she would feel, whether her emotions would start to take over. But she was in control, calmer than she imagined she'd be. Perhaps she'd been resigned to this even before today's announcements. So she didn't stand up. She didn't walk away. This was her station, her life, her tired, depressing, rundown canteen. It was Laraby who had entered her world. It was he who would be leaving.

He seemed to sense her resolve and stood up. Salter could see that he had accepted the situation now. There was finality to his movements, the way he squared his shoulders. There would be no more requests for her to reconsider.

"I hope you've made the right choice here, Lauren," he said, collecting his jacket from the back of the chair and shrugging it on. "Because, you know, for such a good detective, even Jejeune forgets to ask the right question sometimes. Like about Ray Hayes, for example."

Salter was puzzled, shocked. Amid all the turmoil between the two of them, what was Laraby doing dragging up some name she had never heard of?

"We put him away for twenty-five to life. Only he's out now. But the inspector you're so keen to protect has never asked why. Sometime when you've got a moment alone with him, perhaps you'd like to tell him for me. Only when you do, you might want to make sure it's somewhere quiet. He'll need a few minutes to collect himself, I imagine."

Laraby leaned forward to rest his hands on the table across from her. "Ray Hayes was released on an unsafe conviction. Seems there was some dodgy handling of evidence around that time. All of the cases that went through our station during that period are under review. And that would include the one involving the Home Secretary's daughter. Tell him that, would you? Only, a word to the wise, Lauren. You might want to let him enjoy his Christmas first. Because I can guarantee he won't be enjoying much of anything after you get around to telling him."

Salter watched Marvin Laraby's back as he departed. She had been preparing herself for a range of emotions when he left. Trying to work out the complexities of his rivalry with Domenic Jejeune had not been among them. She stared around at the drab walls of the cafeteria. No matter how ugly, familiarity had its own comforts at times.

56

The supermarket's Christmas decorations taunted Lindy with their joy, every blinking light, every twinkling strand of tinsel. Even the cheery piped-in music seemed to magnify her own sadness. She gathered her goods desultorily, on this, perhaps her final *grocery journey* to this shop. But she would dig deep, find that steely resolve again that had been missing since the explosion, blown out of her it seemed at times, leaving only hollowness, weakness, a lack of will. If this was to be their last Christmas in Saltmarsh, she would make it a good one. No tears, no moping around, no regrets.

When her phone rang, she thought briefly about ignoring it. False levity was beyond her at the moment, and no one deserved to hear her sorrow as they were gearing up for their own Christmas celebrations. She saw it was Dom's number. The one person she could speak to, the only one who would understand her inconsolable sadness, who shared it. Except, he didn't sound sad; tentative, perhaps, but definitely not sad. She listened for a few moments as he spoke and then sought out a quiet corner where she could turn her head from the passing shoppers to hide the tears welling up in her eyes.

"Oh, Dom, that's fantastic. It's the best Christmas present you could ever have given me. Did Shepherd say what changed her mind?"

"Only that the position had opened up again, and she hoped I would consider staying. She didn't say why."

"Of course not. She'd be too embarrassed to say she'd had a rethink and come to the conclusion you're the best detective she's ever had, and the station would be absolutely lost without you." She looked down and her cart, her eyes still moist with emotion. "The shopping can wait," she said. "I'm coming home. We're going out to celebrate."

Lindy walked to the door, where a man held it open for her.

"So what's happened to Laraby?"

"No idea," said Jejeune. "I imagine he's off back to the Met. Or Minton. But let's not talk about other people. Let's make tonight about us, and about Saltmarsh, and about the idea that we are staying here after all."

The man's face was hidden in his hoodie, but the spirit of Christmas was flowing freely in Lindy now. Goodwill to all, whether you could make eye contact with them or not. She mouthed a passing thank you to the man as she left.

The man did not let the supermarket door close after her. Instead, he watched her cross the car park, still chatting animatedly on the phone.

"My pleasure, Lindy," said Ray Hayes.

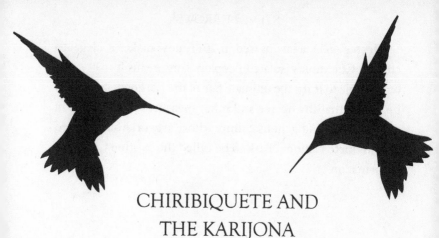

CHIRIBIQUETE AND
THE KARIJONA

At more than 10,000 square miles (27,000 square kilometres), Chiribiquete National Park is one of the largest rainforest reserves in the world. It is also one of the least accessible. In addition to the tepuis, the "Lost World" mountains that are home to the Chiribiquete Emerald hummingbird, the park features waterfalls, rapids, giant granitic domes, and canyons.

It is also the spiritual and physical home of the Karijona. In the 1790s, the estimated population of the indigenous Karijona people of Colombia was 15,000. By early in the twentieth century, introduced diseases and the appalling exploitations of the rubber harvesters had reduced the population precipitously. Today, only around sixty individuals are known to exist. However, research flights over the park suggest there may be at least one isolated tribe of Karijona still surviving in a traditional setting.

Noted for rowing their canoes while standing, wrapping their chests with beaded belts, and piercing their nasal septum with animal bones, the Karijona people also created the greatest assemblage of pre-Columbian paintings in all of Amazonia. Thousands of depictions of people, animals, and objects can be found at sites throughout the park.

Decree 4633, a law passed in 2011, now makes it illegal to contact Colombia's isolated peoples. This means it may never be possible to learn the ultimate fate of the Karijona. It can only be hoped that the decree and other measures will succeed in preserving an indigenous culture whose artworks have caused Chiribiquete National Park to be called the "Sistine Chapel of the Amazon."

IN THE SAME SERIES

A Siege of Bitterns
Steve Burrows

Globe and Mail 100: Best Books of 2014
2015 Arthur Ellis Award — Winner, Best First Novel
2015 Kobo Emerging Writer Prize — Shortlisted, Best Mystery

Inspector Domenic Jejeune's success has made him a poster boy for the U.K. police service. The problem is Jejeune doesn't really want to be a detective at all; he much prefers watching birds.

Recently reassigned to the small Norfolk town of Saltmarsh, located in the heart of Britain's premier birding country, Jejeune's two worlds collide when he investigates the grisly murder of a prominent ecological activist. His ambitious police superintendent foresees a blaze of welcome publicity, but she begins to have her doubts when Jejeune's most promising theory involves a feud over birdwatching lists. A second murder only complicates matters.

To unravel this mystery, Jejeune must deal with unwelcome public acclaim, the mistrust of colleagues, and his own insecurities. In the case of the Saltmarsh birder murders, the victims may not be the only casualties.

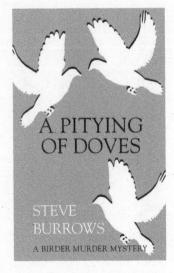

A Pitying of Doves
Steve Burrows

2015 Dewey Diva Pick

Why would a killer ignore expensive jewellery and take a pair of turtledoves as the only bounty?

This is only one of the questions that piques Chief Inspector Domenic Jejeune's interest after a senior attaché with the Mexican Consulate is found murdered alongside the director of a local bird sanctuary. The fact that the director's death has opened up a full-time research position studying birds hasn't eluded Jejeune either. Could this be the escape from policing that the celebrated detective has been seeking? Even if it is, Jejeune knows he owes it to the victims to solve the case first. But a trail that weaves from embittered aviary owners to suspicious bird sculptors only seems to be leading him farther from the truth. Meanwhile, Jejeune is discovering that diplomatic co-operation and diplomatic pressure go hand in hand.

With two careers hanging in the balance, the stakes have never been higher for Inspector Jejeune. And this time, even bringing a killer to justice may not provide the closure he's looking for.